3 402
HARRIS C

D1095256

YA   Purdy
Purdy, Rebekah L.,
The summer marked /
$16.99   ocn889524257

JUN 2 0 2016

WITHDRAWN

The Summer Marked

REBEKAH L. PURDY

To Heather, Tricia, Danie, Rachel, Wendy, Jenn, Phil, Laura,
Cholle, Traci, Barrett, Chase, and Gabby for helping me get
through a rough start to 2015.

This book is a work of fiction. Names, characters, places, and incidents are the product of the author's imagination or are used fictitiously. Any resemblance to actual events, locales, or persons, living or dead, is coincidental.

Copyright © 2015 by Rebekah L. Purdy. All rights reserved, including the right to reproduce, distribute, or transmit in any form or by any means. For information regarding subsidiary rights, please contact the Publisher.

Entangled Publishing, LLC
2614 South Timberline Road
Suite 109
Fort Collins, CO 80525

Entangled Teen is an imprint of Entangled Publishing, LLC.

Visit our website at www.entangledpublishing.com.

Edited by Liz Pelletier
Cover design by LJ Anderson
Photography girl (c) Aleshyn Andrei
Photography roadway (c) Sean Pavone Photo
Interior design by Jeremy Howland

Print ISBN 978-1-63375-009-8
Ebook ISBN 978-1-63375-010-4

Manufactured in the United States of America

First Edition August 2015

10 9 8 7 6 5 4 3 2 1

Over hill, over dale,
Through bush, through brier,
Over park, over pale,
Through flood, through fire!
I do wander everywhere,
Swifter than the moon's sphere,
And I serve the Fairy Queen,
To dew her orbs upon the green;
The cowslips tall her pensioners be;
In their gold coats spots you see;
Those be rubies, fairy favours;
In those freckles live their savours;
I must go seek some dewdrops here,
And hang a pearl in every cowslip's ear.

— William Shakespeare

PROLOGUE

*S*now fell outside, piling up on the deck, the trees bending beneath the harsh winds. Every winter seemed worse than the last. The bitter chill. The darkness. The attempts to break through the gate surrounding our property.

My gaze flitted to where Salome and Kadie sat playing with their Barbies on the floor, unaware of what hid in the shadows, waiting to burst inside. As much as I wanted to keep Salome ignorant of what lurked in the woods, she needed to know. And soon.

Salome turned her gray-blue eyes on me then set her toys on the floor. "Grandma, will you tell us a story?"

I smiled, setting down my cup of tea. "Well I suppose I could. Why don't you two come sit up on the couch while I go and grab a book and some hot cocoa for you?"

Once I had the girls settled in with their warm drinks, I hurried to the hidden room, where I produced a key from my necklace. I made sure the girls were occupied before shoving the door open. The last thing I needed was for them to try to sneak inside. There were too many dangerous, magical things bound up in here.

The scent of herbs washed over me as I went to the shelf and pulled the ancient leather bound book down. It had been a long time since I'd had this tome out in the open. Not since I'd recorded the information and put it away for safekeeping. My hand trembled as I held it against me. Perhaps I ought to pick a different story. Maybe one with less darkness.

No. Salome needs to hear this one.

When I got back to the living room, I found Salome and Kadie bundled up in a blanket, sipping their cocoa.

"Are you two ready?"

"Yeah. You can sit right here." Salome patted a small spot between her and Kadie.

When I got comfortable, I opened the book. The scent of roses washed over me as if I'd strolled into a summer garden. I cleared my throat.

"Once upon a time, there was a small girl who wandered into the land of Faerie. She'd followed the glowing fluttering wings of what she thought were lightning bugs into the woods and up the hill. But little did she know that dangerous creatures stalked her from the shadows. Pixies, red caps, goblins, trolls… they'd recognized her human scent as soon as she crossed the border between lands. And they hungered for her."

"What are red caps?" Kadie asked, her dark brown eyes wide.

I hesitated, not wanting to scare the girls. "Red caps are a type of goblin. They have red eyes, pointy ears, and wear a red cap, which they keep dyed with human blood."

Salome scooted closer to me. "Eww…is that true?"

"Yes. Well at least in our story it is." I prayed that they never ran into any sort of creature like this. Before I could continue, the girls went on to ask more questions about the pixies, goblins, and trolls and after I described each one, I saw the fear on their faces. Better to have them scared than unaware.

"There are lots of monsters in Faerie," Salome said. "I don't think I'd ever want to go there."

I smiled, ruffling her pale blond hair. "Oh, not everything in Faerie is bad. There are beautiful castles, waterfalls, magical horses, tiny fairies who grant wishes, handsome princes, and strong queens. There is darkness, but also light." My hands gripped tighter to the page. "Maybe I should tell you about the Faerie Queen Genissa and how she saved her people."

"Wait, what about the girl who followed the lightning bugs into Faerie, what happened to her?" Kadie said, trying to pull a giant marshmallow out of her cup.

"Actually, their stories kind of crossover and intertwine. You see, this girl would become the only one who could save Faerie. Perhaps all of us. Not by fate. Not by destiny. It would be by necessity."

Salome cocked her head. "But if she's not the chosen one…"

I couldn't blame her for being confused. This was a fairytale unlike any she'd ever heard, because this one was true.

"Let me explain," I said. "There was an evil queen who was trying to destroy all the courts within the fairyland. And the Queen of Faerie knew she had to stop the bad things from spreading. So this child, the one who followed the lightning bugs, when she came into Faerie, Genissa decided to give the girl all of her power and send her into hiding. She knew that one day, this child would grow up into a strong woman and come back and save everyone. But this special girl would become the target of all the bad faeries and they'd want to gobble her up. So Genissa appointed her a guardian to keep her locked away and safe, until just the right moment. You see, Genissa loved her people very much."

Kadie and Salome both stared at the pictures in the text, then back to me.

"Hey, Salome, the little girl looks kind of like you." Kadie giggled.

"She's got yellow hair like me," Salome said, holding up strands of her pale hair to compare it to the child's in the book.

To them, this was just a story—some fairytale. But they didn't know how real it was. How real the monsters were.

I snuck the cloaked child past the sentries posted along the castle walls, hoping no one realized I harbored a human. If they did, it could mean the end for her—and I'd be labeled as a sympathizer. She'd wandered into Faerie and right into a nest of pixies. If I hadn't been out for a walk, I wasn't sure what would've happened to her; maybe she would've died or perhaps they would've led her deep into the forest and left her there. But no matter the outcome, I knew she wouldn't be here now, if I hadn't found her.

"Quickly, child," I said, tugging her arm.

Her gray-blue eyes met mine. "Where are we going?"

"Shh…don't talk. We're almost there." We came to a garden, and my hands slid along the wood as I searched for the secret door. I brushed my fingers against the hidden handle, and I produced a key from the pocket in my cloak, pushing into the private courtyard of Genissa, the Queen of Faerie. The scent of roses clung to the air around us, flowers and unruly vines spread about our feet, while water sprayed in the nearby fountain. A sharp contrast to the creatures that loomed in the forest outside the castle.

A curtain pulled back at the window and the queen peeked outside. A moment later, she opened the door to her rooms, allowing me to enter. "Dorsinae, what is it?"

"*I'm sorry to disturb you, Your Highness.*" I lowered the hood of my cloak. "*But you told me to come to you if I ever found a human child within the borders of Faerie.*"

Her eyes widened. "*Come closer, child, I will do you no harm.*" She held out her hand to the little girl.

The girl stepped forward. The cloak I'd thrown over her slipped from her head. She raised her small head, her eyes shimmering in the moonlight as she stared around her.

Genissa gasped. "*She's come to us at last, the one I was waiting for.*"

"*What do you mean?*" My fingers trembled as I toyed with the ribbon on the sleeve of my dress, my skin still ink-stained from the archives.

"*Grisselle has grown more powerful. She's embraced the darkness. Already Winter begins to spread it claws. Soon, I will be no match for her—my only hope is to slow her progress.*"

"*But you're the Queen of Faerie, are you not more powerful than your sister?*" My gaze met hers; fear coiled in my stomach.

"*Maybe once upon a time. But she meddles with things beyond our comprehension. She will destroy me. I've foreseen it.*"

"*Then we must whisk you away, put you into hiding,*" I said. "*You know the Spring, Summer, and Autumn courts will aid you.*"

"*No. I will not run away. I will not forsake our kingdom. The Faerie Court will fall into ruin. Dark times will be upon us—but there will be hope. A tiny spark that you shall keep safe for me.*"

"*Genissa, please, I beg you—be reasonable.*" Whatever my friend planned on doing, I knew it would cost her everything.

"*My duty as queen is to protect our lands—our people. I would never forgive myself if I deserted my post.*" She clasped my hand in hers and gave it a gentle squeeze. "*I need to know that you'll do exactly what I tell you to. That you will promise to obey the commands I'm about to give you."*

Tears welled in my eyes. "You know I'd do anything for you, Genissa. You need only ask."

"This child will be the key to everything. Tonight, I shall give her all my powers. They will lie dormant inside her until the time comes."

"No, Gen—I— if you do this, it will leave you unprotected. There must be another way."

"There isn't. I've seen the future, and if we seek to save any part of our world, I must make this sacrifice." She leaned down, taking the girl's shoulders in her hands. "You're brave. I sense strength in you. And one day you will be greater than even me. But your courage will be tested, just as mine is now. You will face many horrible things, yet they will make you stronger. So my young queenling, I gift to you the power of Faerie. That you may embrace the light and fight the darkness. All you'll ever need to know is right here." She placed her hand over the girl's heart.

The child's eyes widened. She swayed on her feet, clutching tight to Genissa's arms. "I want to go home," she whimpered. "I'm scared."

"Shh…it's okay, child. The queen won't hurt you," I said.

The ground beneath us quaked, sending bits of rock from the stone gates to the ground. Thunder boomed overhead like giants tromping through the woods. Leaves and rain and snow swept about the courtyard as the door banged open beneath the heavy gusts of wind. The air tasted of magic.

The Queen looked at me. "With the last of my power, I will put a sleeping spell on her. You must hide with her in the human world. She is not to be awakened until after you have a daughter who is barren."

"As you wish," I said. My throat thickened and I took a deep breath. *"My life is forfeit for whatever task you ask of me."*

"You will insert yourself into this child's human family. Glamour yourself as her elder. One of them has recently passed. If you hurry, you can replace her before anyone finds her. Then make sure the girl disappears until she's needed."

My voice shook. "I'll have to absorb the elder's remaining essence, won't I?"

"Yes. You must take her memories and make them your own. You will become that person. Which is another reason you must be quick. The longer you delay, the less of her essence will remain. Otherwise, you may only use your magic to set up safe boundaries around your homestead." She led me into her room and flung open her closets. *"To keep her safe, you will have to lock the child away in this." She gestured to a marble coffin with a glass lid. "I want you to transfer things from Faerie that you will need in the coming days. Weapons. Artifacts. My scrolls. Whatever you feel you may need to rebuild our kingdom."*

"What if I fail?"

She helped the girl to sit on the floor then clutched me to her chest, pressing her lips to my forehead. *"You cannot fail, Dorsinae. I trust you. You will leave Faerie and not look back. Not until the stars align."*

I'd never been away from Faerie. The human world was but a tale to me. The only knowledge I had of it was from books and papers I'd studied as a scholar. But it was one thing to study a place, and quite another to live there. "I will do my best to honor you."

"There are a few friends I trust in our court, I will make sure they watch after you and the child in the human world. The place you take as your home will be guarded by protection spells. You will be this girl's light. Love her as if she were your own."

Bells rang in the distance, signaling the midnight hour.

"*I will.*"

Genissa released me, knelt next to the child once more, and stroked her blond hair. "Sleep well my beautiful girl. May the blessings of Faerie be upon you."

With that, the girl's eyes drifted shut and Genissa placed her in my arms. "You must go now, the changing of the guards is taking place—you'll be able to slip through unnoticed."

"Will I see you again?"

Genissa gave me a sad smile. "Go, friend. Let us not linger on things that cannot be changed. Great things are at stake."

With a wave of her hand, the top of the coffin slid open and I put the small body inside. It'd be years before I'd see it opened again. And Faerie would be on the brink of destruction—my dearest friend long gone, but not forgotten.

"Grandma, are you okay?" Salome tugged on my sleeve, bringing me back to the present.

"Yes, of course, dear." And after all this time, I actually was okay. "I think maybe that's enough stories for today. Why don't you two come help me make some cookies?"

Winter

How like a winter hath my absence been
From thee, the pleasure of the fleeting year!
What freezings have I felt, what dark days seen!
What old December's bareness everywhere!
And yet this time removed was summer's time;
The teeming autumn, big with rich increase,
Bearing the wanton burden of the prime,
Like widow'd wombs after their lords' decease:
Yet this abundant issue seemed to me
But hope of orphans, and unfathered fruit;
For summer and his pleasures wait on thee,
And, thou away, the very birds are mute:
Or, if they sing, 'tis with so dull a cheer,
That leaves look pale, dreading the winter's near.

—William Shakespeare

Chapter One

Salome

The white stallion ran around the fenced ring, tugging at the lead rope Gareth had tied around its neck. Sweat glistened on Gareth's brow, his billowy black tunic unlaced to reveal tanned skin beneath. With his shaggy golden hair tied back, he looked like a romantic hero straight from one of my mom's romance novels. And the galloping horse just added to the picture. I leaned against the gate and smiled. He was gorgeous even with the jagged scar on his cheek. The arrogant fae warrior was tall. Strong. Powerful.

And he was mine.

It'd only been a couple of weeks since I'd broken the Winter Curse and given up my life in the human world to join Gareth in Faerie. So far, I regretted nothing. Well, other than missing my family and friends. But I loved Gareth and wanted to be where he was. And his house on the outskirts of Faerie was perfect. Not too close to the danger, yet outside the boundaries of the human world.

I swallowed hard. My gaze traveled over his biceps, up his shoulders, to his way too kissable looking lips.

Might want to shut off the thoughts.

Too late.

Gareth glanced up from the horse. His mahogany eyes met mine. I knew then he'd heard every thought through our bond. Trust me, a blood bond sounded great in theory. At least until you realized there was someone inside your head, hearing and seeing everything you dreamed, thought, or saw. Okay, so it didn't happen all the time, just when I got distracted and let my guard down.

"*I can't concentrate with you watching me like that, Salome.*" He grinned, then gave me a wink. "Maybe we ought to go for a swim."

The horse whinnied and charged at him as if he didn't like his flirting with me. I stifled a giggle, but Gareth only glared at the beast.

"If I didn't know any better, I'd say the horse was jealous." He released the rope and stepped away from him.

I laughed. "Don't tell me you feel threatened by a horse."

He shut the gate, locking the animal inside. It snorted, pawing at the ground. "Hardly."

In two long strides, he was in front of me, backing me toward the house. I bumped into the stone structure. My heart thudded like a ball falling down the stairs. He propped his forearms on either side of my head then pressed himself against me.

His fingers brushed my cheek, his breath warm upon my skin as he leaned in.

"*Have I mentioned what a distraction you've been?*" he said inside my head.

"*Several times.*"

"*Why can't I get enough of you?*"

"*Because you're not trying.*"

"We'll have to fix that," he said, aloud this time. Gareth

rested his forehead against mine, his fingers tangling in my hair.

I wrapped my arms around his neck, pulling him closer. "Kiss me."

He wet his lips, his breath already warm upon my cheek. His mind opened to me, and I could feel his love and passion and need. My heart pounded so loudly in my ears, anticipating the moment his lips would touch mine. I stroked the back of his neck, letting my fingers dance across his skin, drawing him closer.

"You have no idea what you do to me." He drew nearer, until his mouth brushed mine.

"Hope I'm not interrupting anything." A familiar voice ruined the moment.

I glowered when I saw my kind of ex-crush, Nevin, standing behind Gareth. To tell you the truth, there'd always been something missing with Nevin that I still didn't understand, which all went to say that I didn't have feelings for Nevin, and I was pretty sure he didn't have feelings for me. But that didn't mean there wasn't still a little tension between him and Gareth.

"You are. Maybe you should come back later." Gareth didn't unlock his gaze from mine.

Nevin's blue eyes hardened. "Is that any way to talk to your king?"

Gareth released me, his smile fading as he turned around.

"He was teasing, Nevin." I rested my hands on my hips, glaring at Nevin.

He stepped closer to me, grabbed my hand, and raised it to his mouth, placing a kiss along my knuckles. "Ah, Salome—as beautiful and outspoken as ever."

"And you're still arrogant." I jerked my fingers free from him. Just because I once *thought* I loved him didn't mean I wanted his lips on me. We'd shared one kiss the whole time we'd been together. And that one kiss had killed me. Literally.

If it wasn't for Gareth and our blood bond, I'd still be dead. Drifting in a sea of ghostly bodies. Though it was hard to blame him since my death broke the curse on Nevin and his people, allowing him to return to the Kingdom of Summer and take up his throne once more. But I'd never forget the fact that he'd used magic on me to try and make me fall in love with him. Almost like I'd been drugged. So yeah, Nevin definitely wasn't my favorite person.

His mouth twitched. "You'd do well to teach your girlfriend some manners, Gareth. If she says that to the wrong person they might not be as forgiving as me."

Manners? I'd teach him some. He might be Summer King, but that didn't mean he could just barge in whenever he pleased. Okay, so it did. Ugh.

Gareth shot me a knowing glance. *"Don't let him goad you."*

"As much as I'd love to stand here and banter with Salome — I've actually come here on business." His brow furrowed, while his grin melted away.

When I stared closer, I saw the dark shadows under his eyes. The worry that lined his features. Something was wrong.

"Why don't we go inside? We can talk in private." Gareth led us to the back door with the high stone arch.

Cool air caressed my skin as I stepped over the threshold. We came to the hallway filled with paintings of battles and tapestries of dancing couples. Deep crimson colors interwoven with gold, blue, and black.

Our footsteps echoed off the hardwood floors, the flames on the candles flickering as if a great wind blew through the house.

When we came to the library door, Gareth glanced over his shoulder at me and Felipe, his butler who'd joined us. "We should only be a few minutes. Felipe, bring in the pomegranate wine."

The dwarf bowed and scurried toward the kitchens. Nevin followed Gareth into the room, his dark hair falling across the back of his neck. I waited for Felipe to return with their drinks and watched as he disappeared inside the library. Moments later he came out and hurried toward the kitchen. The library door started to swing shut, but I caught it with my foot, leaving it ajar.

I pressed myself against the cherry wood wall, listening intently.

"What news from Summer?" Gareth asked.

"Grave tidings," Nevin said. "I wish I was here under happier circumstances."

The sound of a glass being slammed down echoed from within the room. I jumped, heart skittering against my ribs.

"The Winter Queen's poison is spreading," Nevin said. "Everywhere we look, winter leaves its mark. Trees are dying. Plants aren't growing. Our people grow weaker every day as this desolate season spreads." His voice faltered. "Gareth, I know I owe you so much already for all the time you spent keeping our kingdom running while I was imprisoned in the human world, but I must ask one more favor of you."

Gareth grunted, but he was a loyalist. I already knew that whatever Nevin asked, he wouldn't turn him down. And that terrified me.

"What is it?" Gareth said.

"You need to come back to the Summer Palace. Perhaps go into enemy territory and search for a way to defeat our foes. I trust no one else with this matter. All around me people are turning against us."

"No!" My thoughts came through loud. *"You already ran*

his kingdom for three centuries because of his foolishness."

I couldn't believe Nevin would ask this of him.

"Salome, he is my king, I need to hear him out. Regardless of how we feel about him, I owe him my allegiance." Gareth peered out the door then shut it behind him. *"I promise we can talk about this later, but for now I need to give him my undivided attention."*

"But it's not fair for him to ask this of you." My fists clenched at my sides.

"You must understand the position I'm in. I'm a warrior of Summer, Salome. When called on, I need to do what I can."

Furious, I marched down the hall and out the back door. If I was Kadie, I'd tell Nevin to shove it up his ass and leave me and Gareth alone. No way she'd take his crap. But I also didn't want to get Gareth in trouble with Nevin by running my mouth. And deep down, I understood why Gareth would do what Nevin had asked. He cared for his people and would do anything for them. That was one of the things I loved about him. If only Kadie was here so we could gush about him together.

Kadie. How long had it been since I'd seen her? I ticked off the months. And it'd been several weeks since we last spoke. I never got to tell her that I'd moved in with Gareth.

A sudden bout of homesickness washed over me. Maybe I shouldn't have come to Faerie. No matter how much I wanted to fit in here, days like today made it clear I wouldn't. There were always private meetings or talks that I wasn't privy to listen in on, although, Gareth usually told me what was going on. He didn't like keeping things from me. So even though he had a duty to Nevin, he trusted me enough to keep me informed on all things Faerie or Summer.

It just sucked that we always had to drop everything for Nevin. That he could come in and interrupt us at a moment's notice. I thought living on the outskirts of Faerie with Gareth would alleviate some of that, but apparently Nevin could magically poof himself to our house whenever he wanted.

With a sigh, I made my way to the training ring where the stallion stood. He eyed me a moment, then trotted over.

"Hey boy." I reached between the wooden planks to pet his head. "I'm beginning to think you're the only friend I have here besides Gareth."

Wow. Was I really talking to the horse? He sniffed my hand then bowed his head. The trees danced beneath the breeze. The scent of honey swirled around, making me heady.

Without another thought, I hefted myself atop the fence, throwing first one leg over, then the next until I stood inside the circled area. Once again, I held my fingers out to the steed.

"Steady boy. I won't hurt you."

Odd. He wasn't freaking out on me like he did with Gareth. Instead, he trotted right up and nudged my shoulder.

God, I might live to regret this. But I was sick of Nevin always butting into everything. He used people to get what he wanted—he'd used me to break his curse and he'd used Gareth to keep his kingdom running, and here he was again, trying to make Gareth go back out there and risk his life. And if Gareth got sent away, I didn't know what I'd do. He was my lifeline out here to understanding Faerie, to staying connected to my humanity. Right now, all I wanted to do was ride the horse. To get away from Nevin and his superiority complex. Because even though I understood why Gareth had agreed, Nevin never should have asked him to do this in the first place.

"Okay, I'm gonna climb on your back." *Please don't let him trample me.* He knelt down before me as if to help me up. *Well this is kinda weird.*

I took a deep breath and slung my leg over. Unsure of what

to hold on to, I tangled my fingers in his mane. The movies always made riding bareback look easy, but I was certain I'd slide off any minute now and land in a pile of horse crap.

I gave his flanks a light tap with my feet. The animal walked slowly around the circle and I tightened my knees against his warm sides to keep from falling. It gave a toss of his head then pawed the dirt. Unfortunately, I didn't speak stallion, so I had no idea what he wanted.

After a second he picked up his pace. The small circles made me dizzier with each pass. Suddenly, I understood what he needed. More room to run.

"If you promise to be good we can open the gate."

I hoped this wouldn't tick Gareth off, but I couldn't stand to be around Nevin, and if I stayed here, I might say something to get us both in trouble. Besides, I wasn't a prisoner here, and if I wanted to go for a ride they sure as heck weren't going to stop me. Back home—well, what had once been home—I'd learned I couldn't go practically anywhere without worrying about being attacked. But here, there were so many guards and magic spells warding the land that I couldn't help but feel safe. As long as I didn't go far, I'd be okay.

Well, assuming the horse didn't kick me off within the first five minutes…

"Don't make me regret this," I muttered.

The horse whinnied and moved alongside the fence. I leaned over and unlatched the gate, opening it wide enough for us to get through.

I expected him to charge into the woods, but instead he took slow, hesitant steps forward. Once I settled myself back in place and held tight to his neck, he dashed toward the wood-line, galloping down the tree lined path.

We zipped by ancient oaks and maples, their green canopies

blotting out the sun. Tiny wildflowers dotted the trail like a burst of rainbows. I ducked beneath low hanging branches, watching butterflies flit out of the way. My hair whipped behind me. What a rush—kind of like riding a motorcycle.

Beams of sunlight kissed my face as we raced wildly through the foliage. I smiled and tightened my grip when we neared a bend in the path. All of a sudden the horse came to a jarring halt. With a screech, I flew from my mount, landing on the ground a few feet ahead of him. I groaned, staring up at the sky. Crap. Had I even made it five minutes?

My head hurt. The horse let out a loud neigh and came to hover over me.

A frigid wind snaked around me like icy tentacles brushing my skin. I stilled. Goosebumps puckered my arms. Puffs of condensation escaped my lips as I breathed out.

What's happening?

I heard several crackling sounds. My gaze swept over the woodland as I attempted to sit upright. I gasped.

This can't be.

Panic gripped me, squeezing until I thought I might pass out. Ice crept across the ground, leaving a layer of frost on the plants and flowers; much like a slug leaves behind a slimy trail.

We need to go.

But before I could get up, a woman stepped from behind a great white oak. Her hair was white as a January blizzard. She wore robes of such a deep blue it made me think of frozen waters. A crystal crown sat upon her head. Her lips had a bluish-purple tint to them, reminding me of a drowning victim. Severe blue eyes narrowed as they took me in. Even though I'd never met her before, I'd seen enough drawings of her to be pretty sure this was the Winter Queen.

A slow sardonic grin spread across her pale face. "Ah, the

human who saved the Summer King—alone in the woods at last. You can't imagine how long I've been waiting and watching you. They must not care enough to protect you."

I sat straighter, my pulse quickening as I slid closer to my horse. "I don't need their protection."

"Is that so?" Her mouth twisted. "Because of you I lost my stronghold on Summer. And for that, I want you dead." She moved closer, gliding across the fern covered ground. The once green fronds snapped off in her wake. "This time I won't send a petty witch for the job."

The horse moved up further like he wanted to protect me from her, convincing me even more that we had to get out of there.

Maybe if I asked her questions I could stall her long enough for me to get on the horse and ride away.

Yeah, that'll work. Just like in the movies.

"Kassandra? She worked for you?"

"And she failed me."

I bit my lip, trying not to think about the gnarled monster who'd nearly killed me in the human world. The witch who'd cursed Nevin and his troupe and had wreaked havoc on my family line for centuries. Until I'd broken the curse, destroying her.

My blood went cold. My body numbed as the queen's magic crept around us. Soon, all that remained green was the small patch of grass the horse and I were on. I sucked in deep breaths, my chest tightening. But I couldn't stop the images flashing through my mind of my childhood self. Drifting beneath the icy waters of the pond. Darkness. The cold. Death.

The queen raised her hands above her head. "I'm the one who gave Kassandra the means to set the curse in place—such a feeble girl couldn't even handle you." In one swift motion, she brought her hands down.

Dark shadows encircled her. Magic exploded, shaking the forest floor beneath us. The scent of sulfur and rotten fruit made me gag. The stallion bucked up, and for long seconds, horror enveloped me—

Warmth flooded through my veins, and my skin tingled like tiny shock waves traveled through my blood. A second later the horse snorted and slammed his hooves to the ground. A bright light flashed then cascaded down like rain and created a magical shield around us. My body vibrated as a loud humming grew in my ears.

Whoa, what just happened? Had the horse protected me? The circle pulsed with the deep greens of the forest. A rocky outcropping sprouted up like walls between us and the queen. The chill melted away and the air became warm once more.

"This power isn't strong enough to shield you forever," she snarled, taking a step back.

A loud *whoosh* sounded, while currents of hot hair blew my hair back. The woods erupted with golden light. "No, but mine is."

Nevin glared at the Winter Queen, his sword already drawn. Beside him Gareth unsheathed his own weapon.

"You're trespassing, Grisselle. And outside your own court, your powers aren't strong enough to take on both me and the king." Gareth took a step closer, the snow melting beneath each footfall. "So what'll it be?"

Beams of sunlight sprung from Nevin's fingertips, burning the hem of her robes. The queen screeched then stomped at them to try and put them out. The stench of burnt material hung heavy in the air.

"This isn't over. I will kill *all* of you." Grisselle raised her arms as if she might fly off then she wrapped herself inside her cloak and disappeared.

I let out a sigh of relief. If they hadn't shown up, I wasn't sure what I would've done. My fingers trembled as I stood and stroked the horse's mane.

I leaned over and whispered in his ear, "Thank you."

He nodded his head, staring down the guys.

Great. I'm in for it now.

Gareth sheathed his blade then turned to me. His eyes blazed like hellish fires. "Do you know how worried I was about you? Damn it, Salome, you can't just run off like that." In two quick strides he had me in his arms, hugging me tight to his chest. I buried my head against him, taking in his scent, his familiarity.

"I'm sorry."

"I know. Just please, next time you're going somewhere, at least tell me through our bond, or better yet, wait for me to finish talking so I can come with you."

"It's just hard having him here. I had to get away…"

He released me then glanced at Nevin. "Get back on the horse, Salome, and go straight to the house." Gareth gave me a knowing look, and I knew he was just doing this for show in front of Nevin.

But before I could move, Nevin jerked me from Gareth's side. His fingers dug into my shoulder as he forced me to look at him.

"You could've been killed." He shook me. "What the hell were you thinking?"

Um—okay, why did he seem angrier than my boyfriend?

"I—I'm sorry. I just went for a ride."

"And almost got killed." Nevin's jaw clenched. "You need to be mindful that you're not in the human world. There are things and people here who will not hesitate to end your life.

Especially now that they know you have powers."

My eyes widened. "Wait, what? I don't have powers, are you freaking crazy?"

"How do you think this magical shield protected you?"

"That wasn't me, that was the horse." I tried to back away from him.

He didn't look nearly as convinced as I wished he would be. "Perhaps. But if you do have powers, it's as I suspected." He shook his head. "This would change everything. I knew Doris had to be protecting you for a reason. And that reason is becoming very clear." His gaze shifted to Gareth, who stood silent, watching the woods. "I'm going to send some of my guards back here to escort you and Salome to the summer palace. It's the only place *we* can keep her safe."

"Yes, Your Highness." Gareth bowed, but already I felt his irritation running wild through our link.

"What the hell's going on?" I thought.

His gaze met mine. *"Winter is closer than it should be. That's what Nevin and I were talking about. Things are about to change. And you might not like some of the changes. But know that I have your best interest in mind."*

Nevin released his hold on me. "I expect to see you both by week's end. You too." He nodded at the horse, who moved closer to me. Nevin grinned.

"What?" I folded my arms across my chest.

"At least I know your virginity and virtue are still intact."

"Excuse me? My virtue is of no concern of yours. Besides, for all you know, Gareth and I have slept together hundreds of times." God, he was such an asshole.

He chuckled. "Now you're just flat out lying, my little human. You see, if you weren't a virgin, then the Horse Prince here, Adaba, wouldn't protect you. He only assists and guards fair maidens with their maidenhood intact."

Well that explained his aggressiveness toward Gareth. I glanced at the horse, who seemed to nod in approval.

"Again, I don't see where any of this is your business." My voice hardened. He caught loose tendrils of my hair between his fingers, studying them as if he thought they might come to life. "You'll soon find out, Salome, everything in Summer is my business."

My vision blurred as rage pounded inside my head. Not just my rage, but Gareth's too. Nevin dropped his hand.

"I will leave you two to prepare for your journey." With that, he faded into the trees and disappeared.

"Do you want to explain what's going on?" My eyes settled on Gareth. "You can't really believe I have powers. I mean, I think I'd know if I had magic. Not to mention how weird Nevin's acting."

"Salome, please let's just go back to the house and get packed."

"So what? Is this going to be like last time? You know things but won't talk to me about them?"

"No. Of course not. I'll try to explain everything later." He stared at some unseen thing in the distance. "But right now, we need to get you back to safety."

I stared at Gareth, and before he could start back, I reached a hand out toward him. He smiled and touched my fingers, clasping them tightly. Together we tromped up the path, toward his estate in silence.

Things were changing. I could feel it. And somehow I knew nothing would be the same again. This journey was about to set it all in motion.

CHAPTER TWO

Kadie

I cranked the music in an attempt to drown out the world. My gaze flickered to the "You're now leaving Texas, come back soon" sign and I glared.

Yeah right. I saluted the stupid billboard with a middle finger.

Good riddance.

People said everything's bigger in Texas. And they were right. Because the world's biggest asshole lived there. Zac. Just the thought of him ticked me off all over again.

I should've seen it coming. I mean, what girl actually moves thousands of miles away from home to follow her high school sweetheart to college?

Yep—that idiot would be me. The same girl who walked in on her boyfriend to find some stupid blond with her head buried in his lap. I'd startled them—too bad I hadn't scared her enough to bite his wanker off.

My fingers clenched the steering wheel and I pushed the gas pedal down as if I had a brick attached to my foot. I passed the pickup truck in front of me, only to gag on the muffler fumes that sputtered from its tailpipe.

I hated Zac. Hated his dumb ass grin. Hated the dimple in his cheek that looked like someone had hole-punched his face. I despised the new tattoo on his arm. Longhorns. I'd like to shove a longhorn somewhere… Yeah, this totally sucked.

Texas hadn't been what I'd thought it'd be. The size of the school overwhelmed me. So many people and classes and buildings. It wasn't like my hometown back in Michigan where everyone knew me and my family. It's like I'd lost myself down there. And the one person I was supposed to count on cheated on me, making me feel more alone than ever. I'd always wanted to get away from Starlynn Village, but it became apparent real quick that I was used to being somebody, and well, down there, it was hard to be noticed at all.

Take a deep breath. I'll be home soon and Salome will make me feel better. She always does.

I glanced at my cell on the seat next to me. Still no call. I'd left her like forty-five messages since this morning and I really needed her. I'd always tried to be there for her, but here I was having a crisis and she couldn't do the same for me. Maybe she was mad at me for being such a crappy friend. I mean, it'd been well over a month since we last spoke. However, that wasn't *all* my fault. She had a phone too.

But I knew better. Salome didn't hold grudges. My chest tightened. God, I missed my bestie. She always knew the right thing to say to make things better. Already, I pictured her standing in her doorway with a box of chocolates, some tissues, and a stack of chick-flicks. She'd hug me like she always did and tell me I was too good for Zac.

Which I totally am.

I smiled through the tears. Nope. I wasn't gonna waste another tear on his sorry butt. I knew several guys back home who'd give their left kidney to go out with me.

My pep talk lasted all of two seconds.

Shit. I still had to break the news to my parents that Thanksgiving vacation was going to last a lot longer than anticipated. As in, I dropped out of college and would be moving back to Michigan. With them. But maybe the fact that I'd already looked at a couple local colleges to transfer back to would lighten the blow. Or maybe they'd take it in stride and be thankful I was home. And all that pilgrims and Indians sharing and getting along crap would rub off.

Right. Who was I kidding?

I'm so dead.

*H*opped up on gas station coffee, I pulled into our narrow dirt driveway. I turned the ignition off and stared at the wraparound porch. White wicker furniture sat on either side of the door. Mom's hanging flower baskets held only dead skins of the summer blooms. Light flickered in the windows, bathing the ground in a golden splash. I sat there for long minutes, trying to compose myself.

Okay. You can do this.

My teeth grazed my bottom lip and I ran my fingers through my dark hair.

The curtains pulled back. One of my younger twin brothers, Casey, peeked out.

Ah hell. Here goes nothing.

The front door burst open like a pair of pants after a holiday meal. My family poured out. Mom, Dad, Casey, and Carter.

"You made it." Mom squashed me to her chest as she hugged

me tight. "I got worried when I saw the snow coming down."

"Nope, I'm fine. Just tired." I gave her a weak smile then turned to my dad.

He ruffled my hair. "There's our college girl. How are you, sweetie?"

"Oh Reed, let her get her stuff and come inside." Mom's gaze drifted to my car. She eyed all the boxes. Her brow furrowed, but she didn't say anything. "You're just in time for dinner." She ushered me toward the house, not even letting me stop to grab the stuff from my vehicle.

Once we got inside, the scent of fried chicken overwhelmed me. The rooster clock chimed on the hour, and I stared at the large fireplace with the pictures of me and my brothers lining the mantel above it. Relief washed over me. I was finally home.

"Do you want to get a quick shower before we eat?" Mom patted my arm.

My stomach growled. "No. I'm starving."

I followed my family to the dining room, taking my seat next to Carter at the table. Mom quickly brought platters and dishes filled with food in. Fried chicken, mashed potatoes, green beans, biscuits, apple pie. All my favorites. It'd been so long since I'd had a home cooked meal. I used a fork to grab the chicken breast, then scooped a large heap of potatoes onto my plate.

After dumping gravy all over everything, I took a huge bite, savoring the taste.

"It looks like you brought everything home with you," Mom said like a bloodhound on a trail.

Damn it. Okay. Tell the truth.

"That's because I did." Might as well get straight to the point. "I dropped out of school."

"You *what*?" Dad's voice boomed behind me.

"Kadie, what the hell were you thinking?" Mom's shrieks outdid his as she dropped her biscuit on the table.

"I'm sorry. I just needed to come home."

"You are not quitting school." Mom glanced my way. "When Thanksgiving's over you're going back to Texas."

"No. I'm not." My jaw tightened. "I can't go back. I dropped my classes."

"Then we'll call the administration office and tell them it was a mistake."

"No. You don't understand."

"Understand? What's there to understand? Tell me why you just threw away thousands of dollars in tuition."

"Because I'm homesick. Texas is so far away from everyone. And I can't get used to the big crowds." Here came the big one. "Plus I caught Zac with some other chick." My fists clenched at my side. "I can't bear to go back."

Casey and Carter looked between us. Dad shot me a warning look. "Why don't you boys go on up to your rooms for a few minutes. You don't need to hear this conversation."

Mom reached across the short distance and grabbed my arm then gave me a strong shake. "You don't quit college over a boy. This isn't high school."

"It's not just about him, it's about me, too! I don't fit in down there. It's not like Michigan, where I had tons of friends. I have nothing down there. No friends. No family. Zac is history. I just can't go back. You've got to understand."

Dad crossed his arms across his chest and stared me down. "Kadie, you can't quit school. You're practically an adult, which means you need to act like one. And adults don't quit school over boys."

The fuck they didn't! "Did you not hear me? This isn't just about Zac."

"Sounds like it to me," Mom said. "We just want what's best for you. Quitting school a semester in isn't doing you any favors."

"You know what? I don't need this." I leapt to my feet. "I came home to get away from everything. But if you aren't going to let me stay, then I'm going to Salome's."

"We didn't say you couldn't stay," Mom said, reaching for me.

But I pushed around her, grabbed my jacket from the living room chair, then hurried outside. With a sob, I jerked my car door open.

"Kadie," Mom called after me.

"Look, I've had a really long couple of days and I can't do this right now. I'll be at Salome's if you need me." My eyes blurred. I slammed the door shut and started the engine.

Mom and Dad stepped back as I threw the car in reverse and peeled out of the driveway. Snowflakes covered my windshield and I turned on the wipers.

"Just get to Salome's," I told myself, my voice cracking. "Everything will be okay." Life sucked. I'd known my parents would be pissed, but I didn't think they'd freak out and not want me back home.

They didn't get it. All my friends in Texas were friends of Zac's, too. Most of them knew he'd cheated on me and never bothered to tell me. I must've been the biggest laughing stock at the frat house. Didn't it mean anything that I'd have told them? Heck, that I *had* told them when I'd seen something like that? But they hadn't returned the favor, and I'd been so busy taking care of everyone else that I hadn't seen what was right in front of my eyes.

And now my parents were pissed. Shit. They didn't even let me explain that I planned on still going to school, just not in

Texas. It wasn't like I decided to be a deadbeat or something.

Hell the only reason I'd gone to Texas in the first place was because of Zac. He might not have been my first boyfriend, but he was the only serious one I'd ever had. But now that we were through, I wanted to be in Michigan where my family and friends were. Where I could at least feel safe and valued.

The sky darkened as I drove the familiar roads to the Montgomery's house. When I got to the wrought iron gate, I pushed the intercom button to be let in.

"Hello?" Ms. Montgomery's friendly voice piped up.

"It's Kadie, can I come in?"

"Oh, sure." She seemed startled by the request, as if I hadn't been here a thousand times before. "Come on up."

When I got through the gate, I parked next to Salome's old jeep. I smiled, eager to see her. I leapt from my car and raced onto the porch, where Ms. Montgomery stood holding the door ajar.

"Hey, Ms. M. I just got back and wanted to come by and see Salome."

"Oh, didn't Salome tell you, sweetie? She moved in with Gareth a couple weeks ago. I don't have their new address yet."

Moved in with Gareth? No way. Salome wouldn't do something that big and not tell me. I mean, we had a best friend code. We told each other everything. I was always there for her and here I needed her more than anything and she wasn't around. And apparently she was keeping secrets from me, too!

"I can let her know you stopped by next time I see her."

What the hell? Something wasn't right. She was lying to me, but why? I mean, there was no chance in hell Ms. Montgomery would let Salome move in with an older guy without at least getting an address and phone number.

My throat thickened. Unless, of course, Salome was avoiding

me. Maybe this really was payback for not talking to her over the last few weeks.

Don't be stupid. She isn't like that.

"Okay, tell her I'll be in town. Not sure where I'm staying yet. But I'll have my phone on me."

"Take care." She glanced at the woods, then shut the door before I could say anything else.

Why's everyone acting so weird? And where the hell is Salome?

Snow swirled across the yard, dusting my jeans. Winter scared the crap out of her. There was no way she'd be out in it. Besides, her jeep was home. Maybe I ought to bust into her house. Salome's room was on the first floor. But even from here, I noticed her window was dark.

I trudged back to the vehicle and slid into the driver seat. Shit. I really needed to find her. I wondered if Gareth still worked backstage at *Club Blade*. I could take a quick trip out there and pop inside. Because Gareth would definitely know how to get a hold of Salome. And I needed my girl more than I wanted to admit. But I remembered the strange things that happened last time I was there. Maybe the club wasn't such a great idea.

My phone beeped indicating I had a text message. I almost dreaded looking it, wondering if it was my parents trying to get a hold of me to yell at me some more. Hesitant, I picked up my cell and slid the screen over only to find a text from Salome.

Mom said you were home. Can you come get me? Gareth and I had a huge fight—I'm at Club Blade. Please, hurry.

Damn! I didn't want her there by herself. I typed back:

On my way.

God, I couldn't wait to see her. I hoped everything was all right.

CHAPTER THREE

Salome

"Make sure you pack light." Gareth tossed a leather bag onto my bed. "We'll need to travel fast."

I stared at his back as he walked out the door. Ugh. Why was he being so aloof now? Okay, so the answer to that should be easy. Nevin. Why did Nevin have to waltz in here and ruin everything? I whipped open my white oak armoire and tugged a few dresses from their hangers. I wadded them up and shoved them into my bag. They'd be more wrinkled than an elderly tit by the time we got to Summer.

My hand ran across the blue silk curtains that framed my four-poster bed. The fire in the white marble fireplace had already been dowsed. Windows hid behind heavy plum drapes. This had become my home. A place I thought I'd spend eternity basking in Gareth's hotness, not running from maniacal winter queens and dealing with ex-crushes.

With a sigh, I walked to the trunk at the far side of the room and unlatched the gold fastenings. Inside I found several cloaks of varying shades of blue, yellow, and black. I pulled out one of each color and secured them in my pouch as well. God, what

I wouldn't give for a pair of jeans and a jacket right now. But according to Gareth, no one in Faerie wore jeans, which was totally stupid.

They don't know what they're missing.

Bag in hand, I trudged from my room shutting the door behind me. I made my way down the dim hall to Gareth's room. His door was ajar, giving me a view of his thick shoulders as he folded a couple pairs of breeches.

My breath caught in my throat. He was so perfect. So beautiful. So—

"Are you finished packing then?" He didn't even turn to look at me.

"Yes."

"Good. Felipe should have our food already bundled." He sheathed a long sword at his side.

I leaned against the doorway. "You said we'd talk when we got back. So what's really going on here? What did Nevin want?"

Gareth stiffened and ran a hand through his hair. "He wants us to come to Summer. He needs me to do some scouting for him into enemy territory, but mainly he wants me to help train the soldiers. We have some veteran warriors, but over the years, we've lost so many. Most of our troops are young and untrained. If we're going to be able to continue to hold our borders, we need to make sure our army is battle ready."

"Is that all?"

"There was also some discussion regarding you, but I'd rather not get into that just now or I'll get pissed off all over again."

"Does it have to do with what he said about me maybe having magic?" I hoped not. Because I still believed Adaba had been responsible for it.

"Yes. But we can talk about that later. And I promise we will speak about that, too. But right now we've got to hurry up and get packed. We need to be on our way soon. After your run in with the Winter Queen, I don't want to chance her coming back with an army."

"Are you still mad at me?" I slipped inside his room, my eyes intent on him.

He spun to face me, his gaze piercing me like a lance. "Damn right I'm mad. This is the second time I've nearly lost you since we've bonded." He dropped his things on the bed and moved toward me. "Do you know what it's like to feel someone you love on the verge of death?"

He caught my chin, forcing me to look at him.

"I said I was sorry."

His brow furrowed as he pulled me into his arms. My blood thrummed at his closeness. Already, his warmth blanketed me. I nestled against him. He caressed my back, moving to my hips, until he pressed me closer against him. My fingers trailed up his chest, stopping only when they cupped his face. I stood on my tiptoes, until my mouth crushed his.

His lips parted and his tongue glided against mine. He deepened the kiss, lifting me up in his arms, until my face was level with his. I wrapped my legs around his waist, my arms slipping behind his neck.

God, I couldn't get enough of him. I just wanted us to stay here, in his room, and not have to worry about Grisselle or Nevin or Winter. I wanted to concentrate on us. On the heat that blazed between us. On the life we were trying to build with one another. I'd hoped when I'd agreed to come to Faerie with him that we'd left the horrors of Winter behind us, that after Kassandra's death, I'd get my happily ever after, which never happened.

He groaned, trailing kisses down my neck. "Salome, we're supposed to be packing."

"I'm already finished." I pulled back so I could stare into his mahogany eyes. "Don't tell me I'm distracting you? I thought you were a warrior? That you could resist anything."

His lips curved up into a playful smile. "Hmm...did I say resist? I meant succumb. I can only succumb to your charms... and if you don't stop now, you might succumb my clothes right off me."

A blush touched my cheeks, and I rested my palm against the side of his face, feeling the light prickle of stubble. "It's good to know that I have the power to seduce you, Gareth of Summer. I was beginning to think you were immune to me, that you had the constraint of a monk."

"Definitely not immune—and does this make you think of monks?" He twisted around until he had me pressed to the wall, his body molded against mine. He traced the contours of my hips, then slipped upward until his thumb brushed against my lips, followed by his mouth. He kissed me until I was dizzy with nothing but thoughts of him and I together. Every breath I took was filled with him. Every scent. Every touch. Until at last he drew back, his teeth taking my bottom lip between them. "You were saying?"

Breathless, I stared at him. He was so perfect, so handsome. I still didn't understand what he saw in me. "No more visions of monks," I said.

"I wish we had time to finish this," he whispered. "But I want our first time to be special, not rushed."

"Too bad you don't have a Holiday Inn close by," I teased. Pressing my mouth against his temple, then his cheek, until my mouth grazed his earlobe.

He lowered me back to the floor and I reached out to

steady myself. Drunk on his kisses, I needed a moment to get my bearings back. He held me up, until I could stand on my own.

"And by the way, don't ever doubt my love for you. You might be from the human world, but you're the most perfect woman for me. Do you understand?"

His gaze slid over me as if he could see right into my very soul. To the deepest depths that no one else saw or knew. And he was mine.

"Let's try and enjoy our journey—it'll likely be our last for a while." He stroked my hair then let his hands fall away as he released me. He bent over to retrieve his belongings from the floor.

"Wait—what do you mean our last journey?"

"Once we get to Summer, I'll be pretty busy, like I told you I'll have to do some training and scouting." He closed the curtains on his bed and headed to the door.

I followed on his heels. "I still don't understand why Nevin can't do it himself. Why do you have to go all the way to the Summer Palace to do this for him?"

"Because he's king and he asked me to."

"Since when do you do what you're told?"

I knew the answer. This wasn't just about doing what he was told. It was about his loyalty and his duty to his people. But I loved him and I missed him already. Was it too much to ask to spend more than a few weeks together before he left again?

He held up a hand. "You know I have a duty to Nevin, whether I like it or not. Besides, this isn't about him, it's about our kingdom. Winter claims more of our people every day. We have to stop the queen. In case your earlier run in with her wasn't any indication."

Guilt gnawed at my bones like a mangy hound with a

rawhide strip. "I know. It's just, well, it seems like you're always the one they send."

He chuckled. "That's because they know I'll get the job done. I'm the best warrior in the kingdom."

"Cocky much?"

"You know you like it."

We pushed through the back door to find Felipe readying the horses. When the dwarf spotted us, he hurried to take our packs.

When he had our bags secured, Gareth caught his arm. "Make sure the house is locked up tight and seek safety as soon as you can. I'll send word when we return."

Felipe bowed then scurried back inside.

Adaba stomped his foot and snorted at us. His head swung back and forth with impatience. Gareth glanced down at me. "I suppose he wants us to hurry."

As soon as his mahogany eyes met mine, I was lost. My heart skittered against my ribs, remembering the kisses we'd shared in his room just moments ago. My blood throbbed with ancient songs. He took a step closer, his arms ensnaring me. Callused hands caressed my cheek.

Gareth's lips were a breath away from mine. "Perhaps we can forget about Nevin for a few more minutes."

Adaba whinnied and shoved between us, his hoof nearly smashing my toes.

"Hey," I scolded. Where'd this horse come from anyway, the dang Dark Ages? Didn't he know nowadays people kissed all the time?

Gareth glared. "I have a feeling he's going to be worse than a chastity belt."

The horse's lips peeled back in a toothy smile. He nudged my shoulder then bent for me to climb on his back. He was enjoying this far too much.

Once settled in on our saddles, Gareth glanced at the sky then at me. "We need to get as far as possible before nightfall. No telling which of the queen's monsters will be lurking."

"What about the soldiers Nevin was going to send?" I scanned our surroundings.

"We don't have time to wait for them. They can meet up with us on the road."

I shivered in spite of the warm sun beating down on me. No way did I want to have any run-ins with any creature. I'd spent eleven years facing the nightmarish beasts in the woods as a child. Being haunted by winter and everything that lurked within its gloom. I'd already faced so many of them when I broke Nevin's curse, and I wanted no more of it.

Wind whispered through the leaves like a soft lullaby. Great oaks swayed beneath the gusts, while the scent of daffodils drifted around us. Gnarled branches entwined above, acting as a gateway of sorts.

Gareth led us through woodlands and across sweeping fields of wildflowers. Soon I recognized the path leading to the lake where we'd danced at prom. I smiled, remembering Gareth in his black and white tux. The way he'd let me into his world that night. It was the first moment I realized there was something between us.

Adaba sidestepped a barberry bush. He danced in place, refusing to go further. My stomach knotted while I inspected our surroundings. I didn't see anything. The birds had stopped singing. Not even the wind rustled.

"Something's wrong." Gareth pulled up on his reins.

"I don't hear the lake. Or smell the sea salt." I rubbed my arms against the sudden briskness in the air. "Do you think it's the queen?"

"No, I don't sense anyone. But we need to proceed with caution."

Adaba snorted, but followed Gareth's steed. As we turned the bend in the road, I gasped. White flakes glittered as they fell from the sky. Giant waves were frozen in mid-air where they'd once splashed against the beach. Everything was barren and covered in snow and ice.

Puffs of breath fell from between my chattering teeth.

"Oh. My. God." I wrapped my arms around my chest in an attempt to keep warm. "Winter's spreading."

Gareth stared at his devastated land, jaw clenched. "She's going to pay for this and for every crime against Summer."

He kicked his heels into the sides of his horse and galloped across the icy landscape. I had no choice but to urge Adaba forward, too. For long minutes, I thought he might keep the startling pace, but as we reached the woods and the summery warmth once more, he slowed for me to catch up.

We continued deeper into the forest, passing by gurgling streams and ducking under low branches. But Gareth remained quiet. The forlorn look on his face unsettled me. It wasn't like him to clam up like this. As the day pressed on, I grew restless. There was only so much silence I could take. And the happily chirping birds drove me crazy.

"Are you going to spend the entire trip not talking?" I narrowed my eyes at his back.

"No. I just need time to sort things in my mind." He glanced over his shoulder. "Why don't we stop so the horses can get a drink and rest for a few minutes?"

Adaba came to a halt and I slid from his back. He glanced at me then made his way over to the stream with the other horse. I yawned, stretching my arms above my head.

Gareth smiled and tossed me a hunk of bread. "Just think,

only a few more days of travels."

I plopped onto the ground and laid back. "Ugh, don't remind me. My ass is already numb from riding."

He took a swig of water from the skin, then frowned. "Is that the proper way a lady should speak?"

With a snort, I propped my head on my arms. "Fine. My asseth is numbeth—better?"

"No. You should be more mindful."

I sat up, staring at him. He'd lost his flipping mind. Then it dawned on me. "Oh my gosh. You're worried about impressing Nevin when we get to Summer. Unfreaking believable. But just so you know, I don't give a crap what he thinks."

"You should," Gareth said, putting the skin back. "But it's not him you'll need to impress—the other Fae nobles will be there, and let's just say they're not all keen on humans."

I sighed and pushed to my feet once more. "You're the only Fae Lord I care about impressing. And you've seen me at my worst."

"And impress me you did. You're perfect to me, even at your worst, but I'm also madly in love with you. The others may see your quirks and behaviors as offensive and off-putting. Because they don't know you like I do." He caught my hand and tugged me beneath a giant weeping willow tree, where tiny beams of sunlight snuck through like dancing fireflies. "I just want you to fit in and feel like you belong with my people."

I sighed. "You're not embarrassed by me, are you?"

"No. How could I be? You're beautiful." He kissed my forehead. "Strong." He placed another kiss on my cheek. "You broke a curse that no one else was able to for centuries." His lips lightly touched my nose. "And you're the kindest, most self-sacrificing person I've ever met in my life." This time he kissed me on the mouth.

Which lasted all of two seconds before Adaba came bounding over. He immediately pried us a part by wedging himself between us.

"Guess that's our cue to be on our way." Gareth glowered at the horse. "Remind me not to invite him to our wedding…"

The horse let out a low nicker that sounded a whole lot like a laugh to me.

After a while we mounted our horses once more and headed through the woods. We rode for several hours, passing through fields so green that it made me envision The Shire, from Lord of the Rings—hills the color of emeralds giving way to miles of blue sky. Soon we came to a crossroad and Gareth studied the terrain. At last, he urged his steed down an overgrown path.

Here the grass seemed more brittle. The flowers that once bloomed in the fields and along the roadside were now nothing but brown husks. Dilapidated cottages and homes dotted the hillside. Weathered stones, bearing the markings of a flower, were nearly covered in dead moss.

"Where are we?" I turned in my saddle to see the stricken look on Gareth's face.

"This used to be the Kingdom of Spring. They were the first to fall to Winter." Gareth brought his horse to a halt and climbed from his back.

"Were there any survivors?" Sadness washed over me as I stared at the landscape.

"Very few. Most died when the king did. There are a few stragglers and half-breeds, but most of them stay hidden."

"I-I see." My throat thickened as we stepped over fallen trees and the remains of destroyed homes.

An old gate caught my eye and I stopped to see the remnants of the old rosebushes. I dropped Adaba's reins and walked across the uneven ground, until I stood inside it. Small statues and a dried up fountain lingered inside. At one time, this had been someone's garden. But now it was just a brown, dead reminder of what once was.

My fingers brushed against the withered roses, brown and moldy with decay. Tears welled in my eyes. This land was another victim of Winter. Just thinking about all the people who hadn't been able to escape and the homes that would never see life again, filled me with a sorrow so deep, that it hurt my heart.

"I wish I could change this," I whispered. "That all could be like it was before Winter came."

"Salome, we need to keep moving. There should be a place ahead where we can stop to get a few supplies, then we'll find camp for the night."

I nodded, letting go of the rose and stepping out of the garden. Not that I wanted Gareth to go to Summer, but I was beginning to understand more now, why it was so important. Although, I wasn't sure how they'd be able to keep Winter at bay when no one else had been able to so far.

Adaba nudged my arm as we walked. "What is it boy?"

He glanced up to where a lone finch landed on a tree branch. I smiled as it whistled a light tune. This had been the first life I'd seen since stepping into Spring. But it somehow gave me hope.

We made our way through the thicket, Gareth leading the way, until we came to a large hut, nearly hidden in the overgrowth. If Gareth hadn't of pointed it out, I would've walked right past it.

"What is this place?" I said.

"A store. The last remaining one in Spring." Gareth took my reins from me. "Adaba, I want you to keep your eyes and ears peeled while we're inside. If you catch even a hint of danger, I want you to alert us."

The horse bowed his head as if he understood and went

to hide in the brush so no one would see him. Gareth and I made our way around the back of the hut, where we were met by a short, grizzled looking dwarf. His gray beard was braided with green and silver beads at the ends. His dark eyes narrowed as they took us in. He wore a dirtied tunic and breeches—his boots had long since seen better days. My gaze flickered to the battle axe he held over one shoulder as if daring us to take another step.

Ancient green and silver tattoos ran the length of both arms, while another peeked out from the collar of his shirt.

"You're trespassing," his gravelly voice called out.

"Lachlin, it's me, Gareth of Summer. We mean no harm. I've just come to see what kinds of weapons you have on hand."

"Been a long time, my friend," He lowered his weapon, resting it on the ground. "I don't have much of a selection anymore—no manpower to create them. Nor do any of us dare to venture back into the caves—too many enemy eyes watching."

Gareth held out his arm and Lachlin clasped it. "We'll see what you got. I need to find a light, short sword for my betrothed, Salome."

As if just noticing me standing behind Gareth, Lachlin shifted his gaze to me. His eyes widened. "She's human."

Gareth chuckled. "Yes, you're quite observant."

Lachlin walked around me, sizing me up. "Is she the one everyone has been talking about? The girl who broke that fool Nevin's curse?"

"Yes, I am—and you can speak to me, I'm standing right here." I waved a hand in front of his face.

This time he grinned. "Ah, and she has some spirit I see. Good for you. Now, let's get inside before someone notices us."

Lachlin and Gareth lumbered into the hut ahead of me. When I got to the doorway, I had to duck down so I didn't hit my head. But when I got inside, I noticed the ceilings were higher than they looked and I stood to my full height. All around me were shelves of trinkets, dishes, clothing that'd been patched a few times over. A few weapons hung on the back wall, behind the short counter.

A painting over a small woodstove caught my eye. It was of a blond man, dressed in all green, a crown made of twisted wood, emeralds, and silver sat on top of his head. Behind him loomed a great castle in the trees, flowers and vines nearly hid it from view. I stepped closer to it. My finger traced the intricate flower carved into the wooden frame.

"Who is this?" I glanced over my shoulder at Gareth and Lachlin.

"*That* is the late King of the Spring Court. He was the best bowman in all the four kingdoms — not too shabby with a sword either." Lachlin crossed himself. "May he rest in peace."

I closed my eyes and tried to imagine what Spring had been like before its downfall. Before the young looking king, his whole life ahead of him, had perished. Before his people had resorted to hiding.

"Have you seen anyone out this way recently?" Gareth leaned over the counter to examine a silvery blade that Lachlin held up.

"No one except for a few families that are hidden in the woods. No signs of any Winter troops or the queen. But you'll want to be careful nonetheless. We've had a lot of bandits along the roads between Spring, Summer, and Autumn. Not sure what kingdom they hail from, but they've caught a few unsuspecting travelers in the last couple of months. Everyone is trying to survive, but they don't realize taking from one another isn't going to help any of us live to fight against Winter."

"Hmm…we'll keep off the main road at night then. Salome,

come here a moment, I want you to try to wield this for me."
Gareth held the short sword out to me.

I took it by the handle and stared at the strange markings
etched into the blade. A sun, a flower, a leaf, and snowflake. It
wasn't too heavy and it fit perfectly in my hand. The silver on it
glinted beneath the flickering candlelight.

"Does it feel all right? Is it light enough for you?" Gareth
came to stand behind me, his hand covering mine on the hilt.
He helped me swing it around for a moment.

A strange vibration crept along the length of my arm, a low
humming sounding in my ear. As if the sword were singing to
me. I closed my eyes. Warmth spread through me, followed by
the scent of flowers and rain. Like the first signs of spring after a
long winter. Words I didn't understand to a song I didn't know
popped into my head.

"Yes, it's perfect," I said.

I opened my eyes once more to find Gareth watching me
closely.

"What did you just say?"

"That it's perfect," I said.

"Before that."

"Nothing." I raised a brow at him.

"Salome, you just sang something in the old language.
Something about bringing Spring back…"

"Oh, I don't know. I was holding the sword and all of a sudden, I thought I heard music. I didn't realize I'd said anything."
Great. Was the sword haunted? Or maybe I was going crazy?

"What kind of song?" Lachlin came around to stand with
us.

Gareth peered at him. "The Song of the Four Kingdoms."

Lachlin sucked in a deep breath. "We haven't heard that
since…since…"

"Since what?" My legs suddenly felt like jelly beneath me. Jeez, why was everyone acting so strange?

"Since before the kingdoms fell," Gareth answered. "It was our anthem before the Fall of Faerie. It was outlawed after Grisselle had demolished our lands and killed our people." He handed the weapon to Lachlin. "We'll take it, but can you get a belt and sheath for it?"

He gave a quick nod, then scurried away, searching his shelves. Once he had the belt and sheath, he wrapped the sword in beautiful blue canvas material, then slid it into a wooden box, which he secured with leather strips.

Gareth reached into a pouch tied at his side and took out some gold coins, which he handed over to Lachlin.

"You don't need to be paying me that much." He stared at the money.

"Take it—you can use it to help some of your people get more supplies. It looks like your food wares are low. At least this will allow you to barter with some of the Summer merchants."

"Thank you, friend—I wish you and your betrothed a safe journey. Hang onto this girl, lad, there's something about her. I can sense it—"

"As can I." Gareth patted him on the back.

A few minutes later we stepped outside, where Adaba stood waiting for us. Once Gareth secured my weapon in Adaba's saddle bags, we led our horses back out to the road. Up ahead, I caught sight of a small caravan of carts. It looked as if these people had packed up all their belongings in a hurry. They were resting beside the path, letting their horses graze.

"Gareth? What's wrong with them?"

"They're refugees, displaced by the war. They were likely run out of their homes by trolls and goblins."

The elfin children's eyes looked sunken in. Their clothes,

dirty and tattered. The parents didn't fare much better. Loose clothing hung about their frames, fatigue painted their every movement. These were not a people who held out hope for something better. And it broke my heart.

Without a second thought, I slipped some bread and cheese from my saddlebags and made my way toward them.

"Hi," I said.

The adults instantly reached for weapons, until they saw that I'd brought them food.

"I mean you no harm," I said.

A little girl came forward, her mouth gaping open. "Mama, it's a human...a real, live human." The child glanced at me, curiosity getting the best of her as she reached for a hunk of bread I held out to her.

"Beatrice, what'd I say about taking food from strangers," the elfin man said.

"Our food is fine," Gareth said from behind me. "We hail from the border of Summer."

I turned to see that Gareth had also brought some supplies over for them. The small group of travelers circled us, taking all that we offered them. And in that moment, I wished I had more to give.

"Thank you, it's been days since we've been able to kill any game for meals," the elfin man said.

"What happened?" Gareth watched the kids run around our legs.

"Trolls, about two weeks back, attacked our village. Most of the people perished in fires or were taken as slaves. We managed to escape through some of the tunnels. We waited until they left our homes, then went back in to salvage what we could. My wife has family near the mountains. We're hoping they can take us in until it's safe for us to return to our village and rebuild.

And with this food, you've renewed our hope."

"I'm glad we could help. We wish you safe journeys." Gareth waved.

"You as well," the man said.

The female elf peered down at me, tears in her eyes. "Thank you for your kindness—we'll never forget it."

I offered her a smile and gave her hand a squeeze. "You're welcome."

"Hey, Da, Mama, look. There's a flower growing." The child pointed at the gate for the flower garden I'd gone into earlier. And there, on the edge of the fence, was a beautiful red rose.

Gareth's eyes widened. "Weren't you just in there?"

"Yes, but the flowers were all dead…"

"Not anymore." He reached for my hand, squeezing it tight. "The light is returning. After all these years, it's awakened."

CHAPTER FOUR

Kadie

My teeth ground together as I searched for the right road. I'd forgotten how out of the way *Club Blade* was. With a sigh, I turned my brights on and squinted. So much for my wonderful homecoming. My parents didn't want me. Salome was in some sort of trouble. And now it was frickin' snowing. I switched the windshield wipers to high. My happy world dissolved around me.

You just need to find Salome.

At last, I saw the hidden track obscured by the trees. I flicked on my blinker and turned down the desolate road.

Shadows plagued the way ahead while limbs scraped the side of my vehicle. I took a deep breath. Maybe coming here alone wasn't such a great idea. Salome would so owe me for this—a large tub of chocolate ice cream and some movies to start with.

Stop being childish. It's just a road with trees, not flesh eating zombies.

The lane twisted with more curves than a porn star. Soon, I

came to the familiar covered bridge, which looked like a gaping mouth waiting to swallow me up. The boards creaked as I drove over them, sending me bouncing in my seat with each bump. On the other side, the forest surrounded the road in front of me like a dark tube. I kept following the serpentine road as it narrowed, trying to ignore the oppressive darkness beyond the headlights.

After a few minutes, I pulled into a clearing, where several cars sat already parked. The purple neon sign flashed *Club Blade*. The violet rays made the black brick building look even more sinister, if that was possible.

Please let me find her right away so we can get out of here.

But no matter how uninviting and edgy it seemed, I was going in.

I found a parking spot near the back of the lot and shut off the engine.

I glanced down at my day old rumpled jeans and stained t-shirt. Okay, I might just be here for a few minutes, but it didn't mean I wanted to look like something straight out of a trash can. Yeah, if I went dressed in this, I'd get turned away at the door.

I reached inside, unlocked the back door, swung it open, and tugged a box labeled "dresser" to the edge of the seat. Without wasting time, I ripped it open and rummaged through until I found a black lace thong, matching bra, and a sexy red halter dress. Once I had my things, I shoved the cardboard box back inside.

My gaze roamed over the lot. *Good, no one's looking.* I whipped my t-shirt and pants off, tossing them on the passenger seat, then tore off my dirty undergarments. Snowflakes hit my bare skin, melting on contact as if my body was a giant bonfire. I shivered.

The frigid air would probably chap my ass cheeks right off. *But as Mom always says, beauty is pain.* I tugged on my thong then finally shimmied into the tight red dress. Once I adjusted my girls, I reached back into the car for a pair of black heels.

I did a breath check in my cupped hand then grabbed my purse from the vehicle. I felt inside my black tote, snagged a hair clip, and then secured my hair in a twist. With a quick dab of Crimson Kiss lip gloss, I was ready to go.

Showtime.

As I neared the building, the steady thump of music beat in time with my pulse. The bouncer barely gave me a glance when I moved toward the entrance—unlike last time, when they checked to make sure Salome and I were on the list.

Nervousness washed over me. This was almost *too* easy. Maybe this was a sign I should turn back around. I mean, why would they all of a sudden just let me in like this? And why wasn't Salome waiting outside for me? Unless her and Gareth already made up?

No, you came all this way, you need to go inside and have a look around.

Warm air whooshed against my cold skin as I pushed inside. Strobe lights pulsed flashing at a dizzying rate. Foggy wisps floated across the dance floor. I took a deep breath, inhaling the sweet scent of incense. Already it made me heady.

Okay, search for Salome, Gareth, or Simeon. If you don't see them then you can leave.

I pasted a confident smile on my face and sashayed the hell out of my ass as I made my way through the club. My gaze flitted across the room. Couples danced, pressed so close together, you'd need a crowbar to pry them apart. People sat in corners, kissing, while others drank and laughed. Typical club scene. But no Salome or Gareth. I wavered. Maybe she'd sent another message and it just didn't come through? *Shit. Okay, you've come all the way out here, you can't just give up.*

I caught sight of the bartender wiping down the counter. Maybe he might know something. So I made my way over to him and perched on a stool.

The music changed to something slower. Kind of New Age, yet ancient at the same time. The low drumbeat beckoned me. Made me imagine drinking and bonfires. Okay. So didn't need my mind going there.

What the hell's wrong with me?

I swallowed hard.

Stay focused. You're here for one thing. And one thing only.

"Hey, is Gareth working tonight?" I batted my eyelashes at the bartender.

He gave me a quick once over, his gray eyes stormy. "Who wants to know?"

"I'm Kadie. Gareth's dating my best friend, Salome. Although I'm surprised you don't remember me." I leaned closer.

He smirked. "Sorry, don't recall you. But Salome, she's that small blond girl, right? Had a few people up-in-arms last time she was here?"

What the hell? So he remembered her, but not me? "Yeah, that would be her."

"Hmmm..."

"So, have you seen her or Gareth tonight?"

"No, but that guy down there, might be able to help you. He knows a lot about Gareth." The bartender pointed down the counter.

My eyes came to stop on a hot guy leaning against the bar. His pale blond hair stood in messy tufts, shocked with blue highlights. Dressed in black from head to toe, his tall frame loomed over everyone around him.

Holy hell. I didn't come in here for a guy, but I sure as hell wouldn't mind leaving with that one.

He raised his head, gaze meeting mine. He glanced away from me, then to a tall dark haired guy leaning against the wall. Maybe this guy was gay—which was too bad. Damn, just my luck.

A moment later, he caught my eye again, and this time he pushed away from the counter and sauntered toward me. Even from here, I could almost smell his confidence as if it were cologne.

"Well what do we have here?" he said in a voice that was both deep and sexy.

I stood straighter, sticking my chest out. "A good time, if you play your cards right."

Salome would cringe if she heard me use that line. Hell, I almost cringed myself and probably would've had he not been so hot. But if this guy had information, I was going to pour on the charm like nobody's business to get it.

His eyes glittered. Just like every other guy, he'd soon be falling all over himself trying to get in my pants. If nothing else, I knew how the male species worked.

"Why don't you join me for a drink?" He leaned over, his breath cool against my now warm skin.

Now should be the time I mentioned I was underage. But tonight, I didn't mind throwing a few back, as long as I got what I came into the club for.

"Sure. And I'm Kadie by the way." I let my hips sway in time with the music.

"Etienne." He placed his hand at the small of my back, leading me to the bar.

God, he's so hot. And his name. Talk about yummy. Forget

the drink; I wanted to gobble him up. No information? No problem. There were *other* things he could give me…

Etienne ordered our drinks, and the bartender didn't even bother to card me. Which seemed kinda strange.

"So tell me, Kadie…" Etienne handed me a goblet filled with ruby colored liquid. "How did you find Club Blade all the way out here?" I noticed him shift his attention back to where the tall dark-haired guy had stood, only now the wall was empty. Was he trying to make that guy jealous or something?

Not wanting to seem unsure of myself, I smiled. "My ex-boyfriend and one of his friends brought me here once. And I'm kind of looking for someone."

His long fingers grazed my arm, sending chills across my skin. "Hmm…maybe I can help you out. What are their names, I might know them?"

"Simeon and Gareth. Although, I'm really here to find my friend Salome," I said, then realized I'd never gotten far enough with the guys to get a last name.

The dark haired guy appeared at my side, his chocolate-colored eyes sparkled like a lit fuse. His lips curved into a broader grin, revealing perfect white teeth. "Simeon and Gareth of Summer — such a pious man, don't you think, Etienne?"

Etienne's grin melted away and he stiffened beside me. "Teodor, what a nice surprise."

"Couldn't let you have all the fun, now could I?" Teodor's gaze slid over me like I was a piece of meat and he was a butcher.

I shivered. Something about him scared the hell out of me. Chills snaked over my skin, and I rubbed my arms.

"So, tell me about Gareth and Simeon," Teodor said.

"I haven't seen Simeon since before I went away to college and Gareth's dating my best friend." I downed my drink. Sweet and tangy, it instantly warmed me. "But I'm actually more interested in finding my friend."

"Are you now?" He smiled once more. "Here, let me get you another one." Teodor took my empty glass and headed over to the bar.

Fuck. Where was she? I scanned the room once more for Salome. Still not seeing her, I slid my cell from my bra and checked to make sure I didn't have any other messages from her. But there weren't any. Maybe she'd went into the bathroom or something. I'd give her a few more minutes to show her face—unless something had happened to her. Damn.

"Look, maybe you should leave now," Etienne whispered when Teodor was out of earshot. "You seem like a nice girl, Kadie."

"Then you obviously don't know me very well," I teased as my stomach clenched with uneasiness. Maybe he was right, maybe I should just get the hell out of here. But then I'd be back to square one. I really needed to find Salome. I just had to stick it out a little longer to see if these guys really knew anything. Maybe it was time to turn on the Kadie charm.

But just then Teodor came back, holding out a drink for me. "A special drink, for a special lady."

At least I'm not the only one throwing around cheesy lines tonight.

I wasn't going to get any information from them by giving them the cold shoulder, so I finished my cup and set it on the counter and turned to Etienne. "Aren't you going to drink yours?"

He chuckled, then handed me his goblet. "No, go ahead."

I picked up the goblet by the stem and tossed it back. Etienne watched me, and his gaze slid down my throat until it reached the low neckline of my dress.

I have you now.

"So, about Gareth and Salome, have you seen them to-night?"

I downed the rest of my drink and let Etienne take the cup from me.

"No, Gareth hasn't been in the club for months now. But enough of about him." He placed the glass on a nearby table then tugged me toward him. "Let's dance."

His fingers clasped mine as he led me to the dance floor. Already my blood burned beneath my skin where he touched me. If we didn't turn it down a notch, I might combust. We found a place at the center of the crowd and he pulled me against him. "You need to stay away from Teodor," he said at last. "He's bad news."

"And you're not?" I whispered against his neck.

I heard a low groan escape his lips. "Oh, I'm bad, too, just a different kind of bad. If you were smart, you'd get out of here and as far away from both of us as you can. In fact, I think you should get out of here right now."

My heart thudded in my ears, and a pleasant buzzing sensation spread through me. It was getting hard to think. And so easy to feel…

"What if I'm not smart? What if I want to stay?"

"Then you'll pay the consequences." He gripped me tighter. "Please, Kadie, just trust me and go."

Beneath his button-down shirt, my fingers traced over sculpted muscles. Even through the fabric, I could tell he had abs like the guys in magazines my mama didn't want me looking at. His hands roamed over my hips. I glanced up, meeting pale blue eyes. He leaned closer until his lips crushed mine.

Etienne tasted of wine, his mouth pleasantly cool. He deepened the kiss, taking my breath away like a crisp December morning. I couldn't get enough of him. He intoxicated me.

He pulled back, his eyes staring down at me as if he could devour me with them. The lights continued to pulse and dizziness washed over me. Etienne's hands moved down my back and he grinded his hips against mine. I gasped.

Why can't I get enough of him?

My vision grew fuzzy; people in front of me blurred. Even the music didn't sound right, like someone had slowed it down too much. I tried to steady myself.

Oh God, did he drug me?

I stumbled, then clasped hold of his shoulders.

"Are you okay?"

My eyes narrowed. "What did you do to me?"

"Nothing. Unless Teodor gave you something."

For some reason, I laughed and kept dancing even though warning bells went off.

Wake up. You need to go.

But I kept dancing and kissing and touching Etienne.

C'mon. Stop being an idiot. Say goodbye and get the frick out of here.

"Kadie, you need to stop now. We have to go," Etienne said again, this time more urgent. He stopped dancing and attempted to tug me off the dance floor, but my body refused to move.

Somewhere in the distance, someone screamed. I raised my head and glanced around. Warm droplets splashed against my cheek like rain. I wiped the liquid from my face and glanced down. Oh shit. Crimson. Blood.

I've got to get out of here. Now. Why can't I move?

I was seriously fucked up. The lights stopped pulsing and flickered. It was then that I noticed Etienne wasn't beside me anymore.

The music faded to frantic voices. People shoved to get to the exits, like they just woke up and realized something horrible was about to happen. Panic shot through me. Where the hell was the door? I spun around, searching for a way out. The lights went out, plunging me into inky blackness.

A shoulder rammed into me and I staggered back. Terrified shrieks rang out from nearby.

What direction do I go?

I was half-tempted to drop to my knees and start crawling, but I was scared I might be trampled.

"Come on, we must go, before he finds us." Etienne's voice sounded in my ear. Strong hands wrapped around my waist, leading me forward. "Hang on to me."

I reached in the dark until I clung tight to him. "What's going on?"

"Shh...don't worry, I'll get you out."

"Going somewhere?" Teodor called out beside us.

"I'm sorry," Etienne whispered. "I'll try to keep you safe."

What the fuck did that mean?

A gust of wind ripped at my dress and hair. The smell of rotten food assaulted me, and I gagged as dizziness took hold once more.

I'm gonna be sick.

Etienne tugged me onward, and I fought to keep up. At last, we burst through the darkness. Relief washed over me when I noticed the moonlit woods. We'd gotten out. But where the hell were we? This wasn't outside the club. In fact, I didn't see the club at all. Damn, was I so fucked up that I didn't remember leaving?

"Let's show Kadie what's really going on," Teodor said with a laugh.

I turned to Etienne and stopped short. Frozen in place, I watched in horror as chunks of his face fell off—it melted away like the wax of a candle.

Oh God.

Green, blemished skin covered the once handsome Etienne. Horns curled up from his forehead, reminding me of a ram. His jagged teeth had bits of fleshy pieces stuck inside and I nearly retched, having moments before kissed that mouth. Emerald eyes glowed with amusement. This wasn't happening. He looked just like one of the goblins I'd seen in Salome's grandma's book.

No. This wasn't real. It couldn't be. I had to be dreaming or hallucinating. I pinched my arm and pain shot up to my shoulder. Oh crap. I was awake. But that didn't mean the drugs they gave me hadn't screwed with my head.

"Welcome to the Unseelie Court, Kadie. I hope you enjoy your stay." Teodor pointed to the freaky creatures stepping from the woods to surround us. Green, blemished skin, horned beings, grotesque things that were half-human and half-monster. Goblins, trolls, red caps—things that should not exist. But there they were, staring at me as if I was an item on the buffet.

I took a step back and turned to where Teodor had been standing, but now in his place was a creature with a wolf like snout and rows of sharp teeth. No. This wasn't happening. My body quaked beneath me. I needed to run, but there was nowhere to go. It was too late.

Etienne was looking at me, and some emotion flashed in his eyes, gone too quickly for me to be sure what it was.

Beyond them, all I noticed was the ice and snow and blood. The creatures from Salome's grandma's books were real. The same monsters Salome had been scared of as a child—the ones I didn't believe in—were surrounding me. And I was their captive. All because I'd come here for Salome—

Oh God. Salome.

"What did you do to my friend?" I said.

Teodor shook his head and chuckled. "You poor girl. You

still think that message actually came from Salome?"

My heart sank as I realized what he meant. The message. It hadn't come from Salome. It had come from *them*.

Shit. Shit shit shit.

"That's why we sent for you," he said. "You're going to help us capture her."

I reached for my phone, only to find that it wasn't there. Fuck. How would anyone find me now? I could only hope Salome would realize I was missing.

*T*he frigid air nipped at my skin and goose bumps broke out across my legs and arms. My stomach knotted as I watched a butt-load of dark creatures pour from the woods like a demonic wave. Some stood tall, with pointed ears and razored teeth, their skin the color of charcoal and eyes red as strawberries. Others were part man and part beast. Twisted horns, blemished skin, claws the size of butcher knives. It was like I stepped onto the set of some effed-up horror flick and I was the first actress to be sacrificed.

I took several steps backward, but Etienne gripped my arm. His slimy skin made me want to barf.

Thank God I didn't sleep with him; I could've ended up pregnant with toad children or something.

"Let. Me. Go." I jerked my arm in an attempt to free myself. But his fingers never moved. I shifted my attention to the ground, searching for some sort of weapon. Anything I might use to fight my way out of here. But there was only snow and trees and darkness.

"I will try to protect you," Etienne said in a hushed voice.

"Please, trust me. Don't cause a scene."

Teodor moved closer to us. "We have uses for a girl with prior connections to Summer."

"Listen, I don't know anything. Please. Just let me go." My feet planted firm on the ground.

Teodor reached for me, his gaze darker. "Etienne, perhaps you should hand the girl over to me. I bet I could make her talk."

"No, I found her and I'll do things my way."

"Is that what you're going to tell the queen?" Teodor's snout full of teeth gleamed in a deadly smile.

Holy fuck. Panic stole over me. No way was I going any further with these two. I had to keep it together. I had to get out of here. Wherever here was. I kicked out my leg, nearly catching Teodor in the crotch, but he dodged out of the way. If they were gonna take me, I damn sure wasn't about to make it easy for them.

But in one swift movement, Etienne uprooted me and dragged me down the path. "We've got a long journey. Someone get her a fur before she freezes to death. She won't be any use to us dead."

A centaur with red swirling paint on his chest trotted up alongside us and dropped a large wolf pelt around my shoulders. The head was still attached, vacant eyes staring at me. For a moment, I expected it to clamp down on my throat with its long teeth.

Etienne peered down at me again, and I saw a flicker of something again in his eyes. Concern? Regret? But then that flicker disappeared and his mask of resolve returned.

"Sweet dreams," he said. He blew his sweet, honey scented breath in my face, and everything went black.

$\mathcal{I}$ came to with a groan, still groggy. Etienne's shoulder dug into my abdomen, each step he took jarring me. I squeezed my eyes shut and opened them again, hoping this was a dream. But when I opened them once more, I was still being held captive, being carried through the gnarled woodland. My body trembled. How long had I been asleep? The dark sky indicated it was still night. But was it the night of my abduction or had I been a sleep a long time?

Soon Etienne set me on my feet and I turned to see a mammoth black gate. Withered vines clung to the wicked, long spokes. Knobby, decayed trees stood along the fence line, while thorns stuck every which way, as if to keep intruders out.

I swallowed hard. The gate screeched open, sounding like thousands of people screaming in pain. My knees nearly buckled and I covered my ears.

Please make it stop.

Etienne glanced at me. "You need a stronger stomach if you're going to survive here."

My gaze shifted to the large castle before me. Where the fuck were we? I knew for damn sure that there were no castles in Starlynn Village. Maybe this was like *The Lion, the Witch, and the Wardrobe*, and we'd stepped into some other land. Or maybe I really hadn't woke up. I shook my head, trying to clear the cobwebs. But every time I blinked or closed my eyes, I was still here.

I stared at the Black spires, which twisted toward the sky like devil horns. Thick, dirty ice caked the bottom stones, while red fluid dripped down the window panes. It looked like blood.

I didn't want to know for sure what it was. Rocks carved like skulls—at least I hope they were rocks—stared down from various balconies and ledges. Only one word described what I saw. Morbid.

My pulse thundered in my ears as we stepped into the main corridor. Black marble covered nearly every inch of the floor and walls. Monstrous paintings depicting death and sacrifice paraded us into a wide-open throne room. Gnarled trees, acted as pillars, while a ceremonial stone table sat at the center of the room. The rock surface crimson from God only knew what. My legs shook beneath me. And not for the first time, I wondered if I'd live to see tomorrow. I bit my bottom lip, then took several deep breaths. My gaze flitted about the room, until it landed onthe oversized throne made of bones.

"Don't tell me you two have been out playing with humans, while I fight Summer." A female waltzed into the room. White hair hung about her shoulders, framing a too-pale face. Deep blue robes swished at her feet. Red stains decorated the hem as if she'd been clog dancing on dead bodies. But it was her cold, blue eyes that held me in place.

Etienne bowed. "Of course not, my queen. This girl will help us bring you Salome and all of Summer."

"Will she now?"

Teodor stepped ahead of Etienne. "She has ties to Summer. To both Simeon and Gareth. If you'd like, I could take her to my rooms and get her to talk."

A thin smile, if you could call it that, spread across her bluish-purple lips. "Does she now?" She sat on the throne, then glowered at my captor. "Stop using your glamour. I can't stand to look at you two in that form."

Etienne released my arm. A light glowed around him as his previous, hot form fell back into place. His now blue eyes met mine.

Oh God, this was his true form? But no matter how good looking he was—and no matter what that flicker in his eyes had signified—I now knew he was a monster.

"That goes for the rest of you. Take your glamour off before you make me sick." The queen settled back in her chair.

All around me, creatures turned from freaky horror movie cast look-a-likes to drool-worthy models. Dark hair. Golden hair. Tall. Muscled. The ones that didn't change back, scurried around grabbing cloaks and cups for the others. Like the uglier ones were the servants.

"Bring in the wine." The queen snapped her fingers and two pig-snouted men entered carrying trays with goblets filled with what looked like red champagne. They offered one first to the queen, then turned to wait on the beautiful people. "Bring one to the human."

I went still. The last time I'd accepted a drink from a stranger, I'd ended up here. "No. I'm fine. I don't want any."

The queen stood, crumbling her goblet in her hand. Glass and crimson sprayed across the floor. "No one refuses me."

Guards moved forward, one on each side. They shoved me to my knees and pinned me in place. Terror washed through me, gripping my gut until I thought I might barf or piss myself. One of my captors caught hold of my hair and pulled my head back, while Teodor forced my mouth open. The queen laughed as they poured the wine down my throat.

It burned my esophagus, and I caught the faint taste of blood. I gagged as they released me, wiping at my mouth with my arm.

"Now—why don't we play a fun game?" Her lips turned up at the corners. "You tell me what you know about Gareth, Simeon, and Summer and I won't kill you."

Fuck. This lady's insane.

"I don't know anything. I mean, I dated Simeon for, like, five seconds. And Gareth went to my school for a few months."

"Fae don't just date humans, there had to be something they wanted," Teodor said. His eyes narrowed as he stared me down. "We *all* want something."

Etienne met my gaze over his shoulder. He looked uncomfortable, almost like he regretted what was happening.

My hands trembled, but I fought to stay composed. "Simeon never asked for anything. Hell, he wouldn't even sleep with me. Trust me, I tried to seduce the man. And like I said, Gareth went to my school and hung out with one of my friends."

Something they wanted?

Shit. We'd gone out a few times, but I barely knew them. I barely…

Oh God.

Salome. The first time I'd hung out with Simeon, Gareth had spent the whole time asking me questions about her. They'd used me to get to Salome. Was she here in Faerie now? If Gareth hurt her, I swore I'd kill him. I sucked in a deep breath.

There's no way I'm gonna tell them about Salome.

The last thing I needed was for them to stalk her. Shit. Shit. Shit.

Fine time to be chivalrous. For once, I should put myself first.

I wet my lips and glared at Teodor. "Look, I don't know what they wanted. Like I told you, I met Simeon at a coffee shop and he asked me out. We went out like maybe three times, then he broke up with me for some girl. And since Gareth hung out with him, I never saw either of them after that."

"She's not telling us everything—I can feel it." The queen pointed at me, her eyes glowing. "Take her to the Red Room until she decides to talk."

I leapt to my feet, fists clenched at my sides. "What? I told you everything—you can't keep me here."

"Oh, but I can." She stepped off the dais and glided toward me. When she was in front of me, she ran a lacquered fingernail down my cheek.

My skin stung, and a droplet slipped down my face. She'd drawn blood.

With a grin, she licked her finger. "Take her away."

"Perhaps, you'd like me to keep her with me instead, Your Highness?" Teodor watched me in a way that made me think of axe murderers and America's Most Wanted Criminals.

"No, I found her and I'll make her talk," Etienne interjected. He snatched hold of my arm, tugging me from the throne room and down a narrow, dark hall before the queen could change her mind. The only light came from a few scattered candles that flickered along the wall. Everything else lay doused in shadow.

"You should've cooperated."

"Fuck off." I tried to jerk free from him.

He came to an abrupt stop, pinned me to a nearby wall, and leaned closer. "Do you think I wanted this for you? I told you at the club you should leave, but you didn't listen. Then to let Teodor overhear you, you left me no choice but to bring you here. If I didn't grab you, then he would've. Trust me, you don't want to be alone with him. He has a way of making people spill their every secret."

His breath was warm against my cheek, the scent of honey and fruit clinging to his skin.

He's too close. I can't think.

This time I pulled out of his grasp, trying desperately to ignore the pulse thundering in my ears. Confusion swirled inside. How in the hell could I be attracted to him? I didn't like the pull he had over me. And I needed to find a way to break it before I did something stupid. Besides, I had a lot worse things to worry about. Like all the monsters and demons that lurked in the castle. All of which could kill me in a split second.

Another wave of fear washed over me. How was any of this possible? How did I not know places like this existed? Maybe Salome's grandma's stories really weren't stories after all. And maybe she was trying to warn us when we were younger.

Once more, Etienne secured me to his side, his grip tighter than before. "Please. I don't want this any more than you do. It'll be over a lot faster if you just tell me everything I want to know."

"Don't count on it." My jaw tightened. If I was going to survive, I had to put my big girl panties on now and be ready to fight.

After several turns down twisting hallways, we came to a stop in front of a pair of hulking wooden doors. Etienne produced a key, unlocked it, and shoved me inside. I whipped around, hoping to get out, but the door slammed shut, and I heard the bolt locking in place.

"Let me out!" My hands pounded on the door. I took a few steps back then ran forward in an attempt to ram my way out. But the wood didn't budge, instead, I bounced off and skidded backward across the floor.

A sob lodged in my throat, panic setting in.

There has to be a way out.

I spun to get a look at the room then froze. Candles came to life, revealing the gruesome décor. Bones and skulls adorned nearly every inch of this place. Human heads hung above a fireplace mantle made of spines, displayed like trophies. The reddish-brown stains covered the walls as if someone had poured buckets of blood on them. Curtains made of skin and hair billowed back and forth as wind snuck through the windows.

I covered my mouth, but it was too late. I vomited, splattering the already stained floor. I heaved, again and again, until nothing was left in my stomach.

I have to get out of here. Now.

A pair of glass doors caught my eye and I ran forward. I fumbled with the handles, but was relieved when they swung open. Brisk air clawed at my bared skin, the cold taking my breath away. I glanced around the snow covered courtyard only to find it just as horrific as the scene inside.

Human skins hung like laundry set out to dry from gnarled tree limbs. A fountain made of bones sputtered bloodied water from its depths. I squeezed my eyes shut, wishing this was just a nightmare. But when my lids came open once more, I was still there.

Tears blurred my vision as I found a wooden bench and collapsed on it.

"Help meeeee…" an agonizing cry sounded from beside me.

My fingers dug into the wooden bench and I shot an alarmed look around me. Then I saw it. The tree in front of me. Only this tree wasn't normal. It twisted so that it faced me, revealing a human face embedded into the bark. My gaze followed the length of the trunk where two legs were rooted into the ground, blood seeping from them. What should've been branches on the tree, I soon realized were this person's arms, covered in thorns and leaves.

"Please…"

As I stared at the tree, I realized I recognized that face. Salome's dad. "Mr. Montgomery?" I whispered.

"Help me…"

No matter how strong I was, I knew then I might not make it out alive.

CHAPTER FIVE

Salome

*A*fter we parted ways with the refugees, Gareth led me into the woods and off the road. When the others were out of sight, he came to a stop and spun to face me.

"What's wrong?"

He grinned. "Nothing, I'm just proud of you." Seeing the way you treated those elves back there…Salome, your kindness is truly one of your greatest gifts. I wish more of the Fae were like you. It's just, these aren't even your people, and yet you want to help them."

"Well, they kind of are my people now. I gave up my human life to come here. With you. Which means I have to do my part to protect them and make sure they survive Grisselle. Besides, I apparently have a reputation to live up to since everybody and their brother seems to know about me breaking the curse. I think they're probably surprised to see I'm just a normal girl."

"You, my love, are anything but normal." Gareth tugged me into his arms; his palm rested against the side of my face, his thumb rubbing the skin under my eye. "Do you not find it odd that things in Spring have started coming back to life the moment you walk through the kingdom?"

I went still, my gaze meeting his. "That wasn't me. Like I told Nevin, I don't have any powers, so if that's what you're getting at—"

"Why is it you don't question all the fantastic things that have come into your life over the last several years, but you question the possibility of you possessing magic?"

"B-because, I'm just some human girl who happened to get lucky in guessing how to break a curse. I don't want everyone thinking I might be able to save them. Believing I'm something I'm not." My head rested against his chest. "Besides, if I had all this power, then how come you kept having to rescue me in the human world?"

"Probably because you liked it when I rescued you." He smirked, his brown eyes boring into mine. "You loved me carrying you in my arms, like this." He hefted me up, cradling me against him.

"Oh, is that so?"

"Yeah. But mostly, I think you hoped I'd do this." He leaned his head down and kissed me.

Just as his tongue slipped into my mouth, a loud snort sounded behind my ear and I felt warm breathing on my neck. I jerked back only to see Adaba's form looming over us. He used his head and butted it against Gareth's.

"Ow, what the hell is his problem?" Gareth set me down, rubbing his forehead. "You, my feisty equine, are about to get on my last nerve."

"You did call him a chastity belt—so now he thinks he has to live up to his new title." I smoothed my dress down, pulse still pounding against my skin.

"This makes me all the more eager to get to Summer. At least then we can shut the bedroom door if we want some privacy," Gareth said.

And for that, Adaba bit him in the arm. This would definitely be a long trip with those two. For the next hour or so we trekked farther into the woods, until we came to a small clearing nestled between some large boulders and thick trees.

"Why don't we make camp here for the night? We can get the saddlebags off the horses, then gather some firewood," Gareth said.

The air had grown chillier now that the sun had gone down some. While Gareth gathered kindling and logs for a fire, I set up our bedrolls. This would definitely be a first for me, sleeping outdoors, under the stars. I hoped nothing came in while we slept and tried to murder us. My imagination conjured all types of creatures that could do us in. I shook off the grizzly thoughts.

Gareth soon came back and set the wood down, then proceeded to work on getting our campfire going. It only took him a few tries to get the flames started. Adaba moved into the woods and posted guard along our outskirts.

I watched Gareth warm some of our meat over the fire. I loved watching the way the firelight played off his features, making his tanned skin more bronzed, his eyes more wild. His golden tattoos on his arm blazed like flames. My eyes followed his every movement. I remembered how many times he'd come to my rescue in the human world. How many nights I'd laid awake thinking about him.

Ever since coming to Faerie, we'd spent almost every waking moment together, either outdoors riding horses or taking walks or swimming. Sometimes we'd just sit in the library together and read. We seemed so far removed from the human world now—and the normal things we'd done back there. Like the waterpark, the carnival, going to prom together—rides on his motorcycle. A part of me missed that life. But I wouldn't give up the one I had now. Wherever he was, I wanted to be.

"Where you are, I want to be also." Gareth thought to me.

"Oh, sorry, sometimes I forget how much I project..."

He smiled. "I don't mind—especially when you're thinking of us and how hot I looked at prom."

"Funny." I took the bowl of venison he handed me.

"We should probably bed down, once we're done eating. We'll have another long day ahead of us tomorrow."

A yawn escaped my lips. "Yeah, I can definitely use some sleep."

I scarfed down my food, then rinsed out my bowl by dumping some water in it and swishing it around. I slid my boots off and crawled into my makeshift bed.

"Do you have your dagger on you?" Gareth glanced at me as he settled into the bedroll beside mine.

"Yeah, it's right next to me."

"Good." He scooted closer to me, until our sleeping mats were right next to one another. He slid his arm across my waist, then leaned down to press a kiss to my lips. "I love you," he said.

I laced my fingers into his hair and pulled him down again. "I love you, too."

"Well, isn't this touching," came a voice from beside us. "Never thought I'd catch Gareth of Summer off guard."

My eyes widened. Elfin bandits, four of them, all dressed in various shades of gray and green. All looking mean and ready to hurt us. Oh God. For long moments, I didn't dare move, wondering what they might do to us.

"Salome, as careful and quietly as you can, slip me your dagger." He was still perched above me.

My fingers inched down to the blanket and closed around the hilt of the dagger. Keeping it as close to my body as I could, I inched it up to Gareth. In one, quick movement, he leapt to his feet, throwing the dagger at one of the elfin bandits.

The blade sliced into the cloak of the elf and pinned him to a nearby tree.

"Maris Elkwood, you should know better than that," Gareth said.

Somehow Gareth now had his sword in hand. I didn't see where he'd grabbed it from. As slow as I could, I climbed up beside him—unfortunately the only weapon I had at the moment were my hands.

The one called Maris chuckled. "Looks like you're not as easy to sneak up on as I thought. What say you, Gareth of Summer? Shall we call a truce?"

Gareth lowered his weapon. "Come sit at our fire and let me do a round of introductions."

Maris jerked the dagger from his cloak and tossed it back to Gareth, who handed it over to me. I put it back in its small sheath and set it on my blanket.

"So you travel with humans now?" Maris watched me from his seat by the fire. His dark hair was at odds with his light green eyes. From here, I spotted several knives and a bow beneath his cloak. Whatever he was, he wasn't an ordinary elf. An aura of danger seemed to roll right off him.

"This human is my betrothed, Salome. You might've heard that she broke Nevin's curse? Salome, this is Maris, Caraval, Tulare, and Byron..." he pointed at each of the men in turn. "They are the last of the Spring Court's soldiers."

"And we've been keeping these woods free of Winter scum. Whenever they wander onto our land, we take care of them." He gave a tight lipped smile as he fingered the blade at his side.

"Are you still camped in the same spot?" Gareth leaned closer to the fire.

"No, we try to move around every so often so Winter Scouts

can't track us. There's also a small camp of civilians that we protect. Some of which are women and children."

"I saw Lachlin earlier."

"Yeah, he said as much. Told me your betrothed had a very important sword choose her today."

I shot Gareth a startled look. "What does he mean, that the sword chose me?"

"A warrior's weapon always chooses them. Just as mine did."

"He speaks the truth; however, I would be lying if I didn't say how surprised I was to learn that it was the Blade of the Four Kingdoms which called to you, Salome."

Confusions swept through me. "The Blade of the Four Kingdoms?"

"Only one of the most powerful weapons in all Faerie. Don't tell me Gareth hasn't been telling you our lore and history?" Maris glanced at Gareth, who was giving him a warning look. "But perhaps, I should leave that story for him to tell you." Maris grabbed a leather flask from his belt, unscrewed the lid, then took a swig. When he was done, he peered at me and Gareth once more. "I saw something strange in the woods today. Buds on the trees, even a few birds have returned. And I tell you, these things weren't here yesterday."

"It's curious for sure," Gareth said, eyeing me. "Only this afternoon, we noticed a rose blooming, where before dead plants had been. Isn't that right, Salome?"

"Yes." Where was he going with this? I hoped he wasn't going to try and claim that this was my doing, too.

"I tell you, the courts are reawakening. I don't know how or why, but I can feel it in my blood," Maris said. "Our time is coming."

Gareth cleared his throat. "Salome, you really should get some rest, or you'll be asleep in the saddle tomorrow."

He and Maris exchanged another look. Maris smiled and slid a wooden flute from beneath his cloak. "I think some music is in order."

The light, airy sound of flute music filled the night air, swirling along the breeze as if dancing with it. The fire popped, sending a spray of sparks up toward the sky as if someone had lit off fireworks.

"*Welcome hooooooooome…*" a voice said on the wind.

I sat upright, my blanket falling from my shoulders. My gaze met Gareth's. "*Did you hear that?*"

"*Hear what?*"

"*The voice. It said welcome home.*"

"*No, I didn't hear anything.*" A look of concern crossed his face. "*But after what you hearing voices led to before, we ought to pay attention to any you hear now.*"

He had a point. Last winter, me hearing voices had almost led to my death. I mean, in a way it *had* led to my death, but, well…it was complicated. And I knew better now than to dismiss something I couldn't explain and hope it wasn't real.

I swallowed. "*What do we do?*"

"*Don't worry love, you are safe among friends. We will keep guard. Just get some rest.*"

Gareth scooted closer to me and stroked my hair, until my eyes became so heavy I could no longer keep them open. With him, I was safe. With him, we could face anything. That thought, his touch, and the music helped me fall into a sweet slumber.

*T*he next morning, Maris and his men led us to the edge of the Spring border. "Gareth, if Summer raises an army to go against

Winter, send word to us. I want to avenge my mother and our king."

Gareth bowed his head. "Your mother Rena was a good woman. I know time does not heal all wounds, my friend. But know that if we go to war, you will be the first person I call on. We can always use more bowman."

"Lady Salome." Maris clutched my hand. "It was good to meet you. May Faerie smile upon you." He leaned closer to me and whispered, "The sword is of importance—it has claimed you, Salome. No one has been able to wield it since the first Queen herself. Ask questions, you have a right to know our history—because soon enough, it might become yours."

I sucked in a deep breath. What the hell did that even mean?

As I climbed onto Adaba's back, I peered behind us only to find that Maris had disappeared. Our horses headed back across the northern border of Summer, and I dug my heels into Adaba's sides to speed up so I could ride alongside Gareth.

"Are you going to tell me about the sword?"

Gareth sighed, his brow furrowed in annoyance. "I really wish Maris would've kept his mouth shut."

"Why? Don't you want me to know what's going on?"

"Of course I do, however, I'm not sure yet of the significance of the sword appearing now, and to you. I wanted to do some research once we reached Summer, so I'd have a better understanding of what to tell you. What I do know from studying in the archives when I was a student is that this sword was created at the beginning of Faerie. It was imbued with the powers of all four kingdoms. Winter. Spring. Summer. Autumn. It was the weapon of our very first Faerie Queen Diana—many thought that it had been buried with her when she passed from this life into the Realm of Heroes. It's been lost since her time, a mere myth until yesterday."

"That makes no sense; how did it end up in Lachlin's little shop? I mean, he had hardly any goods in there. Do you think it's a replica?" I glanced at him, fingers tightening on the horse's reins. Panic coursed through me. I didn't want the appearance of the weapon to mean anything to me. I just wanted to be Salome Montgomery. It was one thing to take on being a Faery and an immortal, but I'd come into this thinking I'd still basically be, *well*...me.

But what if I was meant for something more? Would I be ready? I mean, I had hardly any knowledge of anything Faerie—well, other than the tales Grandma had told me as a child. Gareth was teaching me about Summer and all things Faerie, but I still had so much to learn.

"It's not a replica. I might not be able to wield it, but I felt the magic flowing through the blade. It's genuine. And like I said, I'll have to do some research on the history of it to learn more." Gareth watched me intently. "Salome, everything will be okay. Let's not jump to any conclusions until we have more information."

"You're right. I'm sure it's just a coincidence."

"Well, I didn't say that. There's obviously a reason it appeared now. But let's not dwell on it right this moment. No need to fret until we know more about it." He reached across the distance between our horses and clasped my hand in his.

Up ahead of us, a large, crumbling statue blocked part of the road. Gareth brought his horse to a stop, and Adaba halted as well. The face in the stone looked so familiar, but I couldn't place where I'd seen it before.

"Who is that stone figure of?" I let Gareth help me from my mount as we made our way over to it.

"This was our last Faerie Queen, Genissa."

"Genissa?" Where had I heard that name before? Then I

remembered. She'd been the woman from the story Grandma had told me. Chills grated across my skin, causing goosebumps. If this fairytale was real, how many other ones were? And that raised another question. How in the world had Grandma known?

It's like she'd been aware of Faerie's existence the whole time. I recalled her not wanting me to get involved with Nevin or Gareth. How she raced out of her house when Kassandra attacked me. She'd known about this magical world way before I'd come along...but how? What role did she play? And what role would I play? More than anything, I needed to talk to her—which likely wouldn't happen for a while, at least not until I could convince Gareth or Nevin to allow me to go home for a visit.

"Salome? Did you hear me?"

"I'm sorry, I was so caught up in my thoughts..."

"I know," he teased. "I promise that when things settle down, we'll get you home to see Doris. But for now, we need to keep you safe. How about we get some lunch? When we're done eating, I can teach you a few fatal moves to do with a dagger, should you need to defend yourself."

"Are you sure you want me waving a dagger around at you?" My teeth grazed my bottom lip as I stared up at him.

"I think we'll start you off with a stick—"

"Are you saying you don't trust me with a knife?" I threw my hands on my hips.

He chuckled, holding his palms toward the sky. "I never said that, but I do like all my limbs."

We made our way off the path, this time heading toward a clearing in the wood-line. We ate a quick meal of apples, cheese, and bread. When we finished Gareth had me pull out my dagger so we could find a stick close in shape, weight, and length to use as a practice tool.

When we found the perfect one, Gareth had me stand in front of him.

"Because you're small, most captors will be able to overpower you. So if someone were to come up behind you, like this…" Gareth wrapped his arms around me from the back. "You could feasibly just stab him in the leg or anywhere to get him to loosen his hold. Or if you can't move your arms, then you need to stomp on his foot as hard as you can to get him to let you go."

He had me do a couple practice runs on him, but I worried too much about hurting him to really try too hard to get away.

"You don't have to be afraid to lash out, Salome, you're not going to harm me." Gareth touched my cheek.

"I know, it's just hard to go at you full force. I mean, you're not my enemy."

"All right, why don't we move onto something else then?"

Gareth went on to show me where I could cut someone if I needed a more lethal blow. He taught me how to cut across someone's throat, or use my palm to strike a person and make their nose lodge into their brain. Not exactly self-defense maneuvers I ever wanted to have to use, but I was glad he took the time to show me just in case.

By the time we put the fake dagger down, I was sweating and out of breath. Who knew self-defense could be so much work?

With a sigh, I collapsed in the shade under a big oak tree and sprawled out. Gareth sat down beside me, then rolled over until he was propped above me. "Is this another self-defense lesson?" I laughed.

He gave me a cocky grin. "Hmm…it can be. Because what will you do if someone gets you pinned to the ground?"

My hands moved up his chest until my arms circled his neck. "Maybe something like this."

I tugged him down on top of me, letting my mouth cover his. I parted his lips with mine, letting my tongue move against his. He groaned, pinning my arms above my head so he could trail kisses down my neck then back up again. Using my hips, I thrust him up enough for me to roll him over onto his back. I grabbed the stick we'd been using and held it to his neck.

"I do believe I've won, Gareth of Summer."

His hands rested on my waist; my dress pushed up to my upper thighs. "And if this is the way I get to die, you can best me every time. However, may I ask that you not do this move on anyone but me?"

"Why? Jealous?" I dropped the stick, this time pinning his arms above his head.

"Yes."

Right when we were about to kiss again, Adaba's shadow loomed over us. He pawed at the ground, smashing his hoof down about a foot away from Gareth's head.

"Adaba, in case you didn't notice, she's trying to seduce me, not the other way around," Gareth said from beneath me.

The horse gripped the sleeve of my dress and tugged me off of Gareth. "Well, I suppose that's the end of that then."

I rolled my eyes and sat next to the tree instead, picking flowers from the grass. When I had a pile of them, I weaved them together, until I had a crown of daisies. With a grin, I set it on top of my head.

"So what do you think?" I asked.

Gareth's eyes widened, and he bolted to his feet. "We should get moving so we can get to the border of Autumn before dark."

"What's wrong?" I let the crown slip from my hair.

"Nothing, just realized how late it was. Come on." He offered me a hand up.

But I knew it was more than that. Why the heck had the flowers on my head freaked him out like that?

"Gareth, seriously, talk to me," I said, my fingers brushing against his.

"When we get to Summer, I promise we'll talk about everything, but right now, I just want to enjoy our time together. Because once we get to the palace, our time will be compromised. We won't be able to be alone like we are now." His eyes shifted to Adaba. "Well, as alone as we can be now." His lips twitched.

I sighed. "Fine, but we *will* talk."

When we arrived at the Autumn border, the scent of fall hung heavy in the crisp air. I'd always been scared of this season before; I loved the beauty of the trees changing colors and the smell of pumpkin pie, but I always knew Winter came after Autumn. For once, however, I could enjoy this—or what there was left of it. Withered vines clung to old buildings, while remnants of leaves blew about in the wind.

The gray overcast sky loomed above, with the threat of rain hanging onto the angry clouds.

"We should make camp on the outskirts. It'll be safer for us to travel through the kingdom during daylight hours. We don't want to chance any run-ins with red caps in the ruins."

I'd read enough of Grandma's stories to know I didn't want to tangle with one of those. Just imagining their blood sopped caps made me queasy. We urged our horses closer to the riverbank, where an old cabin with a waterwheel sat. The windows were dark, and it looked as if it'd been a while since someone had lived there. Overgrown brown grass and weeds came up to the bottoms of the first floor windows, while the thatch on the roof appeared to have seen better times, ages ago.

Thunder sounded in the distance, and Gareth hopped off his horse. "Wait here while I go in and make sure it's safe." He unsheathed his sword and crept to the door. Quietly, he tried the handle, and the barrier swung right open.

I held my breath as he moved inside. My stomach knotted as I sat waiting for him to come back out. What was taking so long? My eyes scanned the darkening surroundings. I chewed my thumbnail, never taking my eyes off the front door.

A moment later, he stuck his head out. "It's all clear. I was just trying to move a few things out of our way so we could get our bedrolls laid out. There won't be any fires tonight, though. I'm not sure what state the fireplace is in."

As a low howl sounded in the distance, I was glad to go inside—although I wasn't sure how well the house would hold up. After a quick bite to eat, we bedded down, and night set in. The darkness swallowing us up.

Even though I couldn't see him, I felt Gareth beside me, and that was all the comfort I needed. As long as he was here, I knew I'd always be safe. The wind roared against the cabin, letting cold air sneak in through tiny crevices.

"Welcome hooooooooome..." The same voice from the other night drifted in on the breeze, swimming around in my head.

"Gareth," I whispered.

"What is it?"

"I-I heard that voice again, just now."

He sat upright, drawing his sword. "What did it say to you?"

My hand clenched his tunic. "It said, 'welcome home'."

He glanced down at me then stood, moving to the door. He opened it and looked around outside. After a moment, he shut it once more. "I don't see anything."

"Do you think whoever it is wants to hurt me?"

"I don't know, but I'd assume if they did, they would've already made their move. They've had plenty of opportunities before now. But I'll keep watch again tonight. Just get some rest." He sat back down beside me.

I snuggled closer to Gareth, too scared to sleep, hoping morning would come quickly.

CHAPTER SIX

Salome

"Hey, time to get up." Gareth shook me awake.

"It can't be morning yet, I feel like I just fell asleep." I groaned, wiping the sleep from my eyes.

"You know, you talk in your sleep." He grinned, enjoying this far too much.

"Really? And what did I say?" I crawled from my blankets and began to roll them up.

"Well, I don't want to brag, but you did mention how gorgeous I am, and how much you loved my kisses. And you might've mentioned something about Autumn." He opened the front door and gasped, then turned to me, eyebrows raised. "You're not going to believe this," he said.

"What?" I grabbed my bundle from the floor and hurried outside after him. My breath caught in my throat. Last night when we'd come in, all the trees, leaves, and vines had been withered and brown. Today, the leaves were brightly colored in orange, yellow, and bright red hues reminding me of balls of fire. This is what Autumn was supposed to look like. But how did this happen?

"Holy crap…"

"This doesn't seem possible without some sort of magic at work." Gareth glanced around.

I wrapped my arms around my chest, as the chill of the morning air seeped through my dress. "This is crazy, right? I mean, have you ever seen anything like this happen?"

Gareth secured his bedroll to his horse. "Yes."

"Seriously? When?"

"The seasons used to parade in like this at the Faerie Court when the Queen handed over reign for each kingdom when it was their quarter of the year to rule. But that hasn't happened since Genissa died, hundreds of years ago. Other than Summer, all the other courts have been vacant and dead…their seasons never coming. But now—and yesterday, I can't explain it."

I climbed on top of Adaba, while Gareth shut the cottage up. My mind tried to grasp what was happening around us. Were the seasons truly coming back? Or was this just a trick? Maybe some ploy by Winter to call people back to their homes so they could attack them again?

Gareth chose a path that led further into Autumn. The trees were like torches against the gray-blue sky. All around us colors seemed to burst. We went up a slight incline, and there, standing taller than all the other landscape, was the ruins of a castle. As we passed by the gates, I noticed the maple leaves etched into the stone. In the distance, I caught the distinct sound of waves crashing against the shore.

Our horses followed an overgrown trail, which came out next to what looked like an old watchtower. The rocks were crumbling and covered in moss, but it was the view beyond that that took my breath away. There, below us, was the sea. Salt hung heavy in the air, and the sun and trees' reflections cast a rainbow of color on top of the water.

Empty docks made of stone and rotting wood told the story of a time when many great ships came to this harbor. Even from here, I saw the remains of what must've been a huge fleet, now shattered to pieces against the rocks.

Stone stairs carved out of the side of the cliffs led down to the shoreline, but with the waves thrashing about, I knew it wouldn't be safe. I shivered, tugging my cloak tighter against my body.

We rode away from the steep slope and through what looked like old training grounds. Medieval looking pells still stood, waiting for a soldier to come practice his sword or battle axe maneuvers. The more areas we went through, the sadder I became. So many people lost. And for what? Grisselle to increase her stronghold?

Even though Autumn was falling apart, I saw no signs of battle. Not that I wanted to see bones or blood or anything like that; it just felt as if everyone had up and left. A heaviness hung about my shoulders until we rode out of the kingdom into the outskirts.

"I don't know how you spent the last couple hundred years dealing with stuff like this," I said to Gareth as he came up alongside me.

"Trust me, it wasn't easy. I had close friends at both the Spring and Autumn Courts. And I want to keep Summer from suffering a similar fate. But not a day goes by that I don't remember their fall…" His shoulders slumped and he stared off at some unseen thing.

We traveled in silence for the next couple hours, both of us lost in our thoughts. At last, Gareth found a grassy area for us to stop. I fumbled off the back of Adaba and stretched my limbs. After all this horseback stuff, I might need a masseuse.

Gareth opened his mouth as if to speak then shut it as a loud crash sounded in the brush. He drew his sword and whipped around to face the forest. Adaba positioned himself next to me, his ears perked up.

"Wait here," Gareth whispered.

"What's wrong?"

He put a finger to his lips. My pulse thundered as I scanned the thicket. Branches snapped and the birds and wildlife went quiet. The ground quaked beneath me as if the earth had shivered.

"Mwwhoooa." A loud growl broke the silence.

"Salome, back up." Gareth took a stance next to a nearby oak tree.

Before I could move, a large creature the size of a small car barreled into the clearing. Its rock like skin was dingy and gray. Its mouth twisted, revealing pointed teeth. Orange eyes glowed when they came to rest on me. The creature stood at least seven or eight feet tall and wore only a loincloth made of fur, which was secured in place with a belt made of bones. Every time he moved, the bones clanked together like eerie chimes.

"Oh God." My fingers tangled in Adaba's mane.

"Get away from the troll, Salome." Gareth rushed forward. He swung his blade in an arc, aiming for its knees. But the monster blocked him with a giant wooden club that could've easily been mistaken for a tree.

I took several steps toward the tree line. The troll charged at Gareth, knocking him down. Its mammoth-sized feet stomped at the ground, but Gareth managed to roll out of the way.

"Gareth," I shrieked. Panic coursed through me like a rushing river. All I kept picturing was blood and him dying, which freaked me out even more.

Gareth kicked himself back onto his feet. The silver of his blade glinted as he swung it once more. This time the weapon connected with the backs of the troll's legs, severing the tendons. The troll yelped in pain and collapsed into the ferns.

"Turn your head," Gareth told me.

My throat thickened, and I buried my face against the horse's side. Two more loud howls erupted, then all went silent.

"It's okay, he's dead now."

I pulled away from Adaba and stared in horror at the giant head lying in the leaves, its lifeless eyes still glowed even in death. Thick black blood dripped from the foliage. I covered my mouth as nausea overtook me.

Gareth wiped his sword off and hurried to my side. He clutched me tight to his chest. "Shh…just close your eyes and count to ten."

"I feel sick."

"I know. Just don't look at the body, okay? I need you to stay right next to Adaba while I scout out the woods."

"Wait—you're leaving me alone?" My voice quivered. I *so* didn't want to be left with the severed body. Hell to the flipping no.

"Only for a moment." He disappeared into the undergrowth, not giving me the chance to argue.

Several minutes passed before he reappeared, breathless.

"Are you all right?" I caught his arm. His skin was slick with sweat.

"Get on your horse."

"What?"

"Salome, you have to go."

I swallowed the rock-like lump in my throat. "By myself?"

"Yes—this troll was only a scout. The others aren't too far out."

No. This isn't happening.

"Others? But you'll be killed. I-I can't leave you."

Gareth turned to Adaba. "Take her to the Ruined Court and hide. If I'm not there in two days' time, get her to Summer."

Adaba whinnied and shook his mane as if he understood.

Gareth sheathed his sword and picked me up, his arms tightening around me. His lips crushed mine with urgency, as if he was taking his last breath. And I clung to him, absorbing his heat and his woodsy scent. When he pulled back, he set me atop my mount.

"Gareth, please…" Tears streamed down my cheeks. I reached for him, as if that'd really keep him from going anywhere.

He slid a dagger from beneath his tunic and slipped it into the belt of my gown. "Don't be afraid to use this."

"Please."

"I love you, Salome." He swatted Adaba's flank, and the horse carried me into the woods.

As we rode away, I heard the distinct sound of heavy footsteps tromping through the brambles.

I jerked on Adaba's reins. "Turn back. We can't leave him."

But the horse ignored my feeble attempts and galloped deeper into the forest. A sob raked through me as I realized that I might never see Gareth alive again.

CHAPTER SEVEN

*S*eeing Mr. Montgomery here, in this horrific place, shook me—if this was truly him. I mean, how could I be sure this wasn't someone else using glamour?

Look at his eyes. It's him. You just don't want to admit it because then that will make this more real.

But I refused to forget what he'd done to Salome last winter. I remembered how she'd sobbed over the phone after he'd treated her so badly then left her mom. The guy was a total asshat.

"I won't feel sorry for you—not after what you did to Salome," I said.

Pain filled his gaze, his bark covered cheeks tightened. *"What I've done to Salome? I don't understand."*

I glared at him. "Don't understand? You got drunk and shoved her around."

His mouth turned into an *"O"* of surprise, but it looked more like a knot in the tree than his lips. *"But I haven't seen Salome in over a year—well before Christmas."*

"That's not true. You came home…"

"No. I didn't." He coughed, splattering blood across the fresh snow. *"My wife called to tell me Salome was in an accident. I dropped my last tr-truck load and headed straight for Michigan. The snow—it was coming down so hard. And there was a car that had gone off the road. The woman flagged me down. I stopped to help her. Everything went black. I never made it home; instead, I woke up here…Sssooo. Much. Pain."* His eyes glazed over.

How could I know if he was telling the truth? He could be lying to me—trying to deceive me to get information. And if he was telling the truth, what did that mean? That there was a fake Mr. M running around?

Mr. M had always been so nice to me. And he'd coddled Salome, even went as far as building her that playroom shaped like a ship when she was little after her big winter freak out.

"Okay, if you're really Mr. M, then what kind of Valentine's Day card did she make you in third grade?"

"It wasssss a light house with heart shaped brickssss."

He was right. But was this something that the fake Mr. M might know as well? But the sincerity in his voice made me realize he was the real deal.

"Fine, I believe you," I sad.

Nausea stabbed at my stomach once more—because if this was the real Mr. M, then the man who'd hit Salome was probably some fucked up creature who'd glamoured himself like Etienne and Teodor had to look like Mr. M and get into the Montgomery's house. But why?

Salome.

I chewed my bottom lip then shifted my glance to Mr. Montgomery. "I'm sorry."

His branches shook, and he yelped while more crimson dotted the snow beneath him. *"You must not let them know you're a friend of my daughter's. Don't mention her name. They want something from her and will use you against her."*

A lump lodged in my throat. So he wanted me to protect her? Like I always had growing up. Against bullies. Against her fear of winter. It had been easy to be there for her when it hadn't been my life on the line, but now? What about me? When was it okay to look out for my own skin?

My hands fisted in my lap. I wouldn't betray her, but that didn't mean I had to like the situation. "I won't say anything. But we need to get out of here." Although...Etienne already knew I was a friend of Salome's; would he say something?

"I-I can't leave. I'm rooted here."

I didn't want to stare at his legs, which were buried deep beneath the frozen ground, yet I couldn't take my eyes off them. "There's got to be a way."

"The-there's only one way I can be freed from this place," he whispered. *"Through death."*

"No."

"Yes." His gaze flickered to the darkening sky where heavy clouds moved in. *"Please. Put me out of my misery—I beg you. Kill. Me."*

I shook my head. "I can't. I mean, I won't do it."

"Please..."

My throat tightened as my eyes blurred. This was my best friend's dad. No way did I want this on my shoulders. Salome would never forgive me. Hell, I'd never forgive myself.

"I'm sorry, but I can't do it."

He looked away, dead leaves falling from his arm-like branches as they peeled away like skin. He didn't say anything. But what more could either of us say? Then Mr. M's branch-slash-arm-thing tapped my wrist.

"Someone's coming."

I leapt to my feet and watched as Etienne strolled into the

courtyard.

He smiled, but the humor didn't reach his eyes. In fact, he looked anything but happy—more like sad. "I take it you didn't enjoy your new room?"

"Stay the hell away from me or so help me God, I'll slap the shit out of you." I backed up as he moved closer.

"You don't have to be hostile. I'm sure we can make an arrangement to get you a new room for the duration of your stay."

More than anything, I wished I had something to stab him with. But unless I ripped a branch off of Mr. M, I had nothing. "For what price?"

Etienne's eyes darted around the courtyard and up toward the shadowed windows of the castle, his outward actions at odds with the smirk he wore. "Information on Gareth or Simeon, of course."

"Are you flipping deaf? I told you—I. Don't. Know. Anything. Trust me, if I did know something, I'd give you whatever info you wanted."

"Pretty-pretty Kadie. I really wish we could forego the games." He reached out to touch a loose strand of my hair. His warm breath fanned across my cold skin. "Perhaps tomorrow you'll remember something."

He moved closer, his hand dropping away from my hair. His fingers instead dug into my arm, and he dragged me toward the red room.

"No." I planted my feet. "I don't want to go back in there."

My feet slid across the ground as I tried to stop him from taking me. I jerked back, but his grip only tightened. At that moment, Teodor appeared from the shadows.

"I see our prisoner isn't cooperating yet." He turned to stare at me. "See, if I was in charge of interrogating you, I'd already know all your secrets."

Fear rippled through me. No way did I want him touching me. Behind his handsome face, I saw the psychotic pleasure he got from scaring me. I backed up until I bumped into Etienne. He tightened his grip on my shoulders, pulling me closer to him. This time I didn't fight him but instead kept my gaze locked on Teodor.

"Stay away from me," I said.

"Maybe I can find you a warm bed to lie on." He smiled, revealing perfect teeth.

My heart hammered in my chest. Teodor stared at me, his eyes already stripping away my torn dress. Yeah, I had a reputation with the guys, but this was one douchebag that wasn't getting in my pants. No matter how hot he was—or rather *thought* he was.

"I'd rather sleep with a hand grenade."

His lips tightened into a thin line. "Etienne, perhaps you should clue your captive in on the appropriate way to talk to a Fae Prince."

"Leave us be, and let me do my job," Etienne said from between clenched teeth. "The more you interfere with things, the longer it'll take. The queen has put her in my care."

"So be it. But if you don't follow through with the plan, I'll go to the queen and ask her to reconsider." He smirked at him. "You're too soft; I bet she kills you in your sleep." Teodor eyed me once more. "You better hope you're not left alone with me. Because I promise I'll make you pay for your disrespect. This behavior won't be tolerated."

When he stalked off, I let out a sigh of relief, then spun to face my other captor.

"Try to remember, I'm the only person standing between you, Teodor, and the queen," Etienne said. "The quicker you cooperate with me, the sooner I might be able to get you released."

It didn't take him long to drag me back into the Red Room. Etienne tugged me over to the bed, nudging me until I fell to my knees. He took rope out from under his cloak and tied my hands to the bedpost. He left just enough length for me to crawl into the bed. I eyed the overstuffed mattress. I could only imagine what it was made out of. No way in hell was I gonna sleep on that thing. I didn't care how tired I got.

"Maybe one night in here will change your mind." He bent down so his face was inches from mine. "Try and remember, I'm not the bad guy here."

"You look like the bad guy to me. And just so you know, I'm never telling you anything." My gaze darted to his mouth.

God, he better not kiss me.

"Very well. Don't say I didn't try to warn you or help you."

He clapped his hands and the candles snuffed out, plunging the room into darkness. Then came the sound of the door closing. Everywhere I looked, I saw blackness. My teeth chattered as the chill in the room snaked around me. Maybe I'd be lucky and freeze to death. I pulled my legs as close to my chest as I could.

My eyes burned. Damn, I was tired, but I refused to close them. Instead, I listened to screams echo through the room from outside: high pitched cries of people in pain. I dug my nails into my palms. Fear made my stomach tighten. Would I ever escape this nightmare? I wished I'd never stepped foot into *Club Blade.* I trembled, wondering what tomorrow would bring or if I'd make it to see another day.

Gah. I hated these thoughts. I couldn't give up. I had to fight. I blew a deep breath out from my lips. Okay, I needed to get my head on straight and try to come up with a plan. But first, I had to get the damn ropes off.

I moved my wrists around, trying to tug them free, but

the rope only dug into my skin. I placed my hands between my knees, trying to get leverage to pull out of my makeshift shackles, but again the ropes only burned my wrists. The more I struggled against them, the more raw my skin became. *Fuck.* I pushed to my feet and tried to loosen the knot secured to the bed. To my dismay, it wouldn't come undone. Had they spelled the rope? If I had a knife or scissors, I could cut through it.

But you're locked in a damn room with no sharp objects.

Frustrated, I sank back to the floor. Great. I had no weapons. I was tied up in a locked room. And in the morning—if there was even a morning in this horrible place—I'd have to face God knew what. I needed a plan. However, as my gaze shifted around the room, everything became hopeless.

Please let me get through the night.

A sigh escaped my lips when I watched daylight sneak through the door at the back of the room. Somehow, I'd survived the night. My body ached as I attempted to stretch my legs out, my arms still tied to the post.

Every part of me was numb from the cold, but I was alive. As more light fractured the shadows, my gaze fell to the blood-slickened floors. It looked as if the floor tiles had bled. I buried my face against my shoulder. I wanted to cry but didn't dare show my fear. If they realized how badly this place affected me, they'd find other ways to get inside my head or worse, maybe torture me. A shiver scraped along my spine at the thought.

I need to get out of here. I'm going to go crazy.

A lock rattled then the door flung open. Etienne sauntered inside, his white tunic opened like some seventies porn star. He gave me a sad smile.

"Good. You're awake. The queen would like to see you." He walked over and untied the ropes that secured me to the bed.

I cried out as my wrists were freed. The skin around them was raw and reddened from my attempts to escape.

"What are you, her bitch?"

"You should just give in now, otherwise the Winter Queen will only make things worse."

"Trust me, I'm gonna keep fighting until I get out of this hell hole."

"Good, because you're going to need all your strength to survive this place in the coming days." Etienne pulled me to my feet, his hand resting against my lower back as he guided me from the room. Much like yesterday, the hallway was draped in gloom. Everything reminded me of death. From the dark colors to the skeletal remains, the décor promised pain, suffering, and demise. Paintings of horrific battles and bloodied corpses burned into my vision, while sconces made of bones held dripping crimson candles.

After several turns, we finally reached a large corridor with heavy mahogany doors. Carved faces stared at me from the woodwork, each with their mouth opened in a scream, as if they were forever stuck in the door.

Etienne led me into a large chamber. Ebony marble covered the whole room, like a giant black hole had swallowed it. The floor. The ceiling. The walls. All of them black. The only thing of color was the deep white tub at the center of the room—filled with blood.

My gut churned. The metallic scent made me gag. The queen wrapped a white robe around her shoulders; scarlet droplets streamed down her skin and leaked through the fabric.

She took one look at me and laughed.

"Now aren't you squeamish?" She floated across the room, until she stood in front of me. "Haven't you heard? Ten virgins' blood will forever keep you young."

Oh God. This chick's a psycho.

My mind conjured images from a stupid special I'd seen on TV about the Blood Countess, Elizabeth Báthory, who used to murder young girls and bathe in their blood. She did it to stay young. Maybe this was the same person.

Damn. I so didn't need to think of this right now.

"You're sick," I spat.

She frowned. "You don't know what it takes to run a kingdom for centuries. The sacrifices we must all make."

My hands clenched at my sides. "You sacrifice others — that's hardly any skin off your back."

Her eyes narrowed. "Etienne, you'd do well to silence your pet before I lose my temper."

A hand clamped over my mouth. "Be still," Etienne whispered.

The queen drifted across the room to a vanity made of skulls. She picked up a brush and ran it through her hair. "Has she told you anything more about Gareth?"

Etienne shifted behind me, pressing his chest to my back. "No, Your Highness."

She spun to face me once more. "You're going to be stubborn and fight me every step of the way, aren't you?"

I glared at her, tempted to bite Etienne's hand so I could tell her just what I thought of her. But then again, it might not be a good idea to piss her off more. I had no idea what she was capable of.

"Fine, I tried to be nice. But you force my hand. Take her to the Bone Yard, Etienne. We'll see how she likes to sort things.

Maybe a little time scouring through blood will change her mind."

Bone Yard? Oh shit, I didn't like the sound of that. How much longer could I hold out? I didn't know if I'd be strong enough to deal with much more.

Salome, if you're out there. Please. Help me.

*E*tienne jerked me from the queen's chambers and down several winding hallways. A woman met us at a large wooden door. One of her eye sockets was empty. My stomach churned as I stared at her face. It looked like half of it had been ripped off. Scars covered her left cheek and neck.

What the hell did they do to her?

It was like her head had been fed to a lion or something worse.

"She needs attire for the Bone Yard," Etienne said from beside me.

The woman bowed and scurried inside the door. When she emerged, she handed me a long gray dress and a black apron, along with a pair of knee-high leather boots. Once more, my kidnapper led me down the long corridors until we stopped in front of a curtained alcove.

"You have five minutes to change." Etienne pulled back the drape to reveal Hell's version of a changing room. He shut me in, but I heard him pacing outside the makeshift door.

Not wanting the skeevy bastard to see me naked, I whipped off my torn dress and broken heels, then slid into the nun-like clothing, the only consolation being it was warmer —although the fabric was rougher than I was used to. When finished, I slipped back into the hall.

"That was fast." He smirked.

"Yeah, well I didn't want to give you any ideas." I glared as he gripped hold of my arm.

Just keep pretending like you're strong. Don't let him see how weak you feel. How every horrible thing you see drives in the fact that you might not get out of here.

"I'm not the enemy, Kadie. I'm only trying to protect you. Or would you rather me hand you over to Teodor?"

I cringed. "No, I don't want you to give me to him. But last I checked you brought me here, so if you really want to help me then get me out of this place."

"And like I've said before, I saved you from being killed in the club. Trust me, there are far worse things than finding yourself with me. I can name two right now if you'd like."

I snorted. "Obviously, you've never been the object of your attention." But inside, I knew he was right. God only knew what Teodor or the queen would do to me given the chance. However, would he be able to keep me safe from them? And why would he want to?

My gaze shifted to the double doors ahead of us, with guards posted at either side. The large trolls swung them open, letting us into a nightmarish courtyard. Human assembly lines wound around the square. They sorted body parts and limbs into different piles. The stench of death filled my nose and I heaved again and again, but there was nothing left in me after last night to throw up.

"Oh God." My hand covered my mouth as I watched women toss bloodied arms into gigantic pots of boiling water. "Wh-what the hell are they doing?"

"Melting the flesh from the bones. The queen needs more décor," Etienne said, his voice strained. "When they have the bones cleaned off, they sort them by types into crates. From there they're hauled away to the architects and artists she keeps in the towers."

Blood ran like streams across the tiled grounds, seeping into the crevices.

I can't stay here. There's got to be a way out.

Etienne brushed my hair from my face. "We could end this now. Just tell me what you know, Kadie. Then I'll make sure they send you home." His eyes seemed to plead with me, as if he really meant what he said.

I squeezed my lids shut. No way would I tell him anything. Somehow, I knew Salome was involved in this, and I needed to protect her.

But why? You want to live too, don't you? This is going to be your new home or grave if you don't get the hell out of here.

My eyes opened once more, and I sucked in a deep breath. I had to be strong. "Go screw yourself. I already told you I don't know anything. So you're wasting both of our time by keeping me here." I glared.

Etienne's fingers traced my cheek. "Well, love, if you change your mind, I'll be in my quarters. Until then, enjoy yourself."

He spun on his heel and left me standing in the middle of the courtyard. A troll with a whip lumbered toward me. He pointed to the assembly line.

My mouth went dry as I took small steps forward. A girl no older than me smiled, and her eyes glazed over.

Her long blond hair was stained with blood, while the hem of her skirt was soaked in it. "You're so lucky."

"Lucky?" Hot damn, this chick was insane.

"Yeah. The prince likes you." She gave me a dreamy look. "If you do a good job sorting, sometimes they let you attend the balls and serve them."

"Are you on drugs? This place is fucked up." I waved my hand around.

She giggled then twirled around, holding a severed leg in her hand. The snap of a whip caught my attention as a troll lashed out at Crazy Chick. She continued to laugh and sort her limbs.

Holy shit. Was everyone like this? My gaze drifted down the line of girls. Some wore the same mystified, euphoric look, but most seemed frightened, like me.

"Get to work." One of the guards pointed at me.

My legs trembled as I stepped toward the barrel of severed body parts. My stomach churned again. A dark-haired woman further down the line flagged me over. I glanced around then scurried to her side.

"Here, help me stack leg bones."

"Okay." The bones were hot to the touch as they came out of the boiling pots. But it was better than having to feel rotten flesh.

"Don't associate with the Charmed," she said.

"The Charmed?"

"The ones who look like they are having fun. Stay away from them. They're too far gone to be helped and will only go back to their masters to spill your secrets."

"Lovely."

"Not really." The woman glanced at the two guards standing across the square from us. "What is your name?"

"Kadie. And you are?"

"Demetria." She pulled out another bone and stacked it neatly inside a crate. Dark curls fell around her pale face, her brown eyes troubled. "You're the first new girl they've brought to the Bone Yard in weeks. Lately we've had more going out than coming in." She nodded at the pile of bodies littering the high stone wall that surrounded us.

Chills swept up my spine. My chest tightened. Where had they gotten all those girls? Did they take them from the club like me?

Turing my attention from the bodies, I glanced at Demetria. "How long have you been here?"

She sighed, wiping her hands on her apron. "Too long. I have no idea how much time has passed. It was eighteen ninety-nine when I arrived."

"Oh God," I whispered. "You've been here for over a hundred years?"

She shrugged. "Time moves different here. Even if I get away, I have nothing to return to. It's not to say I want to be stuck here forever, but I have nowhere to go. No family waiting for me."

"But the human world, it's better than being here—I mean, being forced to do this."

A guard walked past, splashing through crimson puddles. The blood sprayed across my dress, making it look like it had polka dots.

Demetria lowered her head. "If there was a way to leave, I'd go. But this place is surrounded by guards. Even if we made it past the gate, I have no idea how to get out of Faerie. If the creatures didn't kill us, Winter would. You don't understand, this land, Faerie as they call it, isn't like our world. There are horrible things that lurk in those woods."

Goosebumps puckered my skin. Then I'd be stuck here forever? In this nightmare?

A skirmish started down the line, and I watched in horror as two girls fought over a severed head.

"This was in my pile—quit trying to take my parts."

It was Crazy Chick.

"No, it was in my bin," another girl argued.

"You will not get more parts sorted than me. It's my turn to be picked by the princes." Crazy Chick shoved the other girl, knocking her against one of the boiling pots. Her head hit it with a loud clang. Her body crumpled to the bloody flagstones, her neck twisted at a sickening angle. Crazy Chick kicked the lifeless form several times.

The trolls hurried over and pulled Crazy Chick out of the way. They picked up the other girl.

"She's dead," one of the trolls said in a garbled voice. In one swift movement, he hefted her up and tossed her into the boiling pot.

Crazy Chick smiled. "I made my quota for the day. They'll be so pleased."

"What the hell was that?"

Demetria shifted her sight on the ground. "That is what life is like here. Nightmares. Murders. Blood. Bones. Eventually, you will get used to it. You'll become numb to everything around you. And eventually, you will be able to sleep again."

"I don't want to get used to it. I want to get out of here." Frantic, I glanced around the Bone Yard. There had to be some way to get out of this place.

"Keep your voice down. You never know who is listening to you." She turned to look at the guards as if to make sure they hadn't heard me.

But the others were nowhere near us. I fought the nauseous pangs prickling inside.

Creak—creak…

I turned to see an ancient woman sitting at a spinning wheel with piles of different colored hair all around her.

"What is she doing?"

"Spinning the deads' hair into rope and yarn."

It was like I was in the middle of a messed up fairytale—the kind people tell kids to scare the crap out of them. But even in Salome's grandma's versions there was always someone who came to save the day. As the blood soaked my boots, I knew my days were numbered; there was no one here who could save me. I had to save myself.

Please, just let me get through this. Let me find a way out of here.

*H*ours later, a bell tolled from one of the high towers made of human skulls and bones. Women dropped the body parts they held and hurried across the courtyard, where they lined up. I dropped one last arm bone into our pile and wiped my hands on my skirt.

Demetria clutched my arm, keeping me close to her. "Just keep your head down and talk to no one. Your sponsor will come retrieve you."

We stood waiting for several moments until members of the Winter Court arrived. Tall beautiful beings, with deadly smiles and looks too good to be true. Demetria released me as she was ushered into a small group and led inside. She gave me one last glance over her shoulder.

I stood by myself, trying not to brush up against any of the others. No way in hell did I want to piss off the wrong psycho. Not that I couldn't hold my own, but I didn't want to chance a trip into the boiling pot.

When most of the crowd cleared, Etienne sauntered outside. His eyes swept over my gross clothes. For a moment, I thought I saw sympathy. "Come along; let's get you in and out of the cold." He gestured for me to follow him.

Servants and workers filled the hallways. Some carried trays of food, while others shoved prisoners toward a flight of stairs that went down. I swallowed hard, glancing at Etienne. Would he have me put in the basement? Not that I wanted to spend another night in the Red Room.

We veered away from the stairwell and along the twisting corridors until we came to a thick ornate door. Carved roses outlined the frame, while trees interlaid with gold decorated the middle. Etienne produced a key and slipped it into the lock. He gave it a turn and the door swung open, revealing a gigantic bedroom.

A bed with blue velvet drapes sat against the back wall. Flames flickered from a white marble fireplace. Already the warmth brushed against my chilled skin. No paintings hung on the walls as they did in the hallways. Here you could almost forget you were in the Winter Court. Blue oriental rugs covered sections of the floor. A mural of a sunrise over a lake was painted on the ceiling. Candlelight glowed warmly from a table at the center of the room. Steaming plates of vegetables sat on top of it, next to bowls of soup and goblets of what I hoped was red wine.

"I've had the maids draw you a bath. You can change out of your garments behind that screen." He pointed at the black panel. "I already have clean clothes set out for you."

He motioned for the servants to leave then shut his door, locking it behind him.

I walked behind the screen and quickly stripped out of my bloody dress and boots. Crimson stained my toes where the blood had leaked inside my shoes. I stepped into the steaming tub and slid down, letting the warm water cover me. My fingers scrubbed at my skin. Tears trickled down my cheeks.

I have to get out of here. I have to find a way.

Steam swirled around me, and I dipped my head beneath the water.

I could end this all now. Just not come up for air. At least then I'd be free.

A vision of Salome popped into my head. Then my family. I struggled to sit upright, rivulets running down my face as I gasped for air.

A towel sat on a nearby chair. I stood, grabbed it, and dried off as fast as possible. Then I slid into the woolen nightgown that'd been laid out for me. When I moved around the screen, I found Etienne sitting at the table, his head in his hands.

"I'm sorry you had to go to the Bone Yard today." He lifted his gaze. "I really didn't want this for you."

Tired, I plopped down across from him. "Then what did you want?"

"I told you. To keep you safe." He stood, walked over to the fireplace, and tossed another log on. Sparks sprayed the air like tiny fireflies.

I stared at the broccoli, corn, and asparagus on the plate. Damn, what I wouldn't give for a burger right now —although I guess I didn't really want to eat any meat here, because I had no idea where it came from. At least the veggies looked safe.

"You should've made me leave the club that night," I said.

"I doubt anyone could make you do something you didn't want to do. Besides, once Teodor heard you talk about Gareth, he wouldn't have let you out."

"So what happens now?"

Etienne moved back to the table and sat across from me. "Now I find a way to protect you. But you'll have to trust me. I know it goes against your nature, but do what I say. Don't question me."

I snorted. "Trust has to be earned, buddy. And right now, there's no way in hell I'm gonna do that."

He sighed. "At least promise to be careful in the Bone Yard. I can't be down there all the time to monitor what happens. If I thought I could get you out of here on my own, I'd sneak you out tonight. But she has eyes everywhere and I'm never allowed out on my own. One of the Winter Princes always accompanies me."

I stiffened, dropping my fork back on my plate. "I have to go back?"

"Yes. The queen has ordered you work there every day until you talk."

"And if I don't talk?"

"She'll find other methods." He frowned. "I can protect you, Kadie. But I don't know for how long."

Fuck. Okay, I didn't want to go to the Bone Yard again. But how could I get out of it?

Think girl. You're smarter than this. But you have no weapons and the one thing they want, you don't really want to give, do you?

I rubbed the back of my neck with my hand and watched as Etienne's gaze followed my every move. Maybe I *did* have a weapon. A very powerful one: myself. I knew I was beautiful and desirable and could be damn sexy when I wanted. So why not use it? I could play seductive Kadie for a while, maybe feed enough information over to keep me from being killed and to keep me relevant—needed.

"Why are you being nice?"

I saw that flicker of something again in his eyes. "Because I'm not really the bad guy here. In front of her and Teodor, I have to act horrible, and for that I'm sorry. But if they think for one moment that I sympathize with you, they'll take you away from me. They'll kill you."

My heart thudded in my chest. I chewed my bottom lip, watching as his gaze softened. He ran a hand through his pale blond hair. There was almost something lost—broken—about him. Geez, I so didn't need to feel sorry for this asshat right now. I needed to remember whose fault it was that I was there in the first place.

"I'm sorry, but I don't believe you. Trust me when I say I've dated enough jerks to know one when I see one."

He grimaced. "Fair enough. Someday you will know I speak the truth."

Dong—dong—dong

My fingers clenched the side of the table. "What's that noise?"

"The queen's way of letting everyone know that the prisoners are to bed down for the night." He stood then grabbed my arm, dragging me toward his bed.

I struggled against him. "You're full of crap if you think I'm sleeping with you."

Panic coursed through me. I planted my feet.

He chuckled. "Good thing you're not going to be in my bed then."

Etienne showed me to a cage beside the wall. A mat and some blankets were piled up inside.

"You're freaking joking, right?"

"You don't have to sleep inside it, but you'll need to lay close enough so you can climb in if someone comes to the door. I could get in trouble for not following the rules. I'm giving you some freedom, so don't make me regret it."

My gaze shifted to his. "You're not going to make me sleep inside it?"

"No." He swung the barred door open and pulled out the

mat and blanket and laid it out next to the cage. "The queen insists that all of our humans be locked up until we have them trained. But I told you, I won't force you to as long as you promise to go inside if someone stops by the room." He watched me as I knelt down, grabbed the woolen blanket, and wrapped it about my shoulders.

"Okay, I promise." Could I sneak out while he slept? Or maybe start working on my plan?

He raised his hand to pat my head, but I gave him a look that was equal parts fire and equal parts tempting. He looked away too quickly for me to be sure, but I swore I saw the hint of a smile on his face. At least I hoped. If seduction was my best weapon, I had to be on my A-game.

He went over to recheck the lock on the door. Once he finished, he sat down on the edge of his bed, watching me.

I felt like his pet, and my hands trembled as I gripped tight to my blanket. My plan to use seduction as my weapon was a double edged sword. The room was locked and I was trapped in here with him. His prisoner. If I took it too far, I'd be in more danger than ever.

Etienne dowsed the lights, and I heard his bed shift as he got comfortable. I had to make a choice. And I had to make it now. With a sigh, I gripped the side of the bed and climbed to my knees. Before I could change my mind, I crawled up into Etienne's bed.

"What are you doing?" He sat up in the darkness.

Time to turn on the tears. "I-I'm cold and scared. Look, I-I just don't want to be on the floor, by myself. What if something tries to kill me in my sleep?"

I felt him throw back part of his covers. "Fine, get under the blankets. I promise I won't let anyone hurt you."

My fingers felt around the bed until my palm slid across

his arm. I moved closer to him, slipping under the comforter. Etienne pulled the blanket up until we were both beneath it. I pressed my body closer to his, the warmth radiating through my nightgown.

I heard him suck in a deep breath. "Get some sleep."

"I'll try." I let my head fall against his chest. Etienne might be Fae, but I knew he wasn't immune to my charms. In fact, tonight proved that I might just be able to get him to help me escape. Convinced my plan might work, I finally closed my eyes.

CHAPTER EIGHT

Salome

My knees ached as I bounced in the saddle, trying to hold my grip on the sweat-lathered Adaba. We'd been riding for hours, which put more distance between me and Gareth—something I didn't want to think about. But it was hard not to let my imagination run wild with gruesome images of his death.

Please. Just let him be okay.

The horse galloped through trees and brambles. Twigs, thorns, and gnarled overgrowth scraped at our skin, but we kept our frenzied pace. With a quick glance over his shoulder, Adaba veered left. Only when we approached a river did he slow. He hesitated a second, then stepped into the water, which rose to his underbelly. I glanced back at the bank and realized he was trying to hide our tracks.

As we splashed further in, the cool currents soaked the bottom of my skirts and boots. My teeth chattered.

How long will I last out here?

My gaze shifted to the sun, sinking in the sky. Soon darkness would fall, and I damn sure didn't want to be stuck out in the woods at night.

Adaba slowly made his way upstream, his movements stirring up the sand.

"She's com-ing…"

I whipped around. My eyes searched the landscape, but no one was there. Just endless vegetation blowing back and forth. My fingers tightened in Adaba's mane. Wind wailed through the forest like women screaming in pain. Goosebumps puckered my skin.

Something's here. I feel it.

Bubbles and foam rose from the river floor as if there was an eruption below. Water sprayed my left cheek. A gurgled snort sounded beside us as a great black horse rose from the depths, river-weed tangled in its mane. This was no ordinary horse. It was a Kolpie. It turned to face me, eyes blazing like hot coals. The beast's lips peeled back to reveal blood covered teeth. *Crap.* If I could reach the saddlebags, then maybe I could pull out the sword Gareth had gotten for me. I leaned to the side, reaching for the buckles. Moving at this pace and bouncing around, I couldn't get hold of it.

Come on.

Adaba jerked to the side in an attempt to get to the shore. But it was too late. In one swift movement, the Kelpie latched onto my arm.

"No!" Pain shot through me like a bullet. I fought to stay in the saddle. My horse kicked out his hind legs, catching the Kelpie in the side. Still the creature wouldn't release me.

Instead it tugged harder, ripping me halfway off my saddle. My knees tightened around Adaba's sides, my fingers loosened as water slickened what grip I had. The Kelpie's teeth sunk deeper into my arm. My hands slipped; my hold lost. Horror washed over me when I plunged into the dark, icy depths of the river. The coldness stung my skin. The creature dragged me deeper, and I kicked my legs, thrashing to free myself from it. Above me, all I saw were the distorted images of the sky as it faded from sight. Weeds tangled around my feet, as if trying to help the monster drown me.

My lungs burned while nightmarish images of my last near-drowning played through my head.

It isn't supposed to end like this.

My chest felt as if it might explode. Black dots danced in my vision. Down I went like an anchor speeding to the seafloor.

I couldn't let it win. From deep inside, I willed it to let me go. A burst of light blinded me. And then, in my hand was the Blade of the Four Kingdoms. Underwater, it was hard to maneuver, but I managed to get it in front of me, slicing at the creatures body. A cloud of blood darkened the water and the Kelpie's teeth slipped from my skin, its grasp lost. A strong tug on my dress dragged me back to the surface.

When I emerged from the river, I coughed, sputtering water, still holding the blade. Holy shit. What'd just happened? How had the sword come to me? Adaba's teeth clung to my clothes as he pulled me onto the bank. I eyed the sword warily and dropped it to the ground, then rolled onto my stomach and sucked in deep mouthfuls of air.

With the sleeve of my dress, I wiped my mouth. Tears trickled down my cheeks. Where had the light come from? My gaze slid to the blade once more. Had Adaba found a way to get it to me? Was it really magic? Or was it all me? I didn't want to believe the latter, but the coincidences were adding up quickly.

"Thank you," I said to Adaba.

He nudged me with his snout, urging me to stand.

With a sigh, I bent down and picked up the sword. The symbols etched into it glowed bright blue—then faded before my eyes. "I better put this thing away before I cut my hand off...." More like before I scared the crap out of myself looking at it. Maybe it was haunted. My legs shook, but I managed to stand, put away the weapon, and climb back on my mount. "I'm really starting to hate water," I muttered.

Once more, we were on our way. Adaba stuck to the shoreline as daylight fought to hang on. The trees became sparse, opening up to rolling green hills and rocky terrain. My pulse raced when I saw a figure standing amongst the rocks.

"Adaba," I whispered. My fingers trembled and I jerked on the reins.

But he continued to trot toward it. Shadows stretched across the ground like elongated hands.

"Sheeeee's here..."

If the horse didn't stop now, I was jumping off. I'd had enough drama for the day. As we neared the dark figure, I cringed, waiting for the onslaught. But it never came. Instead, I found myself face to face with a statue. A mother-flipping statue. A nervous laugh escaped my lips as I stared at the weathered stone face.

My gaze scanned the outcroppings. Large ruined buildings stood amongst them, covered in ivy as if the land was taking them back. Once brilliant gates lay in crumbled piles of stone, no longer protecting grand palaces. Adaba halted, and I slid from his back.

This must be the Ruined Court.

"What happened to all the people?" I asked.

Adaba shook his head then continued up the slope of the hill.

Strong gusts whipped through the tall grass, and the hills seemed to ripple like waves. I stepped over a stone head with mossy clumps clinging to its cheeks and its empty eyes fixed on the sky—forever frozen. With a shiver, I turned away and stared instead at the strange rock circles that dotted the hillside.

As I neared them, I noticed the ancient etchings. Some had leaves carved into them, while others had snowflakes, flowers, or suns. They reminded me of the piece of stone I'd found in the hidden room of my grandparents' house. Had it come from here? And if so, how the heck had they gotten it? The more I remembered from Grandma's stories, the more I believed that she'd been here.

Thunder rumbled from above. I tilted my head, and a giant raindrop splattered on the side of my face. We quickened our pace, hurrying up the slick terrain. Lightning zig-zagged overhead. I squealed. God, if we didn't find shelter soon I'd likely get fried.

Fog slipped between the statues like wispy ghosts. The downpour pelted against my skin. The hem of my skirt caught on a bush, and I jerked it free.

Maybe I ought to just tear the damn thing off.

Mud covered the whole dress, not to mention the wet material was heavier than hell.

At last, Adaba stopped at a rocky overhang which had just enough room for both of us to take shelter under. I unstrapped my bags from his back then unhooked his saddle as well. With a sigh, I unlatched one of the hooks, opened my tote, and rummaged through it for some dry clothes.

Once I found a dress, stockings, and a cloak, I stripped out of my wet garments. The horse turned his back.

"You're kind of a prude, you know."

He whinnied but continued to watch the dark landscape. When I finally had my clothes on, I fumbled to unwrap a chunk of dried meat. I inhaled the food, then took a water skin from my pack and got a drink. With my belly full, I grabbed the dagger Gareth had given me and set it on the ground near my blanket, deciding against taking the sword back out.

Gareth.

His name brought tears to my eyes. Was he okay? Would I know if he died? Exhausted, I slumped to the ground, rubbing my arms in an effort to get warm. Damn Nevin for forcing us to go to Summer.

Right now, Gareth and I should be curled up in front of the fireplace, sipping hot cocoa. Instead, I was stuck out in the middle of some freaky ruined village and God only knew what happened to Gareth. I didn't want to think about it—about him not being here with me. He was my true love, and he was supposed to be here. After everything we'd been through, I didn't want to lose him now. I couldn't lose him.

Adaba lowered himself to the ground beside me, his eyes still focused on our surroundings. I swallowed hard. It was so dark. Shadows swathed everything in sight. The sound of thunder and raindrops drowned out any other noises.

What I wouldn't give for a flashlight. Hell, I'd settle for a lighter—anything to chase away the gloom. The horse nudged my arm, trying to make me lay down.

For a moment, I resisted. But if I was going to be in any shape to travel tomorrow, I'd need rest. I curled up and tugged my cloak tight about my shoulders. Frigid air crept beneath my makeshift blanket. I squeezed my eyes shut. *Mind over matter. Don't think about the cold. Just think of warm beaches. And roaring fires. And hell.* Okay, probably not the last one, but I had to do something to warm up.

We'd only been lying down for a short time when something tugged my hair.

"Crap." I sat up and reached for my dagger.

There, flying past my head and glowing like a firefly, was a tiny blue fairy. Tiny and, hopefully, harmless.

It hovered closer to my face. It looked like one of Nevin's people.

"Be still," it whispered.

For a moment I wondered if maybe this was the voice I'd heard before, but it didn't sound at all similar. This one was too high pitched...which meant that mystery was still waiting to be solved.

Adaba climbed to his feet. The ground beneath us shook, followed by the *thud-thud-thud* of heavy footsteps.

Holy shit. Holy shit. Holy shit.

I clamped my hand over my mouth to keep from screaming. What the frick was out there? Rocks fell from above us, cascading down the side of the hill. My heart catapulted in my throat. Not that I wanted to be all negative and stuff, but we had nowhere to run. Whatever stalked the night was waiting for us to make a dumb move.

Adaba pawed the ground, then blew warm breath against my cheek. Like a canon, he burst from our hiding spot, bolting across the rugged terrain.

No.

He left me alone. He—*woosh*—

The scent of sulfur invaded my nose and burned the back of my throat. The sky blazed with fire, and I watched in terror as a great wingspan filled the night. Adaba raced away from me, leading the dragon toward the bottom of the hill. If something happened to him, I'd be alone out here. But just thinking about Adaba made me worry more. How would he defend himself? He was a horse...facing off against a dragon. I froze in place.

The fairy gripped hold of my hair, then tugged me to move. *"You need to run."*

I'd learned the hard way that following someone who *seemed* friendly was a quick way to getting myself in even bigger trouble, but what else was I going to do with a dragon on my heels?

"Where am I going?" I grabbed the dagger, then stumbled forward into the blackness. My foot connected with a large stone—or at least what I hoped was a stone. "Damn it!"

The night swallowed us up. My ears perked up while I strained to hear above the storm. My hair snapped around my head, the wind's rage punishing. A low growl sounded from behind, and my pulse quickened as I glanced over my shoulder to see a pair of glowing red eyes.

"Move faster. It's coming." The fairy yanked harder on my hair, practically ripping it from my head. If she didn't ease up, I'd need a wig.

"What's coming?"

Teeth gnashed at my heels, followed by loud snarls. My thighs burned as I continued to run uphill. I sucked in deep breaths in an attempt not to hyperventilate.

"Hurry, we're almost there."

Almost where? I wanted to ask, but the creature hunting me latched onto my cloak and jerked me backward. I tumbled to the ground with a shriek, fighting to get to my feet.

My fingers closed around the handle of my dagger. In my head, I tried to recall what Gareth had taught me. Frantic, I slashed out with the knife. The beast yelped and I ripped myself free, pretending I didn't see the doglike-snout filled with enormous teeth or the claws that scraped at the earth below it. I leapt to my feet and took off running.

Crap. I didn't sign up for this.

At last, we reached the ruins, and the fairy glowed once more, giving me a bobbing light to follow.

"Go downstairs and hide. Don't come out for any reason."

My mouth went dry as I stared at the crumbling stairs,

which led into a dark abyss. No way in hell did I want to go in there. If I did, I'd be trapped.

"Maybe this isn't a good idea," I said.

Once more, I heard the snarls of the creature as it charged up the hill. I'd probably ticked it off when I'd cut it.

"Go now."

How did I know this fairy wasn't psychotic? I mean, who's to say it wasn't really a flesh-eating zombie leading me to my death?

You don't. But you don't have a choice.

Either I took my chance in the lower levels of the ruins, or I became dog food.

My legs trembled, but I forced myself down the dilapidated stone stairs. At the bottom was a thick wooden door, which was closed. With no time to reconsider, I pushed on it. It didn't budge. Frantic, I rammed my shoulder against it. After a few attempts, it finally groaned open enough for me to slip inside.

"Close the door and stay in there until someone comes to get you," the fairy said. *"We need you safe."*

I slammed the door shut, then leaned my head against my arms. Pitch blackness surrounded me. A thick, musty scent clung to the damp air. Chains rattled at the back of the room. I went still.

Tap. Tap. Tap.

Something shuffled behind me.

Whispers began in a low buzz, echoing off the walls. I clutched my dagger tight to my chest and slid to the floor. My stomach knotted. My heart raced.

Any minute now, I'm gonna pee my pants.

A sudden burst of light illuminated the room, and I squealed.

"Don't worry, we'll protect you..." a voice hissed like

air leaking from a tire. A ghostly figure floated toward me. Its translucent skin glowed; its eyes were hollow and black. Phantom arrows protruded from its—or rather *his*—heart. He raised a finger and pointed. *"Get away from the door."*

I climbed to my feet but stood where I was. The fairy had screwed me over. She'd led me to be murdered by flipping ghosts.

"NOW!"

I staggered forward right as something rammed into the door. The wood splintered while growls erupted on the other side of the barrier. My eyes darted about the room. There was nowhere to go. Well, other than a creepy ass hallway at the back of the room.

Pop. Other ghosts appeared and shoved tables, barrels, stones—anything they could find—in front of the door. A cold touch on my arm made me scream as the same ghoulish man-ghost ushered me toward the serpentine hall I'd seen just a few minutes ago.

No way. I don't want to go in there.

Yet, I didn't have a choice. If I stayed out here, who knew what the dog from hell might do to me? Okay, so I either got mauled to death or accosted by a phantom.

Ghost it is.

My body quivered as I finally followed after the being. Bluish orbs lit the narrow passageway. Cobwebs brushed against my face. I prayed they didn't have spiders attached to them. Shadows clung to the rock walls, seeping out to trail us. Deeper we went, until at last, we came to a metal door. Carved into its base were the same suns, snowflakes, flowers, and leaves I'd seen on the stones outside.

The door creaked open, and I stepped into a room filled only with a large stone table and several chairs carved right into the rock walls.

Please don't let that be a sacrificial altar.

I stood silent for a moment in an effort to catch my breath. When I turned, I saw an army of ghosts step through the walls and ceiling. "Who are you? An-and what do you want?"

"We are the ruined..." the ghostly man said. *"We've come for you..."*

My knees buckled, and I reached for the wall to steady myself. The transparent people closed in on me.

Gareth! I screamed in my mind. *Help me. Please.* But Gareth wasn't here. I was all alone. And soon, I'd be dead.

CHAPTER NINE

Salome

Zsqueezed my eyes shut, awaiting the onslaught. But it never came.

"We won't hurt you," the ghost whispered, his breath bringing out goose bumps.

My back pressed against the wall, and cold seeped into my bones. At last, my lids fluttered open.

"How do I know I can trust you?" For all I knew, they brought teen girls down here and possessed them or something.

"We saved your life from the Hell Hound."

Well, there was that—although I was the one who'd stabbed it to begin with. My gaze drifted to the lone door in the room. Blue light pulsated from the beings, casting shadows that crawled across the floor. "Why? Why did you save me?"

"Because we need you to set us free." The phantom floated closer. *"We're trapped here, until* she *wants us."*

"She?" Could this guy, or whatever he was, be any more vague?

"The queen." His voice sounded hollow.

I stiffened. "You mean the Winter Queen?"

"Yesss…"

"Oh, hell." I'd had one too many run-ins with her already. I *so* didn't want any more.

"You must help us," he repeated.

Water dripped down my face from my wet hair. I raised a hand to brush it away. "Listen, I'm grateful you saved me—but I have no idea how to free you. I mean, you can probably tell I'm not from Faerie. I'm human. I have no powers."

At least none I was sure of, and definitely none I knew how to access.

He moved closer, his eyes turning a warm cocoa color. For a split second, I saw auburn strands of hair sweep across his forehead, like he'd come to life. He opened his mouth, blowing warm breath over my face. The scent of autumn and leaves wrapped around me. It reminded me of the breeze when Gareth and I had rode through the Kingdom of Autumn.

"But you do have powers—already I feel the court reawakening."

"I don't see how that's possible," I said, even as I remembered what had happened with the horse. The sense of warmth flooding through me and out…

I glanced away, noticing a worn tapestry dangling on the wall behind him. I sucked in a deep breath. No way. No freaking way.

I moved across the room, slowly until I stood beneath it. The tapestry had the same picture as my grandma's fairytale book. It depicted an auburn haired woman—a queen—giving her magic to a small girl. "W-where did this come from?"

"It was made during the time of the Faerie Queen, Genissa. Some say she or one of the elders had had a vision…to ensure this vision was not forgotten, it was woven with magical thread— powerful enough to withstand time. This tapestry was made to

archive what they saw. When the wars broke out, it was brought down here for safe keeping. A reminder that not all is lost." His gaze focused on my face as if he were trying to read me like a book.

"This child, she's supposed to come back and save Faerie?"

"That is how the tale goes."

I stared at it, then back at him. "Who are you really?"

His transparent hand reached for mine and went right through me. My skin pricked with goosebumps once more, as if a frigid wind had swept across it.

"My name is Lord Darach—one time heir to the Autumn Throne," he said. He backed away from me and immediately lost what little color he'd had. *"The others you see here were once a part of either the Spring or Autumn Courts. The Ruined Courts."* His voice burned with anger.

"What happened?"

"What happened?" He gave a bitter laugh. *"The Winter and Summer Courts happened."*

My breath caught in my throat, and I stared at him. "No way did the Summer Court have anything to do with this." I pointed at the ghosts. "Gareth and Nevin wouldn't do something like this."

Darach fingered the two arrows protruding from his chest. *"They may not have shot the bow, but they betrayed us nevertheless."*

"I—I don't understand." I licked my dry lips. He had to be wrong. Nevin might be a giant jerk-off sometimes, but he'd never do something like that—I mean, Gareth wouldn't let him.

Darach drifted to the stone table and sat in one of the chairs. He gestured for me to join him.

I hefted up my heavy skirt then moved to the seat facing his. A couple other ghosts joined us, while the rest gathered around.

"Perhaps I ought to explain to you how we came to be this way."

He glanced at me, and I nodded for him to continue.

"There was a time when the four courts—Winter, Spring, Summer, and Autumn—lived in peace. We took turns ruling the land. Each season had its time. The courts came here to rule with the Queen of Faerie for their season—then, when it was over, they would return to their own estates."

That explained the rock circles with the symbols etched into them, which I'd seen when we first arrived.

Darach focused his attention on the far wall, his features tightened as if he was lost in nightmarish thoughts.

"None of us realized right away how strong Winter had grown. Once the Winter King died, Grisselle found a way to delve into the darkest magic. Some say she traveled to the Forbidden Swells to master her powers—a place where no faerie or mortal should step foot. Soon, Winter became longer—the nights colder, more vicious." He shifted his sight to me, eyes filled with sorrow. *"By the time we recognized Grisselle's power, she'd already attacked and destroyed the Spring Court—extending her hold on the seasons."*

I reached across the table; my fingers clenched his ghostly hand. More than anything I wanted to give him comfort, some sort of reassurance. With a sigh, I wished for him to feel my sympathy.

"Wh—what happened next?"

He gave me a startled look as he squeezed my hand. *"I feel you. How is this possible? How did you do it?"*

"I don't know. I only wanted to offer you comfort."

"Your warmth—it radiates like the sun." His eyelids closed as if he were absorbing me. *"I've been cold for so long…"*

My skin glowed where I touched Darach. Tingles ran up my

arm like a jolt of electricity. "Um—what's going on?"

"I'm unsure."

I drew my hand back. No way did I want any more crazy stuff happening. Instead, I shifted in my seat, avoiding the many pairs of eyes staring at me.

"Maybe you should get on with the story now."

"Of course." Darach floated out of his chair to the other side of the table, as if to distance himself from me. *"As I said, Grisselle destroyed the Spring Court. We knew it was only a matter of time before she came after Summer and Autumn. We devised a plan to ambush her here. Autumn court arrived first. We set ourselves in place around the palace. Nevin promised to send his troops through the woods, near the back of the castle. We'd have her surrounded. But Nevin never came. He deserted me—or rather us."* He gestured to those standing around him, with jerky, anger-filled motions.

"Wait, what?"

"Nevin never arrived. They betrayed us. He betrayed us. We weren't strong enough to fight Grisselle by ourselves. So when she appeared, she easily destroyed us. The spell she used tethered us between life and death. We're stuck here as phantoms—ghosts of our former selves. We cannot move on from this place, nor can we go back to our former lives." Anguish washed over him; his lips were drawn downward and his eyes empty of hope.

My chest tightened. "But Summer wouldn't do that—not intentionally," I said. Nevin was a manipulative jerk, but at his core, he was honorable; he wouldn't have let his kind die. Would he?

Darach's hardened laugh echoed off the walls. *"They never came. No amount of your arguing will change that."*

None of this made sense. Summer hated Grisselle. No way in hell would they have allowed her to just take over Faerie.

Not to mention this still didn't explain why Darach thought I could do something to help them.

"How does this involve me—I mean, how do you expect me to free you or whatever?"

He smiled for the first time and in that gesture, I saw his humanity. His desire to live. *"Because you are not of Faerie, and yet you are somehow marked by us—as if you are one of our own."*

"I'm not sure I follow." I quirked an eyebrow. "I'm human, that's it. I was born and raised in the human world. The only ties I have to this place are my boyfriend. I mean, I knew when I became Gareth's betrothed, that at some point I'd become immortal, but I didn't think that would give me super powers or something."

"Nevertheless, it's you who must free us. I can feel it."

"And how am I supposed to do that?" I leapt to my feet. "I don't know what I could do to help you. I'm just a regular girl." Because even if those weird events hadn't been coincidences— the shield that'd formed around me and Adaba, or the Blade of the Four Kingdoms appearing to me—it was part of a mystery I didn't understand and couldn't yet control.

Darach disappeared then reappeared at my side. *"There's nothing regular about you, Salome Montgomery. Word of you travels throughout Faerie. The girl who broke the Summer King's curse and battled death and won. No. You are the one we've waited for. You will free us. And in the end we will fight side by side."* He pointed at the tapestry as if that answered everything.

Problem was, all my earliest memories were of Grandma and Mom. In the human world.

And the voices in the woods.

I opened my mouth to argue. Who was this guy to think he

could tell me what *I* would do? But he raised a finger to my lips.

"Shhh…someone comes. Whatever you do, don't mention us to anyone."

"Hold on, where are you going? What if this person tries to kill me?" Panic shot through my veins as I glanced around the room.

"You'll be safe, for he has a need and use for you. Until next time, Salome." He bent forward and touched my cheek.

My skin prickled as I watched the ghosts vanish. Then I heard a familiar voice.

"Salome!" Nevin shouted.

Okay, so it was my ex-whatever-you-wanted-to-call-him. How was it that Darach thought I'd be safe with Nevin if he'd supposedly betrayed the Autumn Court? Crap, should I even go with him? If he'd really wanted to hurt me, however, he could've already done so. I glanced around the darkened ruins and shivered. More than anything I wanted to get out of this place.

But why did he come instead of Gareth?

Again I had next to no answers, but I had no choice but to move forward.

"I'm here." Tears blinded me as I moved to the door. I looked behind me one last time to where the specters had disappeared. As much as I hated keeping Darach a secret, I knew I had to until I figured out why Nevin bailed on them. Right now, I had no idea who to trust. A ghost? My boyfriend? The King of Summer?

Or maybe I shouldn't trust any of them. Because in all the stories I'd read as a child, Faeries were always tricksters…and they used humans to get what they wanted. So the question was, what did they want? And how did I fit into the big picture?

CHAPTER TEN

Salome

The door swung open to reveal Nevin and several of his guards. I choked back a sob as he pulled me into his arms; whether from relief or worry, I hadn't decided yet.

"Shh…it's okay, I'm here," he whispered. He smoothed my hair back from my face. "I'm sorry I didn't find you sooner. I tried to send soldiers to escort you to Summer, but the portals to Gareth's were blocked. As soon as I realized I couldn't get the guards to you, I readied my troops and sent one of my faeries to find you."

"Trolls attacked us in the woods. I don't know where Gareth is. And Adaba was trying to protect me from a dragon, and he disappeared too."

His fingers wiped tears off my cheeks. "Don't worry, Gareth is a seasoned soldier. He'll make his way to us as soon as he deems it safe. As for Adaba, his whole existence is driven by the need to keep maidens safe. He chose you as the girl he wants to look after. And he is more cunning and strong than you realize." But I didn't miss the worried lines on his forehead, or the constant glances around our surroundings.

I rested my head against his chest. For a moment, I remembered a time when he was the one I ran to when things went bad. Last winter, I'd spent most of my afternoons hanging out with him at my grandparents. Before the curse was broken—before I realized he'd tricked me and used spells on me in order to convince me I loved him.

"Thank you for coming after me," I said at last. But I couldn't help but wonder why, or if he had some ulterior motive.

"You're welcome." He pulled back. "Come along, my men have set up camp in the woods. You can get some food then lay down for a bit."

"I'm not tired."

"Salome, you need your rest. I know you want to wait up for Gareth, but we still have a couple days' worth of travel ahead of us."

I wanted to argue with him—to demand we send men to find Gareth. But I knew he was right.

We made our way down the hill to a narrow path that led into the trees. Here several tents were set up. The green canvas billowed in the wind, snapping like whips. Soldiers sat next to campfires. Some cooked, while others carved arrows or wiped down weapons. Two elven guards were posted outside one of the tents. It was bigger than the others and crowned with a flag embroidered with trees, which billowed in the gusty wind.

Nevin guided me toward it. "You can bed down in my quarters for the night."

His quarters? I glanced up at him. "Maybe I should eat first."

"I'll have food brought in for you. But for now, you need to relax."

Geez, I wasn't an invalid. I could handle sitting by the fire. "Won't your men jump to conclusions about me being in your tent? I mean, we don't want to give them the wrong idea."

He raised an eyebrow at me. "And since when do you care about what other people think?"

I crossed my arms over my chest. "Since now. Because I'm Gareth's girlfriend—his Blood Bonded…the last thing I want is for people to forget that."

He chuckled, holding up his hands. "Fine. I doubt you'll do as I say anyway. You're always so damn stubborn."

"I'm not stubborn."

"And argumentative."

"No, I'm…"

"See?" He teased, tugging me toward one of the nearby fires. "You can sit out here with us until after you eat, then I want you in bed. Okay?"

"You know, you're kind of bossy." I glared.

"Well, I am the king."

I rolled my eyes but took a seat next to him. Already the heat from the flames warmed my skin. One of the soldiers brought over some type of jerky and cheese, along with a flask of water. Hungrier than I thought, I gobbled down the food.

"So what's the plan?" My gaze shifted to Nevin, who stared at the sky. I wondered if he was more worried about the dragon than he'd let on.

"We'll wait another day to see if Gareth shows. If not, then we'll get you to the Summer Palace where you'll be safe."

"But Gareth told me to wait two days."

"Tomorrow will be the second day, Salome." Nevin turned his eyes until they met mine. "My number one priority right now is to make sure no harm comes to you."

"Why? You didn't seem to care about me in the human world."

"Because you're Gareth's Blood Bonded and he is one of

my companions. He would be angry if I didn't protect you."

"And since when do you answer to him?"

Nevin bristled. "I don't. But there are things you don't understand. Things that concern you and Faerie. Right now, all you need to know is that I *need* you to be safe. I've sent word to your grandmother about a few things, and I hope it clears up some recent developments."

"What the hell is that supposed to mean?"

"I feel responsible for you, all right? You saved my life in the human world; that's not something I'll forget. I owe you a life debt, Salome, but let's not argue tonight. If Gareth isn't here by tomorrow, we're leaving, end of discussion."

"I can't leave without him." My pulse soared as anger bubbled inside me.

"He knows the way to my palace. He'll be fine. Whereas you, a mere human, are in far more danger out here than you realize."

He didn't understand. How could I leave the guy I loved out there by himself? Nevin didn't get the whole concept of love or being in love. All he cared about was himself.

An extra strong blast of wind swept through the camp. I clutched my legs to my chest in hopes of conserving body heat and stared at the orange and yellow flames licking at the wood.

"Your Highness, a horse approaches from the east." One of the soldiers waved for the others to arm themselves.

Nevin leapt to his feet, sword drawn. "I want you to wait by my steed. If you hear a skirmish, you need to get on the horse and ride. Do you understand?"

"Yes." My stomach knotted. I gripped tight to the edges of my skirt. My eyes scanned the surroundings. I half expected a monster to jump out.

A moment later, a white horse trotted into camp. "Adaba!"

I leapt to my feet and raced toward the horse. He seemed all right. There were no burns or teeth marks from the dragon. He whinnied then nudged me with his muzzle.

Nevin lowered his weapon and gave a slight bow. "Adaba. My many thanks for keeping Salome safe."

The horse nickered and tilted his head down. After I scratched behind his ears, I made my way to my spot at the fire. Nevin joined me once more, this time sitting closer as if to protect me.

"I can't believe he's alive," I said. "I thought for sure the dragon had gotten him."

"Adaba is more powerful than he looks. You must remember, not everything in Faerie is as it seems. Magic is nearly a part of every person, place, and animal here."

"Is the dragon dead?"

"No. According to the horse, he led it away."

"So you speak horse now?"

He chuckled. "I can speak to this one."

I shook my head at him. "So you're not worried the dragon will come back?" My mouth went dry. All I imagined was it flying into camp and torching us all.

"We'll be safe. I set up a magical barrier around the encampment, and our archers are on high alert."

I glanced at him. Okay, maybe I was cynical, but I didn't see how a few Fae would be any match for a dinosaur-type creature with a mouth the size of a bus—magic or no magic.

What I wouldn't give to be back in the human world right now. In my bed. Far from trolls, Kelpies, and dragons. Fairytales sounded awesome in theory, but living in one totally sucked balls.

I cleared my throat. "So, what exactly happened here at the Ruined Court? This place looks like it's been deserted for centuries."

Sadness washed over Nevin's face as he stared off into the distance. "It used to be beautiful. Marble towers everywhere, gleaming white oak gates, waterfalls, statues... This was the center of Faerie. The place where each court came to rule during their season."

"What happened?" Of course, I knew Darach's version, but I wanted to hear it from Nevin. I needed to know if he'd really betrayed the people.

"Grisselle." His voice iced over like a lake in wintertime. He cast me a sideways glance, as his fingers squeezed mine. "I apologize, I don't want to talk about this right now. Not here. It's too painful."

Too painful,...or was he hiding something? He released my hand and focused on the glowing embers in front of us.

"Sorry I brought it up."

"It's fine. You couldn't know what we went through. All the lives lost. The people we never got to say goodbye to." Regret filled his every word. "Listen, I think you should bed down for the night."

I stiffened. "I can't sleep. I mean, Gareth's out there all alone. H-he could be hurt. And what about the dragon and who knows what else that is probably wandering the countryside?"

He stood, wiped his hands on his breeches, and then headed toward his tent. A moment later he came back holding a blanket. "If you won't go in to bed then at least take this and lay down out here."

"Thanks." I took the woolen throw from him and covered up.

I listened to the soldiers joke around while the fire snapped and popped. Smoke curled up from the flames like wispy strands of yarn. My eyes grew heavy.

I tugged the blanket up about my shoulders and fought to stay awake, but at last, I found myself drifting off. Maybe tomorrow, Gareth would be here.

And what if he's not? What if he's dead?

My lids snapped open. I swallowed hard. I wasn't ready for that. Not now. Not ever.

"What's wrong?" Nevin asked.

"Wh-what if Gareth doesn't come back?" I whispered.

"I promise, he will." He smiled.

"How can you be so sure?"

"Because he's right there." Nevin pointed to the edge of camp, where Gareth stepped out of the shadows, his clothes bloodstained and dirty.

I jumped up. *"Gareth. Oh God, you're okay."*

He rushed to me and caught me in his arms. *"I've been worried sick about you."*

"You? I thought you'd been killed by trolls."

He chuckled as he embraced me. *"I'll always come back to you"*

"Promise?"

"Yes, I promise."

His fingers grazed my chin as he lowered his head. His lips brushed mine, and I wrapped my arms around him. My blood pounded in my ears as he deepened the kiss.

"I'm beginning to think all you two do is kiss," Nevin said from behind us.

My face burned as I took a step back. "No, we do other things."

"Lots of other things." Gareth grinned.

"Um—do you have to tell him that?"

"Hey, just reminding him you're mine."

"Great, so now you're marking your territory?"

He smirked. *"Don't worry, I swear I won't pee on you."*

"Nice." I rolled my eyes.

Nevin stared between us for a moment. "I need to speak with Gareth for a few minutes. Why don't you go into the tent now and get some sleep?"

"But I told you, I'm not tired." I clung tighter to Gareth.

"Salome." Gareth glanced at me. "You need to rest. Besides, I won't be long."

"Fine." I sighed. Great, he shows up and Nevin wants to talk to him again. What would he ask him to do now?

"I'll be in soon." He kissed my forehead and ushered me toward Nevin's tent.

Two candles on a table flickered to life when I stepped inside. A bed made of furs sat in the center of the shelter. The scent of honey filled the air—a smell I associated with the Fae. I walked over to the makeshift bed and lay down. The furs were soft, and I sank into them. I watched the flames on the candles dance, and I let out a yawn. The rustle of the wind in the trees was like a lullaby, and my lids drifted shut once more

A while later Gareth came in. He crawled under the blankets with me and wrapped his arms around me.

"I missed you," he said in a hushed voice.

"I missed you too. So, what did Nevin want?"

Irritation rushed over me from our bond. "Don't worry about it, I'm not going to let it happen. Let's just get some sleep."

"Not going to let what happen?" I sat up, but he pulled me back down beside him.

"We'll talk tomorrow, okay?" He brushed my hair from my face. *"I don't want the guards listening in on everything we say. But just know that Nevin's worried about our kingdom. The Council is fighting him on every decision he needs to make. After being cursed to the human world for so long, there are some who have lost faith in his ability to lead. So he needs to make some tough choices soon—to show he's strong and that Summer is strongest with him as King."*

"Is that all you talked about?"

"No. But I'd rather not get into that tonight, I'm exhausted, and so are you."

"Why do you always have to keep stuff from me? Seriously? It's starting to piss me off."

He sighed. *"Because I'd like to enjoy what time we have left out here together, without ruining it with talk of things that will make us both miserable. We'll be at the palace soon enough. Once we get there, I'll be busy and won't be able to spend as much time with you...I promise, you will find out everything soon enough. I'm not keeping things from you, as I have every intention of explaining what Nevin and I have talked about to you. Just not at this moment."*

Frustrated, I rolled over and stared at the walls of the tent. Even though he wouldn't tell me what was going on, I knew whatever Nevin had said to him had upset him; I could feel it through our connection. Did Nevin tell him I had to go home? Or was it something more about Gareth going off to defend Summer? Whatever it was, I knew it wasn't good.

CHAPTER ELEVEN

Kadie

The room was still dark, and I had no idea what time it was, I sat up and rubbed my arms. My body was no longer pressed against Etienne's. His close proximity all night, coupled with my surroundings, had made it hard to sleep, but I must have eventually passed out from sheer exhaustion.

What I wouldn't give to be back home, in my room, in *my* soft bed. If I closed my eyes, I could almost imagine the smell of Dad's infamous omelets, or the sound of my brothers arguing over video games—stuff that used to piss me off, but I longed for now. A lump lodged in my throat. I might never see any of them again.

Moments later, Etienne shifted and climbed out of bed. He lit several candles around the room then grabbed a pair of breeches from an armoire.

"Good morning." He gestured for me to get up.

"There's nothing good about it." I narrowed my eyes at him. *Ah*. This whole trying to be nice to him thing might be harder than I thought. But I needed to stay focused.

"I see you're in a great mood today." He chuckled as he

made his way over to a pile of clothes that'd been set next to the bedroom door.

"You try being kidnapped and forced to sleep in a castle straight out of a horror flick and then tell me how flipping happy you'd be, jerk-off." I crawled out from under my blankets then stood. My body ached all over. It was like I'd been run over by a snowplow.

He pointed at a clean dress and undergarments. "Go change. Breakfast will be here soon."

I took them from the floor and went behind the black screen. With a sigh, I wondered what I'd have to deal with today. Etienne mentioned last night I'd have to go back to the Bone Yard. I shuddered. Already my stomach churned at the thought. Blood. Bones. The cold. I forced myself to join Etienne at the table. Maybe I could get out of it by showing him some affection or maybe giving him some meaningless information.

"I—I don't really have to go back to the Bone Yard do I?"

"Yes. The queen ordered it."

An older lady scurried into the room, carrying a tray of food. She set it down then rushed back out into the hallway.

"There's got to be a way out of it." Desperation dripped from my words.

"Kadie," he whispered. "There is only one way. I've already told you."

I shook my head. "But I'm telling you the truth, I don't know anything."

He scooped some eggs out of a dish and put them on my plate, followed by a biscuit and apple slices. "I'm being sent away for a few days, so you need to be on your best behavior. The others are not as tolerant as I am."

My mouth went dry, and I gripped the edge of the table. "Where are you going?"

He glanced at me, then grabbed a biscuit and spread jelly across it. "That is none of your business. Now, my maid Rena will retrieve you from the Bone Yard each day and make sure you are bathed. You're free to use my bed while I'm gone—but know the room will be locked so there's no way to escape."

"So I'm going to be stuck in here, all by myself?"

He shrugged. "Yes, and if you listen to nothing else I tell you then at least try not to cause a stir. I won't be here to defend you against the queen or Teodor."

Etienne stood and went over to a cabinet near the back of the room. He pulled something out then relocked the cabinet. He handed over a small wooden box.

"What is this?"

"It's an iron dagger."

Startled, I shot him a wary look. "You're giving me a weapon?"

"I'm not going to be here to protect you all the time. I want you to have some means of defending yourself should you need to. You can have Rena help you belt it beneath your dress so the guards don't see it."

"Wait, doesn't iron kill faeries?" I thought back to all the fairytale stories and books Salome's grandma had read to me over the years. Tales I never realized I'd have to use for survival.

"Yes. But if you're caught with it on you, I will deny giving it to you, so don't let anyone find it."

"But this could kill you too."

"Only if you stab me and give me a fatal wound with it, which I'm trusting you won't do since I'm your only key to getting out of this forsaken place alive."

Why should he care if anyone decided to hurt me? My eyes met his, and his gaze softened.

My pulse quickened. What the hell?

No way am I reacting to him. This was the douche bag that

got me imprisoned here to begin with.

Damn, I had issues. But the fact that he wanted to keep me safe did earn him a few bonus points—and I now had another weapon.

*E*tienne left right after breakfast and his maid Rena came in. "Come along—Master said you're to be brought to the Bone Yard."

I followed her plump form down the winding halls. Too soon, we came to the large, blood-drenched courtyard. The stench hit me full force.

"I'll be back this evening to retrieve you," Rena said, her red curls springing every which way.

My gaze took in the same horrors as yesterday. Bones. Blood. Bodies. The assembly line was hard at work.

"Get moving," one of the troll guards said. His massive frame lurched toward me, whip already drawn.

I stumbled forward then saw Demetria waving at me. Not needing any more prodding, I ran to where she stood, stacking leg bones.

"Morning," I said.

She smiled. "Morning. I see you survived another night here."

"Barely." My fingers closed around a femur that'd just come out of the pot. It burned my hands. "Etienne is gone for a few days."

Demetria frowned. "Then you need to be extra cautious. The other nobles might take notice of his absence and try to take advantage of you."

"What?"

"Shhh…you don't want to bring attention to yourself. Just come here, do your job, and return to his quarters."

I shivered. "And what if they still take notice?"

"Then you need to be as cordial as possible. Don't give them a reason to become angry."

Oh God. I was the least docile person in the world. I didn't put up with people's shit.

"I'll try."

Another load of severed legs was dropped in front of our pot. Demetria quickly loaded them into the boiling water. As we stood there waiting for the flesh to separate, I watched my friend. She was so kind; she didn't deserve to be here.

"How did you end up in this shit-hole?" I asked.

"I was foolish," she said.

"Well that makes two of us."

She smiled. "Misery loves company, and as you can see, I've got lots of it." She gestured to the lines of girls. "Most of us have similar stories of how we came to be in Winter. How we were tricked or infatuated."

"Guilty of infatuation…" I said, remembering how Etienne had caught my eye. "I should've known it was too good to be true with my history of picking out losers."

Demetria wiped her hands on her apron as she walked over to help me organize my pile.

"Well, I too suffered from infatuation. My family was part of a traveling acrobatic group in Romania. We performed for royal families, nobles, commoners—whoever had money to pay us. Eventually, my father decided to book us passage to America. He said we'd have great opportunities here and could stake our own claim. It was a hard journey, but when we got here, Father managed to arrange several shows for us."

"Shows?" I said. "What kind of shows?"

She stared into the distance as if lost in thought. "I specialized in high wire and tumbling acts, which I performed with my eldest sister. We were working one night, just outside of Boston when a man approached me. He was tall, dark, handsome—one of the most beautiful men I'd ever seen in my life. His name was Teodor, and he invited me to dinner."

My stomach lurched. "Teodor?"

"You've met him?" Demetria said. Her eyes widened. "He didn't hurt you, did he?"

"No, but he—he scares me." I shivered, remembering the way he undressed me with his eyes, the way he threatened me with threats that I knew would become promises.

"As he should. But he wasn't always this cruel, or at least he wasn't when I first met him." Demetria tucked a stray curl behind her ear. "We were attracted to one another right away. He was well traveled, elegant, and he showered me with compliments and gifts—things I wasn't used to getting. After our first meeting, he asked if he could call on me the following night. My family of course said no, as they were afraid it'd interfere with our show. However, my eldest sister, Sonja, thought they were being too harsh and helped me sneak out to meet him."

"Then what happened?"

She gave me a sad smile. "He brought me into the woods where he had a dinner set up near a bonfire, under a full moon. I should've known then that something was wrong, but I was young and infatuated. I liked him more than I'd ever liked someone before."

How many times had I been in a similar situation—some guy trying to seduce me, me falling for it? But then again, how easy had it been for me to seduce and tempt people? There was something exhilarating about the challenge of luring someone in—getting them to fall over themselves for you, yet as I knew, it could be dangerous to.

When my gaze shifted back to Demetria, she continued on.

"Teodor told me he'd come to my performance the next night. I explained we'd be in another town, yet this didn't deter him in the least. Instead, he promised he'd follow me. And he did. For three straight cities, he watched my show then met me after. At this point, my family was conflicted about him. My mother and eldest sister adored him. They believed I'd made quite the catch. My other two sisters, father, and brothers hated him and were convinced he was using me."

Her eyes welled with tears. "When we got to New York, Teodor asked me to dinner again. This time he'd hired a carriage to take us into the country. We arrived in a wooded clearing, where there was a great bonfire. So many beautiful people danced around it. I should've known then something was wrong. Why would people be dancing in the snowy woods like that? It was here that he stole me away and brought me to Winter. He wanted my parents to believe I'd run off with him so they wouldn't look for me. Almost as soon as we got here, he handed me over to the queen as a gift."

"What? That asshole!"

She wiped her eyes with the sleeve of her dress. "At first, Teodor still came to see me. However, it wasn't the same. He'd changed into someone I didn't know or recognize. He was cruel, not the gentleman he'd pretended to be before. I was forced to perform and dance for the court. Gradually they grew bored with me, and I was sent to work in the Bone Yard."

"Did he hurt you?" I grabbed her arm, making her look at me.

"Yes, but he's moved on to other conquests. I'm better off out here than caged up in his quarters, forced to do things no person should have to."

A bell at the center of the courtyard clanged. Everyone dropped what they were doing and lined up. A moment later, women dressed in white walked through and handed us each a bowl and spoon. Two trolls carried a cast iron cauldron outside and another lady scooped soup into each bowl.

When it was my turn, I watched the yellow liquid slosh into my bowl. Veggies and meat floated about as the steam rose from it. I swallowed hard, not sure if I wanted to eat it.

Demetria glanced at me. "Don't worry, it's safe."

"H-how do you know it's not human flesh?"

"Because I've worked in the kitchens—they use chickens."

I took a deep breath. With trembling hands, I slurped some of the food into my mouth. It tasted just like chicken noodle soup, minus the noodles. It wasn't bad, but that didn't mean they hadn't poisoned it.

Once we finished eating, we went back to sorting bones for several more hours, during which time I told Demetria how I was brought to Winter. By the time we ended our work I was exhausted. Rena led me back to Etienne's room, where she locked me in.

I slipped out of my blood stained clothes, took a bath, then sat down to eat in front of the roaring fire. From somewhere deep in the castle, I heard screams. My body tensed, and I covered my ears.

Please. Make it stop.

But they didn't.

So I focused on the flames. Somehow, I needed to plan my escape. The Winter Court had to have some type of weakness. Some way out. Clutching the dagger close to my chest, I laid down in the blankets, counting the moments until daylight and praying I survived another night.

ith a groan, I stretched my arms above my head. My back ached from working in the Bone Yard all day. The only thing I wanted to do was eat, take a bath, then go to bed. Unfortunately, the guards told me and Demetria we had to help serve the Winter Court's dinner tonight, which of course had me in panic mode.

Etienne was still gone. That meant I had no one to protect me if I pissed off the wrong person. Here I thought I'd be glad he was gone—so not the case. Not to mention I spent most of my time jumping at the smallest of sounds. At least when Etienne was there, I knew no one would openly attack me... Well, other than the psycho queen.

Just be on your best behavior. You can do this.

Etienne's maid, Rena, poked her head round the door. "Come along, time for you to go to the kitchens."

When I stepped from the safety of the room, I saw Demetria waiting, too. Some of the nervousness went away, knowing she'd be there with me.

"Hey." I waved.

She gave me a forced smile. "Hello again."

I wiped my sweaty hands on my apron. "So, what do we have to look forward to tonight?"

We walked down the hall and she leaned in to whisper. "I've been told we'll be serving the wine. I must warn you, though, dinnertime can get gruesome."

My gaze met hers. "What do you mean?"

"Be prepared for the worst. Some of the Fae are not very kind."

The scent of pastries and soup wafted in the air as we approached the large kitchen. Cooks bent over stoves, stirring pans of food or preparing trays. Maids bustled back and forth refilling decanters or getting dishes ready.

"You best hurry up." A stocky dwarf woman shoved wine decanters in our hands. "The queen is in a mood tonight."

Demetria cast me a glance over her shoulder. "Follow my lead."

My hands trembled as I walked behind her. Wine sloshed against the sides of the glass container. I slowed my pace. The last thing I wanted to do was spill it everywhere. Obnoxious laughter echoed as we stepped into what looked like a ballroom, with dining tables lined up around the edges.

Candlelight splayed off icicles that hung from the chandeliers. Black and white marble tiles covered the entire floor, while two monstrous fireplaces blazed like hellish infernos on each side of the room.

"I'll take the queen's table," Demetria said. "Why don't you start filling the nobles' goblets? When you're done stand against the wall and wait to be called on for more drinks."

My eyes snapped to three human girls, tied up like dogs at the end of the nobles' table. They sat on their knees, gazing up at the food as if waiting for someone to toss them a scrap. My stomach clenched. *Sick bastards*. How could the Fae treat people like this?

"What are you waiting for, stupid?" A Fae tossed her auburn hair, her finger pointed at me.

My eyes narrowed. I bit my lip to keep from telling her where I'd like to shove one of the icicles on the ceiling. Heart pounding in my chest, I moved forward and poured wine into her goblet.

I went around the table, filling glasses. One thing I noticed right away was that only the beautiful Fae sat to eat. Creatures like the goblins, trolls, and satyrs acted as the help. My nose wrinkled as I stared at the satyrs. They had the body and arms of a human, but the legs, hooves, and tail of a goat. Coarse hair covered them, while goat ears poked out of the side of their heads.

"Good, the entertainment's finally here," a tall, bronzed man said.

My gaze shifted to the doors, where several girls were roped together and led to the center of the floor. Four human men came in next, each carrying a stringed instrument, followed by servants with towels and buckets of water.

Shit. What's going on?

The musicians sat on chairs, while the girls were forced to line up. Most wore the same mystified looks I'd seen in the Bone Yard. But there was one I couldn't take my eyes off. Her face had lost its color. Even from here, I saw her legs shaking and the fear in her gaze.

Something bad was about to happen. And I didn't want to witness it. One of the musicians pulled a harp in front of him. He sat at the edge of his seat. His fingers stroked the strings. At first, beautiful music flowed, and I relaxed some.

The other instruments joined in. One by one, the girls started to dance. Then the screams came. Horrified, I watched the girl who'd been freaked out grab her arms. Every time the musicians plucked or strummed a string, deep, bloody gashes appeared on the dancers' bodies. Like an invisible whip lashed out at them. Blood sprayed across the floor, dripping down their dresses and skin. My hands trembled, and I fought to keep hold of the decanter.

My jaw clenched as the one girl fell to her knees. The others just kept twirling—dancing as if they didn't feel a thing. The Fae laughed and cheered.

Without thinking, I rushed to the fallen girl's side. "Hold on, it'll be okay." I tugged at my apron, trying to wrap it around her bloodied wrists.

"Help me," she whispered.

"I'm trying." But for every wound I attempted to cover up, another one sprung forth.

The Fae pointed and continued their laughter. What I wouldn't give to shut them all up. Demetria hurried to my side.

"You have to leave her be or you'll get in trouble." She jerked me to my feet.

The injured girl clung to my leg. I didn't want to leave her. At last, she released me. "Go, you cannot do anything for me." My stomach coiled as I let Demetria lead me away. I pressed myself against the wall, my body trembling beneath me.

"What the hell are they doing?" I said to my friend.

"This is their idea of fun." Her lips pressed into a tight line. "The music won't stop until one of them dies. You must promise not to do something foolish like this again. If you try to save someone, they will punish you too."

"How can I sit back and watch people be killed?"

"You have to." Demetria's voice cracked. "To do good here is to put a nail in your own coffin."

I closed my eyes. No way could I watch this sadistic crap. One final yelp sounded. The music stopped. The entire hall erupted with cheers and clapping.

"They've taken her away now." Demetria touched my arm.

My lids opened. Tears burned my eyes. "They're fricken monsters," I said. "No one deserves to be treated like this."

"I know."

Servants quickly cleaned up the mess, their once white towels colored crimson now. Moments later the main course was brought into the dining hall like nothing ever happened.

"Teodor is here tonight." Demetria nodded to the queen's table. "He's sitting at the end."

I glanced at him. He was definitely hot—dark hair, dark eyes, golden skin that'd make a sun god jealous—but a monster nonetheless. His arrogance practically slapped me in the face from here, and I frowned as Crazy Chick squirmed in his lap.

He nuzzled her then his gaze shifted to mine. He smiled before taking a strawberry from his plate and popping it in his mouth. When he finished chewing, he turned away, giving Crazy Chick a shove from his lap.

The queen glanced at me and beckoned me over. At first, I didn't move. But Demetria squeezed my arm.

"You better go to her or she'll grow angry."

I handed Demetria my decanter and moved across the floor. When I stood in front of the queen's table her lips turned up in a sneer.

"What's wrong, human? Do you not enjoy our games?"

"Of course she does, your highness." Etienne strolled into the ballroom along with another Fae man. Dark circles painted his eyes as he stared at me. "She's merely missed her prince. But I'm here—she can have fun now."

He pulled me against him. His lips trailed down my neck. I stiffened at the heat of his breath in my ear.

"Play along," he whispered.

I swallowed hard and wrapped my arms around him. A brief sense of safety washed over me, but it didn't last long when I saw the queen's forced smile.

"Etienne—join us and tell me news of Summer." She shoved the woman sitting to her right out of her seat and gestured for Etienne to take it.

He released me and sauntered toward the empty chair. "Soldiers from Summer visited the Ruined Court recently. I'm not sure what they were there for, but there were several of them, including the King."

"What?" She slammed her fist down. Her plate flew through the air and shattered on the floor.

"I'm afraid that's not all, Your Highness. I also found dead trolls in the forest near there."

Her eyes narrowed, while her mouth twisted. "I want all the humans out of here. Now!"

Demetria hurried to my side, and we rushed out into the hall. "Go straight to your room and lock the door."

"What's going on?"

"Whenever she gets bad news, she takes it out on us."

Great. And I happened to be one of her least favorite people. Not needing anymore urging than that, I found Rena, who half dragged me toward Etienne's quarters. Once she had me inside, she locked the door. Then and only then did I sink into a chair near the fireplace. My pulse raced; my body quaked.

If Etienne hadn't shown up tonight, I didn't know what would've happened. I squeezed my eyes shut, trying to forget the sight of the dancing girls.

I can't take any more of this.

I covered my face with my hands, fighting back tears that threatened to escape. Now I owed the stupid bastard who brought me here my life. If he hadn't walked in when he had, I was pretty sure Ms. Sadistic Bitch Queen would've had me dancing on top of flaming logs. Or worse, given me to Teodor.

*E*tienne barged into the room, followed by Rena. "Get your cloak and boots on now," he said as he went to his armoire and scoured through it.

"Why? What's going on?" Panic sliced through me like a machete. Did the queen want to see me again?

"I'm going to try to get you out of here. The queen's fury is only going to worsen as Summer grows stronger. The more time you spend here, the more likely you'll be killed."

I stood, dumbfounded. "You're going to help me escape?"

His blue eyes met mine. "I'm going to try. I never should've let Teodor get in my way at the club. I should've forced you to leave. But I'm going to make it right. Now do as I said."

I opened my mouth to protest, but he held up his hand.

"Now isn't the time to argue about me telling you what to do," he said. "If you don't start making some hard choices, you're going to die here—or you can do what I say and help me get you back home. Those are your options."

Oh God. Home. A place where I could be safe again. Wasn't that worth a sacrifice here and there? Wasn't that worth going against my instincts and making tough decisions?

My hands trembled as I fastened my cloak around my shoulders. I sat down in the chair and tugged my boots on. Once I finished, Rena handed Etienne some food, which he tucked into a pouch fastened across his chest like a pack.

"Rena, tell the others to lay low. I will try to come back for the rest of you as soon as possible." He patted her shoulder.

"Be safe, milord," she said.

"Come along." He caught my arm. "If we're going to make our escape, it has to be now. Grisselle normally has fewer guards posted this time of night, so we should be able to make our escape out the front. Just stay close to me."

My heart hammered in my chest. Oh God, I was going home. No more nightmares or horrific murders. No more blood and bones. I couldn't wait to leave this place.

I gripped tight onto Etienne as we headed out the door. I hated that I had to leave Demetria behind. She'd been such a good friend to me, keeping me safe. If she hadn't shown me the ropes that first day in the Bone Yard, then one of the crazy girls or trolls might've gotten to me. But I knew we didn't have time to go search for her. Maybe I could find some way to have Etienne come back for her. She didn't deserve to be here. None of these girls did.

The hallways were streaked in shadows. Silence reverberated throughout the castle. But the deafening quiet unnerved me, as it made each of our footfalls that much louder. When we rounded the corner near the front door, Etienne pushed me against the wall so he could search for guards.

"Follow me," he whispered, catching my hand in his.

The door let out a low groan as he shoved it open and I braced myself for hordes of creatures to jump out and stop us. But none came. Crisp night air took my breath away when we stepped out into the night. The blackness nearly suffocated me. There were no stars or moon, no light except for a few torches lit along the castle wall.

Snow crunched beneath our feet as we moved toward the main gate. All at once, Etienne came to a stop. He dragged me behind an ice-covered statue. "Shit."

Shaking, I leaned against him. "What's wrong?"

"The queen posted more guards. We can't get out."

"But I thought you said—"

"Listen, we have to go back in. We can't get out this way, not tonight. She must've been threatened by the news of Summer and decided not to take any chances."

My heart fell. *No.* I couldn't go back in there. "Please, help me get out of here. I'll do anything you want."

He clutched me to his chest and hugged me. "I'm sorry. I

didn't mean to give you false hope. I thought this way would be safe. But it's not. I'll keep trying to free you, just trust me, okay? Now come along, we need to get back inside before someone notices we're missing."

Frigid air snaked along the neck of my cloak, and I shivered. Had the entire thing been a sick game? A way to give me hope and then snatch it away?

With reluctance, I let Etienne lead me back indoors. But as we made our way down the darkened corridor, someone stepped out in front of us.

"Well, well, well, what do we have here?" Teodor said, his voice thick with menace.

Etienne went still. "I went out for a breath of fresh air."

"And you took your human out after curfew? Wonder what the queen would have to say about that?"

"Get the hell out of my way or I'll tell the queen about the five human girls you took from the Bone Yard without her permission—two of which you made disappear."

"Didn't realize you were keeping track of what I do," Teodor said. "You know, I could just take this one off your hands. She needs to be broken. The sooner she knows her place, the better."

"Stay away from me and stay away from my property." Etienne shoved around him, tugging me after.

Teodor's gaze slid over me as if I was a last meal. The more I resisted him and Etienne fought to keep him away, the more he wanted me. And that scared the hell out of me. When we made it back to Etienne's room, I slumped to the floor in a heap and buried my head in my hands.

"I just want to get out of here."

"I know. And I promise to keep trying. But we need to be more careful. Teodor senses something is going on. You need to avoid him at all cost." Etienne hefted me up in his arms and carried me over to my makeshift bed on the floor. He slid my boots from my feet then untied my cloak. Once that was done, he laid me down and covered me up.

His fingers traced my cheek, wiping away the tears that trickled down. "Please forgive me, Kadie."

But I only nodded. No words would form. I was a fool to get my hopes up—to believe I might actually get out of here. Etienne sat with me, and my lids drifted shut as he stroked my face. I didn't want to be comforted by him. He was the enemy. But this enemy had tried to help me, so maybe he wasn't as bad as I'd thought.

CHAPTER TWELVE

Salome

daba stuck close to Gareth's horse as we weaved through the greenery. The sun beat down on us, and sweat trickled down my forehead. Everything spoke of summer: the flowers, the warm breeze, butterflies flitting overhead.

Adaba whinnied beneath me, and I scratched his neck. I glanced over my shoulder then frowned. To the southwest, the skies darkened as if a winter storm moved in. I shivered, glad we were headed away from it.

The horses in front of us came to a stop as we approached a large clearing. "Here we are, the border of Summer," Nevin said as he and the others dismounted.

He walked back to me, clutched my waist, and helped me down. He offered me his arm, then led me toward a white oak gate that stood at least twenty foot tall. Carved into the wood were trees, suns, birds, and flowers.

Holy fairytale setting.

This was even greater than the summer estate that butted up against my grandma's property, where Nevin had invited me when I chose Gareth to be mine. Speaking of which, my gaze shifted as I tried to find Gareth. He fell in behind us.

"You can walk with me, you know." My eyes met his as I glanced at him over my shoulder.

He smiled, but it seemed forced. *"You are Nevin's guest here. He wants everyone to know it."*

"But I'm your girlfriend. I'd rather be with you."

"It's tradition, Salome, as his guest and—might I add—his savior, he must be the one to lead you in," he responded as the large gate swung open.

I gasped when I saw inside. Great white oaks reached to the sky. Stairs wound around them, leading to houses in the trees. Waterfalls cascaded down mountainsides, splashing into streams that carried boats with Fae in them.

Pink petals blew across the marble roadway. Fae gathered along the roadside to watch us pass through. They bowed and cheered. Nevin waved with one hand, while he placed the other at the small of my back.

The sound of wind chimes carried on the breeze, bringing back memories of Grandma's house. Trees billowed back and forth. My gaze took in the sweeping gardens, full of wildflowers of every shade imaginable. Gardens opened into courtyards filled with statues and water fountains.

It was like I'd stepped into a Tolkien novel. We made our way under a stone archway, which had two ornate oaks carved into it. On the other side we approached white marble stairs inlaid with gold.

"Holy crap," I said.

My mouth hung open as I gawked at the palace, built right into the trees that surrounded it. It had archways that seemed to touch the sky and balconies overlooking pools of splashing water. Tiny fairies flew by my head, chittering as they darted into the trees above. Beautiful, tall Fae moved with grace, making way for Nevin.

He leaned over, his breath fanning out against my face. "So, what do you think?"

"It—it's gorgeous. I've never seen anything like it…"

"Nor will you ever again." He chuckled, ushering me up into the palace.

Everything was light, pristine, and open. At the center of the foyer was a fountain that sprayed water several feet into the air. Four staircases went off the main level—one in each direction—leading to a balcony that wrapped around the room above. My head tilted back, and I caught sight of the ceiling. Scenes of Summer and entwined lovers were etched into the gleaming wood tiles.

"I can't believe you live here." I spun to take everything in.

Nevin stood, watching me. "Now you know why I was so eager to get back home. My kingdom is everything to me. Not just the palace, but the people—the warmth." He caught my hand, tugging me toward one of the staircases. "Come along, I'll show you to your room."

One of the guards approached him and handed him an envelope. "Your Highness, a message came in this morning while you were gone."

My gaze flitted over the familiar handwriting. "Is that from my grandmother?"

Nevin tucked it away. "Yes, but I'll read it later."

"Why are you corresponding with her?" Alarm bells went off.

"She's likely just asking how you're doing." His posture went rigid as he caught Gareth's eye but said no more.

"What the hell is that about?"

Gareth glanced at me and gave a nearly imperceptible shake of his head. *"Not here."*

Nevin's guards dispersed, leaving only me, Gareth, and him. When we reached the balcony area, two halls branched off in different directions.

"I'll see you later." Gareth kissed my cheek. *"I promise, we'll speak later."*

"Wait, where are you going?"

"My room is in a different wing than yours." He gave my shoulder a squeeze.

"You're not serious?"

"Yes."

"But I thought we'd be together, or at least near one another."

"Here, we don't share rooms unless we're wed. Besides, we had separate quarters in my estate."

"I know. It's just I'm nervous being here. You'll still be able to come see me, won't you?"

"Of course. Don't worry so much. I promise, you'll grow to love it here as much as we do."

"We'll meet up with him for dinner," Nevin said beside me. "Now, let's get you to your room so you can freshen up."

We walked down the narrow corridor. Wind sneaked in through the opened windows above, bringing with it the scent of roses.

At last we stopped in front of a blue door with a golden crown and flowers painted on it. Nevin twisted the handle and it swung open. "Here you are. If you need anything, my room is right next to yours. The maids have already prepared a basin of water and a clean dress for you."

"Thank you," I said, stepping around him.

He stood, staring at me for a moment before he closed the door behind me.

Holy shit.

My eyes widened as I took in the ginormous canopied bed.

The light blue curtains billowed back and forth as air blew in from doors that led to a private balcony. An ornate white marble fireplace sat against the back wall, with two plush, wine-colored chairs placed in front of it.

Scenic paintings decorated the walls—pictures of lovers and gardens. Two mahogany armoires stood at either side of the bed, a chest at the foot of it. My gaze settled on the open bathroom right off my room. A golden tub the size of a hot tub took up the better part the bathroom's space.

Damn, this place was made for a queen. After checking everything out, I found the bowl of water and scrubbed my face and arms. Later, I planned to soak in a steaming bath, but for now, I quickly changed out of my grubby clothes and put on the pale blue dress that'd been laid out for me.

I had just enough time to run a brush through my hair when I heard the knock on my door. When I answered, I found Nevin waiting for me.

"Shall we go to Gareth's room for a bite to eat?"

My stomach growled in response. "Yeah, I can definitely use some food."

We left my new room and headed back the way we came. When we got to a door with swords carved into it, Nevin stopped and knocked.

From inside, Gareth called us to come in. His room was smaller than mine, but still large. Where I had pictures on my walls, he had weapons. His four-poster bed took up the far back wall; blue velvet blankets and pillows covered it.

"Why don't you take a seat?" Gareth pulled out a chair at the table, already laden with food: tiny elegant sandwiches, soup, fruit, some type of red drink filled crystal goblets.

"Thanks."

Nevin sat next to me, but before Gareth could join us, his

door burst open and a tall blond woman barged in.

"Gareth! I heard you were home." She rushed forward, to throw her arms around his neck. Her long hair was pulled back in a simple ponytail. She wore tight breeches and a tunic, which showed off her fabulous figure.

I instantly hated her. Who the hell was this chick? Maybe an ex-girlfriend? Or a lover? My stomach clenched as I fisted handfuls of my skirt and my eyes narrowed.

Gareth glanced at me and grinned. *"Jealous?"*

"Damn straight."

"Well don't be."

"Easy for you to say."

"Salome," he said with a smirk. "I'd like you to meet my sister Gwenn."

"Sister? How did I not know you had a sibling?"

He shrugged. *"It never came up."*

Gwenn turned to stare at me. She frowned. "So, this is the *human* you left us for? Hardly seems worth the time."

"Gwenn that's e—"

Nevin glared. "You will not talk about her that way. Have a seat and keep your mouth shut."

Her jaw tightened, but she did as she was told. Gareth joined us as well, plopping down across from me.

"Don't worry. She'll grow to like you."

"I highly doubt that."

Nevin cleared his throat. "We have a very important matter we need to discuss regarding the kingdom."

Gareth tensed, his hand tightened on the edge of the table, and he averted his gaze to the nearby window.

"What's wrong?" My pulse thundered in my ears. I didn't like how on edge he seemed.

"Whatever he has to say, know that I had nothing to do with

this decision."

My eyes widened. *"Is this what you meant when you said we'd speak later?"*

"Just listen to Nevin. He'll explain everything. This affects you. It affects all of us."

I definitely didn't like the sound of that.

Nevin studied me for a moment, then said, "You've done so much for our kingdom, Salome. You freed me from the Winter Curse, along with several of my troupe. You've given my people hope again. They speak of how you defeated the witch and stood up against Winter. I've not seen them this happy or optimistic in years."

Embarrassed, I stared at my plate. "I'm glad to have helped."

"But it's not just that. I felt power coursing through you when Grisselle cornered you in the woods. And Adaba told me how you scared off the Kelpie with magic."

Wait, wait. Was he confirming I really did have magic? But before I could ask anything, he went on.

"You are strong and powerful. Your grandmother wouldn't confirm anything for sure with me, but she did say you belonged here in Faerie." Nevin slid his chair back, stood, and then came to kneel before me. "You've done more than help us. In fact, it is these very reasons why I want you to be my queen. The Queen of Summer."

My mouth went dry, heart clamoring like a drum set.

What?

Maybe I'd heard him wrong.

But three pairs of eyes watched me expectantly. *Oh hell.* He was for real.

CHAPTER THIRTEEN

Salome

"I s this some kind of joke?" My voice came out high-pitched. I sucked in a deep breath, and my gaze shifted from Nevin to Gareth.

"No." Nevin took my hands in his. "I'm very serious."

I snatched my hands back. "And…and you agree with this?" My stomach clenched as I watched my boyfriend.

"No, of course I don't. I love you. But I also know that our kingdom needs you," he said, his face void of everything, his posture rigid.

His kingdom needed me? What the hell? He spent half his time in the human world telling me Nevin might not have my best interest in mind. Now all of a sudden he wanted to just hand me over to him? To get rid of me?

"He's right, Salome. We need you." Nevin sounded almost desperate. "As soon as I sensed your power in the woods that day, I knew you were the answer to all our problems. Our kingdom will stand stronger with a powerful queen by my side. Besides, your own grandmother said you belong here with us."

My jaw tightened and I pretended not to notice how much

my heart ached. "You gave me a boon. I chose Gareth."

"Will you at least think this over before making a hasty decision? You once loved me, Salome." Nevin moved closer so he stood right in front of me.

"No, that was all a lie. You used magic to make me think I loved you. Everything in my world was fake." There was nothing to think over. I'd already made my choice. Besides, if he'd wanted me to be his queen so bad, he should've made that more apparent in the human world. Instead, he'd nearly gotten me killed. So yeah, he could take that crown and shove it somewhere. "I love Gareth. I'm sorry, I can't be your queen."

"See. She's nothing but an ungrateful human." Gwenn stormed across the room, her blond hair whipping behind her like angry snakes. "You should've just left her in her own world."

I clenched my fists at my sides. "Well this ungrateful human saved your world."

"Enough!" Nevin's head snapped up. "One more word from you, Gwenn, and I'll have you escorted from the palace."

Gwenn's face turned crimson, but she clamped her mouth shut. The steeled look she gave me was deadlier than a hunting knife, and I was sure if she got the chance she'd probably stab me with one.

Nevin sighed then faced Gareth. "Perhaps we should discuss this later, when everyone has had a chance to eat and get some rest."

Later? Um—was he deaf? "I'm not gonna change my mind."

"Salome, I'll be really busy training soldiers, and I might even be sent to do some scouting. You'll be left vulnerable. At least as queen you'll be better protected."

"Better protected? God. Are you really so unhappy with

me?" My vision blurred as my eyes pooled. He could've told me all this and saved me the trouble of leaving my family to come to Faerie. I gave up everything for him. I mean, I'd likely never even see my mom or grandparents again.

"No. Of course not."

"Was this the plan all along? Get me to fall for you, then hand me over to your king?" My fingernails dug into my palms, and my pulse roared in my ears like a vicious animal about to attack.

In two strides he closed the space between us, his hands on my shoulders. *"No. I love you. But I want what's best for you—and for the kingdom. Are you sure you want to be stuck with a warrior and not someone who can give you so much more?"*

"You're what's best for me. And just because he thinks I'm all powerful doesn't make it true. Yeah, a shield sprung up in the woods, and yes, I somehow called on the Blade of the Four Kingdoms to defeat the Kelpie, but those things, they could've been a fluke." And if they weren't? I couldn't ignore that possibility, but ifs and maybes wouldn't persuade anyone. So I had to make one last gamble with what I knew for sure. *"I-I just don't want to lose you."*

"And what about the kingdom? You have to realize that these are my people, Salome. What kind of man would I be if I chose my own happiness over others' lives?"

Sure, now he gives me a guilt trip. But the truth was, I loved him. And yeah, I felt horrible that Summer was having issues with the Winter Queen. But I wasn't ready to give up the love of my life because Nevin suddenly needed a queen. There were tons of other women in Faerie and in the human world he could choose from. It didn't *have* to be me.

"We can't force her to be queen," Nevin said at last. "But perhaps she'll change her mind once she knows our people and gets a chance to see more of the devastation that Winter has caused." He gave me a forced smile. "Why don't I leave you two alone? We can talk later about your new duties, Gareth."

Gareth released me and turned to him. "As you wish."

Nevin walked out of the room, followed closely by Gwenn, who shot me a glare over her shoulder. When the door shut behind them, I avoided looking at Gareth.

"I'm sorry we sprung this on you. Believe me when I say I don't want to lose you. But do you know how guilty I felt knowing you could be the answer to Summer's needs?"

"I know you love your people," I cried. "But I don't want Nevin, I want you. We'll have to figure out some other way to defeat Winter."

"Okay." He sighed, pulling me into a hug. "I love you so much. But I also know you'd make a great queen. I only did this because I want our kingdom to be safe. We need a queen, Salome, or Summer is as good as dead. Alone, Nevin is strong, but the magic barriers that protect our kingdom can only be made stronger if we have both a king and queen."

Through our link, I felt the sense of duty he had for Faerie. His warmth radiated around me.

"Don't ask me to do this. I can't. I told you, I choose you." But another thought occurred to me. "Unless…you don't want me." My throat constricted. Maybe he loved me, but not enough to stay with me forever.

"I want you more than I've ever wanted anyone in my life." He pressed a kiss to my brow.

I stared at the table filled with food. But I wasn't so hungry anymore. "I think I'm going to back to my room and go to bed. It's been a long couple of days."

"Please don't go to bed mad." He brushed my hair from my face. "You've got to understand why I did this."

I doubted I'd ever understand. But I managed a smile. No need to have a breakdown in front of him. "It's fine. I just really want to sleep."

Disappointment washed over me through our link, but I ignored it. I'd eventually forgive, but tonight, I hurt too much to care.

"I'll see you tomorrow then." He hugged me one last time then let me go.

As I made my way to the door, I stopped on the threshold. "Gareth?"

"Yeah?"

"I do love you, you know that right?"

His mahogany eyes met mine. "I kind of figured that out after you told Nevin to basically shove the crown up his ass."

My face burned. "I didn't say that!"

"No, but you wanted to. You forget, I can see inside that lovely head of yours."

I shrugged. "We're all entitled to our opinions."

When I got back to my room, I found a package on my bed. And not just any package—someone had brought me the sword I'd hidden in the saddlebags.

"You've got to be kidding," I whispered as I stared at the etchings on the blade. There, glowing bright blue, was the carved sun, the symbol for Summer, and it was pointed right at me.

Was this a sign? Was the weapon trying to tell me that I should've accepted Nevin's offer to be queen?

Okay, just because it was glowing didn't mean anything. For all I knew, it always lit up. I definitely needed to do some research on this thing, the sooner the better.

CHAPTER FOURTEEN

We'd spent the last twenty-four hours in the Bone Yard. My legs screamed for me to sit down. My arms ached from tossing bones. But it was never ending. I wiped my forehead against my shoulder. My eyes burned, and all I wanted to do was sleep.

Demetria glanced at me, her gaze bloodshot. "We're almost done."

I glanced back at our pile. It looked no smaller than it had a few minutes ago. "Maybe if we repeat those words enough times it'll be true."

She gave me a small smile then started sorting another row of leg bones.

Horns blasted from the doorway of the palace, and I watched as the queen emerged. Her black dress swished at her ankles like dark smog trailing her.

"Good day humans," she called out, her shrill voice echoing off the stone walls. "I wanted to tell you that your hard work has not gone unnoticed. In fact, I'm so pleased with you that I'm throwing a ball in two days. If you're extra well behaved, then I shall let you attend."

"A ball?" I glanced at Demetria. "Is she serious?"

She wrung her hands together. "Unfortunately, yes. But it isn't some place you want to be. If you think the dinner was gruesome, it's nothing compared to the balls."

My body tensed. More horrific? What could be worse than watching girls being tortured by music?

Demetria stiffened, and I shifted my gaze to see what she was looking at. The Winter Princes were strutting around the grounds. They examined sorted piles of bones, but mostly they checked out the girls as if on some perverted shopping spree.

If any of them bothered me, I swore I'd beat them with a femur. I hadn't played softball in a while, but I was damn sure I could still swing a bat, or in this case a bone.

Teodor sauntered across the way, his gaze focused on me. I shifted my eyes, not wanting to encourage the douchebag. Crazy Chick glared at me, her mouth twisted in an angry "*O*".

"Well don't you look pretty today." He reached out to touch my hair. "I do like me a spirited girl."

My palms sweated, and I wiped them on my dress to keep from punching this asshat in the face. "Well, I don't like Faeries."

He glowered, dropped his hand, and turned to Demetria. "Your friend here needs to be taught a lesson. Perhaps you have a suggestion?"

She wet her dry lips. "N-no, master."

"Or perhaps you'd like to take her place."

She went rigid but stood straighter. Oh God. I couldn't let him hurt her.

Etienne swooped in, his eyes hardened. "Hate to interrupt, but Kadie is not available."

"Kadie?" Teodor gave a harsh laugh. "So you've given your pet a name?"

Etienne ignored him and gripped my arm. "Get back to

work—you've got bones to sort." He dragged me closer to my pile.

Teodor followed like a croc stalking a zebra. "Seems a shame to waste such a pretty face. Come, Etienne, what can I offer you for her?"

"I told you, she's not available. She's my pet to do with what I please."

Pet? *What a dick.* This wasn't the damn Humane Society, where you go in and adopt an animal. For frick sake, I was a person. Although, right now, I almost wished I was a rabid dog so I could bite their stupid asses.

"What's going on over here?" The Queen glided over.

"Nothing, Your Highness." Teodor smiled, then caught her hand and brought it to his lips.

"It doesn't look like nothing. I won't have everyone witnessing your squabble over a human. She's hardly worth it."

"You're right. There are plenty to choose from." He leered at Demetria.

The queen focused on me once more. "If you keep causing trouble, I might have to use you in my décor."

My mouth went dry. My nails dug into my palms. I tried not to wither under her scrutiny, but my knees knocked together beneath my dress. Her eyes drilled into mine for long moments, and I was sure she pictured using my bones for a candelabra or something. Soon she moved on to another group.

Luckily, Teodor followed at her heels. When they were out of earshot, Etienne leaned closer to me so his face was only inches away from mine.

"You need to avoid confrontations. How many times do I have to tell you that? They will kill you. I can only do so much to protect you."

Demetria shot me a surprised look when he stalked off.

"He's right, you know. You need to lay low, although I'm taken aback at how concerned he seems for you."

I groaned. "I can't just sit here and let them treat me like I'm a piece of meat."

"One day, you'll learn you have no choice."

"You're wrong. There's always a choice. And I'm choosing to fight." Tossing a severed limb into my pile, I spun around so my back was to the boiling pot. "I think I found our way out." I nodded toward the drains.

Her eyes widened as she followed my gaze. "But it's so busy out here—there's no way we'll go unnoticed."

"We'll have to find a time when everyone is preoccupied."

She started another row of bones then pretended to adjust the skirt of her dress. "The ball. All the nobles attend and the guards don't post at their stations in the Bone Yard. W-we could get put on serving duty so we have free rein to go between the ball and the kitchens."

For the first time since arriving in Winter, I smiled. "We're gonna get out of here, Demetria."

She squeezed my hand, and her face lit up. "Tomorrow, we'll make our plans…"

*T*he next day, Etienne sat watching me over breakfast. I fidgeted beneath his gaze. Did he know I was up to something? I licked my lips and pretended to be interested in the blob of eggs on my plate.

"How would you like a break from the Bone Yard today?" he said at last.

"What?" My eyes widened as I glanced at him.

"Are you going deaf?" He quirked an eyebrow.

My face warmed. "No. I can hear just fine. I thought maybe this was some kind of joke."

He chuckled. "I promise, it's not a joke."

"So, what will I do instead?"

"Keep me company."

I dropped my fork. "In your bed?"

He looked confused then shook his head at me. "No, as much as I'd like to be intimate with you, that's not what I had in mind. I merely wanted to take you someplace."

"Oh." Well, I wasn't expecting that answer.

"If I wanted to take advantage of you, I could've done it anytime over the past few days." He took a sip of orange juice then slid his cup back. "I wish you'd at least give me a chance here. I'm trying to be kind to you—to protect you—but you constantly throw it back in my face."

Why did I suddenly feel guilty? God, I had issues. This guy kidnapped me, not the other way around. I had nothing to feel bad about. But I wouldn't get far if I didn't somewhat play nice.

"Listen, I'm sorry, okay. Which, by the way, I'm not so sure you deserve."

"Let's not fight." He stood with a sigh.

"Fine."

"Oh, I almost forgot. I had a gown made for you, for the ball."

"But I thought I'd be serving." Butterflies in my stomach betrayed me.

"You will be, but I'd like to dance at least one song with you."

Flattered, I offered him a smile. "Thanks."

His emerald eyes bore through me, while warmth sizzled in my belly. Was it normal for me to be kind of attracted to my captor?

Hell no. You've got to snap out of this hot guy stupor before you do something stupid.

"If you're finished eating, I'd like to take you someplace now." He offered me his arm.

With hesitation, I climbed to my feet and gripped hold of him. Against my better judgment, I followed him from the room. We wound our way down several halls which, at the moment, seemed empty. Then I remembered most people would be in the Bone Yard at this hour.

We came to a wrought iron gate with metal flowers twisted into it. He shoved it open and brought me outside. I gasped as I stared at it. There was no blood or bones or gruesome décor.

"This is the old garden. One of the only places in the castle that remains untouched by the queen's horror."

My eyes trailed the frozen flowers and waters, everything caught up in crystallized beauty. Ice clung to the trees like tinsel. Heroic statues stood posed with stone swords and bows, snowy vines looped around their legs.

A stone gazebo loomed at the center of the gardens, a built in fire pit in the middle of it. My fingers traced the carvings in the stone.

"Wow, it's beautiful here," I said. Tendrils of smoke snaked from my lips, and I wrapped my arms across my body.

"Are you cold?" Etienne slipped his cloak off and draped it around my shoulders.

I pulled it tighter, catching his honey scent on the material. "Thank you."

He ushered me to the gazebo where a fire snapped and popped. We sat on one of the stone benches, staring at the flames.

"This is my favorite place in Winter," he said. "It's the one place where I can escape the nightmares."

"Why are you sharing it with me?"

He glanced down at me. "Because you've seen too many bad things since you got here. Faerie can be dark, but not everything in this land is. There was a time…"

"A time?" I prompted.

He cleared his throat, but instead of speaking, his fingers clasped mine, warming my chilled skin. I stared at our entwined hands for long moments, wondering what was happening. His kindness startled me. I wanted to snatch my hand away from him—but instead, I sat content.

Maybe this is another one of his tactics to trick me into telling him something.

But when he didn't ask me any questions, I realized he might be sincere.

Without a second thought, I moved closer until we sat with our legs pressed against one another. My fingers trembled as I took them from his and touched his face, following the contours of his squared jawline. "You've kept me safe since I've been here, and I owe you a huge thank you for that."

He scooped me into his arms. He leaned down, his breath warm upon my cheek. Etienne tilted my head to the side as his lips pressed against mine. He pulled me closer. My body tingled as if I was on fire. My fingers tangled in his hair, my tongue grazed his teeth.

He moaned, trailing kisses down my neck until I thought I might ignite from the inside out. At last, he drew back, eyes blazing.

"There's something I need tell you," he said. "Something I want you to know, so you don't think I'm a complete monster."

I cleared my throat and tried not to stare at his lips. "Wh—what is it?"

He entwined his fingers with mine once more and looked at them as if they were the most amazing things ever. "I don't really know where to start. It's been so long since I've opened up to anyone."

"You could start at the beginning," I said, watching the way his lips turned down at the corners.

"The beginning," he whispered. "I guess that's a good place to start." He ran his hand along the edge of the bench, like his mind had drifted elsewhere. After a long moment, he finally spoke. "I wasn't always like this—stuck here in Winter, forced to be one of *her* princes. I'm really the King of the Spring Court." His eyes darkened, and he released my hand. "Grisselle attacked my kingdom. It was without warning. So many of my people died. So many lives, I failed to save."

Whoa, I wasn't expecting that. But as I watched the pain swim on his face, I knew he spoke the truth.

"I'm sorry."

He ran a hand through his already disheveled hair. "In the end, I chose to surrender, hoping to save what was left of my kingdom. The Winter Queen forced me to pledge my loyalty to her. She turned my people into horrible creatures. And now they're forced to wait on her and the Winter Court like slaves. She made me a Winter Prince—and forced me do her bidding. If I disobey or do something she doesn't like, she tortures what's left of the Spring Court. And here, in her realm, my powers are not as strong. If we were in Spring, I might be a match for her... but here—" He picked up a stone and whipped it across the courtyard. "I'm nothing more than a coward. I've let my people down. I've let so many humans down."

"No. You did all this to save your people." Fuck. Why was I giving him a pep talk?

"And look where we are." He covered his face. "She keeps

me watched so closely that I haven't even been able to get word out to Summer that I'm still alive — that I might be able to aid in their war. Instead, I'm just as much a prisoner as you, only I get the benefit of being one of the queen's confidants."

Not thinking clearly, I pulled him into my arms.

He's a mess like me. Broken. Trying to survive.

If only I could take away his pain. Maybe I should tell him about Demetria's and my plan. Maybe he could come with us?

Damn. No you can't say anything. What if he goes back to her? Then everything will be ruined.

"I've been pleading with the queen to let you go." He peered down at me, stroking my face.

I gasped. "You've what?"

"I fed her some false information and told her it was from you. But she thinks you still know more."

"So you've been lying to her to get me free?"

"Yes."

"If she does let me go, then you have to come with me."

He rested his forehead against mine. "Trust me, I would if I could. But my people still need me. So no matter what she decides, I'm tethered to this godforsaken place."

"We could all go together, escape."

"It's a nice dream. But not something I see happening." Silence enveloped us.

Damn. Talk about making me feel bad. But I couldn't back out of my plan now. Maybe when we got out of here I could let someone know that Etienne was still alive. Maybe someone from this Summer Court he mentioned. When Demetria and I escaped, I kind of hoped he didn't get in any trouble.

Nice. Now you want to show him compassion — even though he totally doesn't deserve it.

Okay, so that was a lie. He'd treated me well enough. Not

to mention he'd intervened with both the queen and Teodor on my behalf. Maybe he wasn't as bad as he claimed to be.

Assuming any of what he said is true. Now is so not the time to let my guard down.

On the eve of my escape, I didn't need to think about him. At all. But somehow, Etienne kept popping into my traitorous thoughts. For a moment, I considered again whether I should tell him all about my plans to leave—to get the hell out of this place. But instead, I bit my tongue, unsure if he'd tried to stop me.

CHAPTER FIFTEEN

Salome

I breathed in the summer air, and the scent of roses tickled my nose. With a sigh, I leaned against the railing. Even from here, I saw the green rolling hills in the distance—trees reaching toward cloudless skies. Birds tweeted, flying and sweeping above rooftops.

My gaze came to rest on a maze, which at any other time would've made me excited. It reminded me of one of my favorite movies, about a girl who had to solve a labyrinth to reach the Goblin King's castle and rescue her brother. Jareth, the king, was kind of hot in an eighties rock star kind of way.

But after last night's announcement-proposal type thing, I so couldn't enjoy any of this. My chest tightened. What I wouldn't give to be back in the human world, riding on Gareth's motorcycle, pretending none of this ever happened.

A knock sounded on my door. With a sigh, I walked back into my room. "Come in," I called.

Gareth poked his head in. His eyes softened, and he smiled. "Hey. I'm here to escort you to lunch."

My heart sped up like the flutter of hummingbird wings at

the sight of him. His golden hair was tied back at his neck. His tunic was unlaced enough to reveal the bronze skin beneath. He met my gaze, and that was all I needed.

I rushed into his arms. He held me tight, smoothing down my hair. "I'm sorry I hurt you last night. Trust me, it was never my intention. I'm pissed at Nevin, pissed at myself, pissed at Winter for causing all this turmoil."

"Just don't ever suggest I leave you again. I mean it. You're the one I want." My head rested against his chest.

"I know," he whispered. His lips brushed mine. "We should get downstairs for the banquet."

"We don't have to." I tilted my head so I could see his face.

He chuckled. "You don't know how tempting that is. But, I promised Nevin we'd be there."

"Ugh, he ruins everything." I pouted.

"Come on." He took my hand and tugged me out the door.

We made our way down a back staircase and into what I assumed was the Great Hall. The spacious room opened to archways, where sun filtered in. Pink flower petals blew across the floor. I gasped when I noticed the tiny river flowing beneath one of the archways, right into the dining area. Long, mahogany tables stretched out at the outskirts of the room, while the royal table sat upon a dais.

The scent of steamed vegetables and fruit wafted in the air. My stomach growled in response. I nearly dashed to the nearest table to chomp down some food.

Easy Bessy.

My gaze took in all the beautiful people. Tall. Tanned. Statuesque. Geez, didn't these people eat? If I didn't know better, I'd think we took a wrong turn and ended up at a model shoot. But underneath, I feared there was something more going on. Something dark.

"Who are these people? Slaves?"

"Servants, of a sort."

"So is this what I'm going to be for Nevin? A servant 'of sorts'? How do I know I won't be treated like this?"

"Trust me, no one would dare." He squeezed my hand. *"Besides, you're a hero in our kingdom, and like I said, Nevin's time in your world did him good. As soon as we got back to Summer, he did away with all the laws that allowed humans to be hurt or imprisoned by Fae."*

Relief washed over me. *"I'm sure that made a lot of people happy."*

"Those people are here of their own free will, Salome. As are you. There are some good people here."

Even if Nevin made me angry half the time, I was glad to hear he'd taken my people into consideration with his new laws. It was good to know they wouldn't be kept as slaves or be forced to perform like circus animals. But I was sure there would still be Fae who did what they wanted. Perhaps that was one more reason for me to take his offer. As the Queen of Summer, I could help enforce his decrees of freedom for all people. Including humans.

From his seat at the front of the room, Nevin waved us over. The noble lady a couple chairs down from him glared at me.

Great. I'm here one day and I already have two people who don't like me. First Gwenn, now this lady.

"Salome, you've made it down for our meal. I trust you slept well?" Nevin gestured to the empty seat next to his.

No. I didn't sleep well. Not after the stupid crap he pulled the night before.

Of course, I didn't voice this aloud. Instead, I pasted on a fake smile. "Yeah, thanks."

He squeezed my shoulder then faced Gareth as he took a

place across from me. "This will be your last decent meal for a while."

"Don't remind me." Gareth eyed the platters of food being set on the table.

"Wait, he said your last meal for a while? When are you leaving?" My hands trembled in my lap as I stared at Gareth.

"The scouting party leaves tonight, under cover of darkness. We should only be gone for a few days. When I return, I'm going to be moving down to the soldiers' barracks to start training the new recruits. I'll need to monitor them and keep them on a strict regime if we're going to be battle ready."

I glared at him. "How come you didn't tell me?"

He frowned. *"I'm sorry. I know I should have told you."*

"Damn right you should have. Gareth, the last time people didn't tell me things like this, I almost got killed. So from this point on, just be honest with me. Okay?"

He nodded. *"You have my word. I'll still be able to see you, just not as frequently as we're used to. Believe me, I don't have a choice. The sooner we find a way to deal with Winter, the sooner you'll be safe—our people will be safe."*

I shifted my glance. When he left, I'd be alone. And he'd be in danger. My vision blurred as I fought to keep the tears at bay.

Okay. Pull it together. You can't cry in front of everyone.

If we were in my world we'd have jobs, so I just needed to think of it that way.

"Lady Salome, I'd like for you to meet some of Summer's noble party," Nevin said, interrupting my moping session.

I sucked in a deep breath and turned my attention down the long table. Nevin went down the line of chairs, introducing me to elven lords, rich Fae ladies, and princes. When he got to the auburn-haired Fae woman who'd given me dirty looks earlier, she stood as if to give me a better visual of her.

"I'm Lady Rowena," she said. "And this must be the *impure* one who kept you both so occupied in the human realm."

Impure? What the hell did that mean?

Gareth's face turned crimson. His chair slid back as he went to stand, but Nevin beat him to whatever he was going to say.

"You will not talk to Lady Salome in that manner again. Do you understand me?" Nevin said.

She smirked but curtsied. "Of course, Your Highness. I beg your forgiveness."

He glanced around the table, jaw tense. "That goes for the rest of you. Lady Salome is *my* guest. If I so much as hear anything unpleasant pass your lips in her regards, you will be punished."

Whoa! Where did that come from?

Gareth met Nevin's eye, but he said nothing as he slid back into his chair. Once seated, he watched me for a moment.

"Ignore her, she's jealous."

"What did she mean by impure?"

He picked up a goblet, swished the crimson liquid around in it, and then took a sip. *"She means you're not Fae—pure blood, like the rest of us."*

After that, everyone ate in silence, other than Nevin's attempts to engage me and Gareth in conversation. Being here made it more evident I didn't belong. And my stay, no matter how much they wanted it to go smoothly, wouldn't.

Gareth stood. "Lady Salome, can I offer to show you the gardens?"

I quirked an eyebrow. Okay, so what was up with the sudden formality? "Yeah, I'd like that."

He offered me his arm and led me from the Great Hall. We walked through one of the large archways to a stone path, which wound around a pond. Wooden benches overlooked the glittering waters.

Gareth ushered me to a private corner, next to a weeping willow tree, which somehow seemed appropriate. Once here, he gathered me in his arms. I choked back a sob.

"I don't want you to go."

"I know. But I promise, Nevin and Gwenn will keep you safe. I'll be back before you know it, and at that time, I'll try to see you as much as I can. And I promise to come up to the palace for any important events…once I get back, if you really need me, you can stop by the training grounds. I don't mind taking a break to see you."

His thumb brushed tears from my cheeks. He leaned down and pressed his lips against mine. I wrapped my arms around him, pulling him closer. His tongue brushed against mine as he deepened the kiss.

Warmth coiled in my belly. My body trembled beneath his touch.

"Eh-hem." Someone cleared their throat behind us.

Gareth leapt back, and we shifted to see Gwenn standing there, hands on her hips. "Nevin wants to meet with you before you leave," she said to her brother.

"Let me see her back to her room, then I'll be down."

"She's fine. Besides, Nevin assigned me as her guard and ordered me to bring her upstairs."

Well didn't that seem convenient? Couldn't I spend a few minutes with Gareth before he left?

He gave me a sheepish grin. "I'll stop by and see you later."

As soon as he left, Gwenn spun on her heel. "C'mon. You need to go inside."

We hurried into the palace, down the hall, and back up to my room. Before she let me go in, she did a quick sweep as if checking for monsters. When she was done, she poked her head out.

"Just so you know. I don't approve of you being with my brother," she said. "He doesn't need to be worried about some weak human. I don't know what he or the king sees in you. But I'm telling you now, I won't coddle you. And don't expect me to be your friend just because my brother has a momentary lapse of sense."

My face burned. What the heck had I done to this chick? "Um—okay."

"Regardless of my feelings, I'm your new guard. So don't do anything stupid."

I shoved past her into my room. "I don't need *your* protection. In fact, you don't need to be near me at all." With that, I slammed the door shut.

If Gwenn thought she could bully me, she had another thing coming. I wasn't the same meek girl I'd been in my world. After everything I'd been through, no way in hell was I going to let some stupid, stuck up girl with a sword tell me what to do. Well…unless of course she drew the sword and tried to kill me.

A sigh escaped my lips. Yep. This would be a long stay in Summer.

A couple of hours later, Gareth barged into my room. He wore his chainmail armor and had his helm tucked beneath his arm.

"Sorry, Nevin had some last minute things to go over before I left." He strolled across the room, set his stuff on my bed, and then wrapped me in his arms.

I sighed, clutching him tightly. "Are you leaving now?"

"I'll be back soon." His fingers traced my jawline, and he cupped my chin in his hand, tilting my head upward. He bent down, his lips crushing mine.

Tingles ran up from my toes to my head. My pulse soared as I pressed myself against him. He backed me against the wall, his hands tangling in my hair.

Breathless, he pulled away, eyes burning into mine. Why did it feel like he was kissing me goodbye for the last time? A lump lodged itself in my throat.

"May-maybe I should just go home," I said. "At least until the training sessions are done."

"No. You won't be safe there."

"And I am here?"

"Gwenn will guard you with her life."

I snorted. "Yeah, right. She hates me."

"She'll grow to adore you, same as I do. Okay, maybe not quite as much as me," he teased then placed another kiss on my forehead.

A knock sounded at the door behind us, and Nevin walked in. "It's time to go. The other scouts are waiting near the gate for you."

Gareth nodded, then picked up his helm. Nevin and I followed him out of my room and down to the main square of Summer. Fae lined the street to cheer on the soldiers. They tossed flower petals at their feet, cheering, and clapping—a proper sendoff. Nevin pulled aside one of the other officers to have a last word, leaving me and Gareth alone for a moment.

As we approached his men, Gareth faced me once more. "*I love you. No matter what, don't forget that.*"

"*I love you, too. Please be safe.*" My vision blurred as my eyes pooled. This wasn't how things were supposed to be. I'd left my world to be with Gareth, and now he was going off to war.

As Gareth mounted his horse, Nevin came back to my side and gave my shoulder a squeeze. "Everything will be okay. You'll see. It won't be so bad not having him around for a while."

I wanted to punch him and blame him for sending Gareth away. If it wasn't for him, we wouldn't be here at the palace. But I knew that even if Nevin hadn't ordered him to do this, he still would've volunteered to do anything he could to help defend his kingdom. He was a warrior: a defender of Summer.

The gates swung open, allowing the riders to go through. A sudden pang of fear stabbed at me. Gareth was gone. I was alone in a world I didn't understand—or almost alone. And somehow, I knew things were about to change. For so long, I'd depended on Gareth to watch out for me and keep me safe. Now all I had was myself.

CHAPTER SIXTEEN

Salome

The seamstress tugged the fabric tighter, cutting off any plans I had of breathing.

"Pull your shoulders back," the woman, Taro, said. "And quit wiggling, or I'll stick you with a pin." She glared at me, her mouth drawn so tight, I doubted anyone could get her lips to part.

Geez, we'd been at this for hours now. My legs killed me, and I wanted to sit down, not be threatened with becoming this lady's pincushion. What I wouldn't give to have a pair of jeans or shorts.

A knock sounded at the door, and Nevin poked his head in. "How are we coming along?"

"Almost done, Your Highness," Taro said, giving him a big smile. The first smile I'd seen since she'd gotten here.

"Good. I want to get Lady Salome out of her room for a while."

"Where are we going?"

He chuckled. "It's a surprise. I'll come back in a few minutes to retrieve you."

When he shut the door, the seamstress frowned at me and hurried to put in more pins. When she finally finished, I'd only been poked about a million times, which I was sure she'd done on purpose.

Once I changed, I went out into the hallway to find Nevin waiting for me. He grinned when he noticed I wore one of the many new dresses he'd had made for me.

"You look beautiful."

"Thanks." My eyes narrowed. "If this is some ploy to try and make me forgive you for sending Gareth away, it isn't going to work."

His smile faded. "Are you going to stay mad at me forever?"

I shrugged. "Maybe."

He offered me his arm and sighed. "I had no other choice. Gareth is the best warrior in the kingdom. And one of the few I trust."

"But you've already asked so much of him."

"Don't you think I know that? He ran the kingdom while I was cursed. He protected our people when I could not. I made mistakes, but I mean to right them. And Gareth agreed to this. He could've said no."

We walked outside, the warm summer air brushing against my cheek like a gentle caress. I tilted my face toward the sun and closed my eyes. What did he mean, Gareth agreed? Gareth had led me to believe he had no choice. Had he lied to me? Or was this another one of Nevin's plans to try to convince me to be his queen?

My lids opened and my fingers brushed over the soft, silky petals of a white rose. The scent of honey permeated around me, making me light headed.

Nevin took my hand, his face suddenly serious. "I want us to be friends again."

"Then quit doing things to irritate me." I snatched my hand back from him. "And don't spring crazy surprises on me."

His lips twitched. "Well, if I remember correctly, I've always irritated you. Even back in the human world. My arrogance. My secrets."

I rolled my eyes. "And the list goes on."

He laughed, leading me to a stone bench, which overlooked a large waterfall. Foam churned at the surface, where the thunderous waters hit the rocks.

"Do you also need to be reminded that you used to love me? That you used to want to spend every waking moment by my side?"

I fisted my hands at my sides. "No. But apparently you need to be reminded that I was under your spell. None of my feelings were voluntary. You manipulated me. Our whole 'relationship' wasn't real. End of story."

His fingers swiped loose strands of my hair back behind my ear. "I'm sorry for that, but you need to realize how desperate I was to be free of that curse. Salome, I really do want us to be friends. I hate fighting with you all the time. Just give me a chance."

Uneasiness ran through my veins. What was he up to? Nevin only turned on the charm when he wanted something from me. "Maybe we'll be friends again, but trust is earned, Nevin."

At the sound of footsteps behind us, Nevin spun around. "Sorry to bother you, Your Highness, but we've received a message from the scouting party," an elfin warrior with dark black hair said.

"Thank you. If you'll take it to the throne room, I'll be there shortly," he said.

As the guard left us, Nevin glanced down at me. "I'm sorry, I'll have to leave you for a while. But feel free to explore the grounds."

Before I could ask whether or not I could go with him, he disappeared down the path. If the letter was from Gareth, I wanted to know what it said. I wanted to know he was okay.

Frustrated, I plopped down on the bench and stared at the churning waters. I picked a blade of grass from the ground. With a smile, I held it to my lips and blew on it, creating a low whistle. My grandpa had taught me how to do that one summer. We sat on my porch, trying to see who could make their grass whistle the loudest. A lump formed in my throat. We'd never get a chance to do it again, because I was in Faerie now.

"If it isn't Lady Salome," a feminine voice said.

I twisted in my seat to see Rowena, the snotty noblewoman from yesterday. "Yep, that'd be me."

"Why don't you join me for a stroll? There's a lovely path that goes above the waterfall. I've even packed a picnic." She stood tall, and elegant against the summery backdrop.

My brow furrowed. This lady was a mega witch with a capital b. So was this some act? Or she was trying to be nice?

"Um—sure." I stood, tossing the piece of grass I held to the ground. My hand swiped the side of my dress, as I made sure I had the dagger Gareth had given me belted to my side—just in case.

She gave me a big smile then led me toward a path hidden behind the lilac bushes. As I stepped behind them, I thought I saw Lord Darach's ghost watching me from below the waterfall. But that seemed impossible; I didn't believe he'd follow me from the Ruined Court.

I gasped and stopped walking. Great, now I was seeing things. I squinted. Maybe it was a play of the light or something.

"You need to keep up. The terrain is uneven up here if you don't watch your step," Rowena called over her shoulder.

With a forced grin, I tore my gaze from the falls and pushed up the steep incline. After a few moments, my thighs burned. *Crap*. I was so out of shape. But we kept climbing, until at last we stood on top of the hill, overlooking the gardens.

"Wow, it's beautiful up here," I said, out of breath.

She grinned, setting her picnic basket on the ground, and spread out a blanket. "Come, have a seat."

"Thanks." I sat down then curled my legs beneath me.

Rowena opened up her basket and pulled out sandwiches, fruit, and wine. "You know, I'm one of the highest ranking noblewomen here in Summer. If you stick with me, you might get into the right circles."

Nice to see she was so timid and demure. I held back a snort and concentrated on the darting butterflies. "I'd like that."

She opened the bottle of wine and grabbed a goblet from her things. "You do know that before the king got stuck in the human world, he courted me."

"No, I didn't." Which would explain her shitty attitude toward me last night. However, it didn't explain the sudden change with her being nice to me. Either she was trying to suck up to me in order to get back into Nevin's good graces or she just didn't know how to be personable.

"Well, I'm hoping to pick back up where we left off." She gave me a thin smile, and her eyes darkened.

"Good luck with that. In case you didn't know, I'm with Gareth and not after Nevin." God, did she think I really wanted to know about her plans with Nevin?

She poured the scarlet drink into the glass cup and handed it me. "I do hope we can be friends."

"Thanks. Me too." I sloshed the drink around in the glass as she watched me intently. It's not that I wanted to be rude, but I wasn't a big drinker. In fact, I'd only had wine one or two other times, and that'd been here in Faerie.

I brought the cup closer to my face and inhaled. It smelled so sweet and fruity—almost *too* fruity. Warning bells went off in my mind, and I sat there eyeing the drink. No way was I going to have any of it.

Just then, Gwenn burst into the clearing. Rowena leapt to her feet, grabbed the cup from my hands, and dumped it out.

What the hell was that? I stood, staring at her as she threw all her things back into her basket and raced down the hill.

Gwenn's chest heaved, and I saw she'd drawn her sword. "Are you stupid?" she said.

"What?"

She bent down, stuck her finger in the spot where the wine had been dumped, then held her fingers to her nose. "You almost drank poison, you idiot. Did you really think Rowena wanted to be your friend? She's been trying to get her claws into Nevin for as long as I've known her."

My head swam, and I leaned against a tree for support. "I wasn't going to drink it. Holy crap. Why do you think I was just sitting there with it?"

She glared. "Stupid human. All it would've taken is her bumping your hand and one droplet of this getting in your system. You're gonna get yourself killed, then my brother will blame me for your ignorance."

She grabbed my arm and marched me back down to the gardens, where we found Nevin coming through the gate. A look of alarm spread over his face when he saw Gwenn's blade.

"What's going on?" he demanded.

"Rowena just tried poisoning human-dearest here."

He glowered, jerking me away from her. He searched my face, neck, and arms. "Did you drink anything?"

"No, I didn't get the chance."

He shifted his attention to Gwenn. "How do you know it was poison?"

"Because I could smell the sickly sweetness of her wine. And there's only one thing that gives off that scent."

"Faerie Fire," Nevin said. "That potion was outlawed."

"Well, apparently Rowena has a way of making it."

"Did you retrieve the cup or bottle it was in?"

Gwenn sheathed her sword. "No. She took off before I could do anything. Besides, I was trying to make sure Lady Salome wasn't harmed."

"I can't convict her without proof. The Council will want evidence. And it'll be a human's word against a noble Fae."

"What about Gwenn?"

"I'm not in the Council's favor." She stiffened, her eyes suddenly darkening.

Great, I almost get murdered and my humanity stands in the way of Rowena getting punished.

I rubbed my temples. Faerie was so not agreeing with me. I wanted to go home.

Nevin's hand rested at the small of my back. "Don't worry. This won't happen again. I'll have guards with you at all times from here on out."

I glanced at him. "Are you serious?"

"Yes. I won't let anyone hurt you. Gwenn, see Salome back to her room. And let the other guards know they're to post outside her room in shifts."

She saluted him. "As you wish."

Nevin kept his palm on me as he led me back toward the palace. Gareth was wrong when he said I'd be safer here than in the human world. Now I knew just how dangerous Faerie was—and I knew what lengths some would go to get rid of me.

CHAPTER SEVENTEEN

$\mathcal{D}$emetria carried three bone candelabras to the royals' table while I straightened the crimson seat covers. Somehow, we'd gotten stuck on decorating duty. And here I thought helping set up prom senior year would be the worst dance-related event I'd ever have to deal with. God was I wrong.

When I finished with the chairs, I walked over to Demetria, who held a tray of goblets.

"Last night, they placed me on clean up duty," she whispered. "I had to scrub blood from the Bone Yard stones. The barred doors for sure open into the drainage ditch. There are no locks on them."

I smiled. "Oh my God. That's the best news I've heard in forever."

She handed me a couple of cups to place on the tables. "Be warned, the ditches are filled with water and blood. It'll be a horrific flight from here. But I'm certain the tunnels lead to the nearby creek."

"Let's hope so, because I for damn sure don't want to get stuck down there."

A couple of other humans wandered in with stacks of plates. We moved to the back table so they wouldn't overhear us.

Demetria's hair fell across her face like a silky wave. "You'll need to pack some warm outfits. Wrap them up as best you can so they don't get wet. And make sure you have your stash of food packed."

"Already done. I got my supplies and things last night while Etienne slept."

"Good. The only things left to get are the water skins, which I'll hide outside once the ball gets underway."

Excitement raced through my blood.

I'm gonna get out of here.

No more bones. No more nightmares. As happy as I was, a niggling feeling settled in my stomach. What if something went wrong? What if we couldn't get to the Bone Yard?

No. Failure isn't an option. I either get out of here, or I die trying. I can't take any more of this place.

Soon Etienne retrieved me and led me back to his quarters. "I have a surprise for you."

My eyes widened when he pulled out a beautiful scarlet gown. The top was tight, with strands of gold and white threaded through it. The skirt was like a red silken wave.

"Wow. It's gorgeous." I took it from him, held it against me, and twirled around.

He smiled. "Glad you like it."

I stopped spinning and glanced at him. "Thank you for the dress. And, well, for protecting me. I know it hasn't been easy."

He closed the distance between us. His gaze burned into me as he swiped strands of hair from my face. "I wish I would've met you under different circumstances."

My pulse sped, racing through my veins. Warmth clutched me.

What's wrong with me? Why do I feel so strange around him?

I'd felt attracted to plenty of guys, but this time it felt… different. Deeper. More permanent.

My lips twitched. "You mean like some place that wasn't ruled by a mega-psycho bitch?"

He chuckled, a beautiful sound in my ears. "Yes—that. Listen, I should probably go so you can get ready for the ball. I'll see you later."

I waved as he left me alone. Once the door shut behind him, I gathered my things. Demetria would be by soon to pick up laundry as well as sneak my things outside.

With trembling hands, I managed to slip into my new gown. I paced the floor for a few minutes until I heard a knock on the door.

"Laundry," she said from outside.

"Come in."

She pushed inside and gave me a quick nod. "Are your things ready?"

"Yeah, just a second." I grabbed them from the chair and handed them to her.

She placed them into her large hamper, covering them with dirty sheets. "I'll find you later at the ball."

With that, she was gone.

*E*tienne stepped into the room a while later. "You ready to go?"

My breath caught in my throat. Holy crap, he looked hot. The dark green tunic brought out his already brilliant blue eyes.

Heat crept up my neck. Okay, that wasn't the reaction I wanted to have.

"Um—yeah."

He offered me his arm, and we made our way to the ballroom. When we stepped inside, I was nearly blinded by the beautiful Fae. But the arrogance in the room was suffocating. The scarier imperfect creatures, like the goblins, satyrs, and fauns, hurried around fetching things for the other Fae.

Music carried on the air as human musicians warmed up.

"There you are, you're needed in the kitchens." A dwarven woman caught my arm.

"Don't worry, I'll find you for a dance once the meal's been served." Etienne gave my hand a squeeze then made his way over to the royal table.

When I got to the kitchen, someone handed me a tray of appetizers: tiny cheeses, fruits, and crepes. With a deep breath, I pushed back to the ballroom. In the middle of the floor, some people were already dancing. Relief flooded through me when I noticed Teodor swaying back and forth with Crazy Chick.

I held my tray in front of me, allowing Fae nobles to grab food. Geez, I felt like the Waitress to the Stars with the way they waved me over so they could snatch it up. If one more person called me "human" or "pet," they'd likely have a strawberry sticking out of their eye. Or more likely they'd pluck my eyes and eat them.

When my tray emptied, I spun to go get more.

"I think it's time for that dance you promised me," Etienne said. He took my tray from me and handed it to someone else.

"Okay." My voice came out sounding more breathy than I wanted.

He wrapped an arm around my waist and guided me onto the dance floor. Once there, he clutched me close to him as the soft music surrounded us. I inhaled deeply. My heart pounded against my ribs, like someone playing the xylophone.

"You're the most beautiful woman in here," he whispered, his breath hot against my cheek.

"Thank you." I shifted so my gaze met his.

Oh hell, he's so gorgeous.

I knew better, but I couldn't deny my attraction any longer. Worse, I didn't want to.

We swayed back and forth, bodies pressed close. His fingers traced my jaw-line, and my hands tightened around him. At that moment, I lost myself in him and in the music. The way he looked at me made me feel like a precious jewel.

He leaned down. His lips were a breath away. "Kadie." My name fell from his mouth like a whispered promise.

"Yes?"

The queen clapped her hands. "Humans, bring in the main course."

Etienne took a quick step back, as if realizing what almost happened. "Thank you for the dance." He gave a slight bow then moved to his place at the head table.

Trying to slow my pulse, I hurried to the kitchen again, retrieving a tray with roasted pheasant on it. It was probably for the best that we hadn't kissed. I didn't need an attachment to one of the winter princes, especially since I'd likely never see him again. I just wish there'd been some way to repay his kindness to me while I was imprisoned here.

I went from table to table, putting meat on plates. When I ran out, I caught Demetria's eye, and she nodded toward the hallway. With my tray still in hand, I followed her out of the room.

"Quick, we can put our dishes in the changing rooms," she said.

With a quick glance over my shoulder, we raced away from

the kitchens. Once we got to the curtained rooms, we ditched our trays. My body quaked as waves of nervousness clenched my gut. We slipped back into the shadows, our backs pressed against the walls. We crept to the door leading into the Bone Yard.

I sucked in a deep breath. This was it.

*D*emetria opened the door, and we hurried outside into the bitter cold night.

"Our packs are in that empty pot," she said.

I followed her to one of the large cauldrons. She bent down and grabbed our sacks. I secured mine to my back then ran for the barred door to the drainage pit. Demetria joined me, and I clutched hold of the metal grates and tugged.

Nothing happened. *Oh God. Please. Don't do this.* Fear wriggled into my mind. I braced myself and pulled again.

"It's not budging," I said, frantic.

"Here, let me help."

We both gripped tight, jerking and tugging with all our strength. My fingers tightened around the bars.

Creak.

At last, it swung open. We dropped to our knees, crouching to get through the small hole. Demetria dropped in first, and I heard the splash as she hit the water below. With a deep breath, I slid in backward so I could shut the barred grate behind us. It swung back easier than it had when we tried to open it. With the grate secure, I fell into the putrid bloody water. The stench made me gag as it sloshed around my waist and the walls of the tunnel.

I didn't want to think about the nasty stuff floating in here.

It's a way out. Just hurry.

In the darkness, we continued to push forward, neither of us sure what we'd find at the end of the long tunnel. My teeth chattered as the cold seeped through my skin. We wouldn't last long out here. My feet caught on uneven rocks, and I reached for the wall to steady myself.

For long minutes, we fought our way through, until at last we saw a miniscule amount of light ahead. As we got closer, we came to a similar barred door. It led into a creek. We braced ourselves against the frigid bars and pushed. The door budged, and we tripped out into the open.

"Quick, get out of the water and get changed." Demetria tugged her pack from her back.

The winds whipped through the trees, sending tiny tornadoes of snow spiraling at our feet. How long would we survive in this cold? Numb, I stripped out of my wet gown and tugged my dry clothes from my bag. As quickly as I could, I slipped my dry garments on and secured a cloak about my shoulders. I then shoved my feet into a pair of fur-lined boots.

"Toss your wet garments into the drainage pit and let's go," I said, wadding up my bloody things. I threw them inside then waited for Demetria to do the same.

After that, I kicked the door shut from the shore.

I glanced at the woods ahead of us, then turned and smiled. "We're free."

She clutched my hand. "Not yet. Come along, we need to get as far away as possible."

With that, we ran into the forest. At last, I'd leave Winter far behind. I couldn't wait to get home…and away from this nightmare.

*M*y lungs burned, but we pressed on. Darkness covered the woodland except when pockets of moonlight pierced through the trees. In those moments, the ground sparkled like giant blankets of glitter, making me forget we were running for our lives.

The wind picked up, whipping snow into our faces. My teeth chattered and I hugged my cloak closer.

"We should cross this stream." Demetria pointed ahead. "At least then if they use hounds to hunt for us, they'll lose the scent."

"Okay," I said, out of breath. We splashed through the shallow water, and I prayed it didn't soak into my boots. The last thing I wanted to do was die from hypothermia or frostbite. I hadn't risked my life to escape the castle only to be taken out by a fricken snowstorm.

We moved further into the thicket. Branches and thistles tore at my hands and cloak. I tugged free, falling to my knees. Demetria glanced over her shoulder and came back to help me up.

"We've got to keep moving."

"I know. Sorry."

Swishhheshhhhhh…

The noise came from the forest around us.

"It sounds like the trees are whispering." Demetria's head tilted as she looked up.

Chills snaked across my skin. "Let's not think about that. The last thing we need to do is get freaked out."

But even I couldn't ignore the uneasiness clenching my gut. All I imagined were trees coming to life and attacking us, kind of like that scene in *The Wizard of Oz*.

We stumbled onward. My muscles cramped, my entire body crying out for rest. The frigid temps sent tingles through my skin. I kept sight of Demetria's form ahead of me. She was much better at navigating the woods than I was, although neither of us really knew where the hell we were going. What I wouldn't give for my GPS about now. But since I didn't have it, we just kept heading away from the castle.

After hours of trudging through the deep snow, the sky lightened.

"We need to find a place to rest for the day," Demetria said. "They'll find us too easily if we continue to travel during daylight hours."

"I don't think there's anywhere to hide." My gaze took in the woodland.

"Our best chance is to continue to follow this stream." Demetria tugged me along. "We'll need to start brushing our tracks away, though."

Too tired to argue, I turned to face behind us and swiped at them with my hand. My back ached from bending over. I dug my teeth into my lip to distract myself from the pain, but a whimper still sounded from deep in my throat.

You can do this. Just think of how warm and happy you'll be when you leave this shitty place.

At last, Demetria came to a halt. "I've found us a place to hide."

I climbed to my feet, brushing snow from my cloak, and turned to see where she pointed. Up ahead, the stream emptied into a large river. On the other side of the river there were hills and formations of rocks, and above the crevices I saw several small caves.

She dropped to her knees beside me and helped finish covering our tracks. Then we rushed into the freezing waters once more. We splashed over to the other side of the stream but stayed in the water so as to not create more tracks. When we reached the slippery rocks, we pulled ourselves up. My fingers dug into the icy stones, my skin stinging. Tears trickled down my face. My nose ran, but I hefted myself upward. Demetria picked a path along the rocks, and I trailed after her.

Soon she found us a cave nestled behind thick shrubbery. It wasn't very deep, but it went back far enough to get us out of the cold and keep us hidden from view. When we got inside, I collapsed on the ground.

"We need to eat and drink something," Demetria said beside me. She took her pack from her back and rummaged through it. "And change out of your wet stockings so you don't catch your death."

Numb, I sat up and grabbed a roll, as well as a pair of woolen stockings. I could barely move my fingers, as I fought to tug my boots off. Shit. I'd never been so cold in my life. My teeth chattered. I cupped my hands together and blew on them. My breath warmed them some, but they still ached.

"God, I wish it'd warm up."

Demetria snorted. "That isn't likely, my friend."

I climbed to my knees and managed to get my stockings pulled down, then I fell on my butt and took them the rest of the way off. With a sigh, I tossed the wet garments aside, then pulled on the dry ones. Once I finished, I snagged my extra cloak from my bag as well and wrapped it around me. It warmed me some, but not much.

I took a bite of my roll. It was hard, but food was food.

"You need to lay down and rest." Demetria patted the spot next to her. "If we curl up together, we'll stay warmer."

With a nod, I crawled next to her and plopped down. She hugged me tight, reminding me of my mom. "Do you really think we'll get out of here?"

She squeezed me tight. "The hardest part is already over. We got out of the castle."

"Do you think they know we're gone yet?"

"Yes. They would've noticed at bedtime."

"Then they're already on our trail."

"Perhaps. They might think we're still on the castle grounds. They'll check there first. They're too arrogant to believe we'd ever escape."

We lay in silence for a few minutes. "Demetria?"

"Hmmm?"

"Are you scared?"

She patted my arm. "A little. But for now, we need to sleep or we won't make it far come sundown."

Fear coiled inside me like a snake, but eventually fatigue won out. My heavy lids shut, and I drifted off.

I'm not sure how long we slept, but when I awoke, darkness covered everything.

"Time to get up," Demetria said, shoving her extra garments back into her pack. "Grab a quick bite to eat, then relieve yourself outside the cave."

"Um—you mean use the bathroom?"

"Yes. We won't have time to stop once we descend."

Great. I'd probably freeze my ass cheeks off. But I did as she said.

When we'd both eaten and "relieved ourselves," Demetria led me down the rocky incline. She picked a game trail along the riverbank. The moon peeked out from behind clouds, and the trees billowed beneath the gusts of wind. We fought through deep snowdrifts. My legs burned as I pushed forward. It was hard to run, but we sped along as quickly as we could. At last, we made our way back into the forest, where we'd have better cover.

Pine needles crunched beneath my footsteps, while the branches above crackled with ice. The air nipped at my exposed nose and ears. My limbs numbed. Every step I took hurt, but we needed to keep moving. Shadows seemed to pour into the woods. Soon, I could barely see my hands in front of my face.

Luckily, Demetria reached back and clutched hold of my arm. Together, we maneuvered between the shrubs and trees. From somewhere behind us, I heard horses whinny.

We went still.

"Run," Demetria said, gripping a handful of my cloak.

We bolted deeper into the forest. A branch scraped my face, nearly hitting me in the eye. But I continued to sprint.

The sounds of hooves pounding the ground erupted behind us.

"I don't want to go back," I cried.

"Quick, get in the tree." Demetria jerked me to the side. She leapt for a low hanging branch and hefted herself up. She offered me a hand and tugged me up.

Heart pounding out of control, I climbed the snow covered branches, clutching hold of the rough bark for dear life. We managed to get several feet up when we saw the riders coming.

I pressed myself as close to the tree as I could. My body quaked as terror thrummed in my veins.

Please don't let them look up.

I wrapped my arms and legs tight around the branch.

The horsemen rode past, but neither of us moved. I took a staggered breath, closed my eyes, and prayed. We sat still for a long time. By now, I couldn't feel my hands, feet, or body for that matter.

"Is—is it safe?" I whispered. My teeth chattered.

"I think so." Demetria lifted her head and scanned the tree line, or at least what she could see of it.

Geez, what I wouldn't give for a hot tub or a sauna right now. I was seriously beginning to understand why Salome hated winter so much.

Demetria tapped my arm and pointed down. As quietly as we could, we climbed down a couple of branches, then dropped from the tree. My legs tingled like I'd landed on a porcupine. I bit my cloaked arm to keep from crying out.

Demetria headed in the direction we'd come. "Come, we need to go back this way."

A twig snapped in the woods. We only made it a few steps before we were surrounded.

Teodor rode into the moonlit clearing and blocked Demetria's way. "I told them you grew up in the woods and that you'd take to the trees. We just needed to wait you out."

"Run, Kadie." She glanced at me and we both darted toward the river.

A large horse stepped in front of me, and its rider, Etienne, peered down at me. I turned to run, but in one swift motion, he bent to the side and swept me up in his arms, placing me on the horse in front of him.

"So this is the repayment I get?" His harsh words came out. "Haven't I kept you safe? Haven't I found ways to keep the queen from harming you?" His fingers dug into my arm. "She'll want her revenge now, and there's nothing I'll be able to do to stop it."

"I—I'm sorry." I sobbed, watching as Teodor grabbed hold of Demetria's hair and dragged her into the saddle. He tossed her onto her stomach, so she hung over the side of the horse.

Horror washed over me. They'd found us—and now we'd have to go back. More blood. Bones. Death. Maybe running had been a bad idea. All I could hope for now was that the cold killed me. Then I wouldn't have to face the queen's wrath. But as Etienne held tight to me, I knew I wouldn't be so lucky. Winter had won, and I'd be its next victim.

CHAPTER EIGHTEEN

Salome

Nevin reached across the table to pour me some more sparkling cider. For the first time in a while, it was just the two of us. He'd ordered a private dinner in my room tonight, which made me nervous.

"How do you like Summer so far?" He smiled, setting the decanter back down.

Other than almost being murdered?

But instead of saying that, I cleared my throat and shoved my plate aside. "It's beautiful. And warm."

He chuckled then took a sip of his drink. "That it is. But I didn't want to have dinner with you to discuss the weather."

Nevin slipped a golden box with pearl inlay from behind the basket of rolls and handed it to me.

My mouth went dry. "Wh—what is this?"

"Open it and find out."

This better not be another attempt at trying to make me his queen. Just because Gareth was gone didn't mean I'd change my mind. When the top finally opened, I gasped. Nestled against the blue velvet interior was a sapphire and diamond bracelet.

"Nevin, I can't take this."

"Of course you can." He took it from me and hooked it on my wrist. "Think of it as a gift to cheer you up."

The cool stones kissed my skin. This thing had to be worth thousands of dollars. "Wow. I mean, thanks."

His gaze softened. "I know you miss Gareth. So I wanted to do something nice for you. To make your stay easier."

"I appreciate it, but you don't have to give me gifts." My thumb traced the dark blue gems.

"I wanted to. Besides, you'll need something to wear to the ball tomorrow."

"Ball? As in dancing, dresses, fairytale stuff?"

He stood. "That's exactly what I mean. I know how much you like ballroom dancing. It'll give you a chance to mingle more with our people and forget how far away Gareth is."

He'd obviously never been in love before. You don't just forget someone because they're not with you. With a sigh, I forced a smile. "Sounds fun."

Nevin caught my hand in his and gave it a squeeze. "I'll see you tomorrow then."

He ushered the maids in to clean the table off. When they finished, he waved goodbye and left me alone. By now the sun was sinking beneath the treetops as nightfall crept in, and I walked onto the balcony. I rested my elbows on the railing and watched tiny stars flicker to life like glitter caught in beams of light.

My chest tightened. *"Gareth, can you hear me?"*

But there was no answer through our link. Maybe he didn't want to be distracted while on his missions.

"I miss you." The thoughts poured out before I could stop them. My hands clamped the railing as I waited. Still no response. My gaze scoured the sky. In the distance, I noticed the large

clouds that loomed, threatening Winter's darkness. I wrapped my arms across my chest and shivered. Gareth was somewhere out there…and who knew what kind of danger awaited him.

Nevin offered me his arm as he led me down the staircase and into a lavish ballroom. Twinkling bulbs of light floated above us, like our own starry night. The scent of flowers tiptoed on the breeze that blew through the opened room. Nobles gathered along the edges of the floor, chatting and laughing. A few whispered when they saw me enter. Nervous tingles fluttered in my stomach.

Please don't let me screw up any dance moves.

A group of elven musicians raised their instruments: wooden flutes, a harp, something that looked like a lute, and a violin.

"Smile," Nevin whispered in my ear.

I glanced at him, my lips quivering. "Sorry, I'm just freaking out a little."

"Why?"

"Um—I haven't danced in a while."

He chuckled, giving me a pointed look. "You'll be fine. If I remember correctly, you told me you used to do the ballroom and swing dancing competitions. Not to mention you seemed to handle yourself well during our date in the woods."

"Why do you keep doing that?" I snapped, glaring at him.

"Doing what?"

"Trying to bring up what happened in the human world? I don't know what you're up to, but I don't plan on dumping Gareth. The sooner you get that through your freaking noble head, the sooner I might consider being your friend."

Nevin frowned. "Fine, if that's what you wish. Let's just dance and forget about everything between us."

"Again, I haven't danced in ages. I'd hate to embarrass you and myself."

"You won't. Besides, one does not forget how to dance."

I glared at him. "Says the man who's had centuries of practice."

His hand slid to my waist, and he led me to the middle of the floor. The musicians struck up a haunting tune, and Nevin swept me into his arms, twirling me about the room.

"See, you're doing it." He bent forward to whisper in my ear.

Others stopped to watch our intricate movements as we glided, dipped, and spun. I closed my eyes for a moment, letting myself relax and enjoy it. Soon the music changed to something more upbeat.

Fae laughed, weaving in and out of one another. I laughed too, clapping my hands as Nevin released me to follow behind a group of men. They bowed to the ladies then spun us around. I lost myself in the line of gyrating bodies. Even if I didn't want to admit it, this was fun—and exactly what I needed.

Then how come I feel so guilty?

Because Gareth was out trying to fight Winter, or at least find out what they were up to, and I was prancing around at a ball.

My smile faded. Nevin's arm wrapped around me once more as he tugged me to his chest.

"What's wrong?"

"I—sorry, it's just I somehow feel like I shouldn't be doing this. I mean, my boyfriend's gone, and I'm partying."

He caught my chin, tilting it upward. "Trust me, he wants you to continue to live. He doesn't expect you to spend every waking moment in your room pining after him."

With a sigh, I stepped back in an attempt to put distance between us. "It just doesn't feel right to be celebrating and enjoying myself."

Nevin followed me as I made my way off the dance floor. "Salome, please wait."

His fingers brushed my shoulder and I stopped in a shadowed alcove. "I appreciate what you're trying to do, I really do. I just…"

He spun me to face him. "There's nothing wrong with missing him. But there's also nothing wrong with enjoying yourself—with living. You want him to come home to more than an empty shell spent from worry."

Tears blurred my vision, and I tried to let his words comfort me, but it was no use. I missed Gareth, and nothing he could do would change that.

"Why don't I go get you a glass of punch? You can stay over here and get yourself together." He glanced down at me. "I'll send Gwenn over with you until I get back."

I sniffled, wiping the back of my hand across my face to get rid of any evidence of my breakdown. The last thing I wanted was for Gareth's sister to think I was a crybaby. "Sure, thanks."

I backed further into the shadows and leaned against the wall. My fingers trailed the blue lace fabric of my dress as I listened to the music swell. Everyone was having a good time. Why couldn't I?

Because you have a conscience.

Okay, so maybe that was unfair. The Fae probably missed their soldiers too. But as my gaze traveled the room, I realized no one seemed fazed in the least. I saw Nevin catch Gwenn's attention, then a moment later, I watched as she weaved her way through the crowd.

"Well if it isn't the human again," a feminine voice said beside me.

I spun and found Rowena glaring at me. "You. You tried to kill me!"

She sneered. "Prove it."

My pulse raced through my veins. I took a step away from her. "Nevin will be back soon."

"Nevin? Are you on a first name basis with the king now?" Her too-red lips formed a thin line. "He'll soon grow tired of you, human. And then you'll become another one of his pets. "

"Nevin's my friend, he wouldn't do anything to hurt me."

"Wouldn't he? Our people use your kind for toys and entertainment. You're nothing but animals to us."

My jaw clenched. My gaze burned into her. "That's because you're a monster."

"You have no idea." She smiled, leaning closer as if to intimidate me.

The air around us sizzled. A low hum resonated beneath my feet. I stumbled back, the need to get away from this crazy lady overwhelming. My hand went to the dagger Gareth had given me, belted at my side. Would I be quick enough to defend myself?

"Hey!" Gwenn stepped into the alcove with her sword drawn, eyes piercing and out of breath.

Rowena lowered her hands and rushed into the crowd. Air hissed from my lips as I released my breath. "Thank you."

My guard's head snapped around, and she stared me down. "Can't you stay out of trouble?"

"I didn't do anything," I said. "Nevin left me to get punch, and she cornered me."

"Yes, that might be the case, but you're trouble because you can't defend yourself. You're an easy target for her."

My body trembled as rage swirled through me. "Well, I didn't ask for this. I never wanted to come to Summer to begin with. And it's not like I've had tons of extra time to train. Gareth managed to show me how to use a dagger, but that's about it."

"Too bad, because you're here now. And starting tomorrow, you'll learn how to fight. I can't be here to jump into all your battles for you."

I swallowed. "Wait, what?"

"You're to meet me down by the soldiers' barracks after lunch. I won't go easy on you just because you're the king's *guest*."

"What if I refuse?"

"Then I'll come drag your sorry arse down here. Now, go on up to your room, I'll tell Nevin you got sick. Tavyn, escort Lady Salome upstairs." She waved one of the other guards over.

He nodded and ushered me away from the festivities.

I rubbed my forehead. God, what the hell did I ever do to her—or Rowena for that matter?

And so what if I'm human?

Besides, if the Fae were so strong and powerful, how come they could never free Nevin in the human world? Assholes.

Not wanting to deal with anything else, I stormed out of the ballroom, following close behind my guard as we went upstairs. More than anything, I wanted to go home—to see my family. Or maybe take a trip to Texas to see Kadie. I chewed my bottom lip. I missed my best friend. Right now, she was probably making out with Zac and having a good time; she always had a good time. If only she was here to make this better.

CHAPTER NINETEEN

Kadie

The horses raced through the night, as if hellish fiends chased them. When the wicked, needle-like spires of the castle came into view, my stomach twisted and my body quaked beneath me. I squeezed my eyes tight, trying not to imagine the horrific punishment I'd receive.

I shouldn't have run. They're going to kill me now.

Panic rushed through me. Could Etienne come to my rescue again without putting himself in danger?

A whimper sounded from beside me, and I turned to see Teodor's horse come to a halt. He shoved Demetria off the side of it, then hopped down next to her, hunched over and whispering what I was sure were horrific things in her ear.

"Knock it off!" I screeched, jerking free from Etienne and bolting off our horse. "Haven't you caused her enough pain?" Without a second thought, I jerked my dagger from its sheath and raced the short distance over the frozen landscape. Teodor turned just in time to see me lunging for him.

My blade sliced across his face. He grabbed me by the throat and threw me to the side. He touched the fresh cut along his cheek, then fisted his hand. "You scarred me? You will pay for this, you human bitch."

Before he could strike me, Etienne caught his arm. "No. She's my prisoner."

"You would keep me from punishing her? You really are a traitor. You're choosing her over us."

"No, I'm not, but the queen will deal with them soon enough." He turned to me. "You might want to hold your tongue," Etienne whispered. "You're in enough trouble. Don't give him more reason to hurt you."

"I doubt it's gonna matter at this point if I stand up to Prince Asshole."

"Enough." His arm tightened around me. "We can still salvage you."

Salvage? I wasn't some junked out car. Besides, once the queen got hold of me, I'd likely become a new lamp in her bedroom…or worse.

Grisselle emerged from the gates, guards at her heels.

"Bring them to the throne room," she ordered.

One of the guards jerked me and shoved me forward. I caught myself on the stone wall, my legs weak beneath me. I wasn't sure I'd be able to deal with what was to come. I swallowed hard, biting back the fear that paralyzed me. Maybe now would be a good time to turn my dagger on myself. At least then I could make it quick and not be tortured.

Oh God. I can't go back in there. I can't.

"Get moving," the troll growled.

Demetria staggered inside ahead of me, Teodor giving her a shove as he went.

Hatred burned through me, and it was all I could do not to chase after Teodor and kick him in the nuts. My hands fisted as I glared after him. Another push from the troll sent me stumbling down the hallway toward the throne room. When we stood before the throne made of bones, Grisselle sat, back rigid, with her face frozen in a horrific sneer.

My gaze flickered around. There were four guards, Etienne, Teodor, Demetria, me, and the queen. And at the center of the room sat a large stone block. I couldn't breathe. What did they plan to do to us?

Grisselle stared at me. "I know this plan to escape was your idea. Teodor's pet wouldn't have dared such a thing if you hadn't put her up to it. But nevertheless, she'll be taught a lesson. You'll know I'm not playing games with you."

My chest tightened. I stiffened and took several staggered breaths as my heart pounded in my ears.

"Bring your pet here," the queen said to Teodor. She stood, long black gown swishing at her feet. Excitement radiated from her as she made her way to the block at the center of the room.

A troll guard stalked forward with a large axe propped over his shoulder. Teodor gripped hold of Demetria's dress and pulled her across the marble floor. When they got to the stone, he heaved her onto her knees, then shoved her body across it so that her head and neck hung off the edge.

A sob retched through me as I attempted to run for her, but one of the guards caught my arm and tugged me back.

"No—please…" I begged. "Maybe I can tell you some information you need—if—if you spare her. I'm begging you."

"No, you had your chance," Grisselle said. "You should've thought about this before you chose to deceive me." She sat back down, cradling a wine goblet in her hand as if to watch a show.

"It's okay, Kadie. I'm ready to meet my maker," Demetria said. Tears flowed down her face.

"Please. Don't do this," I shrieked. "I'll tell you whatever you want to know about Salome." Except I knew that if it came down to it, I couldn't tell her everything she wanted to know, which meant I was playing a very dangerous game. I couldn't betray my friends, but I also couldn't stand here and let her kill Demetria.

"My, aren't you cooperative now? And so quickly you turn on your dearest, closest friend. But no matter; whatever information you have will not save Teodor's pet." She turned away from me. "Off with her head," Grisselle said, pointing at Demetria.

I squeezed my eyes shut, refusing to watch. A *thwack* echoed through the room.

"Open your eyes—see what you've caused," Grisselle said.

Her head had been severed from her body

"I should've had your head too, but to see you suffer like this, watching your friend die, is much more pleasurable."

An angry sob erupted from my lips. "You're a sick fucker! You all are. And I hope one day that you burn in hell."

The queen's head snapped around. "You'd do well to keep quiet or you'll be the next one put on the block. Now get this wretched girl out of my face. In fact, I think another night in the Red Room will do her some good."

Etienne caught me around the waist. "You, come with me."

"I just want this over with," I whispered, my shoulders hunched.

He led me down the familiar hallway. When we got to the room, he gave me a sad look. "Be strong. You're alive, which means you still have a chance to get out of here." He turned to leave, then stopped and said, "Do you think Demetria would have wanted you to give up?" With that, he locked me in.

My head pounded, and my body ached. I swallowed hard, but my throat was raw from crying. Not even stopping long enough to glance around the room, I rushed into the courtyard to where Mr. Montgomery's tree-like form still stood. It looked more ragged than last time I'd been in here. The bark-like skin seemed to be peeling off, and his rooted feet bled into the already dingy snow.

"Kadieeeee...what's ha-happened?"

I collapsed at his trunk, and one of his branchlike arms touched my shoulder. "It's all my fault. D-Demetria's dead because of me. I-I tried to escape. I thought we'd make it..."

A low moan sounded from Mr. M's lips. *"But you're alive—th-that's what matterssss."*

Then how come I didn't feel that way? Maybe if I *had* told Grisselle whatever she wanted to know....Maybe if I'd spilled everything I knew about Salome and Gareth and...

What good was holding on to these secrets if people died anyway? If it led to me dying, too? I couldn't help anyone if I was dead. And I'd rather live to regret a mistake than not live at all.

I nestled closer to Mr. M's treelike form. I was never gonna get out of here, and sometime soon, the queen might decide to do to me what she'd done to so many others. Deep down, I was a fighter, but even I couldn't hold out forever.

They'd gotten what they wanted. I was broken.

*M*y bloodied cloak clung to me as I lay on the stone bench. Snowflakes drifted from the sky like ashes from a crematory and landed on me. My head throbbed from crying, and I didn't want to move—ever.

"Kadie, you should go inside. Y-You'll freeze to death out

here," Mr. Montgomery said. Thick, gooey, blood-like sap spilled from the corners of his mouth.

"Maybe that'd be for the best." I tugged my knees to my chest, curling into a tight ball. Too bad I couldn't shut my eyes and just have it be over.

"No. Don't s-say that. You're a fighter. You always have been." His hollow gaze met mine. Kindness radiated from him, despite the horrific mess he'd become. *"You can't give up. Not until you draw your last breath."*

If only it was that easy. Every time I fought back, something bad happened. And right now, I couldn't bear anything else.

With a sigh, I sat up, shaking the snow from myself. "I want to go home, Mr. M. And I'll do anything to get there."

He bent beneath the wind, the breeze rustling what was left of his leaves. *"Goooood."*

He wouldn't be saying that if he knew what I'd be willing to give up to get there. The lump in my throat made it hard to breathe as tears streaked my face again. I'd spent my entire life protecting and looking out for everyone else. That was easy when there was so little at stake. But with my life on the line? Now I had to do whatever it took to survive.

I buried my face in my hands, wishing for the ground to swallow me whole. I had no fight left within me.

The crunch of footsteps roused me, and I glanced up to see Etienne trudging into the courtyard.

"Come along, let's get you out of the cold." In one swift movement, he swept me into his arms and carried me inside.

When we got to his quarters, Rena stood waiting. Hot water steamed from the tub, and the scent of roses was heavy in the air.

"Get her cleaned up and into something warm," Etienne said. "I'll be back soon with some soup. The queen wants you to see her later tonight."

"What?" I snapped my head up and glanced at him. "Is she going to kill me?"

"She wants to talk. That's all I know. But tread lightly."

He slipped from the room, leaving me with his servant.

Rena tugged off my cloak for me and tossed it to the floor. "That was a brave but stupid thing you did." She spun me around and undid the buttons on my gown. "No one's ever made it as far as you."

I stared at the logs snapping in the fireplace. "Yeah, well, it got my friend killed."

Rena moved to the front of me. "Yes, but you've given people hope. That there might be a way out of here."

"And again, someone died."

She patted my arm, gave me a curious look I didn't understand, and then left. She'd never talked to me before, and I wasn't sure why she had now. But I didn't want anyone using Demetria as a martyr to encourage them to try and break out of here. I didn't need any more deaths on my conscience.

I tugged my dress down over my hips, and it fell to the floor in a heap. Goosebumps puckered my chapped skin as I made my way to the tub. At last, I climbed in. The hot water scalded me, but I forced myself to sink into it. I sobbed, laying my head against the edge of the bath.

My fingers trembled as I reached for the soap. Furiously, I scrubbed my body, scratching and scraping until I was raw. Then I fell back into the water, letting it cover my head.

Under the water, I could pretend I was anywhere else but here. No more pain. No more nightmares.

A hand jerked me up, and I sputtered.

It was Rena. "You've a visitor coming soon. You need to get ready."

She dropped a towel around my shoulders as she ushered me from the bath.

I grabbed the cloth and dried off. Rena handed me a long nightgown, which I pulled on over my head. The older woman disappeared, and then a moment later, my visitor—Etienne—came in.

His gaze flickered over me. "Why don't you sit near the fire so you don't catch your death?"

"Why is everyone so concerned with my well-being?" I asked as I trudged to the overstuffed chairs and plopped down.

Weariness settled in as the heat from the flames made me sleepy. A sense of defeat washed over me, and I sank further against the seat.

"I never wanted this for you," Etienne said. "I've failed you. I meant to get you out of here, and all I've done is make things worse."

My gaze met his, and I watched the sadness enter his eyes. He caught my hand in his. Such a soft touch. So gentle. His kindness confused me.

"I want out of here so badly," I whispered.

"I know. But I'm not sure if we'll get any more opportunities. The queen has doubled the patrols."

My vision blurred as tears welled. I was never going to get home. I'd forever be stuck in this nightmare…unless the queen decided to make an example of me tonight.

Maybe I should have stayed underwater. It was looking more and more like death would be my only escape.

CHAPTER TWENTY

Salome

My footsteps crunched on loose gravel as I made my way to the soldier's barracks. I *so* wasn't looking forward to my training session with Gwenn, but at least I got to wear breeches. Okay, so they weren't jeans, but they were way better than the frilly dresses I'd been decked out in. The breeches seemed to be the only positive thing that happened to me since arriving in Summer.

Something shimmered out of the corner of my eye. I whipped my head around, and for a moment, I swore I saw Lord Darach's ghost flicker near the fence post. I took a few steps toward it, but when I blinked, it was gone.

"Great. Now I'm seeing things."

"Who are you talking to?" Gwenn stalked out from behind the building, carrying two wooden swords.

"Um—no one." My face burned. Sure, she chose *now* to show up when I sounded like a raving lunatic. As if she needed any more reason to hate me.

She shook her head, a frown creasing her lips. "Here, take this."

Gwenn tossed one of the practice swords at me. It flew over my head, smacking the side of the barracks with a resounding *crack*!

She glared. "This is going to be a long day."

"Well, I didn't ask for your help." I trudged to pick up my weapon.

"No, but you'll get it regardless."

That made absolutely no sense at all. If she didn't want to be here then why was she? Then it dawned on me. *Gareth and Nevin*. It'd be nice if the two of them quit meddling in my life.

"The first thing you have to do is hold the damn weapon correctly." She marched over and twisted the wooden piece in my hand. "Your fingers need to grip the handle here. If you hold it the other way, you'll probably chop your leg off."

Why did I feel like a kindergarten student learning to color between the lines?

After making sure I had a firm grip on the sword, she moved in front of me.

"Now, you need to work on your stance."

I stood there, staring at her. "Um—I'm not sure what you mean."

With an exasperated huff, she came closer. "Spread your feet apart until they're shoulder width. Bend your knees a little more."

My boots scuffed the ground as I moved into position, mimicking her stance. "Like this?"

"Yes. Now, I want you to swing your weapon around. Get used to the feel of it in your hands."

My teeth grazed my bottom lip, and I spun the sword in a wide arc like I'd seen in the movies. Somehow, I lost my grip, and it sailed through the air and almost hit Gwenn in the face. If she hadn't ducked, she'd probably look like a unicorn right now, with a wooden sword sticking out of her head.

"Sorry. I'm so sorry." *Crap*. I didn't do this bad when Gareth was trying to show me how to defend myself with a dagger.

Probably because you didn't have him yelling at you for no reason.

Instead, I'd spent half the time kissing him, which was probably why I hadn't caught on too quickly.

"You're not supposed to let it go when you swing it. For shit's sake." Gwenn picked it up and tossed it back to me.

This time, I caught it, but barely, and I ended up hitting myself in the stomach. If I survived this training, it'd be a miracle. The only plus side was at least we weren't using real blades; otherwise we'd both be dead about now. Although I bet if I had the Blade of the Four Kingdoms, I wouldn't be so clumsy. Something about that weapon gave me confidence — and it felt almost alive in my hands. Like the day in the river with the Kelpie. But it was a real blade, and I didn't want to chance killing my future sister-in-law — even though she was kind of pissing me off at the moment.

For the next few hours, Gwenn attempted to show me how to wield a sword. She went through different movements and stances, none of which could I master. Gwenn's irritation poured off her like rain.

"I want you to go on the offensive," she said.

I sucked in a deep breath, my heart pounding. "What if I hit you?"

She smirked. "I don't think we need to worry about that."

Jerk. Just for that I hoped I gave her splinters in her face. Trying not to overthink it, I stepped toward her, my fake blade moving in an arc. With a quick flick of the wrist, she disarmed me, then rushed forward, knocking me to the ground.

Damn it. I leapt to my feet once more and retrieved my

weapon. My chest heaved as I tried to catch my breath. No way would I ever get this.

"Again," Gwenn said. "This time don't rush into it. Watch my movements."

"I'm trying. Believe it or not, we don't do sword crap in my world."

"This *crap* might save your life one day. Because *believe it or not*, you might not always have guards to protect you."

"That's not what I meant…" I kind of wanted to tell her that I'd already saved myself once, but I doubted she'd believe me, and I didn't want to sound like I was bragging.

She glowered. "Get into position. This time you'll be on the defensive."

My fingers clenched the wooden handle. I squared my shoulders. Gwenn rushed at me. I barely had time to lift my sword. *Thwack.* Her weapon struck mine, jarring me. I tried to hold my ground, but I stumbled backward beneath the force.

Once more, I found myself on my butt, with my makeshift blade several feet away from me. I rubbed my elbow. Tomorrow, I'd be nothing but one giant bruise.

"Okay, I might need a minute to rest," I said as I climbed to my knees and rested my hands on my thighs.

Gwenn stared at me, eyes narrowed. "You know what? I think we're done with our lesson. You're far too fragile. You'd think if my brother was going to pick a human woman, he'd at least make sure she had a back bone."

Tears burned my eyes as I shifted my gaze to the ground. Screw her. And this stupid place. I bit back the lump in my throat and fought to compose myself. No way in flipping hell did I want her to see me cry. After a second, I pushed to my feet only to find Gwenn stalking off.

I picked up my sword and flipped it over in my hand. *What*

am I doing here? Seriously? I should've just made Gareth take me home where I belonged.

The scent of autumn leaves filled my nostrils. A slight chill swept across my skin.

"Here, let me help you." Lord Darach came up behind me. I gasped as I felt his ghostly touch.

Okay, I was pretty sure I shouldn't be able to feel him. Yet I did. One more mystery to add to the mix. *Awesome.* "Darach? Wait, how are you here?"

He just smiled. *"You looked like you were having a hard time wielding your weapon."*

I rolled my eyes. "Was I that obvious?"

He chuckled. *"All you need is a teacher with more patience."*

"Good luck with that. I doubt I'll ever learn what I'm doing."

"You will, I promise. Now, let me guide you through your movements. They'll seem strange at first. But hold them, let your body get used to them."

His fingers moved up my arms until his hands covered mine. Together we lifted the sword. He led me in several different maneuvers. We swiped the air, arcing and poking and swinging. When my wrists or arms started to go in the wrong direction, he'd catch us mid swing and get me back on course.

Warmth radiated through me as he pressed against my back. For a second, my skin tingled and my blood heated. I glanced down as his fingers disappeared into my flesh.

Oh God, what's happening?

Somehow, he'd sunk inside me—almost as if he'd possessed me. When he realized what had happened, he jerked back, taking with him the sudden heat I'd felt.

"I-I'm sorry. That's never happened before."

"No, it's okay." I spun to face him. In that brief connection,

I'd seen a flash of his humanity. Of the guy he used to be. He reminded me a lot of Gareth.

Giggles erupted from across the yard. A few nobles walked past me with strange looks on their faces.

"Can they see you?"

"*No, so far you're the only one who can.*"

My gaze met his. "Why are you here in Summer?"

He shrugged, then gave me a smile. "*I don't know. Ever since you came to the Ruined Court, I've felt attached to you. Like I have to be where you are. Besides, someone needs to watch after you to make sure Nevin doesn't do anything foolish. I don't want you to suffer the same fate as me.*"

My fingers traced the wooden sword I still held. "So you've been here since I arrived? Keeping an eye on me?"

"*Yes. I traveled with you from the Ruined Court.*"

I gasped. "Wait, you haven't watched me bathe or change, have you?"

He chuckled. "*No. I'm an honorable ghost.*"

"Y-you better be." My eyes traveled over him, coming to rest on the two arrows protruding from his chest. "Do you want me to try and take those out for you?"

He nodded. "*I don't think they'll budge. The winter queen spelled them. They're what kept me tethered to the Ruined Court. To her and her bidding. That is until you came.*"

I placed my weapon on the nearby fence post then turned to him. My fingers trembled as I gripped hold of one of the thin shafts. With a tug, it pulled loose. Then I moved to the other and dislodged that one as well. When I glanced down, I realized they were real. Not ghost arrows. But actual wood.

He gasped. "*You've freed me from the tether.*"

"The arrows, what do I do with them?"

A burst of eagerness and anticipation crossed his face.

"Break them."

I held the two weapons up and snapped them in half. Tendrils of smoke flared up as they lit on fire.

"Holy crap." I dropped them and watched as flame consumed them. Soon it burned out, and there was nothing left of them.

Darach eyed me, but his smile slipped away. *"You've got company. I'll see you soon, Salome."*

And like that, he disappeared right as Nevin sauntered over to me.

"Ah, there you are. Gwenn said she started your training today."

I snorted. "Yeah, if you want to call it that."

"I'm glad you decided to learn how to wield a sword. It never hurts to know how to defend yourself. And Gwenn is a good teacher."

My mouth gaped open. "Um—yeah, I don't think she likes me. At all."

"Just give her time."

Why did everyone think we'd be best friends? Didn't they get it? Gwenn hated me. And if I was honest, I didn't care for her either.

Nevin ushered me toward the palace. I glanced over my shoulder to find Darach sitting on the fence, watching me. For the first time since I'd arrived here, I realized I might have an ally and a friend.

Too bad he's a ghost.

CHAPTER TWENTY-ONE

Salome

$\mathcal{I}$ slipped into a pair of breeches, then tugged a tunic over my head. For the last couple of days, Gwenn had had me out training with her. She'd pushed me to the point of exhaustion and had treated me like her own personal battering ram. I had the bruises to prove it.

I didn't really see any improvement during her practices. She just kept beating the crap out of me, which might have been the whole point.

But once she finished with me, Darach would appear and run me through different drills. He said it'd take me more than a few days to get used to the movements and feel competent enough to fight. He claimed it could take months or years before I developed the skills I needed, but his kindness and patience made me want to be better.

With a sigh, I tied my hair up in a ponytail, then sat on the edge of my bed to pull on my boots.

The scent of autumnal leaves surrounded me, and I sighed, already sure who I would see. Darach appeared next to the balcony door.

"Morning," I said, standing to greet him.

"Morning to you." He grinned. *"I got to thinking last night, while you slept."*

My eyebrows rose. "About?"

"How would you like to show up Gwenn today?"

I snorted. "Um—are you on drugs?'

He gave me a quizzical look. *"What?"*

"I mean, you're joking right? You've been at all my practices. I have absolutely no chance at winning. She's too good."

He ran a ghostly hand through his auburn hair. *"What if I helped you?"*

"But what if someone sees you?"

"They won't. I told you, you're the only one who can." He smirked, floating over until he stood in front of me. For a moment, he seemed taller than normal—stronger. He touched my hand. *"It'll be fun."*

He was right. It'd be fun to finally show Gwenn I wasn't this prissy, weak human she thought I was. Besides, it wasn't like I could do any worse than I already had.

"Okay, I'm in. I sure hope this doesn't backfire." My gaze met his.

"It won't, I promise. It's about time they start giving you the respect you deserve. You've done so much for Summer by freeing the ungrateful Nevin from his curse and risking your life to come here." His eyes darkened.

Whoa, I wasn't expecting that. "Well, thank you. I suppose we ought to go then."

When I arrived at the training grounds beside the barracks, Gwenn stood with her arms crossed, waiting for me. "You're late," she snapped.

"Sorry, I was getting dressed."

She tossed my wooden sword at me. This time, I caught it

midair.

"Thought I'd stop in and see how your training is coming along." Nevin sauntered over to the fence and leaned against it.

"Be prepared for the worst, Your Highness." Gwenn frowned. "Your hu—guest isn't taking to it as quickly as we hoped."

"Don't listen to her." Darach popped up next to me. *"She's jealous that you're getting so much attention."*

I nodded but didn't dare answer him. The last thing I needed was for them to believe me insane. My pulse quickened, nervousness coiling in my belly. I hated having an audience. Trust me, I was bad enough without having the added pressure.

"Relax," Darach whispered in my ear. *"I'm going to take control now, okay?"*

I gasped as I felt his warmth beneath my skin. My body tingled I closed my eyes for a second, feeling two heartbeats thrumming within me. This seemed so intimate, the way his movements meshed with mine. Our breathing leveled until it was the same.

This was so much like putting on a favorite sweater. Did it feel the same for Darach? Did the same warmth encompass him? But then another thought flooded my mind. What if he permanently possessed me? Was this some guise to take control of me? Maybe I should order him out of me and just face Gwenn on my own.

"Are you ready?" Gwenn's voice broke through my thoughts. My arms raised as Darach lifted his. "Yes."

"Relax," he said. *"I won't hurt you. You have my word."*

But what did I really know about him? Thing was, he'd had plenty of opportunities to do something to me before now. And I needed this small victory if I wanted to move forward. If it came to it, I'd fight Darach for control of my body. But for now? It was time to show Gwenn a nice surprise.

So I shoved my doubts aside and let him control my actions.

If nothing else, it let my body get used to the maneuvers of fighting, which would only aid me in the future.

She smirked, bringing her weapon in an arc and jabbing at my chest. But Darach stepped to the side. He then swung our blade upward. It caught Gwenn's and sent her makeshift blade flying. Her mouth gaped as if she didn't believe what just happened.

"Well wasn't that a lucky defensive movement," she said when she picked her sword up from the ground. "Bet you can't do that again."

A small thrill wriggled in my chest. *"We'll see about that,"* Darach whispered.

His words made me smile, and we took our stance once more. This time, Darach didn't wait for Gwenn to come at us. Instead, he hefted our weapon and charged forward. She raised her sword to block our advance. But we dodged to the side and brought our blade upward, catching her in the ribs.

Her face reddened, and she rolled to the side and came up behind us. Darach spun us around, lifting our practice sword right as hers was about to come down.

The wooden swords collided with a loud *thwack*. She attempted to shove me backward with her strength. But with Darach's help, I held my ground. My leg came up and caught her in the stomach, separating us and giving me enough room to drive my fake blade into her shoulder.

Sweat dripped down my forehead, burning my eyes. I blinked, then wiped my face on my sleeve. Gwenn let out a low growl and came at me again. But Darach twisted to the side then took our weapon and jabbed her in the ribs. She fell to her knees and stared up at me like I'd grown three heads.

"You've certainly improved. I'll give you this round. But tomorrow, we're having a rematch." Gwenn gave me a forced smile. "Congratulations. Looks like you're better than you let on. Or maybe you're just better with an audience."

I held my hand out to help her up. But she avoided it; instead she stood on her own, then wiped her palms on her breeches, her glance shifting when Nevin joined us.

"What a fabulous match. See, Gwenn, I told you that if anyone could teach her, it was you."

If they only knew. But I grinned, too. Although Gwenn didn't look happy about losing to me, I saw a brief moment of respect in her eyes, which was more than I could've hoped for. Maybe she'd eventually accept me, or at least be nicer.

Nevin reached for my arm, and I took a step back. He came up short and gave me a sheepish smile. "I'm proud of you. You've worked really hard. Gareth will be shocked to see how much you've learned in his absence."

At that moment, I heard Darach whisper goodbye. All at once, my body went cold. My skin puckered with goose bumps. The fullness I'd felt before was gone. I guess he'd meant what he'd said, and I'd been right to take a chance on him. He had no intention of possessing me forever. He just wanted to help.

Over Nevin's shoulder, I saw Darach. He glowed brighter, as if he'd been dipped in sunshine. His gaze met mine, and he gave me a lopsided grin.

I mouthed the words "Thank you." He nodded then disappeared.

"The three of us should have lunch," Nevin said, escorting me toward the palace.

Gwenn came up on my other side, carrying our weapons. "I underestimated you. But I promise, I'll never do that again. You're the first one to best me in years. But don't think I'll let it happen again."

Pride bubbled inside me. Okay, so I'd had help beating her, but it felt so good. My smile widened. "It's okay. I understand."

When we crossed into the gardens, a sudden, sheer pain overtook me. "Oh my God."

I dropped to my knees. A scream tore from my lips, and I clutched my chest.

Something's wrong.

Everything hurt. My body felt like it was on fire, and I fell forward onto all fours.

Please make it stop.

"Salome? What's wrong?" Nevin dropped down beside me.

No. This isn't happening. I gasped for air. My lungs burned. I couldn't breathe.

"Salome? Answer me. Are you okay?" Nevin tilted my head back.

It was then I realized it wasn't my pain I felt. It was Gareth.

"Gareth!" Damn it! "What's wrong? Please. Answer me!"

For a brief second, I thought his mind opened up to me. But then the doors slammed shut.

"Gareth."

Tears ran down my cheeks. Nevin quickly lifted me into his arms. "Salome, answer me? What's wrong?"

"I-I think something's happened to Gareth." I sobbed, burying my head against his tunic.

"I'm sure he's fine." He glanced at Gwenn.

"Nevin's right. Gareth's the strongest soldier in Summer. He'll be all right."

I wanted to believe them, but I'd sensed his pain. And he wouldn't have closed me off like that unless he was trying to hide it from me.

"Let's get you to your room." Nevin carried me into the palace and upstairs. "Everything will be okay."

But somehow, I knew it wasn't. Gareth was hurt. And I was too far away to do anything about it.

CHAPTER TWENTY-TWO

Salome

The hot bath water did nothing for my nerves. Steam rolled up around me like mist in a graveyard.

"Gareth, can you hear me? Please, answer."

My wrinkled fingers gripped the sides of the tub as I waited, but still he didn't respond. I hadn't sensed him through our link in a couple of days.

What if he's dead? I swallowed hard. *No. I won't believe it. He's probably just healing.*

I squeezed my eyes shut. *"Gareth, if you can hear me. Please talk to me. I need to know you're okay. I need you."*

Tears trickled down my face, and I pushed myself to my feet. Rivulets of water trailed down my skin. I grabbed the towel and wrapped it around me. Summer air blew through the opened balcony doors, but despite its warmth, goosebumps broke out over my body. I shivered and hurried to dry myself off.

Once finished, I slipped into a long white nightgown and sat on the edge of my bed to brush out my damp hair.

Okay, there was no need to freak out yet. I mean, the same thing had happened when Gareth fought the trolls. We'd lost contact then, and he'd still come back to me.

But this is different.

I set my brush on the trunk at the end of my bed then slid beneath my silken covers. The scent of my rose shampoo wafted in the air as darkness settled in. I propped my head up on my pillows and stared at the star cluttered sky.

With a sigh, I rolled on my side, and my eyelids fluttered shut. The light sound of wooden flutes drifted into my room, relaxing me like a lullaby.

The room is filled with bones and ice. In the corner, someone cowers, hands covering her face. When she looks up, I gasp. "Kadie?"

But she doesn't answer, instead she stares across the ice glazed room to where a girl is propped on a stone block. A blade gleams beneath the candlelight. Before I can turn away, I watch in horror as an axe comes down, severing the girl's head from her body.

Blood sprays the snow colored floor. Kadie screams.

A laugh echoes through the room. I turn to find Grisselle sitting on a throne made of skeletons, giggling and clapping.

So much blood. So many bones.

Winter.

Winter is coming for me…

"Noooo…" Kadie yells.

"Nooo!" I bolted upright in bed, sweat running down my forehead.

My door burst open, and Gwenn rushed in, sword drawn. "Salome? What's wrong?"

"Oh God, I-I saw the blood and bones and snow. Grisselle was there. She had my friend." I choked back a sob, shaking as I knotted my blanket in my hands.

She lit several candles, her face pale. "I think I'd better get Nevin. He's better suited to dealing with human emotions."

Gwenn hurried from the room, and I sucked in a deep

breath, trying to calm myself. For a moment, I thought I saw Darach's image in my mirror, but it disappeared when Nevin busted in.

"Salome? Are you okay?" He sat on the edge of my bed.

"I had a horrible nightmare," I sobbed as I went on to explain the gruesome details.

He tilted my head upward and gave me a startled look. "Are you sure you saw Grisselle?"

"Yes, she's not someone I'd ever forget."

He smoothed my hair from my face. "Don't worry, everything will be okay."

I sniffled. "I-I don't think I'll be able to go back to sleep."

Nevin stood, then hefted me into his arms. "You'll stay in my chambers tonight. I promise I won't let anything happen to you."

We walked down the hall to his room. A lone candle burned near his king-sized bed. Dark blue drapes were tied back at the posts, revealing a mountain of blankets and pillows. The rest of the room was in shadows, but I made out a few marble statues, and the weapons rack near the far wall.

He set me down on his mattress. "Here, climb under the covers. I'll sit in the chair and keep an eye on you tonight."

"A—are you sure? I don't want to impose."

"Yes. Now get some rest."

The scent of fresh cut grass and honey tickled my nostrils as I tugged his blankets about my shoulders. My gaze met his, and he plopped down into the chair next to me. He reached out and stroked my face.

"Sleep well, Salome."

I yawned, fighting the tiredness until at last, sleep won out.

*S*unlight spilled into the room. I stretched out and, with a sigh, flung my legs over the edge of the bed. I noticed Nevin asleep in an overstuffed settee. His dark lashes brushed his cheeks. Without the worry lines creasing his brow, he seemed so innocent and young.

For a moment, I watched him, trying to gauge if he was truly asleep or not. My gaze slid over his room once more to a mahogany desk in the corner beneath a tapestry of a wild stag. On top of it, I noticed the letter from my grandmother.

Quiet as I could, I moved across the floor. With a glance over my shoulder to make sure Nevin still slept, I picked the note up and slid it from the envelope.

Nevin,

I received your letter in regards to Salome having powers. I cannot answer that at this time. The only thing I can tell you is she belongs in Faerie. There was a reason I discouraged her from falling in love with you here in the human world. I feared she would lose her life to the curse, and that would have forsaken us all. She has a greater purpose than you can imagine. And my life has been spent preserving her and her innocence. If Salome falls, so do we all.

You must keep her safe while she's in Faerie, for her time is coming to do great things. I do not know what your intentions are, but I hope you will heed my words and not do anything foolish. Tell Gareth he must do everything in his power to keep her from Grisselle's clutches, which means it might be time to move her to the Summer Palace where your magic is stronger.

My borders are still holding, but I don't know how long

they will remain safe. Things are coming to fruition which were foretold long ago. Send my love to Salome. Tell her we love her and miss her. Remind her she is strong and she'll know what to do when the time comes.

Always,

Doris

My fingers trembled as I read the note again. What the hell did this mean? Why did I need to come to Faerie? Did I really have powers after all? If so, was that why Nevin had pushed so hard to have me be his queen? None of this made sense. And if Grandma knew something, why hadn't she told me?

Nevin shifted in the chair, and I quickly shoved the letter back in the envelope and pretended to stare out the window. After a moment, I glanced at him again and kept looking, wondering when he'd wake up. Then his eyes opened, and he caught me staring.

"Why do I feel like an art piece in a museum?"

"Sorry, I didn't mean to wake you."

He stretched his long legs, then stood. "No, I needed to get up anyway. I hope you slept well?"

"Surprisingly, yeah." I wanted to ask him about the note, but I didn't need him to think I was snooping around. Damn. I wondered if Darach might know anything.

"Listen, why don't I walk you back to your quarters so you can change. Then I'll take the rest of the morning off—take you someplace special."

"Really? I mean, I don't want to keep you from anything."

"Trust me, I can use a break from court for a few hours. The Council has given me enough headaches in recent days."

When we stepped into the hallway, several servants turned

to stare at us. Mouths gaping, they went about their tasks, whispering to one another as they nodded and pointed in our direction.

"What's up with them?" I asked when Nevin let me in my door.

"Um—they think we're together."

My eyes widened. "What?"

"They saw you come out of my room disheveled."

"Nevin!" I swatted at his arm. "You have to fix this. Last thing I need are rumors spreading through the kingdom that we spent the night together. Especially since everyone knows I'm with Gareth. How do you think that makes me look?"

"It's fine. I promise to take care of everything. Now get changed, I'll be back in a couple minutes."

Ugh. Sometimes Nevin was so infuriating—like now. I didn't want everyone to think I'd been with him. With a groan, I whipped off my nightgown, tossed it on my bed, and grabbed a clean dress from my armoire.

Once I had it on, I twisted my hair up in a braid and waited for him to come back. It didn't take long for him to reappear. When we left my room, he offered me his arm.

"So where are we going?"

"To my private gardens." He ushered me down a back staircase to a large oak gate. There he produced a key from around his neck. He inserted the metal into the lock and twisted it. Soon, the barrier swung open and he led me inside.

"Wow." I sucked in a deep breath as I spun to glance at the roses, violets, and lilies that grew along the walkway. Fountains sprayed overhead, like a water archway. "I don't know if I'm gonna ever get used to how gorgeous this place is. Sometimes I feel like I've stepped into one of my fairytales."

"That's because you have." He smiled, tugging me toward

large stone stairs.

We climbed upward, the sound of waterfalls crashing as we neared the top. Beams of sun splayed across a grassy field, while trees rocked back and forth beneath the breeze. Nevin guided me to a great white oak on the edge of a creek. As we neared it, I noticed a swing hanging from its branch.

"Hop on," he said.

"Seriously?"

"Don't tell me you've never been on a swing before?"

I rolled my eyes. "Of course I have. Geez, I was like the queen of playground swings when I was in elementary school."

I turned around, scooted on the swing, and clung tight to the ropes.

"Hold on." Nevin gave me a push.

With a squeal, I whooshed through the air. I pumped my legs, going higher and higher. As the wind licked at my face, I felt like I was flying. I closed my eyes, imagining I soared through the sky.

"If you keep your eyes shut, you'll miss the view," Nevin said.

I opened my eyes and stared in awe. From this place, I saw the entire kingdom. The palace. The waterfalls. Trees. Flowers. It was so perfect.

"Amazing," I said, glancing at him.

"I thought you might like it." He reached out and slowed the swing. "I know things have been tough for you lately, but I want you to know that you're welcome here. And I want you to enjoy everything you can."

"Thank you." For a brief moment, it felt like we were back in the human world. Back when he and I used to sit for hours on my grandpa's hammock just talking, when I believed him to be one of my best and closest friends. Before I found out it'd been an act.

Guilt set in. I shouldn't be having fun. Not when my boyfriend was out there somewhere defending Summer.

Maybe spending time alone with Nevin wasn't such a good idea. Underneath all that arrogance, I knew he could be charming, and I didn't want to fall for that trap again.

"What's wrong?"

I gave him a forced smile. "Nothing. Just worried for Gareth."

He frowned. "He'd want you to enjoy things. Not be cooped up in your room the entire time he's gone."

Before either of us had a chance to say anything else, one of his guards appeared. "Sorry to bother you, Your Highness, but the Council has requested your presence."

"I ought to tell them to wait, but I'm sure they've heard some rumors this morning that I should set straight," he said to me.

"Actually, Your Highness, we've received word from some of our border patrols that Winter kidnapped more humans."

Nevin's eyes darkened. "Tell the Council I'll be along shortly."

My mouth went dry. "What does he mean, Winter kidnapped more humans?"

He glanced at me. "Grisselle has been doing it for centuries. We've been able to shut down some of her trafficking points, but she always finds new routes. Trust me, Salome, I'm not happy about this. When she does things like this, it makes people question what's going on. And if enough people pay attention to what's going on around them, then eventually they find the answers they seek—which could lead to the discovery of Faerie."

"So Winter's filtering into the human world? Grisselle is taking my people?" This hit closer to home. Not that I didn't care about Faerie—I mean, of course I did. I cared about the children who'd been displaced by this war. About the refugees who had to keep moving in order to outrun Winter's soldiers. About the kingdoms that'd been destroyed—whole lines wiped out. The thing was, my family was in the human world, which meant they, too, were in danger.

"Don't panic; we'll figure this out. I promise." He tilted my chin so I looked at him, then bent forward. His lips brushed my forehead. A strange tingle pulsed across my brow, like tiny ants marched on my skin. Nevin took a step back, eyes wide.

"What?"

"If you ever had any doubt about being my queen, this should prove you're meant to be." He guided me to a shallow pool of water and pointed down. "Look at your reflection."

There, on my forehead, was a golden tattoo of a crown. "Um—okay, what is that?"

He rested his hands on my shoulders. "All royals or Fae nobility are branded by magical tattoos. They only appear when a noble is born or before a coronation to indicate who should rule."

"Holy crap. You're not serious." I touched my face, tracing over the tattoo.

"Yes, I'm very serious."

"H-how do I know you didn't just put a spell on me or something?" Freaked out, I took a step back. This couldn't be true. I was supposed to be with Gareth. It had to be a lie.

"Salome, I can't do spells like this. I'm speaking the truth. You've been marked by Summer. I had no hand in this."

"But you've been bugging me since I got here about being your queen."

"Because I sensed magic in you. Strong power that could save our people, Salome. I wanted you for my queen, but that didn't mean you'd necessarily have been marked. But you have been, and that means something, something greater than I think you realize. You're the first human to ever be accepted by Faerie—to be chosen as one of her court."

"S-so the land chooses?"

"I guess you could say that."

If that was true, then fate didn't care about love. Summer wanted me to be with Nevin for the good of the kingdom.

What was I going to do? If Gareth was here, he'd tell me whether to trust Nevin or not. *Gareth*. Oh god, what would I say to him? Would he be mad? Did this mean I couldn't be with him? So many questions swarmed my mind.

Anxiety seeped in, and I took several deep breaths. Okay, I just had to calm down. I peeked at my reflection once more and even went as far as getting my hand wet and trying to rub it off. But it only sparkled more, glinting in the sun as if it were a real crown. Holy shit. It looked pretty real to me. I just needed to be rational and not freak out.

When I'd calmed myself some, I turned to Nevin. "Do you have one? A tattoo I mean?"

"Yes. I was born with it."

"But it's not on your face."

"No."

"Then where is it?"

He quirked an eyebrow. "Are you sure you want to see it?"

"Well as long as it's not on your butt cheek or something."

"Definitely not on my backside." He unlaced his tunic and pulled the sky blue material open. There, on his chest, was a golden tattoo of a crown. Golden vines spiraled down his chest and navel. Intricate spirals; in the sunlight, it almost looked like golden armor.

"I should probably go see the council before they send the troops for me," he said. "I'm not going to mention this to them yet, but they'll see it or hear about it soon enough." He gazed around his garden then back to me. "You can stay out here if you'd like. I can leave one of my guards with you."

"No. It's okay. I'd actually like to check out the library." I dodged away from him. My foot caught on a clump of grass, and I went sailing forward.

Nevin grabbed my arm, steadying me before I face planted on the ground. "That last step is a bastard."

"So I noticed." I laughed, shoving my hair over my face to hide the tattoo. I didn't want the attention, not until I figured what was going on and how the hell I'd explain this to Gareth when he came back.

We made our way down the hill and into the palace, at which point we went our separate ways. I followed the rose shaped tiles to a ginormous archway, which opened into the biggest library I'd ever seen in my life.

It was four stories, floor to ceiling filled with books. Ma hogany spiral staircases wound upward to the top level. Tables occupied several areas, along with wicker hanging chairs.

"May I help you?" A short bald man appeared in front of me.

"Um—I wondered if you had any books on the Ruined Court?" I covered my forehead with my hand, hoping he didn't notice anything out of the ordinary.

His mouth fell open in a surprised "*O,*" and his beady eyes narrowed. "And what would you like it for?"

Hmmm…touchy subject?

"I traveled through there on my way here. I was just curious about it." I gave a noncommittal shrug.

"I'm afraid the only information I have is a book on the Great Betrayal. When Winter destroyed Autumn and Spring."

Okay, so in a library this big, they didn't have one article, tome, or book on the Ruined Court? He had to be lying. But I gave him a smile. "Sure, I'll take a look at that instead."

He scampered away like a mouse being chased by a cat. His small form disappeared behind the stacks only to reemerge a moment later with a tome almost as big as he was. "Where would you like to sit?"

"Near the windows, please." I gestured to the back of library, hoping for some privacy.

When we got to the furthest table, he dropped the book with a loud thud. "If you need anything else, please don't hesitate to ask."

When he left, I settled into the high-backed chair and flipped through a few pages. Illustrations of Grisselle popped off the paper. Even from this depiction, she pulsed with evilness.

Darach zapped in beside me. *"I see you're feeling much better after last night."*

"Holy shit!" I jumped, covering my chest with my hand. "You scared the crap out of me."

"Sorry. I thought you saw me." Darach leaned closer.

I glanced at him. "I'm glad you're here. I-I've got to ask you a question."

"Go ahead."

"Have you ever seen anything like this?" I pulled my hair away from my head to show him my tattoo.

His eyes widened. "Yes. You've been marked. This is unbelievable." He leaned closer, his ghostly hand swiping over the gold etching. "When did this happen?"

"In the garden when I was with Nevin." I took a deep breath, fingers trembling. "So what does this mean?"

"It means that the Kingdom of Summer has claimed you as their queen. I knew when I first met you that there was something special about you, Salome." Sadness seemed to wash over his features.

"But I can't be queen, I don't love Nevin. Maybe Summer got it wrong—like maybe Faerie is breaking down and accidentally marked me."

"Markings are not accidental. Faerie knows your heart. And it chose you."

"What about Gareth? I can't just not be with him? We are Blood Bound."

"You don't have to choose anything right now. But at least consider what's at stake—"

At least I knew Nevin wasn't lying to me when he'd said I'd been marked. A part of me wished he had been. I didn't want the weight of the kingdom's well-being on my shoulders—or the thought of losing Gareth.

Darach glanced over my shoulder. *"What are you reading?"* I held it up so he could see the title. His smile slipped away. "Are you okay?"

He nodded and slid into the chair next to mine. Even though he was a ghost, I could see the sorrow etched on his face. *"Yes. It's just hard to see the life of my people summed up in an ancient volume and tucked away on a shelf somewhere. Like we're only a history lesson, nothing more."*

My chest tightened, and I reached for his ghost-like hand. When my fingers touched his, warmth shot through me. "You're not a history lesson. Besides, I thought I might be able to find some way to help you."

"Help me?"

"Well, when we first met, you mentioned being stuck here. I—I thought maybe I might find a way to free you."

"Do you think you'll find information here?" He quirked an eyebrow.

"Probably not, but it's worth a try. I mean, I did accidentally find a way to break your tether to the Ruined Court."

"That you did." His eyes shifted to the window, where a red rose pressed against the glass. *"Salome, there's something I wanted to talk to you about."*

"Sure, what's up?"

"Last night, something happened to you…"

I fiddled with the leather binding on the book. "Um—yeah, I had a nightmare."

"No. It was more than that. I think you're coming into power. That dream you had might've been a vision."

Startled, I sat up straighter. "How could that be? Kadie's not in Faerie. She's in Texas. Besides, Nevin would've told me." Right, the same way he'd told me what my grandma had said.

Wasn't he the first one to suggest I had powers? That I'd somehow conjured a shield in the forest outside Gareth's? All this time, I'd hoped those coincidences had been just that, but what if I did harbor magic? That would mean Nevin had been right and he wasn't hiding secrets from me again. Didn't that mean he would have told me if Kadie was somehow in Faerie?

Darach sighed, his body shimmering as sunlight hit him. He clasped hold of my hand. *"Would he tell you?"*

"I—yes. I think so."

"You don't sound so sure."

"Listen, I'm not sure what's going on with me—I mean, I am standing here talking to a ghost—but wouldn't I have sensed something, I don't know…bigger? More earth shattering than a few tingles on my skin or whatnot?"

"Not necessarily. It might not work the same for you since you weren't born in Faerie. Just be careful. Nevin seems to withhold a lot from you. I don't want to see you get hurt." He gave my fingers a squeeze.

"Would there be any way for you to know for sure if I had powers?"

He stared at me for long moments. *"If you breaking my tether to the Ruined Court isn't a sure indication, then I don't know what is. But perhaps we could try a few spells to see for sure."*

"When?" The need to know the truth burned throughout me. I needed a purpose, something else to focus on while Gareth was away. And if it was true that I had magic, I wanted to know how to use it.

"We could try to test you now. It's been centuries since I've been able to wield magic—but I think I can explain to you how to embrace it and use it."

"Okay, just tell me what I need to do."

Darach moved closer to me. *"I want you to focus on this book. Visualize the air around it. Now, I want you to use the air to lift the book. Imagine the air blowing in from beneath it and carrying it."*

I concentrated on the leather bound book. In my mind, I willed the air to sweep under it, like Darach said. At first, nothing happened. Then all at once, the tome went flying through the air, crashing into the wall, and falling to the floor.

My throat nearly closed off as I choked back a scream. Holy crap. Had I done that?

Darach watched me. *"Well I'd say we've confirmed you have power. But just how strong, we will have to see."*

A dark haired noble woman turned to glance at me and picked up the book I'd sent flying into the wall. "Yours?"

I took it back from her, hoping she hadn't seen too much. "Yes. Thanks."

She nodded and started to turn away, then stopped and said, "Who are you talking to?"

Right. No one could see the ghost. "Sorry, I was reading aloud to myself and dropped my book. I didn't mean to disturb you."

Her lips curled up in a sneer as she turned away.

Great. Now the whole castle would definitely think me crazy. But more than that, Darach's words made me doubt whether Nevin knew more than he'd let on about my nightmare.

I hoped for both our sakes he didn't, because I damn sure didn't want that bad dream to come true. However, I was kind of scared to have figured out what everyone else said was true: that I'd come into magic. Would this now make me a bigger target for Grisselle? And should I tell Nevin and Gareth, or just keep it a secret? I mean, they already had an idea that I might have some abilities, but now I wasn't sure if I wanted to confirm them. What was I capable of, and how would these powers change everything?

I cradled my head in my hands. Damn. I didn't know what to do about any of this. The magic. The marking. The nightmare. Everything just kept getting more complicated.

CHAPTER TWENTY-THREE

Kadie

I stood in a long green gown. The top of it fit snug against my chest, covered in white and emerald pearls. The silken skirt swished at my ankles as I walked.

"Hold still," Rena ordered as she twisted my hair atop my head. "Otherwise your hair will look like a pine cone."

"Sorry," I muttered.

At last, she finished. Not meaning to, I glanced at Etienne. His eyes sparkled.

"You look beautiful."

My face flushed, the heat rushing up my neck. No matter how real it felt, the attraction between us was just a means to an end now. I had to get out of here. I had to escape before something else terrible happened.

"Thank you," I said.

"It's time we go see the queen. Whatever you do, stick close to me. Or at least try to."

I chewed my bottom lip. The last place I wanted to be was with the queen tonight. She might've let me live after the escape, but that didn't mean I was off her radar. Who was to say she didn't have something horrific planned for me over dinner?

Sweat beaded my brow, and I fought to keep composed — to show no emotion.

Etienne led me down a hidden hallway that I'd never been through before. There seemed to be more light here; the décor was less gruesome. There were tapestries of sunshine beaming down on glittering snow; deer and antelope were drinking from a nearly frozen spring. Crystal snowflakes seemed to float in the air above our heads, glittering and glistening beneath the light.

Tiny windows let in the drab daylight, but it was better than the constant darkness I was used to seeing in the castle. At last we came to a pair of ornate golden doors with snowflakes and holly etched into them.

Two troll guards swung them open. The scent of turkey, potatoes, fresh baked bread, and pine wafted in the air around us. I gasped when we stepped inside. Instead of the macabre blood and bones I was used to seeing, there was a large white marble fireplace, with strands of pine boughs hanging above it. The ceiling had pictures of sleighs and bonfires and dancing couples. The walls were draped in white and red and gold. A chandelier with crystal snowflakes hung above a long table, which was filled with all my favorite foods.

The queen stood, wearing a long blue silky dress, sapphires fastened at her throat. She smiled. And not the menacing one she normally gave me. I noticed the only other people present were a few of her winter princes, minus Teodor.

"Kadie, come, have a seat next to me at the table. I've had a feast made in your honor." She gestured to the two ornate chairs near the head of the table.

I glanced at Etienne. What the hell was going on? Maybe she'd poisoned the food and wanted to watch me die a slow, painful death. Or maybe this was like my last meal. My legs trembled beneath me as I looked around the room.

Etienne gave my hand a squeeze, but I had no idea if it was meant to be encouraging or if he was warning me of something. Either way I had my guard up because the Winter Queen didn't *do* nice, at least not that I'd witnessed.

Etienne led me to the place beside the queen, where a servant pulled my chair out for me. Hesitant, I sat down, trying to ignore the uneasiness in my stomach. I gazed about the room once more, searching for any hidden weapons or torture devices—something that might tell me my fate. I didn't spot anything, but then maybe that was the point. She didn't want me to see it coming.

A satyr dished food onto my plate, then poured me a glass of wine. When he finished, he took a step back and went down the line, getting stuff for everyone else.

Etienne nudged my leg, nodding for me to eat. I picked up my silverware and dipped it into the steaming pile of potatoes.

Well, here goes nothing.

"My dear Kadie, I think you and I got off to a bad start," the queen said, watching me eat.

No shit. That was an understatement. I'd seen the victims in the Bone Yard and in the castle. What the hell was she playing at?

"You see, I can be very nice when I want to be. It's only when my patience is tested that I get angry. And lately with the things going on in Faerie, I've been doubly stressed. I've got a kingdom to maintain and take care of, but there are others in these lands who mean to take that from me. So I must defend what's mine, which means I have to show my strength. Make people fear me."

"But how does this concern me? I didn't want to come to Winter. I just want to go home," I said, setting my fork down on my plate.

"You have some vital information that could aid me in the war against my enemy. Most prisoners break the first night without any interrogation at all. But you, you're stronger than most. Such a curious thing. I really hope you don't force my hand further. I want to be nice, Kadie, but you will realize that I shall not be denied anything."

The hair on the back of my neck bristled. So that's what this was about? She thought I'd spill what I knew. I'd already given her a couple details that I really hadn't planned on giving, hoping to save Demetria, my friend, who she'd ordered to be murdered. "And how do I know you won't do to me what you did to Demetria or any of the other girls? That you aren't going to just get information from me then kill me?"

Her piercing blue eyes met mine. "Demetria was punished for disobeying me. She lived way beyond her human years here in Faerie, longer than she would've survived in your world. I can be a reasonable person. But sometimes it's hard to trust people. And that, Kadie, is where you and I are alike. I can offer you the life you deserve. You will be second fiddle to no one. You will have the best dresses and the finest chamber. I can give you jewels and any choice of the Fae Lords here, including the Winter Princes. You will want for nothing—you will be crowned as a Winter Princess, the first our kingdom has had in centuries."

She reached a pale hand forward and caught hold of mine. Her skin was cool, like a December breeze. "Thus far, I've forgone any formal interrogations because I believe we are kindred spirits. We don't have to be enemies, Kadie. You will become our Winter Princess, and all I ask in return is for you to provide me with what information you know."

Holy shit. Was she crazy? I wanted to go home and get out

of this fucked up place.

But to what? The tiny, poor life I'd left behind? The desperate search for respect? Riches? Hot guys? Fame? She was offering me all of that and more.

Tempting, but I doubted she'd keep her end of the bargain.

As though reading my mind, she said, "You won't have any more cheating boyfriends or a family who doesn't understand you. You will no longer have to live in Salome's shadow, or be her protector. Here, you will be revered as my right hand."

Yeah, because being her right hand would be so amazing. I could torture people with her. Maim them. Murder them. And in the end, I'd still be her prisoner, just under another name.

But at least I'd be alive...

"I'm flattered, but I'm not sure I'm the person you want for this. Besides, you hate me and have told me so on several occasions."

Crap.

Don't you dare consider this.

Yes, it had sucked over the years constantly being Salome's watchdog and keeping an eye on her. But wasn't that what friends did?

She's one of the reasons you got imprisoned here. You went looking for her, and they caught you. And the only reason they've kept you locked up is because they want information on her and her boyfriend.

Yeah, the boyfriend she'd never even told me she'd moved in with.

I shook my head. Salome was my best friend. I blushed with shame thinking of how angry I was toward her. God, I felt sick to my stomach. But all I could think about were all the times my parents had made me drop my plans to go hang out with Salome because her mother or grandma called. How I'd missed out on dances or parties, opting to stay inside during the winter because Salome was too scared to go out. My life really had always been about Salome.

Was that what had gotten me into this awful situation? Was choosing something different what would get me out?

"How do you know so much about me?" I shot a quick glance in the queen's direction.

"You wear your heart on your sleeve. And when you came into the club, you were searching for your friend. I just hate to see you hurting. You remind me so much of me at that age. Believe me, you're not the only one to betray herself because she cared too much about others. To put herself on the line time and time again." Her mouth turned down in a frown and her gaze darkened. "But that's a story for another night. Finish up your dinner, and then I'll have Etienne show you to your new room. I really do think we can both come out of this ahead. Why don't I let you sleep on it?"

I still didn't trust her. To tell you the truth, right now I didn't trust myself, either. But I also didn't know how to get myself out of this, so I'd take her offer and buy myself some time while I figured out what to do next.

"Okay," I said. "Your Majesty."

"No. No. That won't do. Please, you must call me Grisselle." She stood, gave my shoulder a squeeze, then turned to Etienne once more. "I want Kadie to have the Gold Room. You may stay with her if you'd like, and we can all meet back here for breakfast tomorrow. And, Kadie, to show you just how much I'm hoping you will truly consider my offer, I'm letting you off from Bone Yard duty for the remainder of your stay here." With that, Grisselle left the room in a flurry of skirts.

The Winter Princes followed soon after, until only Etienne and I remained. We ate in silence. *Shit.* I had no idea what to do.

Maybe I could barter for my release.

Yeah, and go home to what?

Your family is pissed at you. Salome's not around. And you have no place to stay at this point. But do you really want to be stuck in this terrible castle?

I couldn't give in. Not after everything I'd been through—after everything I'd seen. Yet if I refused her, I might be signing my own death warrant.

"If you're finished, I can show you to your room now," Etienne said. His brow furrowed as he stood and helped me up beside him.

I dropped my napkin on the table and took the arm he offered me. We left the formal dining room and headed further down the corridor. At the end of the hallway, there was a stained glass window depicting a woman holding a sword, and to the left of that was a large wooden door.

Etienne led me to the door and with a turn of the handle it swung open. Candles already flickered inside, and I gasped. Damn. Now this was a room. A large canopied-bed sat against the back wall, with pine green velvet drapes tied back with golden chords. A fire roared in the fireplace, which was decorated in light marble and gold-foiled holly leaves. There were two dressers, one on each side of the bed, along with a settee of green, gold, and red at the foot of it. The ceiling had a scene painted on it of a couple ice skating on a pond, surrounded by trees.

There were two overstuffed chairs in front of the fireplace, and in the corner of the room was a white marble tub with golden fixtures.

"Oh. My. God." I released Etienne and spun around. I hurried to the bed and ran my hand along the soft white furs that covered it. Then a beautiful scarlet gown caught my eye.

It'd been laid out for me, along with a wooden box, which contained a ruby necklace, earrings, and ring.

"Is this for real?" My gaze met Etienne's as I held the dress up against me. It was just my color. *Ah.* I wanted to try it on.

"Yes," he said softly.

"You've been here a long time, what do you make of what the queen said? Do you think she'll kill me if I give her information or do you believe she'll keep her word?" I chewed my bottom lip. What the hell was I thinking? But look at this room! I bet Hollywood celebrities didn't even have stuff this nice.

Etienne moved the short distance between us; his hand cupped my chin, forcing me to meet his eyes. "Tread lightly, Kadie. Grisselle might be a woman of her word, but she also knows how to manipulate people into doing things for her."

"But she let you surrender and save your people."

"And look where we're stuck—in a place worse than hell. She kept her pact and didn't kill my people, but instead she imprisoned us here and turned most of the Spring Court into hideous creatures." Etienne's words were filled with acid. "I'm forced to do Grisselle's bidding, as my magic has been diluted by her. The only freedom I have is the freedom to fall asleep in my own room."

"You're alive. And that's something."

Would I really trade everything just to keep my ass safe? And what would Salome want if she could tell me what to do? Wouldn't she tell me that sometimes a person had to be selfish? That sometimes a person had to do whatever it took to survive?

Etienne glanced at the fireplace. "You should bed down for the night. The queen will wish to speak with you early, and you'll want to have your wits about you when you do."

I clutched my arms to my chest, staring at him. His shoulders sagged some, and his eyes focused on anything but me. He looked defeated.

"If this isn't the right choice, then tell me what you'd do in my place. Sit back and wait to be killed? Try another escape?"

"I just want you to be safe, and right now, I don't think any of the above options are going to help keep you that way. But the decision is ultimately yours; just beware of what choices you make." He sighed, then stepped away from me.

I swallowed hard. No matter how luxurious this room was, I didn't really want to be left alone. I knew what lurked in the rest of the castle. With my luck, this area would dissolve away in my sleep, and I'd be stuck in a pile of bones.

"Do you think you could stay the night with me?" My gaze locked with his. For once, this wasn't about seducing someone. I needed him. The only time I got any rest in Winter was when I knew he was close by. Eventually, maybe I wouldn't need him in order to sleep. But for now, he was the only person I trusted.

"Kadie, I—"

"Please?" I touched his arm. "I don't want to be by myself, even in here."

"Okay. I'll let you get changed, and I'll come back once I've let Rena know where we're at. I don't want her worrying."

"Thank you."

When he left, I hung up the scarlet gown, then searched through the dressers for a pair of pajamas. At last, I found a cream colored nightie made of thick, soft material. I slipped out of my clothes and into the PJs. For the first time in days, my hope was restored. I might still make it out of here alive… unlike Demetria.

My throat thickened as I pictured her last moments. I needed to be strong. I needed to survive, and in order to do so, it meant I had to make some sacrifices. There couldn't be any harm in sharing some small bits of information with Grisselle — just enough to keep her from hurting me. And in the meantime, I could take some small comforts, safely locked away in my new room.

You don't know what you're saying. Fight harder. Don't give in.

I quieted the voice inside me.

Sometimes, you had to know when to throw in the towel. And for me, that time was now.

A knock sounded on my bedroom door the next morning; I set down the hairbrush I'd been holding and went to answer. I wondered if it was Etienne, back from his meeting with the guards.

"Grisselle," I said. Surprised, I took a step back to let her in.

"I hope you slept well in your new room?" Her purplish-blue gown swept the floor as she came inside.

"Yes, thank you."

"And everything here is to your liking?"

I smiled, smoothing down the scarlet gown she'd given me. "It's perfect, everything is perfect. I feel like a princess."

Grisselle touched my arm, her skin ice cold. "As you should. Now, I came here this morning because there's someplace I'd like to show you. A private area that I don't allow most people into. But I feel close to you — like I can trust you."

She ushered me from my room and across the hall to where a large tapestry of a sleigh going into the woods hung. Grisselle tugged it back away from the wall to reveal a hidden staircase.

The jagged stone stairs were dimly lit by the dancing flames from candles situated in sconces the whole way up. Shadows stretched and contorted against the stones like dark ghosts drifting along. Grisselle took my arm and brought me upstairs. When we got to the top, she produced an old-fashioned looking skeleton key and slid it into the mammoth size door. I heard a click, and the large barrier swung open.

My breath caught in my throat as I stepped inside the large suite. White tiles with blue snowflakes in them covered the floor, along with several white, fluffy rugs. There was a large bed with white lacy curtains sitting at the back of the room. A fireplace with differing shades of blue and white tile sat near the frosted double doors that led onto a balcony. There was a vanity perched in the corner, complete with large mirror, brushes, perfumes, and ribbons.

But it was the painting above the fireplace that caught my eye. It was a portrait of a much younger Grisselle standing next to a girl with auburn hair. I watched as Grisselle glanced at it, too, her face visibly shaken, almost like she was nervous. "Are you okay?"

Her lips turned up in a shaky half-smile. "Yes. Sorry. Sometimes I still get emotional coming in here. This is my old room from when I was a child. Believe it or not, I wasn't always the person you see before you now. There was a time when I was much happier—when I too had dreams of the perfect life. That girl in the picture with me, she was my sister—one of my betrayers."

I stiffened. "Your betrayer?"

"Come, sit down on the bed, and I'll tell you a story." She moved over to the vanity, her fingers trailing over the items on it.

"Are you sure? I-I don't want to bring back bad memories." My stomach tightened, wondering where she might go with this.

"Yes. I want you to understand me, and know that when I'm offering you favors, I'm putting myself in a position to be hurt again. I'm telling you this so that you know I'm not making this offer lightly. I have trust issues too."

I took a seat on the edge of the bed, my hands fisted in my lap.

Grisselle picked up a sapphire necklace from the vanity and held it, watching it spin around and catch the light coming in through the glass doors. "Once upon a time, there lived a family at the Winter Court. This family was all powerful. Nearly all the crowned royal females of this line were marked to become the Queen of Faerie. There'd only been a couple of the other seasons who'd ever been marked as such." She glanced at me and set the jewelry down once more.

"When I was thirteen, Faerie marked me as its next queen. I was powerful. My parents pushed me to study with the best scholars. I spent most of my days doing lessons and training to use my powers. My duty was to my family and my people, which meant I wasn't able to have a normal childhood, but still, I knew how special and privileged I was to be marked. There were times when I'd go days without seeing another person other than my sister. She'd come up here into my room, and we'd play games or do one another's hair and talk about our futures. Because I'd be Faerie Queen, my sister would be next in line to take her place as the Winter Queen. Our relationship was a lot like yours and Salome's."

My eyes slid around the room, landing on a table set up with an unfinished game of chess. Most of the pieces were still on the board, but I noticed that the black had more left than the white. A chill snaked across me like a serpent gliding on sand.

"During my seventeenth year, I grew tired of all my training and being pushed so hard to become stronger for everyone else's sake. I wanted a break. To see more of Faerie, to experience things. So on the Winter Solstice, I snuck from these very chambers and followed one of the Faerie Troupes into the human world." A playful smile tugged at her lips. "It was this night that I met Leonardo, a human artist who'd been in the woods working on a painting of the scenery. It was love at first sight for me. We grew close and became lovers despite knowing how my family despised humans. So I had to meet Leonardo in secret. Sometimes I'd sneak away from my lessons to go see him. Other times I waited until the household was asleep and used a portal to go into the human world. For the first year, no one knew what I was doing. But one night, after a grand ball, drunk on pomegranate wine, I told my sister of Leonardo and how I wanted to bring him to Faerie to be my consort when I was crowned queen. This would prove to be a big mistake. For once, I wanted to put my needs before everyone else's, to have something special. My whole life, I'd been trained to think of Faerie and only Faerie, and all the sacrifices I'd have to make to keep everyone safe. My role as queen was to protect, serve, and rule. But it was so much pressure—and to never be allowed to have the things I loved…it was difficult to think about. But you can relate to this, yes? How much of your life you spent doing things for everyone else—for Salome?"

I nodded my head as she gripped tightly to the edge of a chair, her fingers turning whiter than normal. Fury washed across her features, and I saw the hatred burning in her eyes.

I swallowed hard, not wanting her to get pissed off. "Are you sure you want to continue?"

Grisselle peered at me as if not even seeing me. "Yes. I want you to know. I, too, have lost things I loved because I cared too much about others and not enough about myself…"

"Okay," I whispered. My gaze slid to the doorway, wondering

if I'd be able to escape if she got too angry.

"The next night I sneaked into the human world again. Leonardo met me in the woods along the lake with a picnic. We'd just begun to kiss, but then my parents and sister burst into the clearing. My parents were furious and dragged me away. My sister had spilled my secrets and had told them everything. As punishment, they got with the other elders from around the kingdoms and they decided to strip away my title, even though Faerie had marked me as her next queen. Even though I'd sacrificed my whole childhood to finding ways to be the best queen I could. I betrayed myself by caring so much for my people—and then, they couldn't even allow me this one small thing: the love of a human. The elders soon found a powerful spell to take away all but my winter power. It was like being hooked to a lightning bolt and struck over and over again." Her eyes welled as she stared at me.

"Your sister betrayed you?" For fuck's sake, how could someone do that to family?

"To a point, yes. My closest companion—my own flesh and blood had let me down, but I'd dedicated so much of my time to Faerie, that in essence it was my own fault for being weak."

"That's horrible," I said, wondering how twisted her relatives could be.

"My parents took my title and gave it to Genissa, who was now marked by Faerie. She took everything from me, her own sister. After all this happened, I decided I didn't want to be here any longer. So I packed a small bundle and snuck into the human world. My plan was to run off with Leonardo. But when I got to our spot, I found him with another woman—a human woman. This was my breaking point. Hatred burned through me, and I turned the girl into a tree on his property so he could watch her and suffer as she died slowly. This is why I came to hate human women and the Faerie court. The elders and my parents wouldn't allow me to be with the person I loved; my sister stole everything from me. When I realized that I wouldn't get my happy ending, I went to the darkest caves at the edge of the Forbidden Swells—a place where dark magic flows. I'd studied enough in my lessons to know how to delve into it. It was here that I embraced my darkness and let it consume me. I had a new plan—to get even with my sister and the royals for all that they'd done and taken from me. No one in Faerie, not one person from any of the courts came to my aid against those that chose to strip me of everything. They could've saved me, but instead, they helped in my demise. That was their biggest mistake—they underestimated just how powerful I was and what I could now do, thanks to the black magic. I was just so tired of giving everything of myself, only to have those around me not appreciate me or understand everything I sacrificed for them. I was at my breaking point, and this was my only defense—to take back what should've been mine."

"I'm sorry that they did that to you. It was wrong." Jeez, she was more fucked up than I was. But now, I understood better why she'd done what she'd done. And after all she'd given up to train and study to become their queen? She'd sacrificed her whole childhood for them—is that what I'd done for Salome?

"Thank you for your kindness. Very few would be so compassionate. We truly are kindred, Kadie. I felt it the moment I met you." She gave me a shy glance, then picked up her handheld mirror.

The queen went still; her fingers gripped the sides of the vanity. Her face twisted, in anger. "No! This can't be." She slammed her palm against the mirror, and it cracked beneath the force of the blow. Blood dripped down the jagged, broken pieces onto the furniture and floor.

But she didn't seem to notice the wound as she squeezed her eyes shut and took several deep breaths before turning toward the door way. "Teodor! Etienne!" Her voice carried like the sound of someone scraping a fork across a blackboard—as if magic carried it down the stairs, echoing throughout the castle.

"Your Highness, you called for us?" Etienne rushed into the room, Teodor close behind. Both were breathless, glancing at me, then back to her, with almost confused looks upon their faces.

"They've escaped—they're all gone."

Teodor crossed his arms. "Who's gone?"

"The Autumn Courts' ghosts. They're no longer tethered to the Ruined Court. That means I no longer control them."

She stormed across the room. Her hands swept the glass figures and bottles from her vanity. They crashed to the floor, sending a spray of broken glass everywhere. Her once cool demeanor shattered like the pieces lying on the floor.

"Someone has undermined my plans—I want to know who," Griselle snapped, visibly trying to regain her composure. "You will find out for me." She raised a finger and pointed at Teodor. "You've spent too much time bedding humans and very little helping to preserve our kingdom."

"Yes, Your Majesty." He bowed.

"Go—now!"

Teodor rushed from the room like the flames of hell licked at his ass.

Etienne hurried to my side, grabbed my hand, and jerked me to the stairs. We hurried down.

"Something big is about to happen in Faerie. Light magic is returning." Etienne squeezed my fingers.

I glanced at him. I didn't know exactly what that meant, but I was sure it might not be good for anyone on Grisselle's bad side—which cemented my choice to do everything in my power to keep her happy. I wouldn't make the same mistake that had cost Demetria her life. I would stay strong. I would survive.

A part of me wondered if Grisselle really was a woman scorned—a woman who had given everything to others and been burned in return. Was she just misunderstood? Not that I agreed with all the girls she'd killed, but I could see why she'd done it— why she'd decided to get back at her family, her sister, Leonardo, and Faerie. They'd done her wrong first, or so she said.

Hadn't I been in the same position? I'd made sacrifices for Zac, all to keep him happy and keep us together, but he had screwed me over, and I'd wanted nothing more than to rip his balls off and shove them down his throat. And what about Salome? I'd taken stupid risks to help her, and look where it had gotten me. I wasn't saying I'd never help anyone again, but from now on, I had to ask myself what was in it for me. This could be the fine line between life and death and I damn sure preferred to live.

Now it was my turn to get what I desired—what I deserved. In turn, it'd help Grisselle out, too. Maybe I could convince her to quit killing people. She might just need a friend: someone to listen to her, someone she could trust, someone who understood where she was coming from. Why couldn't that person be me?

"Etienne, I need to go back and talk to Grisselle."

His eyes met mine, and his jaw tightened. "I don't think now is a good time to be around her."

"Look, it's really important that I speak with her, now."

"Kadie, I—"

"You can stop worrying about keeping me safe. After tonight, I won't need your protection any longer." I stopped and looked him up and down. "But maybe there's something else you can be for me besides my protector." I trailed my fingers down his cheek, until they brushed against his lips. "She promised that I could have any Fae lord I want…"

He grabbed my hands and pulled them away from him. "Look, let's talk about this before you make a decision you might live to regret—or worse, get killed over."

"I've spent my whole life worried about how actions would affect other people. I'm done with it. Today and every day from here on out, I'm looking out for me. And since you don't seem interested in me, I'm going to talk to someone who is. Now will you bring me to Grisselle? Or do I have to go myself?"

"Very well, but don't say I didn't warn you. And don't expect me to come to your rescue again. This—what you're doing here," he waved his arms around, "is foolish and asinine. You're just begging to find yourself in a bone pile in the Bone Yard." He reached out, clutched me by the shoulders, and gave me a shake. "Are you really going to honor Demetria's memory by siding with the enemy?"

I jerked free from him. "Well, if Demetria had been smart, she would've tried whatever she could've to get out of here. I'm not going to sit back and be subjected to the same fate as her. I'm doing what I can to survive—and there's nothing wrong with that."

He snorted, his mouth turning down into a frown, eyes hard as the stone walls. "Nothing wrong? Try condemning yourself to a lifetime of hell." He shook his head. "There are worse things than death, Kadie. Believe me. But if that's what you want, then go on, run to Grisselle. But mark my words, you will regret it, and it'll be too late by the time you realize it."

Ugh. What an asshole. He was such a fucking hypocrite. He'd done the same thing that I was about to do. There was no dishonor in trying to stay alive…and I wanted to live to see my next birthday. Tonight, I'd be something—somebody. I'd be Kadie Byers, Winter Princess.

CHAPTER TWENTY-FOUR

Salome

Unnerved by everything that'd happened, I decided to head back to my room. Maybe in there, I could let things digest a little more. Was there any way to con Nevin into sending for my grandmother? I had a feeling she knew exactly what was going on.

It seemed like I was in the dark about so many things. I needed answers—about the Blade of the Four Kingdoms, why I suddenly had magic, and why Faerie had marked me as the next Summer Queen.

As I turned the corner to enter the hallway to my room, a door appeared out of nowhere, blocking my way. I jumped back, startled. What the heck was going on? The air around me buzzed with what felt like static. The hair on the back of my neck stood on end. A low humming sounded, and all of a sudden the door whipped open and I was sucked toward the entrance.

I let out a low scream, attempting to dig my feet in and grip my fingers tightly to the doorjamb. It was useless, though, and once I was sucked all the way in, the wooden barrier slammed shut behind me and disappeared.

Oh God. Where was I? I spun in a circle as candles lit themselves around the room. Shelves of what looked like ancient books lined the stonewalls. There was a lone table at the center of it—with two books already flipped open, as if someone had been studying and left abruptly.

The ceiling reminded me of a night sky—complete with blinking stars. I gazed at it for long moments until I saw a star shoot across it. Was it magic? Whatever it was, it was beautiful.

My eyes continued to take everything in, from the ancient relics that were displayed on shelves and hung on the walls to the strange crystal boxes that sat in a glass case that stretched from the floor to the ceiling.

"Answers are here, if you know where to look..." A low whisper echoed around me.

I twisted around and around, searching for the source of the voice. "Hello? Who's there? Can you tell me where I am?"

"You are in the Room of the Past. What has already happened is here, and what has yet to happen will find its way here... Time is precious. Seek and you shall find. Remember what you see and recognize what you don't see. But be swift, for time cannot stand still for long, even for those who are marked as a sister of Faerie. When the stars align, you must go..."

Okay, what the hell did that mean? But as I peered up at the ceiling once more, I saw the slow movement of the stars in the sky. Was that my timer?

Not exactly sure what it was I was supposed to be looking for, I moved toward the table. As I got closer to it, the pages in the book began to turn on their own, until it opened to a section with a crudely drawn picture of the Blade of the Four Kingdoms. The text below it was faded, but still legible. It read:

*T*he blade of the Four Kingdoms is imbued with the essence of Spring, Summer, Autumn, and Winter. This weapon was wielded by the first Queen of Faerie, Diana. She battled against the Fomorians, saving Faerie Kind. She was selfless. Her love for Faerie and humanity was greater than the love she had for herself. Some say that is why the blade worked for her then disappeared after her reign. The queens who followed her were self-indulgent and did not have the true markings of Faerie. The four courts began choosing their own queen based on votes and not the will of Faerie. Because the weapon was created to protect and not serve, it is said it disappeared and will return only when

The weapon would reappear when what? The page had been torn off. However, that didn't stop the involuntary shiver that ran through my body. What were the chances that a sword missing for centuries had just happened to fall into my hands?

More pages on the book flipped like an old movie projector. It stopped once more on a painting of the crystal boxes I'd seen in the case.

*M*emory Boxes house all the important memories and events of Faerie. From the first Faerie Queen to the most recent, these dream-like visions replay when the boxes are opened. They cannot be destroyed by magic or weapons, for memories are never truly lost. They are pieces of our past. They are warnings for our future.

The boxes. My gaze slid over them. I wondered if this was what I was supposed to find. I swallowed hard and ambled across the room until I stood in front of the crystal boxes. I didn't see any latches to open the case, but as I slid my hand against the glass, it opened of its own accord.

Whisperings surrounded me. At first, I thought people had entered the room with me until I realized the noise was coming from the boxes themselves. My hand hovered over each of them, unsure which to choose. But as my fingers trailed over each lid, I felt a tingling sensation run up my arm, and when I came to the last box in the last row, the vibrations grew stronger.

Cautious, I picked it up and brought it over to the table, where I sat down. My stomach knotted, wondering what would happen when I opened it. I prayed I wouldn't unleash something.

Body quaking, I gripped a hold of the top and pushed it up. A tiny cloud pushed out and spread above the table until it looked like a movie screen. Then the images began to appear. There was a horse carriage, transporting what appeared to be a glass coffin through Faerie. Mourners stood on the sides of the roads and paths, tossing flowers and leaves at the feet of the horses. I leaned closer, making out the body of a woman— Genissa, the Queen of Faerie. Her auburn hair spread out on the white pillow her head rested on; a white gown made her appear angelic. She held a bouquet of violets in her hands. But as the carriage rounded the bend, I noticed there wasn't a body in the coffin any longer.

"Whoa, wait a second." I wondered if there was a rewind button on this thing. The carriage disappeared around the corner. Then the memory replayed again. This time, I paid closer attention. Right when the horse drawn contraption got close to the bend, I saw the slight flicker—almost like a glitch or something. And then, again, the body wasn't there.

What the hell did this mean? I sat there for long moments. Where was the body? Unless the body had never been in the carriage to begin with…Maybe someone had used magic or glamour to make it look like Genissa was there. And if she wasn't, then where the heck was she—or rather, her body? Wariness crept in. Someone or something had wanted me to see this particular memory box, but why?

"Time to go…you must seek out the Matron of Faerie—the archivist must remember…she holds the key. The warden holds the map. The sister holds the doorway open. The other is made of darkness. Beware of the girl who calls herself friend."

"Wait, what does that even mean?" But before I could get any more answers, a light burst into the room, revealing the door once more. It swung open, and I was thrown back out into the hallway where I'd started.

In a matter of seconds the door and the room were both gone. I leaned against the wall for long moments, wondering if I'd imagined the whole thing. Crap. Whatever this was, I knew it was important. But did I have all the pieces to put the puzzle together? The thing was, I didn't know who might be able to answer some questions for me. Darach? Nevin? Maybe I was on my own for this one.

*N*evin pulled my chair out for me as we sat down to dinner. Tonight, we were dining outside beneath the moonlight. Blue, yellow, and green paper lanterns floated in the air above, their soft lights glittering off the river.

"Don't worry, I only invited nice people tonight," Nevin said.

I smiled, but my mind was on anything but dinner. "Well, I can definitely do without Rowena for a while."

His brow knit. "Trust me, I'm looking into things where she's concerned. The only problem is Gwenn isn't a viable witness, at least not according to the Council."

"Why? She's a noble lady and one of the royal guards."

He leaned closer. "Because she was kicked out of Council. Let's just say they don't see eye to eye. And she and Rowena have a long history of clashing. Gwenn believed we should train like our soldiers so we could better defend ourselves. However, most of the nobles disagreed, especially when she tried pushing it into law."

My gaze shifted to my guard, trying to picture her in a dress and sitting around like the others, but I couldn't.

Laughter filled the room, and I turned to see Fae children weaving in and out of the tables. Some peeked at me from behind their parents, while others inched closer to us. People glanced at me, curious looks on their faces. For once, I sensed no animosity simply because I was human.

"So who are all these people?"

"These are guests from the kingdom. Only two nobles amongst the group."

A young man poured pomegranate wine into my goblet. He briefly glanced in my direction before returning back to his post.

"Why are they all staring at me?"

Nevin chuckled. "Because they want to meet the woman who freed us from Winter's clutches. You're a legend amongst the masses."

My brows raised. "You're teasing me."

"No. I promise."

An elven boy wandered through the crowd. When he saw

me, he grinned and pushed through the people until he stood beside my chair.

"The others bet me I wouldn't come talk to you," he said. "But I wanted to know if you really broke the king's curse."

Nevin leaned across me. "Yes, she did. She killed the witch and freed me and my troupe."

"Ha, I told them it was true." He glanced over his shoulder at his friends who seemed overly enthralled with me. "Just so you know, I think you're the prettiest girl I've ever seen." His ears turned pink.

I touched his cheek. "Thank you, I think that's the nicest thing anyone's ever said to me."

With that, he bowed and rushed back to his buddies.

"Looks like you have yourself a fan," Nevin said. "Soon all the boys in the kingdom will be lining up to get a glimpse of you."

I laughed, catching Gwenn's eye across the yard. She acknowledged me with a quick nod, then went back to scouring the area. Did she ever take a break and just have fun?

In the distance, the sound of horns broke through the festivities.

I faced Nevin. "What's going on?"

His gaze searched the darkness as men on horses galloped to the edge of our eating area. "I'm not sure." He stood.

I recognized some of the soldiers from Gareth's scouting party. Dust clung to their wrinkled uniforms, and fatigue showed on their faces.

One of the men approached Nevin. "Your Highness, we bring grave news."

My stomach clenched as I climbed to my feet beside Nevin.

"Gareth?" I called out in my mind.

Silence.

Oh God. Please don't let it be him.

"What is it, Darvin?"

"Lord Gareth has been injured in battle." He pointed to Gareth's body, slung over his white stallion. "He was cut down in the mountains, east of here by an iron blade. His body is shutting down. The iron poisoning can't be stopped."

"No," I whispered. My throat seemed to close off. I couldn't breathe. Tears blurred my vision. This had to be a mistake. It had to be. I reached for the table to steady myself.

Several people cried out at once.

"Silence," Nevin shouted. "Everyone is excused save for Lady Salome, Lady Gwenn, and Darvin."

The dinner party broke up, everyone scattering until just the four of us remained. I dared a glance at Nevin, who'd paled; grief and worry flooded his eyes. But Gwenn hadn't budged. She stared ahead, her jaw tightened.

Nevin turned to Darvin. "What happened?"

"Winter ambushed us near the border. They struck three days ago. It happened so fast, we never had a chance to react."

Three days ago? That's when I'd felt the shot of pain through our bond. This wasn't happening. He promised me to always be here. He gave me his word.

"There has to be something we can do. For God's sake, you have power."

"Salome, iron poisoning for Fae is deadly…"

My heart shattered like crystal as a sob wrenched through me. "No, that's unacceptable."

Nevin came to my side and drew me into his arms. "Bring him to his chambers and send for Elder Briar—he's our best healer. I'm not making any promises as to whether he'll be able to help him or not. I'm truly sorry, Salome—I swear upon my life that we *will* avenge him." He pulled back, his fingers wiping tears from my face. "Gwenn, see Salome to her room."

"I need to be with him." My legs wobbled beneath me, but Gwenn offered me her arm.

"Until they have him settled in, you'll only be in the way," Nevin said.

Anger poured through me. "Listen here, Gareth is my boyfriend and my betrothed, and I'll be by his side."

"For now, you need to go to your room. I promise as soon as we can get him laid out and have the elder come in, I'll send for you. Now please, we're wasting time here."

Defeated, I let Gwenn lead me into the palace. Somehow we made it up to my quarters. When we stepped inside, she patted my arm.

"My brother's a good man—if he dies, know that he did so protecting the people he loved. It's an honorable way to go."

God, I wish she'd quit talking about him as if he was already dead—as if he would for sure die. All I could manage was a nod. How could she be so nonchalant about her brother's situation? Didn't anyone care?

"You have my word," she said. "I'll keep you safe, no matter what. Even if you are a human, my brother loved you, and it's my duty to protect what was his." She moved to the door and closed it behind her, leaving me alone.

I slumped onto my bed, crying. My arms wrapped around my chest as I curled into a ball.

This isn't how things are supposed to be.

I chose Gareth. He loved me. We were supposed to be together forever. Bonded. Inseparable. Damn it! If Nevin hadn't sent him away, none of this would've happened. Gareth couldn't die. He couldn't. He'd faced so many enemies and always won.

"Please don't leave me." I sobbed. "Please."

But there was no answer from him. And there might never be again. Gareth might die…which meant I might lose him forever.

CHAPTER TWENTY-FIVE

Salome

I watched as the elder put the poultice on Gareth's wound. His skin was clammy and beads of sweat slickened his forehead. The wound had caused his flesh to darken like spoiled meat along the ridge of the cut mark. His face and body were otherwise pale, the normal bronze sheen gone.

"There's nothing more I can do," the elder said. "I'm afraid he won't last the night—"

"No, that can't be. There has to be something you can do. Some sort of magic that will fix this." I leapt to my feet. "Please, I beg you."

The elder's eyes filled with sadness. "I'm sorry, Lady Salome, but there's no power strong enough to combat the iron poisoning that has entered his system. Take comfort in knowing that he at least made it home, so you could say your goodbyes." He spared me a glance, but with nothing left to say, the tall elfin man left the room.

With a sob, I sank into the chair by Gareth's bed, taking his limp hand in mine and pressing it to my lips. No. The elder had to be wrong. He couldn't die on me. He couldn't go back on his promise—he'd promised to always be here for me.

"You can't leave me, you hear? You brought me back from the dead, you called me back to life and I came. So don't you dare give up on me now." My eyes welled. *"Please, fight. For me. Fight for us."*

His breathing seemed more labored. Fear racing through me, I turned to Nevin, who stood solemnly near the door. "Nevin, please, tell me there's something we can do? I-I hadn't wanted to tell you earlier, but you were right. My powers are real. So help me figure out how to use them to save Gareth."

"It would take more magic than you could possibly have, Salome. Death is one of the most powerful spells…"

"But Gareth brought me back. Couldn't we do the same for him? How did he do it?"

"I don't know. I'm not lying to you—I don't know. I only remember him calling to you. Him and your grandmother both. What do you remember of your death and resurrection?"

"I was stuck in an in-between, and I heard his voice, and I followed it."

"Maybe he's in a place where your voice won't come through. Perhaps the poison keeps you from reaching him."

"Nevin, come on. There has to be something we can do."

He lowered his head. "There might be another way. But I'm not sure you'll like it"

I shot to my feet, letting go of Gareth's hand. "What is it? I'll do anything to bring him back."

"You could become my queen," he said.

Anger erupted inside me. Oh. My. God. My boyfriend was dying and he was trying to convince me to be his mother-effing queen. This was low, even for Nevin. "I can't believe you'd try to manipulate me right now, when the love of my life is dying—"

"I'm not trying to trick you. As the Summer King, I can tap

into some of the powers of the kingdom. However, my magic is not, and will not, be at its fullest until Summer has a queen. When both a king and queen rule, all the power is available, both the feminine side and the masculine side of it. I believe that together, with Summer's powers behind us, that we could beat away this darkness that keeps him from returning to us."

My fingers knotted into balled up fists at my sides. "Is this another one of your grand schemes? Your tricks? How do I know you aren't lying to me again? That you won't deceive me—deceive Gareth?"

Nevin straightened his shoulders. "Gareth is one of my closest companions and has been since we were children; he was the only person I trusted enough to watch after Summer when I was stuck in the human world for all those years. Do you think I want him to die? That I wouldn't do everything in my power to save him? Because I would—and right now, I'm telling you that on our own, neither of us is strong enough to bring him back. No, I can't guarantee this will work, but doesn't he deserve a chance? Isn't that what you're asking me to give you?" His eyes burned with fury as he glowered at me.

I swallowed the lump in my throat. What would I be willing to sacrifice to bring him back?

Everything.

If only Gareth could communicate with me—let me know whether I was making the right choice. I could choose to forego my happily ever after in order to ensure that the man I loved would live to see another day. But what if it didn't work? What if it was a trick? What if my sacrifice caused more harm than help?

"I need time to think about it," I said at last.

"Time is something we don't have much of."

"I know. Just give me tonight." I plopped back down next to

Gareth, clutching his hand to my chest.

"Very well. Try and get some rest."

I nodded, but I knew I wouldn't sleep. Once Nevin left, I cried, leaning my head on Gareth's pillow. "I wish you could tell me what to do. You mean everything to me, I can't lose you…"

*N*evin came into the room the next morning and sat in a chair beside me. "You've been locked up in here all night now. You need to eat."

My head throbbed as I turned my crusty eyes to look at him. "I don't feel like it."

"Gareth wouldn't want you to waste away. *I don't want* you to waste away." He reached for my hand, cupping it in his. "Everyone is worried about you. The people of Summer look to you as a savior—you give them hope. And now, they worry for your health."

"I didn't ask for them to put me on this pedestal," I said in a hoarse voice. "Besides, your nobles have a very different opinion of me."

He gave me a sad smile. "Perhaps, but the heart of the kingdom stands behind you. Please don't take their hope from them. It's all they have—all *we* have."

Irritation radiated through me. How dare he make me feel bad? "The man I love is dying—can't I mourn for him? For shit-sake, this isn't like some beloved pet or stranger. This is the man I planned on spending the rest of my life with."

"I understand you're hurt, but right now, you need to take care of yourself. Hiding out in here isn't helping you."

My bottom lip trembled as tears burned my raw cheeks.

"What do you know about losing someone?" I glared. "I can't come out, and I won't. Just leave me be."

"You can come out." He took my chin in his hand and made me look at him. "I'll give you until tonight—then I'll force you from your room, even if I have to carry you out myself. You can't be sitting in here, watching him waste away."

He released me, stood, and then walked out of Gareth's chambers.

With a sob, I screamed, picking up a cup off the dresser and throwing it at the wall. God, Nevin didn't get it. Gareth's life was on the line. He might not come back. And right now it felt like I had this giant hole in my heart, like a piece of my soul was missing. I wasn't complete without him.

The scent of autumn encompassed me.

"He's right, you know," Darach said. *"You can't hide away forever. Sooner or later, you'll have to face the world."*

"But it hurts so bad, just the thought of him not being here." My eyes burned as tears that I thought were all dried up started to stream down my face again.

"I know." Darach's arms surrounded me, blanketing me against the world. He felt so solid.

I faced him, still in his embrace. "I loved him so much... H-he promised to never leave me. He promised."

More sobs raked through me like waves crashing on the ocean.

"Shh...Salome. Come here." He tugged me closer, and we sank together. It was like being in a cocoon—surrounded in his very being, his spirit. Like that alone could shield me from the hurt I felt.

A sense of security settled over me like a soft whisper.

"You'll stay with me, won't you?"

Mahogany eyes met mine. *"I can't promise forever, because*

I don't know how long I'm here for you. But I'll stay as long as I'm able to."

A strange glowing aura wrapped around us, and for a moment, I swore I heard his heartbeat again.

But that's impossible. He's a ghost.

"Thank you," I whispered.

We stood in silence for long minutes before Darach spoke again. *"How did you meet Gareth and Nevin?"*

I swallowed the lump in my throat then went on to explain my fall through the ice covered pond when I was six. How Nevin saved me. And I told him of my fear of winter. He listened intently as I reminisced about Nevin and Gareth, and my final decision to come to Faerie.

Remembering my time in the human world with Gareth brought on a fresh set of tears. If I closed my eyes, I saw him standing across the pool at the water park; I pictured him in his tux when he agreed to bring me to prom. My heart ached for him. And it killed me that I'd spent my last night with him angry.

"I think you were meant to come to Faerie. To be a part of our lives. To be a part of something even bigger than us. Nothing happens without reason."

I opened my eyes, and the droplets that'd clung to my eyelashes splashed down my face. He wiped them away. Maybe he was right. Maybe everything had led to this very moment for a reason. I had to make a decision, and I'd have to make it soon, no matter how hard it was.

"I'll have to leave his room, won't I?"

"Yes, the sooner you face reality, the sooner you can heal."

But somehow, I didn't think it'd be that easy. Besides, I didn't want to exist in a reality where there was no Gareth. Where my light was plucked out. "Thank you," I said again, clasping his hand.

"*No. Thank you. If you hadn't come to the Ruined Court I'd still be tethered there, stuck in misery.*"

I wanted to remind him he was still stuck in this world, between life and death, and that I didn't think I'd done him any favors. But his smile changed my mind.

"Instead, you're anchored to me—and I'm not exactly Ms. Happy right now."

"*No. But you will be.*"

Is he right? Will I ever get beyond the sadness?

As he attempted to comfort me, my thoughts drifted to Gareth.

"*I wish you were here,*" I thought.

But instead, I settled for the ghost who'd become my best friend.

CHAPTER TWENTY-SIX

Salome

A maid slipped into the room, a new gown draped over her arm. She glanced at the bed where Gareth was and gave me a sympathetic look. "I'm sorry about Lord Gareth, milady."

"Thank you.

Darach scooted away from me. The security that'd surrounded me through the night slipped away. But I felt refreshed—like a battery put on a charger.

Gwenn and Nevin came into my room.

Nevin glanced at me. "Salome?"

"Um—I'm right here." I waved.

The worry lines in his forehead disappeared, and he let out a relieved sigh. "How are you feeling?" He reached for me, pulling me into a hug.

"Better."

"You look better—more rested." He stared at me.

Over his shoulder, Darach glowered and crossed his arms.

"I have a meeting with the guards this morning, but I thought perhaps we could have lunch together." Nevin released me. "You need to keep your energy up."

"I-I don't know. I'm not sure I want to leave Gareth."

"I can sit with him for a bit. If there are any changes, I can send word to you," Gwenn said.

My chest tightened. What if something happened to him while I was gone? Did I want to chance not being here? But as Gwenn met my eye, I realized that maybe she wanted some time alone with her brother. I nodded. "Okay."

"I'll send someone up to help you bathe and get changed."

"Actually, I'd like to do it on my own." Even though I'd been in Summer for a while now, I still didn't like people helping me. Besides, I was capable enough to wash myself.

"Very well. I'll see you later." He sauntered out.

Gwenn hung back for a moment, watching me. "Are you really going to be all right?"

"I think so," I lied, because right now, I wasn't sure. For today, I had to wear a mask, one that said I was fine even though on the inside I felt like shattered glass with tiny, broken pieces strewn about that might not be able to be glued back together. Today, I'd have to determine what to do. Either I became the Summer Queen and possibly got enough power to save Gareth, or I let him die peacefully in his sleep, losing him forever.

Put like that, it didn't seem like such a tough choice anymore.

Gwenn peered about the room, her gaze focusing on everything but her brother as if she was scared that he'd pass away if she looked at him. She seemed so uncomfortable. "If you need anything, let me know."

"I will." My lips brushed Gareth's forehead before I left his room. I went back to my quarters to get ready for a quick bath. I stared at my hands. Maybe I wasn't ready to get up yet. Maybe I'd never be. What I wouldn't give to be back home with Grandma right now. She'd know how to help me. She and Grandpa always made things better.

"Grab a change of clothes," Darach said.

"What?"

"I'm bringing you to the best place in Summer." He bowed, shooting me a quick grin.

I glared, not in the mood for jokes. "You're from the Autumn Court—how would you know the best places here?"

"Believe it or not, Nevin and I used to be good friends. So I visited for balls and other such gatherings. Back when..."

"Back when what?"

He floated across the way until he stood by the doors to the balcony. A dreamy look encompassed his features, he gave a wistful smile. *"Back when, Nevin and I used to be in love with one another."*

"Whoa, wait a second, come again?" My brow raised.

"Nevin and I used to be together, before the fall of Spring and Autumn, before he ran away to the human world—before he betrayed me and my kingdom."

"What happened? I mean, you've been pretty anti-Nevin since we've met." I clutched a clean dress in my arms and moved to his side.

"Nevin and I were schooled by the same scholars and trained by the same Master of Arms. It was during this time that we fell in love with one another. We'd spend nights studying together or practicing sword in the training yard. We were always together." He smiled sadly.

"So you fell in love with him while at school?" I stared at him; to say I was surprised, was an understatement.

"Yes. I knew right away, that there'd never be anyone else for me. We kept our relationship a secret for a long time—especially after we both were named heirs for our kingdoms. But eventually we got tired of sneaking around to see one another and decided to be open about our coupledom."

Even in his ghost form, I noticed his hands clench and the anger in his eyes.

"Darach?"

"The kingdoms' elders did not agree with our union, nor did the Queen of Faerie. We were told that because we were both heirs to our throne, we couldn't be together or our kingdoms would fall. They told us that we would need to marry women in order to control all elements of our powers—both the feminine and masculine side. We were forbidden to be together."

"Oh God. Darach, I'm sorry, I didn't know," I said.

"I know. It's not your fault. At first, I thought Nevin and I would still be able to find ways to meet up, even if it meant being only lovers. We knew we couldn't choose ourselves over our kingdoms. And since Faerie had chosen us to rule, we could not in our right minds abandon our people. But that didn't stop Nevin from becoming angry and wanting to get back at the elders. So he decided to visit the mortal world and bed human women, because the only thing the elders hated worse than two kings being together was the thought of Nevin with a human. He did it to show them they weren't going to control him." He floated back and forth, as if trying to diffuse his feelings.

What did this mean? If Nevin was truly gay, not bisexual, then I had to rethink what he was asking me to do. He wasn't being selfish, and this wasn't a ploy to get me to be with him instead of Gareth. He was giving up the chance for love, too, all to save Gareth and his kingdom.

I swallowed. "So, does that mean Nevin likes boys *and* girls?"

Darach shrugged. *"He can be with either gender, but his heart belongs only to one. Of course, I hated seeing him be so free with himself—to lay with women and dismiss me as if he'd never had my heart. As if my love meant nothing to him. Not too long after this, Grisselle attacked Spring. Nevin came back to Faerie, and that is when we'd made our plan to try and stop Winter...and you know the rest of that story—that he never came, and soon after, he got cursed to the human world. He deserted me. If only he'd stayed with me. If only we'd stood up for what we had... And that, is why I am so bitter...so angry."*

"Then you must really hate me," I said.

"No. I don't. I wanted to—because you have access to Nevin—and it's you he's asked to be his queen. But I find myself wanting to protect you, to be here for you. You're kind. You're powerful. And you see the best in everyone, even those who treat you badly. But if I had to choose all over again, between Nevin and my kingdom, I'd have to put my people first...no matter how much I love him." He shook his head. *"So you see, I understand what he's asking of you. He loves our people. And so do I. Enough to make hard sacrifices."*

I swallowed hard. "It wasn't fair what the elders did to you and Nevin. They should've allowed you to be together. They should have searched for a way."

He reached for my hand, his ghostly fingers brushing mine. *"A dream for a life now passed. But thank you for your kind words."*

With a sigh, I walked to the door, and Darach ushered me from the room. Servants bowed to me as we made our way down the hall.

Kind smiles and sympathetic looks followed me all the way to the foyer of the palace, but I didn't want their sympathy. I wanted Gareth to wake up and be okay. I wanted to go back to my room and hide under my covers—to close my eyes and pretend this had never happened. As we turned the corner, my body went rigid when I saw Rowena standing in the doorway with a couple of other noble ladies.

She sneered, eyes gleaming with hatred. "Well if it isn't Lady Salome, looking lovely as ever."

My cheeks burned as I glanced down at my nightgown. Wisps of loose, dirty hair clung to my face. I probably should've cleaned up before I left my room.

"Ignore her. She's just jealous," Darach said beside me. *"Come this way."*

We veered away from her hateful watch and went down a long, arched hallway. After a couple of minutes, we came to a doorway and took steps down into a large garden area.

"These are the outdoor elven baths." Darach nodded ahead of us.

Waterfalls cascaded into small pools and splashed on rocks. Steam rose from the gleaming, Caribbean-blue waters. Stone walkways led to each separate bath—kind of like a Faerie spa.

"Milady, welcome. Can I help you?" I turned and saw a tall, beautiful elven woman. Dark hair hung past the middle of her back. Her pointed ears poked through the dark waves, and a long green dress swished about her bare feet. A young girl peeked out from behind her and gave me a shy smile.

Darach tapped my shoulder. *"Tell her you'd like to bathe."*

"Um—I heard this was the place to come for a bath?" My face went hot.

"Of course. We've got a private one available at the back of the gardens. Unless you're expecting someone to join you?"

My eyes widened, and I covered my chest with my arms. "No. I'll be bathing alone."

I shot a quick glance at Darach, making sure he understood. No way did I want him to pop up in the water next to me. Ghost or not, I still needed my privacy.

The elven woman nodded. "Very well—follow me."

The little girl stepped out from behind the woman, giving

me a good view of her bouncing golden curls. My mouth went dry when I noticed the long scar that ran down her cheek to her neck, but I averted my gaze, not wanting her to think I stared.

We followed a stone path between trimmed rose bushes and daffodils. The scent of honeysuckle hovered on the breeze. Butterflies fluttered between the plants, landing on tiny leaves.

The elven woman brought me into a hedged off area. My breath caught in my throat as I saw the pool. Lilies floated in the bath; the constant splash of the waterfall sprayed me with warm water. It was beautiful—like a tropical movie shoot. This would've been a perfect place to spend time with Gareth.

My throat thickened. There were so many things I'd wanted to do with him. So many places I'd wanted to go. But I might still be able to, if I chose to accept Nevin's offer. It just meant that we wouldn't have the future together we'd wanted. But at least he'd be alive. I thought about Darach and all he'd been forced to give up—how hard it must be seeing Nevin with someone else.

Could I do that? Watch Gareth find someone else? Or would I be able to put him through that, knowing of our blood bond? But was it more selfish of me to let him die when I had the means to possibly save him?

The small girl handed me a bar of soap and a glass decanter of shampoo, snapping me out of my stupor.

"Run along now, Moira." The elven woman shooed the child away.

"If I can ask—what happened to Moira?"

Her smile faded. "Her village was attacked a few months back. Trolls from Winter murdered most of the people, save for a few children. I-I took her in when our soldiers brought her here."

A lump lodged in my throat. "D-does this happen a lot? I

mean the attacks?" I remembered the refugees we'd seen in Spring.

Her eyes welled. "Yes, Milady. Winter grows closer to our borders every day. But don't you worry about such things. King Nevin will stop them. He'll find a way to protect us." She wiped the moisture from her eyes. "I apologize. Enough of this talk — why don't you get into the bath?"

"Thank you."

She nodded. "If you need anything — anything at all — just ring the bell." She pointed to the silver bell on the stone table.

She hurried down the path, leaving me alone. I stripped out of my clothes and stuck my toe into the water. It was so warm. With a sigh, I slid into the depths. The hot current cascaded over me as I found rock seats built into pools. I dipped my head back, letting the heat relax my muscles.

When I closed my eyes, I saw the scar running along Moira's face. Why would anyone want to hurt an innocent child? Damn it! Someone had to stop Winter. They created nothing but horror, death, and chaos. They took everything from me. And not just from me — from the people of Summer, Autumn, and Spring. Tears burned my eyes. And Gareth — they'd wounded him, left the love of my life on death's doorstep.

Now I might never be able to tell him I love him again. All I'd have were memories. Hatred burned in my blood like acid.

It sickened me how easily Winter could destroy homes and people with so little regard. I gripped hold of the bar of soap and scrubbed my skin as if I could wash away the sorrow.

"Ah, there you are. I finished my meetings early," Nevin said.

I squealed, covering myself with my hands. "Nevin…"

"Don't worry, my back is turned to you." To be fair, his back really was turned to me, but still. "Moira here escorted me to you. She's got a towel for you to dry with."

Moira walked over and handed me the large white cloth. Shyly, I waited for her to turn around, too, and then I climbed from the bath and dried off as fast as possible. I quickly grabbed my clean dress and tugged it over my head, letting my wet hair hang about my shoulders.

"I'm dressed now, you can turn around."

He spun to face me then bent down. "Moira, can you let Lady Alma know that I'd like to take lunch down here today?"

She curtsied, giving him a big toothy grin. But before she left, Nevin handed her a gold coin.

My eyes welled. "I'm sorry—I didn't know." I pointed at Moira's retreating frame. "I-I didn't realize how bad things were. Or at least, I didn't want to admit it."

Nevin's gaze softened, and he walked to my side, reaching for my hand. "Shh…it's okay. There's still time to stop Winter. They haven't won yet."

"We have to destroy them. They've hurt so many people—taken so much." My body shook as another round of sobs tore through me, and I thought about Gareth being cut down. About Darach's people, my family—Moira.

Nevin pulled me into a hug as if that would comfort me and make me forget what was going on around us. But it wouldn't. Nothing would.

"We will, I promise."

With a sniffle, I pulled back and wiped my face on the sleeve of my gown. Would the pain ever go away?

Servants soon arrived with a table. Once they had it set up, they laid a lacy cloth over it then set plates of food down. Nevin gestured for me to sit in one of the chairs that'd been brought in. We sat in silence as we ate.

When I glanced at Nevin, I noticed the dark rings circling

his eyes. He'd lost weight, too.

"You need to take better care of yourself or you'll be no good for Summer."

He offered me a pained smile. "Sometimes it's easier said than done. It just feels like the weight of Faerie is on my shoulders." He set his fork down with a *clink*. "Summer is the last court who can stand against Winter."

I reached across the table and caught his hand in mine, giving him what reassurance I had, even if it wasn't much. "You're not alone in this."

He stared at my fingers for long moments before he raised his gaze to mine. "Salome, I know you've been grieving for Gareth and will continue to do so. And this hardly seems the time. But I must ask again. Will you be my queen?" He let my hand go and stood, pacing back and forth.

His offer carried a different weight now that I knew his secret history. Would he hate me if I revealed to him I knew his secret? Or would that make it easier for him to admit what he was giving up, too?

"It doesn't have to be a match made of love," he said. "I know your heart belongs to Gareth and always will. And to be honest, I don't know how to love someone, as you already know. But I *need* you. Summer needs you. And I trust no one more than you. No matter how much you've denied it, I know there is strong magic inside you. We just have to find a way for you to harness it." He watched me expectantly, his gaze boring through me. "Even Doris knows Faerie needs you—she will not tell me exact details, but she knows you're important to us. Please, I'm begging you, and you know I'm not one to beg. If not for me, and if not for Summer, then for Gareth. You taking the throne could be the very thing that saves him."

I swallowed hard. At eighteen, this wasn't something I was

ready for. Yet didn't I owe it to Gareth? He'd risked his life for me and for the kingdom he loved. And didn't I owe it to Moira? She'd lost her whole family to Winter. And what about the humans who'd been kidnapped from my world? If I didn't put a stop to Grisselle's reign, what would keep her from taking more of my people?

My heart clamored in my chest, and I took a deep breath. I held his gaze then looked away. Somehow, I got the feeling this moment had been in the making since he'd pulled me from my grandparents' pond. I would never love him, and I knew he'd never love me. He *couldn't* love me, not like that, even if I had felt that way about him.

But could I live with that? Would being able to save Gareth and get my revenge on Winter be reason enough to agree to be his queen? Nevin was right about one thing, Grandma had said that I needed to be here—was this what she meant? Or was there something else I had to do? Only a couple weeks ago, my life had already been figured out. Gareth was my true love. We were going to get married and live out our happily-ever-after in Faerie. But Grisselle had taken that from me—maybe not directly, but she'd started this war.

Then another thought struck me. What was to keep Winter from killing my family? They knew where Grandma and Mom lived. For as long as I remembered, Grisselle had had a hand in my life and in my nightmares. Her having Kassandra curse Nevin was only the beginning. How many of my ancestors had died because of the Winter Curse?

She had to be stopped. If she wasn't, everything would fade into legend, and the worst horrors would be released on the world. Could I live with myself then, knowing I'd had a chance to put a stop to it, but I'd chosen to do nothing?

I glanced at Nevin once more. In my heart, I knew I didn't

love him. Hell, most days I didn't even like him. But maybe he felt the same way about me. And maybe, too, we both wanted the same thing: Winter to be stopped. No matter how much of a pain he'd been, Gareth had always stayed by his side. Maybe part of it was out of duty, but he obviously cared enough about Nevin to keep him alive—if not because they were friends, then for the kingdom.

Some sacrifices had to be made for the greater good.

"Yes, I'll be your queen. But there will be boundaries on how we handle this. Not to mention there are changes I think need to be made here at the Summer Court. And as soon as I'm crowned, I want your word that we'll heal Gareth."

"Yes of course." He quit pacing, circled the table, and drew me into his arms. "Thank you. I don't think I'll ever have enough lifetimes to make this up to you. I'll send messengers out right away to those dwelling closest to the kingdom. We'll have your coronation tonight."

Tonight? Oh, God. I so wasn't ready for this.

CHAPTER TWENTY-SEVEN

Salome

By the time I got back to my room, the panic set in. My palms became slick with sweat, and my stomach knotted as if someone had tied it in a bazillion shoelaces. Oh God, what was I thinking? I couldn't be queen.

"Darach?" I glanced around my room.

"I'm right here." He appeared next to me with a pop.

I paced back and forth. "I just agreed to become the Summer Queen."

His gaze swept over me. *"I think you'll be a great queen."*

My eyes widened. "What? You can't be serious. I don't know what I'm doing. I'll fail and…"

His hands shot out, gripping me by the shoulders. *"No, you won't. You're destined for this. Don't you see? You broke the curse on Nevin. You freed me and my people from Grisselle's clutches. You're exactly what Faerie needs."*

"I'm scared. I don't want to mess things up."

"It's okay to be scared. But trust me when I say this is the best thing for Summer. They need a queen. With both a queen and a king, the power will flow more freely. They'll be able to put

*up better magic defenses along the borders. You'll be able to do
everything that I wished I could."*

I opened my mouth to say more, but a knock sounded on the door behind us. "Salome, it's Gwenn. Nevin told me to bring the seamstresses up to get your measurements. This will be the fastest dress made in the history of dresses."

Darach gave me a nod and disappeared.

"Come in," I said.

Gwenn ushered in three elven women. They had measuring tapes, different shades of material, ribbons, and pencils.

"Nevin told me the news," Gwenn said as she stood watching me get fitted for a coronation gown.

I gave her a weak smile. "I'm still in shock that I accepted."

"Well, you're definitely moving your way up the ranks," she said, her voice hardened.

"Look, I didn't agree to this just because I wanted a title." My eyes narrowed. "I-I'm trying to help."

"We'll see about that. But at least you finally came to your senses. You made a real fool of Nevin the last time he asked you. As a human, you should be grateful for this kind of attention."

Choked up, I turned my head so she wouldn't see the tears. Sometimes Gwenn could be a real bitch. Was she mad because I'd accepted the offer so soon after her brother was hurt? Or did she just hate the fact that I was human?

Once the seamstress took my measurements and fitted me for my gown, I opened the door to my room and headed down the long hall. I needed to get out of there for a little while.

Gwen stopped me. "Where are you going?"

"I just need a few minutes, okay?"

"You can't go anywhere without an escort."

I pushed around her and headed to Gareth's room. Taking a deep breath, I turned the handle, surprised to find it unlocked.

Gwenn came up short, her eyes watching me carefully, but she didn't follow me inside.

Gareth's scent overwhelmed me as I closed the door behind me. I inhaled deeply, half expecting to see him come in from the balcony or pop up from behind the four-poster bed. But he didn't. I envisioned his heart-melting smile and his touch, and the way he'd hold me like I was the most precious treasure in the world. Instead, I stared at his pale, weakened form.

Everything I looked at reminded me of him. The swords. The large mahogany furniture, which matched the color of his eyes. The way the sunlight spilled in the glass doors, like the light that he'd been in my world. My chest tightened, and I sat on the edge of his bed, laying my head just above where his heart was. I listened to the faint beat.

I couldn't breathe without him. I fisted the quilt and took in his familiar outdoorsy smell, and then I lay back, trying to keep from crying. What I wouldn't give to feel his arms around me.

"I need you," I whispered. "So much. You can't leave me. I-I might be able to heal you, but if I do and you wake up, things will be different. I wish you could tell me I'm making the right choice. That you'd rather live a life without me than die."

"Salome?" Gwenn poked her head in the door. When she saw me crying, she just stood there. "You should go back to your chambers now. I think they're just taking in a ceremonial gown for you."

I nodded then stood, not saying a word as we went back to my room.

When she made sure my quarters were safe she turned to me, her gaze softened. "I'm sorry for what I said earlier. And I'm sorry my brother got hurt." With that, she left me once more.

Nervous flutters tingled in my gut. I took a deep breath in an attempt to calm myself.

Just breathe. You'll be fine. I'm sure no one's ever died during a coronation.

I smoothed the light blue skirt of my dress down with my clammy hands. The gold roses embroidered in the material seemed to gleam beneath the soft glow of candlelight. What if I fell down the stairs when I was introduced? Or what if I barfed? Yeah, that would not be pretty.

"Salome?" Nevin stuck his head in my room.

"Yeah?" I glanced at him. He was more dressed up than usual. His light blue tunic matched the color of my dress, and he'd tucked the legs of his white breeches into his brown, leather boots. A gold and sapphire crown rested upon his head.

His sky colored eyes met mine. "You look beautiful." He stepped inside, securing the door behind him.

"Thanks. I'm nervous as hell though."

"That's to be expected." He chuckled, then pulled a decorative wooden box from behind his back. "I wanted to give you this. A gift from the king to his queen."

With trembling hands, I took the box from him and unlatched the clasp. I gasped. Inside I found a sparkling sapphire necklace, along with a matching ring.

"Oh my gosh, it's gorgeous."

He smiled. "Why don't you turn around and I'll help you put it on?"

I spun to face the wall, then lifted my hair as he secured it to me. The stones were surprisingly warm against my skin. With the necklace in place, he walked around until he stood in front of me. This time, he took the ring and slid it on my left ring finger. He set the box on a nearby table, then stared at me.

"I hope I don't embarrass you or myself in front of all those people." I fidgeted with my hands.

"You won't," he whispered. "Listen, before, when you said I had no idea what it felt like to lose someone or love someone, I wanted you to know that I do."

Was he going to come clean about Darach? I watched the sadness swim in his eyes.

"Do you want to talk about it?"

"No, not really. Just know that I once loved someone so much it hurt. And when he was taken from me, I swore I'd never let anyone near my heart again."

My glance flickered to Darach, who was sitting on my bed. "What was his name?"

Nevin lowered his head, refusing to meet my gaze. "You know, I think this might be a tale for another time, Salome. We need to both be sound of mind for the coronation. And you need to make sure that your tattoo is visible for all to see tonight. They will not be able to deny you becoming queen, not when Faerie has marked you. They cannot ignore that."

With a sigh, I shifted my gaze from him. "I sure hope you know what you're doing by making me your queen."

"I do." He offered me his arm. "Are you ready?"

"As I'll ever be." I looked at Darach.

"Don't worry, I'll be there the whole time." He stood to follow us, his face flushed.

I was sure he'd heard Nevin's confession. Maybe that'd change how he felt about Nevin now. Maybe it'd offer him some small comfort to know that Nevin still thought of him.

When we stepped into the hall, several royal guards fell into place both in front of us and behind us. We went down a back stairwell. At the bottom were two enormous white oak doors with crowns carved on them. At our approach, they swung open. My heart clattered against my chest like someone clanging against metal bars. My pulse leapt to my throat as I gawked at the crowd that'd gathered in the throne room.

My eyes wandered the room. Most faces bore hopeful looks, smiles, or tears. But when I saw Rowena, I knew not everyone was happy. She glared, her animosity almost choking me.

Nevin led me before the throne. He released my hand and turned to address the crowd. "Good people of Summer. We have gathered here today to witness the crowning of our Summer Queen—the first in centuries."

Cheers and whistles erupted around the room. My legs knocked together.

Please don't let me pass out.

"Lady Salome has dedicated herself to our cause—but most of all to us. She broke the Winter curse in the human world. And today, the land has found her worthy—as I've found her worthy."

Nevin's fingers brushed against my skin as he pulled my hair back to reveal the golden tattoo on my forehead. Gasps and more cheers went up.

"Let there be no more doubt. My dear people, we've at last found our queen. Lord and Lady Claudius, bring forth the crown."

The masses parted as two Fae entered the chambers. One carried a blue velvet pillow with a crown resting on top of it. The other held a white oak and sapphire scepter. They climbed the four stairs to the dais I stood on.

"Lady Salome, I ask that you please take a seat." Nevin's hand rested on my arm as he helped me to sit on the throne. He turned first to Lord Claudius for the scepter. "Lady Salome, I give to you the power, love, and sanctity of Summer. From here on out you will be the heart and voice of our people, as I am the shield and sword. Do you, Lady Salome of the Human World, accept this gift?"

I wet my lips. "I accept the Scepter of Summer—I will be the heart and voice of our people."

He gave me a reassuring smile and placed the scepter in my left hand. Next, he turned to Lady Claudius. He raised the jeweled crown above my head. "Lady Salome, as the sovereign King of Summer, I choose you above all others to be my queen. I entrust our lands, our people, our magic, and our love to your hands. As my queen, you shall sit by my side and help to rule Summer. Your life is my life, as my life is your life. We are one. We are Summer. Lady Salome of the Human World, do you accept your queendom and profess to protect it at all costs, even if it means the ultimate price?"

My erratic pulse drowned out everything, but I slowed my breathing and stared straight ahead. "I accept the Crown of Summer. I will protect our lands, our people, our magic, and our love. Your life is my life, and my life is your life. We are one, Nevin of Summer. We are Summer."

Nevin lowered the crown until it rested on my head. My body prickled with electricity as if a magical blanket had been thrown over me. There was no denying it—power flowed stronger in my veins. He offered me his hand and helped me stand.

"I present to you Queen Salome of Summer. May she reign by my side forever more."

Whoops and hollers echoed around me. I smiled, tears welling in my eyes.

This is for you, Gareth. I promise I won't let you down.

"Now, it is time to present the queen to our kingdom." Nevin rested a hand at the small of my back as our guards fell in once more.

We exited the room and headed up a grand gold and white marble staircase. "Where are we going?"

"The Grand Balcony. You can see the whole kingdom from there. And it's where royals are presented after a coronation."

I glanced at him and for the first time in a long time, I noticed some of the strain had melted away. The smile he gave me reached his eyes. He looked rejuvenated, hopeful, and happy. I gave his hand a squeeze.

"Summer really will be okay now," I said. "I—I have a feeling things will be set right."

"I feel it too. The tides are shifting."

When we reached the top landing, a line of stained glass doors stood before me. The setting sun shone through the colored glass, sending brilliant rainbows bouncing across the walls and floor. Even before we walked onto the balcony, I heard the roar of the crowd.

"Ready, my queen?" Nevin whispered.

"Yes, my king."

Together we moved onto the opulent deck, high above Summer. Down below were thousands of Fae—elves, satyrs, centaurs, even some humans. Nevin raised our hands together, and we both waved.

Everyone shouted and screamed and cheered. Their love and hope washed over me. They'd been waiting for me. Darach's words came rushing back to me.

You're destined for this. Don't you see? You broke the curse on Nevin. You freed me and my people from Grisselle's clutches. You're exactly what Faerie needs.

And somehow I knew he was right. As I waved to *my* people below, I noticed the dark skies in the distance—Winter's threat closing in on us. In that moment, I would never doubt my choice to become queen. Others might've been pushing me to take the throne, but in the end, this was my choice. And now, I had one more thing to do—A life to save. I only prayed I wasn't too late.

CHAPTER TWENTY-EIGHT

Wood popped in the fireplace, spraying sparks in the air. My gaze rested on Grisselle, who sat eyeing the chessboard. She took deep breaths as if to calm herself. I hesitated in the doorway for long moments, wondering if I should disturb her or not, but at last, she looked up at me and waved me in.

"You don't have to stand in the doorway," she said. "I didn't mean to scare you. It's just that things around me feel as if they're falling apart."

I nodded. "I understand completely. Look, I've had a chance to think about the offer you made the other night. I mean, I'd like to take you up on it. If I share what information I know, then I want your word and promise that you won't kill me."

Excitement and fear raced through my blood: fear that she'd decide I wasn't worth it and have me sent back to the Bone Yard; excitement for what my life could be if she let me live. I'd be trapped here, but at least I'd be alive.

And if I decided I wanted to visit the human world, I was sure I could convince Grisselle to let me. She needed me just as much as I needed her.

"Kadie? Are you sure?" She floated to my side, her hands clasping mine. "If you do this, then you'll be here with me, forever. You will be like the sister I was supposed to have. And you'll have to understand that sometimes I will have to ask you to do things you might not agree with, but whatever those things are will be for the betterment and survival of our kingdom. If you go through with this, then I promise to name you as my Heir. You will be my everything. Together we will rule all of Faerie one day. You will answer to no one but me, and I will never kill you so long as you never betray me. I'm putting my trust in you."

She didn't have to say the threat laced through her promise. I didn't really have a choice. I could be her confidant, her sister, her heir, or I could turn her down and lose my life as quickly— as horribly—as Demetria had lost hers. But it wouldn't be enough to simply agree to her offer. I had to make her believe I wanted it. I had to make *myself* believe I wanted it.

"I won't betray you. I've had enough of that in my own life. We both deserve better than what we've been handed over the years." I squeezed her hand back.

"Then let us make this official." Grisselle produced a silver dagger.

My heart leapt into my throat and suddenly I couldn't breathe. "What's that for?" I took a step back.

"If we are to be sisters then we will do it in blood. You will become of my blood and I yours. We shall be blood sisters." She took the blade and slid it along her palm.

I watched the crimson fluid bubble up in the wound. She handed the knife to me. I squeezed my eyes shut. *Please don't let me regret this.* My hand trembled as I opened my eyes once more. I pressed the cool metal of the dagger against my skin and sliced. A sharp pain flared in my hand, and I cringed.

Grisselle clasped our wounded palms together, letting the blood intermingle. "From this day forward, we are sworn sisters bound to one another. Your thoughts will be my thoughts, and mine will be yours. We shall always know where the other one is. We swear in this moment our allegiance to each other. I will protect you and watch after you like a sister and you must do the same for me. Do you swear, Kadie, by your blood?"

Not like I had a choice.

I wet my lips. "Yes, I swear upon my blood."

Even as the words left my mouth, I realized what I was doing to myself—how I was making myself a more certain prisoner in a way I might never escape. But I would do it, and I would do it to survive.

"Then you are, as of now, a Winter Princess and Heir to the Winter Throne." Grisselle pulled her hand from mine, then kissed my brow. Her lips were as cool as ice cubes against my warm skin.

I snaked my arms around her and gave her a hug. It was done. I'd secured my safety. Grisselle embraced me back, rocking me back and forth.

"I'm glad we're sisters now," she said. "Now come. Sit with me and tell me all you know of Salome, her family, and Gareth…"

The queen asked lots of questions about Salome's grandma after I explained how she seemed to know a lot about Faerie. I told her some of the stories Doris had read to us when we were younger, and how Salome was only allowed to go certain places, but never far from their property. I even explained about Gareth and how he was always at the right place at the right time whenever something happened with Salome and how the only places I ever saw him in the human world were Perky Joe's and anywhere Salome was.

I didn't know what kinds of information she'd find important, but she absorbed every detail I gave her: odd things I'd noticed about Salome over the years, the people she hung around with, her family and what roles they played in her life.

The odd thing was that the more I opened up to her, the easier it felt to tell her whatever she wanted to know. Like I could trust her, even though I knew I shouldn't. I shuddered as I wondered whether the blood bond she'd forged between us would have deeper consequences than I'd realized.

When I finished, she thanked me and hugged me, telling me I'd given her all the information she needed and tonight we'd have a celebration in my honor, to introduce me to her kingdom as her heir.

As I stood in my room getting ready, I slipped into the beautiful red gown she'd laid out for me. There were snow-flakes sewn into the hems of it, made of white lace. I then put on the ruby jewelry she'd given me, as well as the small crown, which fit atop my dark hair perfectly.

Rena, Etienne's maid, handed me a pair of red satin slippers. "You are ready for dinner now."

"Thank you. Where's Etienne?"

She frowned. "In his room, getting dressed." She took a step back from me. "Kadie, I can't help but think you've made a mistake. Etienne's worried about you."

I laughed, hoping she couldn't hear my anxiety. I couldn't afford for Grisselle to ever doubt my commitment. This was my life now. It was the price I'd pay for staying alive. "There's nothing to worry about. I'm fine. Besides, look at everything the queen has given me. She and I are friends now."

Rena nodded. "I see. Well, if you don't need me now, I'm going to go back to check on Etienne."

"I'm good, thank you."

Soon a pair of guards came to escort me to the dining room. I noticed they were leading me back to the original macabre part of the castle. However, when I got to the dining room door, Grisselle awaited me.

"Ah, you look beautiful, sister. Red is definitely your color."

I looked at the ground. "Thank you."

"Are you ready to be introduced?"

"I-I think so." My nerves seemed to twitch beneath my skin like a fish flopping on land.

Doors opened to reveal a less dark room. I noticed Grisselle didn't have any bones in there tonight, nor did she have any disturbing tortures set up to watch. Relief flooded over me.

When we entered, everyone stood: humans, royals, servants. Grisselle clutched hold of my arm and smiled down at me.

"Good people of Winter, I want to introduce you to our newest Winter Royal, Princess Kadie. You will treat her as you treat me, and you will obey her. She has been vital to me over these past few days and is like a sister."

My gaze drifted across the crowd. I saw the surprise etched on some of the Fae lords' and ladies' faces, like they couldn't believe the queen had given me a title.

And as terrible as I felt knowing Grisselle could harm me at any moment, that strange warm feeling came over me again, the same I'd felt when sharing with her my secrets about Salome. There were benefits to being her prisoner. There were benefits to earning her favor.

No more would I have to serve those bastards. Now they'd have to listen to me. But more importantly, I saw the resentment and horror on Crazy Chick's face, and I smiled. She'd been trying for years to get in with the royals, constantly throwing herself at Teodor and the other princes, but I was the one granted this. I was the one the queen had chosen.

"*They will respect you, you will see…*" I heard Grisselle say, even though her lips never moved.

"Wait, how did you do that?" I whispered.

"*We're blood sisters now, which means I will always be able to hear your thoughts, and when I allow it, you'll hear mine as well. We'll be able to communicate without everyone else butting into our conversations. Just think the words and I'll hear them.*"

"*Like this?*" I thought.

"*Yes, exactly. Now, come along, let's not keep our guests waiting.*" Grisselle guided me over to the head of the table, where we took our seats.

Immediately servants began to fill our goblets and plates. Some of the humans eyed me warily, but I kept a smile on my face. Were they sickened by the choice that I had made? Did they think I'd sold out? Or were they jealous? I was sure that if any of them were given the opportunity as I was, they would've taken it, if only to stay safe. I wouldn't let them make me feel bad. It wasn't like this had been my first choice. I'd tried every other option first. But the idea of staying alive won out. And I'd do anything to preserve myself.

As I took a bite of broccoli, my glance fell on Etienne. He watched me closely, never taking his eyes from me. I studied his chiseled face, loving the way his pale blond hair stuck up in messy tufts. How his sea colored eyes undid me. Ever since I'd met him, he'd tried to protect me, but now I didn't need him to. We'd be on more even ground now, both of us Winter Royals. Grisselle already said I could have any man I wanted, and I wanted him.

I smiled at him, and he nodded in return before switching

his attentions to the food on his plate.

Just then, Teodor burst in, carrying a gust of cold air with him. He stalked toward the head table and bowed.

"I bring news from Summer." His jaw twitched as if he was nervous, which was odd for him. Nothing ever bothered him, so whatever he was about to say would be the nail in someone's coffin.

Griselle lifted a goblet filled with crimson liquid to her lips then set it down on the table. It turned her lips scarlet, making me think of vampires.

"Well, what's this news you've interrupted my feast for?" She narrowed her eyes.

"Summer has crowned a queen."

She leapt to her feet, knocking over her cup. Blood soaked the tablecloth as she clenched her fists. Through our bond, I felt her hatred and anger burning like acid thrown on my skin. A cloud of blackness swirled in my mind, her emotions going wild as if they'd been sucked into a cyclone.

"What?" She growled and swept her arms over the table, knocking plates, cups, food, everything off. "Everyone out! Now! Teodor, gather the princes and go to my quarters."

Etienne climbed to his feet and hurried to my side. "Get to your room. Don't unlock the door for anyone."

"What's going to happen? She won't hurt you, will she?"

"I don't know. But if something goes wrong, Rena will come for you."

"But I don't understand."

"If Summer really crowned a queen, it means Winter is losing or will lose its grip on Faerie."

And if that happened, it meant Grisselle might lose everything, which in turn meant I might lose my newly found safety.

CHAPTER TWENTY-NINE

Salome

Nevin and I hurried from the balcony to Gareth's room, where one of the guards stood vigil over him.

"How is he?" I asked, hurrying to Gareth's bedside.

"Hanging on, Your Highness. But his heart grows weaker. The elders stopped in to see him for a moment and they were surprised to find him still with us. He's a fighter—"

I sucked in a deep breath. We were running out of time. If we were going to do this, it had to be now.

Nevin scooched in next to me. "Jacob, you can leave us now."

The guard bowed and slipped out of the room. Nevin turned to me. He looked as nervous as I felt. "Are you ready?"

"I-I think so. Just tell me what I need to do." Nerves twisted in and out of my belly like a whirlpool. My heart collided with my ribcage.

"You must place one hand on Gareth and give me your other one. Together, we will call upon the powers of Summer to heal him. You must open your mind to receive the magic. Stay focused, for it is easy for a new user to burn themselves out on it."

"Okay." I took a deep breath.

Nevin clasped my hand then laid his palm flat against Gareth's chest, just above his wound. Trembling and praying this worked, I placed my fingers right above Nevin's on Gareth's skin.

"Listen to my words, Salome. Repeat them. Embrace them. And feel them," Nevin said. "As King and Queen of Summer, we call upon the power of our land—upon the essence of life—to heal one of our own. Use us as your instruments. Let whatever your will be, happen."

I repeated the words in my head, clutching tight to Nevin. Warm tingles vibrated beneath my feet, racing up my legs and chest and through my arms, until beams of golden light flowed like a stream from my fingertips.

Gareth gasped, then his body shook violently, making the bed move beneath him. Fear embraced me, but I felt Nevin squeeze my hand tighter.

"Focus, Salome. Don't lose sight of what you want."

What I wanted was to have Gareth healed. I needed him. I did as Nevin said and focused harder. Gareth twitched and tossed, until I saw a dark cloud explode from his wound. In that moment, Nevin released my hand and shot a sun shaped orb from his hand, which hit the blackened mass in midair. I watched the thing that'd come from Gareth be devoured by the light until it no longer remained.

Gareth gasped again, and this time, his eyes flew open, and he sucked in a deep lungful of air, as if he'd just emerged from a lake.

"Salome." His voice sounded gravelly as he reached for me. His arms gripped hold of me and he pressed me against his sweaty body. His fingers traced over my face.

My heart leapt into my throat. Like a warm blanket, I felt him in my mind, filling me with his presence.

He went still, his gaze landing on the tattoo—Summer's Mark. Then I felt his rage, swarming me like a nest of angry hornets. For someone just moments before on the verge of death, he moved super-fast as he leapt from the bed, eyes narrowed.

"What the fuck did you do?" Gareth stalked toward Nevin. In one swift movement, he clutched Nevin by his tunic, dragging him away from the side of the bed and slamming him against the wall.

"Need I remind you that I'm your king?" Nevin shoved him back.

"And apparently my betrothed is now your queen—

"Oh God, Gareth—I didn't betray you. Summer marked me before your return." Tears burned my eyes. *"You were injured and the elders told us you wouldn't make it. We tried everything to heal you, but it wouldn't work."*

He glared at me. *"So you married him?"*

"Nevin said there was a chance that if I took the throne as Summer Queen and answered the marking that our powers together would be able to heal you. I had to take the chance to save you... You have to believe me when I say that I did this because I love you, and I would never do anything to hurt you."

He turned his brown eyes on me. "I know you would never do something like that to me. But he would, after everything I've done for him." He glared at Nevin. "This was your plan all along, wasn't it? To take her from me?" His fist connected with the wall.

Nevin glowered. "No, it wasn't. When she chose you, I was okay with it. I had every intention of letting you have your happily ever after. But things changed when I found out she had magic. Look at her head, Gareth. Look at the tattoo. She's been marked by Summer. She was meant to be our queen. If it's any consolation, I don't love her. But I do need her...as does our kingdom. And if she hadn't become queen to save you, you'd have died. She did this just as much for you as she did for our kingdom."

I caught Gareth's eye. "I felt your pain when you first got injured—then you didn't answer me when I called to you. Do you understand the hell I went through? Watching you come back to Summer on the back of a horse, practically dead?"

"I'm sorry. We got ambushed, and I was injured. I, and a few other soldiers, took refuge in the mountains so I could heal, but if I would've known this would happen, I would've found a way to get back sooner."

My legs shook beneath me. "I will not let you make me feel bad for saving you. Yes, this wasn't the perfect option to do so, but I did it out of love."

Nevin glanced at Gareth. "I didn't do this to be selfish or heartless. I did this for Faerie. Do you think I liked betraying the trust of one of my closest friends and most loyal warriors? Because I didn't. My job is to protect the kingdom, and I have to do it by any means necessary. And I needed you to be here, alive, to help us fight the battle against Winter just as much as I needed Salome as my queen."

Gareth hit the wall again. "She was mine, Nevin. And I was hers."

Nevin ran a hand through his hair, his brow knit with worry. "I know. But I screwed up once, and it nearly cost me my kingdom. I couldn't take another chance. Gareth, you know I gave up the love of my life in order to protect our people. He died, and I couldn't even save him. I wasn't about to let the same happen to you and Salome. Yes, I need her. But it wasn't me I was looking out for. It was our people."

Gareth shook his head. "I just need a few minutes to absorb all this. Please leave." He opened his door, ushering us out.

Tears stung my eyes as I stormed to my room and buried my head in my hands. I hated seeing the hurt on his face—but he had to know I loved him. Couldn't he feel it through our bond? And yes, I knew Nevin's intent since I'd arrived in Summer was to make me his queen, but I honestly didn't think he'd use Gareth as a vice to get me to agree to this. He wasn't doing this to seduce me.

But was it possible he had some other ulterior motive?

Moments later, Nevin swept into my chambers. "Salome, listen, I'm truly sorry. I never meant for you to get hurt. That wasn't my intention. Just let me handle Gareth, okay? This was my idea and my doing."

"Would you stop telling me what to do? Let me take part of the blame—because, you know, I was the one who said yes. I could've told you to screw off or told you I didn't want to be queen." I glared.

His shoulders sagged, but he grabbed hold of my arm and led me onto the balcony. "I didn't go about this the right way, but I needed you. *They* needed you." He pointed to the kingdom below. "Winter is spreading, Salome. And I meant it when I told you I trusted no one else to become my queen. Please believe me."

"Ever since we met, you've manipulated me into doing stuff for you. First in the human world when you pretended to care about me so I'd break your damn curse, with the way you used magic to make me think I loved you. But this, I don't believe you did this to be malicious. For once, I think you actually tried to do the right thing."

He took my hand in his, uncurling my fingers. "My caring about you was never a lie—as far as people go, you're probably one of the few I can tolerate. And I doubt I'll ever be able to express how sorry I am for bringing you into this. But I don't regret you ruling by my side. You were meant to do it."

I stared at my hands then turned to him. "I want to be alone for a while."

He nodded. "I'll be in my chambers if you wish to speak later."

When he left, I went back inside. "Darach? Are you here?"

He appeared next to me, his face hardened. *"Yes."*

"Gareth is alive," I said.

"Yes, I heard. I was in his room when he came to."

My throat constricted. "What am I supposed to do now? Gareth was so angry."

"Maybe you should ask him." Darach nodded as Gareth came into my room.

"Nevin's assigned me as your new guard," Gareth said. "Gwenn will still help out when needed."

He remained quiet for long moments then he gripped hold of my arm as he spun me to face him, opening his mind to me.

"Do you know what kind of hell I've been through—cut off from you?" he asked.

"You? I thought you were going to die. I agonized over you—not a moment went by that I didn't miss you or think of you."

"I know, Salome," he whispered. His fingers traced my face. "I didn't dare reach out to you because I didn't want you to know how injured I was. For that I'm sorry. If I could take back all of this, I would. I've missed you so much."

I blinked back tears as my hand covered his. "What are we supposed to do now? Can I get out of being queen?"

He frowned. "Only through death."

"Then I'm stuck with Nevin?"

"No—you're stuck being *our* queen. It doesn't mean you have to be *his*," he growled.

"I wasn't ready to be thrown into this position. I agreed to it because I needed to save you and I wanted to avenge you. Avenge the people of Summer who've been hurt by Winter. I'm only eighteen, for God's sake. Not to mention, human." Tears streaked down my cheeks.

"And powerful," he finished for me. "Our people love you and they rally, united for the first time in centuries, all because of you."

"I never meant to hurt you."

He stroked my hair. Warmth traveled through our bond, ensnaring me like a tidal wave of heat. "I know. You don't know how pissed off I am right now. Pissed that Nevin went behind my back after you'd already told him no and we agreed that he'd let you be. Pissed that Nevin has any type of claim over you—even if it isn't built on love or intimacy, I don't like it. But at the same time, I can't deny what's in front of my face. You've been marked by Summer. Salome, I love you, and I'll be yours until the end of time, but I think you were meant to be our queen."

He leaned closer, his lips capturing mine. His mouth parted mine; his tongue traced inside it. His hands slipped down to my waist, pulling me against him like a suit of armor.

It'd been so long since I'd felt his touch—felt his lips upon mine. Heat raced through me like a horse on a track, and I clung tight to him, taking in his familiar scent and letting his warmth wash over me.

Breathless, I pulled back. "What do we do now?"

"You can have a consort. It's not exactly what I had in mind when I brought you here, but I'll settle for it as long as we can be together. And Nevin *will* know that you're physically off limits to him."

Heat raced to my cheeks. "Are you sure you can live with that?"

His mahogany eyes took me in. "Yes. When I bonded with you in the human world, I took my vows very seriously. Nothing will tear us a part. Not death. Not some idiot king making you his queen."

"Do you think Nevin will be okay with this?" My teeth grazed my bottom lip.

"I don't give a shit what he thinks. He's the one who broke my confidence—he made you queen. Yes, he helped save my life, and I owe you both for that. But if he won't agree to our terms, then I'll take you back to the human world right now."

My lips twitched. "Didn't you just say I couldn't get out of this queen gig?"

"Yes, but I'd move the world to be with you—even if it means becoming an enemy of Faerie to do it."

I nodded. "Then he either accepts our deal or we're gone."

"Do you want me to send Gwenn to get him?" Gareth released me.

"Yeah."

Gareth poked his head out the door to where his sister stood guard. He whispered something to her and she disappeared down the hallway.

A moment later Nevin came into my room. He eyed us, running a hand through his hair, his eyes downcast. "I said I was sorry. And I meant it."

"I know." And I did. His people meant everything to him. "You did what you had to do. We both did. And I will remain your queen. *Our* people need us. *But* I do have a few stipulations."

He glanced at me, giving me a wary look. "Such as?"

"I won't consummate our joining or marriage or whatever this is. There will be nothing physical between us."

"Understood."

"And I want to be with Gareth."

Nevin closed his eyes and rubbed his temples, then opened his eyes again. "Fine, but it will have to be in secret. If the council believes our joining to be a farce, they will try to have me removed. The kingdom and the council must believe we are together. You will have to attend public functions with me. Gareth has been assigned as your guard so he can be near you, and once night falls, he may come to your chambers as long as you're discreet."

"*Gareth?*" I glanced at him, wondering if this would be okay.

"*I'm agreeable to this as long as you are. This isn't my ideal choice, but given that you are marked, I don't want to take you away from Summer—nor do I want to lose you. And be assured, tonight, Nevin and I are going to have a very long talk.*"

"*Just be careful, he is your king, and I don't need you getting imprisoned for killing him.*"

"*We're gonna have words, that's all.*"

At last I looked at Nevin, who stood silent, watching us. "It looks as though I'm still your queen."

Hesitant, he took several small steps toward me. When I didn't back away, he hugged me. "Someday, I'll make this up to you."

"There's nothing to make up for. We both have a duty to the kingdom and to Faerie."

"I know." He released me and gave Gareth an uneasy glance. "Tomorrow, Salome might need to move into my chambers."

"The hell she will." Gareth fingered the sword at his side.

"For show, Gareth. I don't mean to bed her. There is a secret passage that runs between our rooms, so she doesn't have to sleep in there. But I can't take any chances."

Damn, Nevin just kept dropping one bomb after another. Soon I wouldn't be able to keep Gareth from kicking his ass.

"It's fine. We'll make it work," I said, coming to stand between them.

"Salome?" Gareth fixed me with his gaze. "Are you sure about this?"

"We don't need anyone to doubt I'm the queen."

"I'll let the servants know that your things will need to be moved soon." Nevin gave my arm one last squeeze then left the room.

When the door shut, I bit my tongue. This wasn't how I'd pictured my life in Faerie would be.

Gareth gave me a sad smile, and I rushed into his arms. "Please stay with me tonight. I—I just need someone to hold me."

He brushed tendrils of hair from my face. *"I'll stay as long as you need me."*

My head fell against this shoulder. He felt so solid—so real. I lifted my cheek and stared into dark brown eyes. His thumb traced my jaw, and when I didn't pull back, he leaned down, his warm breath fanning against my face, sending sparks shooting like stars down my spine.

Tonight, I didn't care if I overstepped any boundaries. After everything I'd been through, I wanted to feel something other than hurt and pain. I tilted my head.

"Salome?" Gareth's thoughts trickled into mine.

I stood on my tiptoes, snaking my arms around his shoulders. Not needing anymore prodding, his lips caught mine. A burst of heat simmered inside as he sucked on my bottom lip before letting his tongue dart inside my mouth. He tasted of apples and pomegranate wine and everything sweet. His fingers tangled in my hair as he pressed me closer. He seemed to consume me, like a forest fire. His kiss deepened and warmth coursed through my belly, spreading until I felt as though we were falling into one another.

Breathless, I pulled back, amazed to see the golden glow forming around us. He raised our entwined hands watching tiny looping flashes of light wind through them.

"What's happening?"

"I don't know."

But the tender look he gave me made me realize that things were about to get a whole lot more complicated. I was seriously beginning to think I'd become a character in a paranormal romance book.

I was the Summer Queen, whose king happened to be my ex-boyfriend. My "boyfriend" was now my guard, and he had given me permission to be my ex's queen. Oh, and I also had an invisible best friend that no one else but me could see. So yeah...things were crazy.

CHAPTER THIRTY

Salome

"Hope you're ready to jump into a pit of vipers," Gwenn said as she watched a servant help me secure my crown.

I groaned. "Please, don't remind me. I'm not sure I'm ready to face the Council."

She sneered. "Trust me, no one's ever ready for that bunch of pompous arses."

"You're not helping, you know." My fingers toyed with the white lace on my sleeves. "I'm already nervous as hell."

"Hey, you wanted honesty, so I'm giving it to you." She grinned, revealing a dimple in her left cheek. Her golden hair was secured at the nape of her neck with a turquoise ribbon. Her sword blade glinted in the sunlight as she stood near the balcony door.

It'd been two days since my coronation and the Council, although unhappy with a human as their queen, accepted the fact that I'd been marked with authentic tattoos. It still pissed me off that I'd been forced to allow them to investigate the validity of them.

Imagine a bunch of snotty nobles touching and prodding

you, even going as far as calling in a practicing spell caster to make sure we didn't trick anyone with the tats. Because yeah, every girl I knew wanted flipping ink on her forehead. Well, in this case, golden markings, but still.

At least when it was said to be legitimate they'd shut their mouths. Nevin might be king, but several nobles seemed hell bent on undermining him, even though the people as a whole loved him, despite his many years imprisoned in the human world.

Nevin admitted a lot of the continued support and love had a great deal to do with Gareth, who'd kept things running in his absence. He'd protected their people, reigned in his place, and kept the Council in check.

Speaking of Gareth, Nevin had him helping with some newly recruited soldiers this morning, although he'd promised to have him back in time for the Council Meeting.

"You're ready now, Your Highness." The servant bowed to me.

My cheeks warmed. "Please don't bow to me."

"It is the way things are done." She smiled.

Gah, I'd never get used to this.

"Let's get you to the meeting." Gwenn walked across my room and opened the door for me.

Sweat beaded my upper lip, and already I felt my pits getting wet.

You can do this. Just stick to your guns and don't let those idiots bully you.

We wound down the long corridor and moved downstairs, where Gwenn took the lead and ushered me through a stone archway and into a private room. Already several Council members were seated at the long, mahogany table. Nevin sat at the head of it, an empty place to his right. That seat was where Gwenn guided me.

"What's she doing here?" Rowena pointed to Gwenn. "She

was banned from the Council, or have you forgotten your place?"

Gwenn's shoulders went rigid, and I placed a hand on her arm. "She is my guard and goes where I go."

"Are you insinuating that you're not safe in the Council Chambers?" Rowena smirked.

That stupid cow. She was trying to make me look bad. I glowered. "Of course not. However, my guard made an oath to never leave my side. And since I'm here, she's here. Furthermore, you will address me not as your equal, but as your queen."

Several pairs of eyes followed my every movement as I took the chair next to Nevin. Gwenn bit her lip, and I could tell she was trying hard not to laugh. Beside me, Nevin took my hand, giving it a squeeze. A moment later, I watched Gareth move into the room and stand near the wall.

Rowena opened her mouth then shut it again.

"My darling, you've made it." Nevin leaned over and kissed my cheek, which I was sure was for show. "Since the queen is here, we can get underway. As you all know, we've gathered to discuss the continued threat from Winter."

"I hate seeing him kiss you like that." Gareth's eyes met mine.

"I know. Trust me, I'd much rather have your lips on me than his…"

"Maybe we can arrange that later?" He gave me a quick wink, then turned back to watch the Council.

"I think we need to march on Winter with a surprise attack," a man sitting to Rowena's left said.

Nevin sighed. "As much as I respect your answer, Lord Ballock, I don't see this working or being advantageous. We've lost too many soldiers as of late. We can't march into Winter in the dead of the cold. Our men would never survive. We need to find a way to try and draw more of their forces out before we set siege to them."

"Then what do you suggest, Your Highness? To continue to let Winter's armies take out our outer lying villages?" Lord Ballock said.

"No. What I suggest we do, is send word to our people and have them move back within our walls. Then we can better protect them. Right now, we need to strengthen our borders. And with a new queen, we have the power to do just that—without sending Summer's armies to their death. Besides, Lord Gareth was able to draw some intelligence from a guard who worked at the Winter Palace. It seems like there might be another way inside. But before we can try to attack, we need to make sure our own people are safe first. We'll also need to find more volunteers for our armies." He braced his hands against the table and I noticed his nails digging into the wood, like if he didn't keep them there he might use them to strangle Lord Ballock.

"I agree—we know we can hold our own borders, you've been doing it for centuries," I said. "And if we can train more people in combat, it'll give us bigger numbers to work with."

Rowena slammed her fist on the table. "Are we going to listen to a human who has no idea how to run a kingdom?"

My blood boiled hot as a volcano beneath my skin. I gripped hold of the table, half tempted to punch her in the face.

Geez, I sound like Kadie.

Nevin shot to his feet, his gaze hardened. "You, Lady Rowena, will never address our queen as 'some human,' nor will you speak to her that way again. You will apologize. Now."

The room fell silent as death.

Rowena's face turned crimson as she lowered her eyes. "I'm sorry."

Nevin heaved. "That goes for the rest of you too. One more snide comment or remark about my queen and I'll have you removed from the Council. She has been marked by Faerie, which means she was chosen to rule our kingdom and you will respect her." He glowered at them each in turn. "For now, we will plan on strengthening our borders. In the coming days, if any of you should come up with a better strategy, then I will take it into consideration. At this time, I will adjourn this meeting. Everyone is excused to prepare for tonight's ball. I expect to see you all at the celebration to welcome our new queen."

Chairs scraped across the floor as the nobles stood and left the room. When they were gone, Nevin glanced at me.

"You did well today. You showed them they can't push you around." He smiled.

"Um—did you miss the part where I kind of pissed everyone off?"

"No. But they'll get over it. It's time they realized they're not the ones running the kingdom. They're here to give input and guide our decisions. However, they are not the final say. As of late, I don't think they know what's best for our people. They're more concerned with protecting themselves. Besides, we've tried twice now to storm Winter's walls. Both times have failed. We need a new plan. We need more manpower. If the Spring and Autumn Courts still existed, then I'd humor another well launched attack on Winter."

With Gwenn and Gareth at our heels, we made our way from the Council's Chambers and upstairs.

"Don't worry, we'll figure something out."

When we stopped outside my door, Nevin cast a glance down the hall. "The rest of your belongings should be moved into my chambers soon."

My mouth went dry. "I know."

"We just need to make them believe we've consummated our marriage. Nothing more, as I promised you and Gareth."

Fake or not, I hated that we had to do this. Nevin was

gaining my trust as a friend, but just pretending to be his true wife felt like a betrayal to the man I actually loved. With a sigh, I went into my room to get ready.

Nevin swept me into his arms as we glided across the ballroom floor. Music floated on the air—beautiful, twinkling songs, wrapping me in invisible arms.

"You look lovely tonight," he said, one hand resting on my waist, the other entwined with mine.

"Thanks." I gave an uneasy smile, trying not to notice all the people watching us...including Gareth. It was so hard pretending to be in love with Nevin when all my eyes and heart noticed was Gareth. Especially tonight, seeing him dressed up in his tan breeches and dark blue tunic, his skin shimmering bronze beneath the glow of the lights. I sucked in a deep breath and drew my attention away from him.

Instead, I glanced about the room. Candles floated in the streams of water that wound about the outside of the room. Flower petals covered the marble tiles.

We spun around, and I lifted my head. Other Fae clapped their hands and swung about the room. Laughter filled the area as people joined in the dances. Everyone was having fun.

Nevin dipped me back, my loose hair nearly grazing the ground. He pulled me back up with a snap, and my hands caught his biceps. He spun me out then brought me in again.

It seemed that everyone had forgotten their troubles, at least for the moment.

Even I was having fun. But then my thoughts drifted to Gareth. I swallowed hard, the smile slipping from my face. It was hard to have a good time, knowing that we had to sneak around just to talk with one another. We'd never get the chance to dance in public like this or show affection unless it was behind closed doors.

Thoughts of him sobered me.

Nevin caught my chin. "Are you okay?"

"Yeah, I—I think I need some fresh air."

He stared at me, seeing through my lame excuse. "Is it really fresh air you need?"

"No."

"Why don't I have Gwenn see you to your room?"

"Are you sure?"

"Yes. I'll see you later, okay? Sorry I didn't send Gareth, but I don't want any rumors starting tonight. Not with this being so new."

"I understand. Thank you."

He waved to Gwenn, who hurried over to us. "The queen isn't feeling so well; can you bring her upstairs?"

She bowed. "Of course. Come along, Your Highness."

I gripped hold of the arm she offered as we made our way out of the ballroom.

"It's all right to live your life, Salome," she said. "There are some of us with whom you need not pretend who your heart belongs to."

"H-how did you know?"

She gave a soft chuckle. "I'm getting good at reading you."

"Great. And here I thought you hated me."

"We might not always see eye to eye, but it is my duty to protect you, and I take my job seriously."

When we arrived to my quarters, she went inside and looked around. When she determined it was safe, she flagged me in. "Gareth wants you to be happy. Trust me, he'll find ways to see you, but he knows all that's at stake. And don't worry about all the dramatics between Gareth and Nevin. They'll blow over like the summer breeze, they always do."

"Even knowing he's okay with this charade doesn't make it any easier." I sighed.

"No. He'll always be a part of your life, but that doesn't mean you can't make new memories and be happy." She patted my back. "If you need me, I'll be posted outside your door."

When she left, I took off my crown and pushed out onto my balcony. The cool air kissed my skin. Moonlight reflected off the river below; the trees swayed in the breeze. Stars pulsed and glittered above like tiny lightning bugs. For a moment, they reminded me of home, where I used to run around with Grandpa in his backyard, trying to catch them in jars.

"You look beautiful tonight." Darach came up behind me, resting his hands on my shoulders. *"You don't know how hard it is to only be a bystander at the ball."*

I turned to face him, my back pressed against the railing. "Well, you could've come down to dance."

"Can you imagine the gossip about the queen twirling about the room by herself?"

I chuckled. "Um—yeah, I see your point." My gaze met his, and my smile melted away. "It must be hard for you. To be here, yet not be a part of this world." *To see me with Nevin*, I wanted to add.

"It is." He caught my hand and brought it to his chest. *"But I can feel your touch. And you can see me and interact with me. Even if I have to live out the rest of my days like this, I can still find moments of happiness. You've been a good friend to me, Salome."*

The scent of autumnal leaves and spices hung heavy in the air. "Since you've been helping me learn how to wield a sword, the least I could do was offer you a dance. So would you like to dance?"

"More than anything," he whispered. With a gentle tug, he brought me into his arms. Music from the ballroom seemed to echo in the night. We glided across my balcony, the moonlight shining down upon us. I clung tight to him as if he were here in the flesh and blood and not just a ghost.

I rested my head against him, and for a second, I swore I heard the loud thump of a heartbeat. This was the third time I sensed a life force within him. My gaze shifted to his. His eyes glittered, and I could almost feel his happiness pouring out of him.

With a smile, I took a step back. I faced the kingdom below again. From behind me, Darach's arms wrapped me into a loose hug.

"Sometimes, I forget I'm dead."

"Believe me, you feel very much alive to me."

He chuckled. *"I think that's the nicest thing anyone's said to me in a long time."* He embraced me from behind and placed a light kiss along the back of my neck. A tingling sensation spread across the base of my neck, much like it had the night Nevin kissed my forehead and my tattoo appeared. *"If only we could've met before all this,"* he whispered. *"When we could have had a normal companionship."*

"I promise, we'll find a way to help you. To free you for good."

"If it means leaving you and Nevin, I'm not sure I want to do it."

My throat tightened. What drew me to him? Made me rush to him when things seemed to get out of control?

Because he reminds you of Gareth and Kadie all rolled into one.

Which could prove troublesome. It'd be hard to explain my sudden close friendship for a ghost —a man who was no more but wanted so much to be in our world.

Chapter Thirty-One

Kadie

For long hours, I waited in my room for Etienne's return. My nerves frayed, wondering if Grisselle would take out her frustration on the princes. As long as she didn't hurt Etienne, because I had plans for him—or rather, to be with him.

Rena poured me a cup of hot tea. "You should get some rest. There's no telling how long the queen will keep them."

I blew on the steam swirling up from my glass. The scent of cinnamon and apples made my stomach growl. I took a sip. The hot liquid trickled down my throat, warming me.

"I don't think I'll be able to sleep until I know he's okay."

She gave me a knowing smile and then squeezed my hand. "Etienne is a good boy. He's been through so much. Not a day goes by that he doesn't blame himself for what happened at the Spring Court. But I'm glad he's found you; you make him happy. And you give him hope for a future that isn't tainted by Winter."

Maybe this was my chance to actually fall for someone. Salome used to lecture me about waiting for the right guy, but I'd always shoved the idea aside because my friend spent too much time with her head buried in fairytales, believing in true love, romance, and all that flowery Valentine's shit.

But for the first time, I considered maybe she'd been right. Well, at least if Etienne and I could explore a normal relationship—as normal as anything could be around here, anyway. Maybe tonight, we could take everything to the next level. He'd wanted me ever since the night at the club. I'd seen it in his eyes then, and I'd seen it even here in Winter.

The door to the room burst open. Etienne stood at the threshold, breathless. "The queen wishes an audience with you. I think you might be the only one to make her see reason."

Rena cast a nervous glance between us. "Well, come along, child, you don't want to keep her waiting."

When I reached the door, Etienne offered me his arm.

"Everything will be okay," he said.

"I know. The queen and I are blood sisters now, she'd never hurt me."

Etienne went still, his eyes widened. "You're what?"

"Blood sisters. I know she's angry, but not with me. I can hear her in my head."

"Damn it, Kadie, do you not have any idea what you've done? She's bonded to you, which means she can get inside your head…she can use you."

Rena grabbed Etienne's arm. "Enough talk. There are ears everywhere."

Etienne went silent and jerked me out of the room and down the hall. He wouldn't even look at me. What the hell was his problem?

When we arrived at the queen's door, Etienne knocked.

"Come in," Grisselle called. We found her standing near a window, overlooking the snowy landscape below. When the guards left us, she spun to face me, a smile upon her blue tinted lips. "Ah, Kadie. I'm glad you could join us."

She gestured to Teodor and two other princes seated on furry rugs in front of her fireplace. My arms crossed my chest.

Etienne ushered me closer, and the queen took a seat with the others. "As you know, you and I've grown very close over the last few days. I've given you gifts and a title and my trust. And now, I must ask you to do a favor for me in return. Before I ask this of you, I want you to know that if there was any way to accomplish this myself, I'd do it. But for various reasons, there is no way I'd be allowed close enough to pull this endeavor off. That is why, my little sister, I must beg this of you."

Inside, I felt her opening up to me. The dams were breaking and she was letting me see her fear as if it were my own. The darkness. The worries of being alone. Of dying. But mostly the fear of losing everything she'd worked so hard for. That everything she'd fought the last couple hundred years for was going to crumble around her.

I cleared my throat, my mouth dry as desert sand. "What do you need of me?"

She pulled a dagger from her sleeve, the blade catching the faint gleam of flames.

Oh hell. Already, I dreaded what she was about to say.

"As you know, Summer has become a thorn in my side. They know all my trusted advisors and soldiers, so I can't get close to their borders. However, I realized that no one in Summer, save for Gareth and Salome, know you. What I need you to do is kill the Summer King or Queen. To help protect what is ours and help get rid of our final enemy."

My heart sped up. "You want me to kill someone?" A wave of nausea washed over me. "I don't know how you think I'll be able to get close enough to the king or queen to do so... I'm a human."

"Yes. But the queen isn't so strong yet. Kadie, trust me in this. If we're going to save our kingdom, I'll need your help."

A wave of fear rushed through me. I heard the unspoken threat in her words. She needed my help. And I knew what would happen if I didn't give it.

"I just don't know why Summer would let me anywhere near their queen…"

She reached for my hand and gave it a squeeze. "I've got it on good authority that your dear friend Salome has been crowned Summer Queen."

"Salome is…she's what?"

Grisselle smiled, almost as though she took pleasure in seeing me unnerved. "She has been crowned Summer Queen. No one told you?"

I shook my head. "No."

"Now you can see why this is perfect. She wouldn't question you at all. In fact, she'll welcome you with open arms. And all you have to do is cut her with this spelled dagger. One tiny prick to her skin will kill her."

My eyes closed, and I sucked in a deep breath. Holy shit. Could I really kill my best friend?

"Kadie, I'd send one of the princes to do this deed, or go myself, but the Summer Court knows who we are and can see through any glamour we'd use. We'd be killed before even stepping over the border. You are the *only* one who'd be able to get close enough to do this."

But it was Salome.

Darkness and despair swam through my mind, and clouds of sorrow washed over me. *"Kadie, please, I beg you. I've been kind to you. I've given you everything that I can. Even made you my heir. If we don't end Summer now, then we'll be destroyed. You'll lose everything, and so will I."*

Everything. So much contained within that one word.

"But this is Salome..."

"Who has done nothing but use you over the years." Grisselle stared at me, her eyes welling with tears. *"I didn't want to tell you this, but Salome knew you were imprisoned in Faerie. She could've sent troops or someone to rescue you at any point. But she didn't. To her, you weren't worth the trouble. You were dispensable."*

"She knew I was here?"

I took a staggered step back. Was it true? Did Salome care so little for me that she couldn't be bothered with rescuing her best friend? Most of my time spent in Winter, I'd tried my hardest to protect her, to keep her safe. Giving up my secrets about her had been to save my life. I didn't want to end up like Demetria—I deserved better.

As though Grisselle could sense the doubt in me—and given our blood bond, maybe she could—she said, *"Remember all the times she ruined your life. All the times that she made you put her first. Kadie, you deserve better than that—and I promise when this is all over you will come back here to me, and we'll rule side-by-side. You and I will make Faerie perfect. But I need you to do this. I'm begging you."*

"What exactly would I need to do?" I said out loud this time.

"This dagger is spelled to sense royal blood—and as soon as it's activated, it'll open a portal near the border of Summer, and you can walk out of there and back here to Winter. It shouldn't be too hard to get close to Salome. She won't suspect a thing. And to ensure that you get there safely, I'll send Etienne with you. Nevin and Gareth will recognize him as the King of the Spring Court. They don't know of the bargain he made with me or that he's been here since the fall of Spring. He can tell them he was imprisoned but managed to escape—bringing you with him. They'll trust those answers and let you in."

Etienne paled beside me but remained quiet.

Maybe I was dreaming? But as I stared around the room at the expectant faces, I realized they meant it.

Grisselle's voice sounded in my head. *"If you agree to do this, I'm entrusting you to go through with it. You can't use the blade to cut yourself or an animal. It'll only work on one of the royals. Kadie, please do this for me. If you do, I'll never ask another thing from you. It might be our only chance to be free of Summer. If you don't and Salome and the rest of Summer catch wind that you've bonded with me, they'll kill us both. We have to get to them first."*

Another wave of fear washed over me. I closed my eyes. This was it. Any chance I'd had at saying no to her or trying to out-smart her was gone. She was in my mind. In my soul. If I said no, she'd kill me now. And if I said yes but tried to run as soon as I was away from here? She'd find me. She'd follow the bond between us and drag me back here for a fate worse than Demetria's.

I couldn't let that happen. I couldn't.

"I'll do what you want," I said. Willing certainty into my voice, hoping she believed me even as I didn't want to believe it myself. "But I want it to be remembered that I'm risking everything for you."

And then another thought occurred to me. I knew what Grisselle would do to me if I failed her, but...what if Salome caught me? What if Summer discovered I was an assassin meant to kill their queen? They'd hurt me just as bad as Grisselle. Maybe worse.

"Speak your mind," Grisselle said, as though she couldn't read my thoughts. She knew what she was doing by forcing me to speak the words.

"You've given me a lot over the last couple of days, so I'm

going to look at this as a return of favor," I said. "But if something goes wrong, I want to know that you will come for me."

A look of relief flashed over Grisselle's frigid features. "You're making the right choice." She smiled, then caught my hand in hers. "I will always come for you. You have my word."

Etienne stared around the room, refusing to meet my gaze. I wanted to know what was going through his head. Did he think I was being foolish? But then again, what did it matter what he thought? He couldn't help me get out of this. I'd killed that hope when I'd mixed my blood with Grisselle's.

"We'll provide you with maps and food—everything you'll need to make the journey. Etienne will accompany you tomorrow."

"Thank you," I whispered.

"No, thank you." She smiled as she placed the dagger in a scabbard and handed it to me.

I clutched it to my chest like a treasured possession. She waved her hand, dismissing us. Etienne and I were silent as we made our way back to my room. Once inside, I turned to him.

"I'm glad you're going with me," I said.

He cupped my face. "You don't have to do this, you know."

I jerked away from him. "Yes, I do. I need to prove myself to Grisselle."

"And you think the Summer Court is just going to let you waltz in there and kill their queen and then let you waltz right back out again? Have you thought none of this through?" Etienne asked. He made his way to the door then turned back to face me. "I'll send Rena down to help you pack."

"Etienne, wait." I hurried to his side. I didn't want him to be mad at me. Surely he understood why I'd agreed to this? Before he could go anywhere, my lips captured his. With a low groan, his mouth moved against mine in desperation. I dropped the dagger and tangled my fingers in his hair, pulling him closer. He trailed small kisses down my throat, his hands gripping hold of my hips and pressing me against him.

"I want you," I said against his mouth. "Please, spend the night with me tonight."

He held me at arm's length, his gaze melting me from the feet up. His forehead touched mine, and I clung to him. Finally—a guy who made me feel something.

"Kadie, I'm sorry, but I can't. Not with her in your head. I don't want to share my intimate moments with her. She's taken everything else from me, but I don't want to let her have this."

"So you don't want me?" My voice cracked with emotion.

"Not like this." He tugged free from me. "I've got to get my things in order. I'll see you in the morning."

When dawn came, I sat up. Today I'd start my journey. Last night I'd had nightmares about what it would mean to kill Salome...for me, for Winter, even for Summer.

"No doubts, little sister. Everything will work out. Just stay strong." Grisselle's words filled my mind.

"I know."

I climbed from bed, stretched, and hurried to get my clothes on. My pack already sat on the floor near my dresser. Rena had helped me with my things the night before. Once I struggled into a pair of breeches and tunic, I slipped on a pair of boots.

A knock sounded on the door, and Etienne poked his head in. "Are you about ready to go?"

"Listen, I need to do something before I leave. It's important."

He gave me a quizzical glance. "What is it?"

I swallowed hard. "I'd rather not say, so if the queen asks

later, you can answer her honestly when you tell her you didn't know anything about it."

"Okay, now you're scaring me." He watched me closely.

"Can you get me an axe?"

He frowned. "If you're planning on taking out Grisselle, it's not worth the risk. Many before you have tried and failed."

My eyes widened. "Um—that's not what I need it for. Besides, I meant it when I said she and I are sisters now."

With a sigh, he finally nodded. "Okay, I'll get it for you."

Etienne left the room, and I glanced around, taking in the vision of my safe haven one last time. How many nights had I spent in here, under Etienne's watchful eye? He'd risked everything to protect me, and all he had in his own quarters were a few remnants of Spring.

You need to keep it together, girl. There's no turning back now.

I reached for a fur-lined cloak hanging up on a hook by my door. Hopefully it would keep the cold from seeping in while we trekked through the snowy woods.

After a few minutes, Etienne reappeared, carrying a large axe. "I hope this will work."

My stomach twisted, but I didn't feel right leaving until I took care of this. "Yeah, it's perfect. Can you bring me to the Red Room?"

He held the door open and gestured for me to follow him. We made our way to the nightmare-inspired room. When we got there, I turned to him.

"I need to go in by myself," I said. "I won't be long."

He grunted disapproval but did as I asked and locked me in. I picked my way through the scarlet room, ignoring the curtains made of skin that hung about the windows. With quick steps, I darted past the human heads that hung above the mantel. At last, I found myself in the wintry courtyard.

Mr. M's tree-like form sagged. His leaves were all gone. Shredded bark littered the ground at his roots, which used to be legs and feet.

"Mr. Montgomery?" I said.

His knothole eyes opened and he glanced at me. *"Kadie... you're back."*

"Yes. I've come to say goodbye. I've made a deal with the queen for my safety."

"Goood—tell...tell Salome I love herrrrr..."

My vision blurred as tears burned my eyes. Fuck. Why did he have to say that? "I will."

"Please. Put me ou-out of my misery. So much pain."

I touched his twig fingers. "Th-that's what I've come to do, Mr. M. Forgive me."

With a staggered breath, I raised the axe. I struck the tree three times before it finally cracked and fell to the ground. When it hit the icy surface, I watched as the old tree turned into Mr. Montgomery.

I knelt by his side. He gasped for air, his hand catching mine. "Thank you—b-be safe, Kadie."

His head rolled to the side, and he took his last breath.

A sob raked through me as I pressed a kiss to his cheek. "Rest in peace, Mr. M. You're in a better place now—some place where Winter will never touch you again."

I dropped the axe and stepped away from him. A part of me had done this to put him out of his misery, but the other part didn't want to see his hurt when he learned what I'd agreed to do to Salome. When he learned that I'd traded her life for mine. And at least now I didn't have to think about him stuck out here, alone, in the ice and snow. At least now he wouldn't have to suffer.

I wished it was so easy to do the same for myself.

CHAPTER THIRTY-TWO

Salome

My maid helped me into my dress, and I lifted my hair up out of the way so she could button it. When I did, I heard a loud gasp behind me.

"For the love of Faerie," she whispered.

"What's wrong?"

"I think you ought to have a look at this, Your Highness." She spun me around then gave me a hand held mirror.

I tilted my hand held mirror until I saw my neck. There, spiraling up the back of my neck, were more golden tattoos. Only these ones looked like tiny maple leaves. "Um—how did I get them?"

"I don't know—but that's the mark of the Autumn Court. It means you're to be their next queen, but I don't understand how this is possible. Their king has been dead for many years. Autumn has always been ruled by the male line."

I set the mirror on my vanity. My eyes widened when I remembered Darach's light kiss on the base of my neck last night. Had that triggered it?

"Listen, can we just keep this between us for now? At least

until I can figure out what it means?"

"As you wish, Your Majesty." She curtsied then finished buttoning my dress. "I'll let Lady Gwenn know you're ready for your walk."

"Thank you." When she scurried off, I let out a relieved breath and made sure my hair covered my newest Faerie ink. Geez, if I kept this up I'd be tattooed from head to toe. All I needed now was a leather jacket and a motorcycle. I frowned. The thoughts of motorcycles brought with it the image of Gareth and prom night, when he'd picked me up on his and then we'd spent the whole night dancing on the beach beneath the moonlight. It seemed so long ago and yet just like it was yesterday. I hated that he wasn't here with me, that we had to pretend he was my guard and nothing more—although, for the last couple of days Nevin had had him working with the younger soldiers. By day he helped with training, and at night he was assigned to me.

Gwenn strolled into my room and leaned against the wall.

I turned my head so she couldn't see the tears as I hurried to brush them away. If nothing else, I had to pretend to be strong.

"So where do you want to go today?" she asked.

With a shake of my head, I cleared my mind and pasted a grin on my face. "I've wanted to go through the labyrinth since I got here." At last, I moved across the floor until I stood in front of her.

She rolled her eyes. "You're queen now and the best thing you can think of to do is run through a damn maze?"

"Please?"

"Ugh. Fine. But I'm not going in. I'll wait at the exit for you."

"Are you chicken?"

She snorted. "No. But I used to play in there when I was a

kid—I've outgrown it."

My lips twitched. "Whatever—I'll have you know it's okay to have fun every now and then."

"Then let me know when you need a sparring partner. Maybe tomorrow we can challenge a couple of guards to a fight or something." Her fingers traced the hilt of her weapon.

We made our way into the gardens until we stood at the entrance of the hedge maze. My gaze traveled over the thick greenery.

"Come on, I might get lost. You don't want to have to come find me at midnight, do you?"

"Fine, I'll go with you, but only because Nevin would have my head if I lost the queen." She followed me in the entrance. "Don't run too far ahead of me."

I grinned. "I won't."

The sun warmed the top of my head as I slipped into the labyrinth. I ran forward, zig-zagging right, then left, then right again. Within moments, I ran into a dead end. I backtracked and took a left then another left. I came to a fork in the maze.

"So which way should I go?"

She rolled her eyes. "You're the one who wanted to do this."

Gwenn stood with her arms crossed, watching me. Obviously she wasn't going to be any help.

Okay, this looked way easier from above. I chose the middle path and came to a bench with a stone fountain sitting next to it. Beyond the spouting water, I saw another path. Climbing roses grew along the maze walls here, adding splashes of pink and scarlet.

This kind of reminded me of the corn maze Kadie and I had done our sophomore year during a Halloween Festival in town. Of course, she and I were the last ones to come out, but only because Lon Pinder, who was dressed as a werewolf, chased us until we ended up turned around.

I laughed at the memory. Luckily for her, she'd come to her senses where he was concerned. The guy had been a total druggie and no good for her. It always astounded me how she picked up some of the worst douchebags. She should be home from college for the holidays now—probably basking in a hot tub with Zac or some other piece of eye candy. My eyes welled. Man, I missed her.

"Look what we have here." Rowena stepped out from behind an apple tree situated between two hedgerows. "They left the queen all alone."

"She's not alone." Gwenn drew her sword and went to stand between us.

But with a swipe of her hand, Rowena sent Gwenn sailing through the air and into a nearby statue. Her weapon skidded across the ground, her body still. My eyes widened as I waited for her to move, but she didn't.

Hands shaking, I backed up, running into the side of the labyrinth. "What do you want?"

Her too-red lips turned up into a wicked smile. "That's easy. Your death."

My pulse raced. "Stay the hell away from me."

"Or what, human? You are powerless against me. You see, you took something from me—or rather someone."

"You mean Nevin?"

Her eyes narrowed. "Yes, of course. I was supposed to be his queen. We courted before you came along, and he would've chosen me had you not come to Faerie."

Shit. She's out of her freaking mind. I glanced at the path to my left. Would I have enough time to make a run for it?

But before I managed to move, she raised her hands. Green light sparked from her fingertips, lighting the air like sparklers on the Fourth of July. Vines uncurled from the walls and slithered like snakes. I turned to run, but the long green vegetation caught hold of my ankles, jerking me to the ground. They crept up my legs. Darach appeared next to me.

"Salome, get up. Run!"

I crawled back on my hands and feet. In one swift movement, Darach wrapped his arms around me. Dizziness washed over me, and my stomach churned. Everything blurred for a moment. A second later, we were in a different part of the maze.

"Darach...? What happened?"

He looked as confused as I felt. *"I think I just transported you."*

"Thank you—"

But before I could give him my gratitude, a part of the hedge separated from the rest. I gulped as I realized that Rowena sat atop a lion made of shrubs and plants. Its crimson eyes glowed brighter than embers.

"Get her!" she ordered.

The beast opened its mouth, and when it roared, flames shot out, scorching the ground in front of me.

"Go." Darach shoved me down another walkway.

Crap.

I'm gonna die. I'll be killed by a flipping labyrinth.

"Gwenn," I screamed, running into a dead end. Was she even still alive? If so, I hoped she heard me, or that someone else in the palace did. My legs trembled as I turned to face my nemesis.

Rowena laughed, her hands pulsating with light once more. Vines shot out of the hedgerows, and this time I couldn't dodge them. The long ropes of greenery caught hold of my neck, wrapping around my throat.

I gagged. My fingers pried at the vegetation as they tightened like a boa constrictor.

I can't breathe.

Frantic, I slid down the wall, dots dancing before my eyes. *No. It can't end like this. It can't.*

"Fight it, Salome." Darach's hands grabbed for the plants. *"It's not your time. You can't let her win. Fight it,"* he whispered in my ear.

My hands fell to the ground; my fingers dug into the dirt.

No. I won't let her kill me.

A burst of light filled the labyrinth—almost like rays of sunlight—and lightning struck the earth. At that moment, the ground shook beneath me. A crack formed and surged toward Rowena until a great chasm opened up and swallowed her up to her neck.

Holy shit! What'd I just do?

She shrieked, and the vines around my neck loosened, allowing me to start tugging them free.

"Salome," Gwenn hollered. She hacked through a section of the maze. When she emerged, I saw the blood along the side of her forehead. She glanced at Rowena then rushed to my side to help untangle me from the plants. "Whoa, what happened?"

I sucked in several deep breaths. "She attacked me, and I—I…"

Rowena's hand clasped the side of the hole, and she tried to pull herself out. "You won't win—he'll never love you."

Something glinted in the air, and I watched in horror as she released a dagger. It sailed toward my head. I rolled to the side, acting more on instinct than conscious thought, and fortunately I moved fast enough that the blade missed me and stuck into the bushes behind me.

Anger surged inside me. The earth rumbled beneath my feet once more. This time the dirt filled the deep ditch I created, like a cave in.

"No." Rowena's eyes widened. "She'll bury me alive."

"Good, it's no less than you deserve." Gwenn raised her sword.

"No, she deserves much more than that," Nevin said as he appeared along with Gareth. "You made an attempt on my queen's life. You're a traitor and will be treated as such. Gwenn, hand me your dagger."

Rowena cried out. "No. You can't mean what I think you do. I won't survive."

"You should be glad that's all he does, because if it were me, I'd have your head." Gareth seethed, his gaze intent on me. *"Are you okay?"*

"I think so."

"I heard your cry for help and came as quickly as I could. I should've gotten here sooner."

"I'm fine—please don't worry."

Nevin glowered as he took the blade from Gwenn. He reached forward and let the knife slice across Rowena's shoulder—one of the only body parts not covered in dirt. He then reached down and laid his palm against her skin.

"Rowena Thornwood, I hereby strip you of all your powers. And from this day forward, you are banned from the Kingdom of Summer for your crimes against the queen."

A stream of light filtered from Rowena as if her very essence was being vacuumed out. She shrieked, her eyes wide with both fear and hatred. When Nevin finished, two of his guards lumbered through the hole in the hedges that Gwenn had created.

"Give her a change of clothes and a pack with food, then take her beyond our borders and leave her."

"Yes, Your Highness." They bowed and went to dig her out.

Gareth glanced at me, then at Rowena. *"I should help them."*

"Go. I'll be fine."

At last, Nevin turned to me. My legs wobbled beneath me.

"It's okay, I've got you now." He took my hand and helped me stay on my feet.

"Sh-she tried to kill me."

"I know. I'm sorry I didn't get here sooner. Come. I'll take you back to your room."

"But Gareth…"

Gareth looked at me from where he was kneeling to help the guards with Rowena. *"Go. I'll stay here to ensure this monster never has a chance to hurt you again."*

I nodded at him, then at Nevin, and he guided me out of the labyrinth, where a small crowd of people had gathered.

"Now there can be no doubt that you belong to Summer," Nevin said. "Your powers are growing stronger, Salome."

"I don't understand how."

"Shhh…we have plenty of time to talk of it later—in private." Nevin made his way into the palace and upstairs without so much as breaking a sweat. At last, we arrived in my room. He set me on my bed then proceeded to tuck me in. "You need to rest—using that much power all at once, and without another Fae anchor, can drain you."

"I'll be fine." I gave him a shaky smile.

"You scared the hell out of me today."

"He's not the only one," Darach said over his shoulder. His gaze met mine; worry lines were painted on his ghostly head.

"If you want, I can stay a while." Nevin touched my face, forcing me to look at him.

"I'll be okay. I promise. Besides, I think you've got to break some bad news to the Council about Rowena."

He groaned. "Yeah, that'll go well." He gave me one last hug, then stood to go. "I'm posting three guards outside your chambers, so if you need something, let them know."

When he finally left, Darach drifted to my side. The mattress dipped with his pressure as he sat down next to me.

I slid forward, lifted my hair, and bent down to reveal the tattoo that adorned my neck. "Can you tell me what this means?"

He exhaled loudly as his fingers traced it. *"It means, if I was alive, you'd be the Autumn Queen and rule beside me."*

"Wait a second, I'm already marked by Nevin and Summer—how did this happen?"

He glanced down at me. *"I don't know, but I've told you from the beginning there's something special about you."*

"We need to find out what's going on and soon."

"Are you going to tell Nevin?"

With a sigh, I scooted against my headboard, resting my head against the cool wood. "No. Not yet. I want to keep you a secret, for now." At least until I knew what this could mean. I'd just started to get accustomed to this new situation. Telling Nevin about Darach might throw everything back into chaos.

He grinned. *"Hmmm…this could be fun. Think of all the havoc we could wreak. Maybe we could cause a stir in the council meetings. Or we could try and best another Summer Warrior."* He reached over and tugged on a strand of my hair.

I shifted my gaze. "As fun as that sounds, I think I should probably just rest now."

"You're right. Sweet dreams, my queen."

Darach's form faded and disappeared, leaving me with yet another unanswered question. What did this second tattoo mean?

I sat on the throne beside Nevin as the Summer Council stormed into the room. Lord Ballock led the group, his face crimson and his eyes narrowed.

"Is it true, Your Highness? Did you banish Lady Rowena?" he asked.

Nevin glanced at them as if they were nothing more than a swarm of gnats there to annoy him. "Yes. She's lucky that's all I did."

"The Council should've been a part of this decision. We can't just have our nobles dismissed without a hearing."

"She had her hearing, in front of me—when I caught her trying to murder my queen. And, may I add, your queen as well." Nevin stood, came to my side, and tilted my chin to reveal the burn marks along my neck made by the vines. "The Council may offer advice, but I am still King, Lord Ballock."

"I beg your pardon." He bowed, gaze darting to the other Council members who remained quiet. "Rowena wouldn't have attacked, Your Highness—she's been with the Council for so long. She knows our kingdom needed a queen. Many of us thought for sure you'd choose her."

"Are you calling me a liar?" Nevin glowered. "Because I assure you, I wouldn't have acted against Rowena had she not done something. And if the Council doesn't want what's best for our kingdom or our queen, then perhaps it's time to do away with this archaic government."

Gasps went up in the small crowd of nobles, and several of them paled.

One of the other lords stepped forward. "Lord Ballock doesn't speak for all of us, Your Highness. You have the majority support in this."

Six of the others raised their hands to indicate they were a part of this majority. Only three, including Ballock, seemed opposed to the decision.

"Thank you, Lord Maelen." Nevin returned to his throne.

Lord Ballock opened his mouth to say more, but Nevin held up his hand, gesturing for Gareth to come forward. "Do you have reports on our soldiers?"

"Yes, Your Highness. We've had over five hundred new recruits come in in the last couple of days from the outer borders of our kingdom. Most are younger, but they're willing to fight. They have rudimentary skills, but I believe with a little time, we can have them battle ready."

"Very good. Please keep me updated as to their progress. Lord Maelen, could you please send word to some of our farmers that we'll be looking to buy more corn, oats, and vegetables? We need to make sure we have enough food on hand to feed our army and our people, should it come to that."

"Of course, Your Highness."

"Now, if the Council is quite finished, there are things that we need to be doing. Please know that if any of you reach out to Rowena or I hear that you've communicated with her, you will be joining her in her banishment. Is that understood?"

They nodded their understanding, but I could tell by the tight lips and glares that they weren't all happy with this. I hoped they didn't cause more trouble down the line for us.

My gaze moved to Gareth's tall frame, taking in his beautiful eyes. Having him in here with us brought me a strange reassurance that everything would be okay, at least for today. But I quickly turned away. I couldn't let on that I had feelings for him, especially not in front of the Council, who were already looking for reasons to have me and Nevin overthrown.

CHAPTER THIRTY-THREE

The wolves disappeared as dawn set in, just like Etienne had said they would. Every night after that we made sure to find shelter where they couldn't get in.

My feet ached as I plowed through the thicket. Thorns tore into my skin. I licked my chapped lips, cringing when it felt like they split. I'd been traveling for days now and all I ever saw was snow.

A familiar sound in the distance caught my attention. "Oh God, is that what I think it is?" I glanced at Etienne.

We both jogged forward. There, up ahead, was the river—and on the other bank, I saw beams of sunlight. I walked along the side, trying to find a place shallow enough to cross. At last, I noticed an area where it was only up to my thigh.

With a splash, I stumbled across, the current almost knocking me over. Cool water seeped through my clothing and into my boots. My cloak dragged behind me like a net. Rocks along the bottom made me unbalanced, so I slowed down.

As soon as I climbed up the embankment on the other side, I fell to my knees. My fingers gripped hold of the soft grass. Warm breeze licked at my wet skin. The scent of flowers filled the air. I tilted my head toward the sky: so much blue, no clouds, no snow. Birds twittered in the distance, flying between branches. Bees buzzed around violets and lilies.

But if I thought I was in awe, my reaction was nothing like Etienne's. His face beamed as he raised his hands to the sky, as if he could touch the warmth. He sucked in a deep breath, and his fingers dug into the grass as mine had. I wondered how long it'd been since he'd seen the sun or stepped out of Winter. Seeing the joy in his eyes almost made me feel bad that we'd have to go back someday

A twig snapped, and Etienne's gaze shifted. Paranoid, I climbed to my feet, ready to run.

"Don't move," a voice called behind me as a blade pressed against my throat.

"P-please don't hurt me. W-we've just escaped Winter." My legs trembled beneath me. If they didn't buy this, then we were so dead.

"Then why do you carry a pack and supplies?" The guard came around to stand in front of me, his blade still at my neck.

My eyes welled. "I stole it from one of the storerooms a couple of weeks back. Because I was on kitchen duty, I had access to food. Listen, I'm just trying to get back to the human world. I-I heard talk amongst the servants that Summer was a safe place."

He nodded. "Summer is a safe place, and we plan on keeping it that way. However, we don't know if you're a spy sent here by Winter."

"I'm not. I promise." My voice quivered. "They kidnapped me from the human world. Just please. Help me."

The guard didn't look convinced. He turned to Etienne. "And what about you? Were you a prisoner, too?"

But before he could answer, the guard shoved gags in our mouths and proceeded to tie us up. "Put them on the horses, Shand. We'll let King Nevin decide their fates." Another man stepped out from behind a tree.

We could have fought back. There were two of them, but with Etienne's fighting skills, we might have won. But we didn't fight back. This was part of the plan. We were supposed to be easily captured. How else would we convince them to let their guard down?

They took my pack after they had bound my wrists. With a nudge, they led me to a chestnut colored horse. Shand climbed up first, then reached down to grab my arm while the other guy lifted me. After a moment, they had me situated in front of Shand. Luckily, they didn't pat down my inner thigh to find the dagger—my only lifeline out here.

Etienne hadn't been treated as kindly as me, and I saw that he'd been tossed haphazardly over a horse on his stomach, with a soldier sitting behind him, keeping him from being able to move.

We rode for a while. The saddle hurt my butt, and it felt like my knees might actually fall off. I'd probably walk bowlegged for the rest of the day. The smell of horse made my nose wrinkle. I so wasn't a big fan of animals. Give me a car any day of the week. Hell, I'd settle for a bike at this point.

At last, the hills and woods opened to a large white oak gate, which had carvings etched into it. My mouth gaped open as the doors creaked, allowing us to enter. Everywhere I looked there were waterfalls and flowers. Houses were built into trees. Great archways gave way to gardens and fountains. Holy crap. I half expected to see Orlando Bloom step out dressed like Legolas.

Shand tugged on the reins of the horse, bringing us to a

stop. More guards met us, and I was handed down to them, while others worked to secure Etienne beside me.

"We found them crossing the river from Winter into Summer. She claims they escaped and are seeking refuge," Shand said.

"I'll have Camlin take your horses—why don't you bring them into the palace," the other guard said.

Shand slid from his mount, his dark hair hanging to his shoulders and his armor gleaming in the sunlight. "Thanks."

He gripped my arm tightly and pushed me up a marble stairway into a huge foyer. Four sets of staircases jutted to upper levels. Marble tiles covered the floor, while streams ran through arched doorways.

"Come along." He jerked me forward.

My mouth went dry. Now came the true test. If they didn't buy my story, I'd end up either imprisoned or dead. "Wh-where are we going?"

"The throne room. The king and queen are holding court as we speak."

"Good, you're doing great," Griselle said in my mind. *"You're right where you need to be. Don't be scared. I'm with you. And I'll be with you when you make your move."*

Don't be scared.

But she knew exactly what her voice in my head would do to me. She wanted me scared—just not of Nevin and Salome.

Two guards met us at a set of double doors. They nodded at Shand as we approached, and then they opened the doors for us. Heads turned to watch us as we made our way down a crimson carpet.

"Your Highness, we found this human crossing into Summer near the Winter border. She claims to have escaped, but we thought it'd be best if we brought her in for questioning."

My gaze shifted to the raised dais, and my breath caught in my throat. There, sitting on one of the thrones, was Salome.

"Kadie?" Her eyes widened as she stood. "Release her at once. I know her."

Shand glanced to the king who nodded. "Go ahead, untie her."

The guard held out a knife and cut the bindings on my wrists. I rubbed the raw spots and twisted my hands to get the feeling back in them.

"I want to see her in private," Salome said.

"No, I don't think that's a good idea." The king caught her arm.

She glared. "Nevin, I'll be fine. She's my best friend."

Gareth moved from his place behind her chair. "My queen, you need to take precautions. Regardless of your relationship with Kadie, your safety is our utmost concern."

She moved from the dais and came to my side, wrapping me in her arms. Everything about her smelled like summer: flowers, rain showers, freshly cut grass. Gone was the familiar coconut lotion she used to wear. She squeezed me tighter, as if she thought I wasn't real. And for a moment, it comforted me—made me feel like I was at home. I savored the sensation. This could be the last time I felt like this again.

She drew back, her eyes welling with tears.

Oh God. Salome…I couldn't do this. Maybe if I told Salome everything, she'd be able to arrange to get me out of here.

But then I felt Griselle's presence in my mind once again. I felt the weight of my hidden dagger. More than anything, I felt the fear of what Grisselle would do to me if I failed.

Salome released me, then turned to Gareth as she started to guide me along by my arm, her golden gown dragging behind her. "Please see us to my drawing room."

Gareth sighed but fell in behind her, then turned to the king. "I'll post guard outside her door."

Nevin watched me closely. "If you do anything to harm her, I promise you won't leave our dungeons, is that clear?"

"Yes." I nodded.

"Don't worry, I will get you out of there should something go wrong," Grisselle said. *"So long as you prove your loyalty to me, I will show my loyalty to you."*

"And what about this one, Your Highness?" Shand drew Etienne's head back.

I heard any audible gasp from Nevin as I moved away from him. "It can't be…Etienne?"

But I wasn't able to stay and see how Etienne would handle Nevin. Salome reached for my hand. She was quiet as she led me from the throne room and down a hall decorated with marble statues. We came to a stop outside a door etched with roses. She pushed it open and pulled me inside.

As soon as the door drew shut, she hugged me again. "I'm so glad to see you. I-I just can't believe you're here."

I hugged her back, my throat constricting. "Me too. God, I've missed you."

Truth in lies. It made what I had to do all the harder.

"How did you get here?" She pulled back, wiping the tears from her face.

"After I caught Zac cheating on me, I left school. When I got home, my parents and I got in a huge fight. So I went to your house, but you weren't there. I got a message from you to meet you at Club Blade, but I'm guessing now it might not have been from you." My lip trembled, and I closed my eyes and took a deep breath. "I decided to go to Club Blade by myself. That's where I met Etienne, a fae prince. He brought me through to Winter. I—I was there for a long time." I swallowed. "The things

I saw. The things they did to me... It was horrific."

She clutched me tight as I sobbed, telling her about the blood and sacrifices and Demetria's death. I even told her about falling for Etienne, though I left out his true identity.

"Now, Kadie. You must do it now." Grisselle's words echoed through me.

Salome stepped back but held my hand in hers. "I'm sorry you had to go through all that. If I'd known you were there I would've found a way to come for you." She stroked my hair, reminding me of my mom.

"I know you would have come for me," I said. "It isn't your fault. You didn't know."

"I can't help but feel guilty," she said. "I'd do anything to keep you safe."

I swallowed. "It's too late for that," I whispered.

She stopped and looked at me. "What do you mean?"

"Now," Grisselle shouted in my mind. *"Do it now!"*

"There's something else I need to tell you," I said.

"What is it?"

I moved away from her, fumbling to tug the dagger from its sheath on my upper thigh. My eyes blurred as salty drops raced down my cheek. It was either her or me.

Her gaze flicked to the dagger. She went still. "Kadie?"

"Don't worry, it'll only hurt for a second."

She took several steps away from me. "Kadie, you don't have to do this."

"I don't have a choice," I whispered. "You don't know what she'll do. What she's already done."

"Whatever threat she made, we'll find a way to keep you safe. You still have a choice. I promise. Just hand over the dagger, and we'll figure this out."

Grisselle's essence flowed through me, a reminder that

the situation wasn't so simple. I would never be safe again. Wherever I went, whatever I did, Grisselle would be with me.

Someone began to open the door, but Grisselle's power lashed out of me and shoved the door closed then knocked over a cabinet to bar the door and keep anyone from entering.

"Salome!" Gareth shouted from outside. "What's going on?"

"Gareth, help me." Salome staggered away from me and toward the barred door. She attempted to push the cabinet out of the way. When it wouldn't move, she spun to face me, her skin draining of color as disbelief painted her features.

"We have her, Kadie. Finish it."

I raised the knife to do as Grisselle ordered, but I hesitated, and Grisselle made me pay for it. My mind flooded with images of what she would do to me.

My body laid on a board as the skin was stripped from my bones one limb at a time—

A glimpse of myself being shoved into a boiling pot still alive, while trolls beat me back down every time I tried to climb out.

Musicians seated in the ballroom, playing a song until I bled to death.

I focused on blackness, nothingness, anything to shut out the wave of fear. Only then did I realize what Grisselle had done, filled me with nightmares of torture so powerful that while I focused on keeping them at bay, her power surged through me, forcing me forward as easily as she'd closed and barred the door.

Unable to stop myself, I lunged forward with the blade and stabbed it in Salome's chest.

She screamed, her face already pale. She reached for the knife, trying to take it out, but I pressed forward, and she stumbled backward.

"Kadie…" She stretched her fingers out toward the wall to steady herself, but she fell to her knees then sagged to the floor in a heap, her sunshine colored hair spilling out around her like a halo while blood soaked into the ends of it from her wound.

My hands trembled as I stared at her, watching her gasp for air. "I'm sorry. I didn't want to. I didn't mean for this to happen. I—"

The door burst open. Gareth took one look at me. I knew then that I was screwed. There'd be no clean getaway.

"Take her to the dungeons. Now. And get the king." Gareth dropped down beside Salome.

Hands dragged me toward the door. "Let me go. Please. Listen to me. I had no choice. I had to do it. Please. Let me go…"

CHAPTER THIRTY-FOUR

Kadie

*M*oisture dripped from the ceiling, splashing with a ping against the rocks. I drew my knees to my chest. Salome had looked so pale when the guards dragged me out: her lips blue, her eyes vacant like death veiled them. I'd done it. I'd killed her.

My stomach clenched. Oh God. I'd killed her. Panic set in as I stared around the tower room dungeon that held me. They'd used magic to get me up here. There were no stairs. No windows. No way to escape. Would Etienne or the queen be able to rescue me?

"Kadie? Are you there?" Grisselle's voice rang out in my mind.

"Yes." I sobbed.

"You did what I asked. You truly are my sister now. Ah, to see the disbelief on her face when you stabbed her will forever be one of my happiest memories. Summer will surely fall now. They thought they were being so smart crowning a queen. They thought they could destroy us, but we showed them."

I shut my eyes. The things I'd now done... I couldn't help

but remind myself that I'd done them to survive. That in the final moment, it had been Grisselle who'd pushed my hand and the knife into Salome. I pushed those thoughts away. I'd chosen to make this bond with Grisselle. I'd opened myself to her to save my life. Everything I'd done and everything I would do now was my fault.

"Please, come get me."

"Soon."

"Nevin sentenced me here. I'm never gonna leave this place if you don't get here. Gareth was going to have me killed outright, but Nevin thinks I have information he can use. They'll torture me."

I dug my fingers into my palms and rested my head against the stone wall behind me. Darkness fanned out all around me. The only noises came from the dripping water and scuttle of rats. The stench of must and mildew made me gag. The only good thing was at least it wasn't freezing up here.

"I'll send a friend for you. We'll break you out and leave for Winter. I won't let anyone hurt you," Grisselle said. *"And you're sure Salome is dead?"*

"You saw me do it," I said.

"And what of Etienne, where is he? Can he not help you?"

"I don't know; he was still in the throne room when I went with Salome. I haven't seen him."

My stomach soured, and acid burned the back of my throat. What if she changed her mind and didn't get me? What if that would turn out to have been an empty promise? I would be stuck here, every day reminded of how my mistakes had led to the death of my best friend.

CHAPTER THIRTY-FIVE

Salome

*F*reezing air burned my lungs while streams of ice chilled my veins. I sucked greedily but couldn't breathe. Dots danced before my eyes.

I'm so cold.

Darkness settled over me as pain pricked at my skin and body like thousands of needles poking me at once. Kadie had stabbed me. Kadie, the girl who'd been my best friend since childhood. But why? I didn't understand.

A burst of light exploded inside my head, and I watched as tiny snowflakes fell before me.

"You're ours. All of ours." A chime-like voice I didn't recognize carried on the wind.

A wooden bridge formed at my feet, and I walked over the creaking boards. "Hello? Is anyone here?"

"Salome? What're you doing here?" Darach's face paled as he caught me in his arms.

"Here? I don't know where I am?"

"Between life and death. You're not supposed to be here. It's not your time. It can't be your time." Panic washed over his

features.

"Maybe it is my time. I've cheated death twice already. Maybe it's finally caught up to me." I touched his face. "And would it be so bad if I stayed here with you? You said we were friends and that you were lonely."

His gaze softened. *"No. But there's still much for you to do in Faerie. Summer needs you, Salome. Their land will fall if you're not there to stop Winter."*

"And how do you know I can defeat Grisselle? I might be queen now, but I'm still very much a human."

And remembering what Kadie had done to me, I had all the proof I needed about how well a human would fare against Grisselle.

Darach pulled back. *"You have never been just a human. I've told you before your destiny is something greater. If you won't go back for you, will you go for me or for Gareth? For Nevin and the people of Summer?"*

"I'm so cold."

"It's always like that here. You can never get warm. The only time I feel any sort of relief from it is when I'm with you, in Faerie."

"Salome," Gareth called my name. *"Please, answer me. You've got to come back. You can't die. I didn't let you pull me back from death only to have you leave me."*

"Go to him." Darach hugged me. *"Do what I cannot. Be with the person you love."*

With a sad smile, I stepped away from him. "Someday, we'll find a way to bring you back, too."

"I know. Now go, before it's too late."

"Salome," Gareth hollered from the bridge I'd just moments ago crossed. *"You've got to follow my voice. You've got to come back."*

"I'm here," I said, rushing toward his voice. When I made my way over the wooden walkway, I saw Gareth standing there.

Heat radiated through my body, thawing me. The iciness melted away as he swept me in his arms. In one swift movement, he hefted me up.

"Don't ever scare me like that again. You understand?" He turned his frightened gaze to search mine.

"You—you came for me," I said, resting my head on his chest.

"No matter what, I'll always come for you. I love you."

We walked back through the cold and darkness until the warmth came back again. The scent of honey hung around me.

"Open your eyes, Salome."

With a gasp, my lids shot open to find Gareth, Nevin, and the man who'd come in with Kadie bent over me.

"You scared the hell out of us." Nevin searched my face. "I'm never letting you out of my sight again. I don't care who's with you."

A strand of my hair fell into my eyes, and I lifted my hand to push it back. "Holy crap. What's this?"

The piece of hair was entirely blue, but that's not what freaked me out most. It was the glittering, intricate ice-blue tattoo of swirling snowflakes that wound up around my arm.

"Somehow, you've been marked by Winter," Nevin said, helping me to sit up.

"What? How's that possible?" Oh hell. This was crazy. First I'd been marked by Summer, then Autumn—which Nevin still didn't know about—and now Winter?

Maybe now it was time to come clean with him—about everything. Last year, I'd almost died because people had refused to share what they knew with me. Now here I was hanging onto precious knowledge like that could keep me safe. Instead, I was in more danger than ever. I had to take a risk and share with them what had happened to me. Share what little I knew. Whatever was coming, we needed to face it together.

"We don't know. But I'll have one of our archivists start looking into it. There's got to be some significance. The only person I've ever known to be marked by more than one kingdom, was the Faerie Queen."

With help, I managed to make it to my feet. My eyes wandered around the room. Fear settled as I remembered what'd happened. "Where's Kadie?"

"In the dungeon, where she belongs." Venom laced Gareth's words.

"I-I can't believe she stabbed me. It was like something dark came over her—the things she said to me, it wasn't like Kadie at all. I just don't want to think that she'd intentionally hurt me."

"It was no accident," the man said.

"W-who are you?"

"My name is Etienne. I'm the King of the Spring court." His blue eyes blazed as he gave a slight bow to me. "I'm sorry I was unable to warn you sooner, but I couldn't risk saying anything until Kadie was away from me. We're just lucky we arrived before she could finish the job."

"You knew she intended to murder me?"

He glanced at Nevin, who held up his hand.

"We'll talk more about it when we're out of here," Nevin said. "But for now, just know that Kadie has been put someplace where she won't be able to hurt you again."

"But she had to have been spelled, she wouldn't do this on purpose," I said. But deep down, I wondered if that was true.

"Stabbing you with a dagger is a far cry from an accident," Gareth said. "She's given herself over to Winter. But I promise she will not hurt you again. We've taken precautions."

"But why would she do this?"

Etienne's brow furrowed. "She made an agreement with Grisselle to save her life. She forged a blood bond with her. It's changed her...turned her into a person who would kill you to survive. I'm not sure if you'll ever get the old Kadie back."

Nevin placed a hand at the small of my back. "I'm sorry, but I think the best place for her right now is the dungeon. We're just lucky that Etienne was able to warn us about what was going to happen. Now let's get you to *our* room. We'll all come up later and explain everything."

Gareth's eyes narrowed, and I saw him clench his fist. He wasn't happy that my stuff had finally been moved into Nevin's quarters, but I'd held off long enough. People had started to talk, and we didn't need that.

When we reached Nevin's room, both Gareth and Gwenn posted outside the door. "I really wish you'd reconsider letting Kadie out. She's been through a lot. And she came here for sanctuary."

"No, she didn't. She came here to kill you. I'm sorry, but I won't budge on this." He helped me into the bed then pulled the blankets up to my chin. "Get some rest. I'll be back once I've had a chance to brief the Council."

When he left, the bed shifted beside me, and I glanced up to see Darach staring down at me. *"You frightened me today. I thought you'd died."*

"I'm a hard person to kill." I smiled. "My guard and king have a way of keeping me alive."

He frowned. *"That's not funny."*

I rolled my eyes. "If I don't laugh about it, I'll cry. Besides, I'm not lying when I say they keep me alive. Those two have saved me more times than I can count. They're like my own version of a bulletproof vest."

"You need to be more careful. When the queen learns you still live, she'll try again to destroy you and Nevin."

I swallowed hard, because I knew he spoke the truth. Grisselle wouldn't give up until Summer was destroyed. And I needed to stop her at all costs. As I sat there, all I kept seeing was Kadie's twisted face. I couldn't believe that she'd tried to kill me. I wanted to believe she'd done it simply because she was afraid of dying, but if what Etienne had said was true, she'd bonded herself in a way to Grisselle that had changed her. The Kadie I knew was gone—maybe forever.

If Grisselle could get someone as strong and tough as Kadie to crack, then what chance did I have at defeating her?

CHAPTER THIRTY-SIX

Salome

I glanced up as Nevin came into our room, his dark hair disheveled, his blue eyes tired.

"There you are, I've been looking for you." I smiled. "What's wrong?"

"Nothing. Just another long meeting with the Council. Ballock is trying to cause doubt in our ruling Summer. He's trying to convince the Council that we got rid of Rowena in order to gain more control. I'm about two seconds from strangling him."

"And what of Etienne?"

"I've got him hidden away. No one from the Council was in the throne room when they arrived. Most of the newer, younger soldiers didn't recognize him. For now I'd like to keep him a secret from Ballock and some of the others. Gareth should be bringing him over shortly."

I slid from the settee and went to him. He looked so vulnerable and tired. Without really thinking, I wrapped my arms around him for a hug, and he gave me a startled glance.

"Things will get better," I said.

Hesitant, he returned my embrace, resting his chin on my

head and letting out a sigh. "I hope your night has been better than mine."

"Well, I'm still alive, so that's something." I smiled.

"Yes, but here I bring you to Summer and you've nearly met your demise twice now." His shoulders sagged, and a twinge of guilt shot through me as he walked to the French doors that led onto the balcony. He went outside and leaned against the railing. I followed after him.

With a nervous breath, I moved to stand beside him. Shit, what was I gonna do? This wasn't Nevin's fault, and I didn't want him blaming himself for something he couldn't have prevented. "I'm sorry, I wasn't trying to upset you," I said.

"I know." He spun to face me, moonlight glinting off of him. "And I hope you understand that I'm trying to protect you. Everything hangs in the balance, and you don't realize just how deceptive Grisselle can be. To have her send someone into our kingdom and our home to kill you is showing just how desperate and cunning she is. She'll stop at nothing to kill us and our people."

His gaze met mine, and in it I saw just how serious he was.

"Pardon me, Your Highness," came Gareth's voice. He was standing in the doorway. "The scouts came back from the border. You told me to get you when they arrived." He glanced at me. *"What's going on?"*

"Nothing." I shrugged. *"We're just talking about Grisselle and Etienne and Kadie."*

"Gareth, could you send for Gwenn and Etienne now? We can talk with him more now that the Council is in their rooms for the evening."

He nodded then left us alone once more.

*E*tienne sat across from me at the table in Gareth's room, his eyes focused outside the glass doors leading to the balcony on the sun setting over the horizon. We were waiting for Nevin to return. He had to tell a few guards that we weren't to be bothered unless there was an emergency.

At last, he waltzed into the room and we all stood.

"Etienne of Spring—I still can't believe you're alive after all this time. This does my heart good to see you, my old friend. Sorry we didn't have time earlier for a proper greeting, but as you know, my queen's safety was at hand."

"Nevin." Etienne held out his arm to him.

They clutched one another's wrists and bowed. "I know you mean to leave Faerie for a while, but first, I think we need to talk."

Etienne closed his eyes, took a deep breath, and then nodded. "Very well, but you must understand that I need to leave here as soon as possible. It is only a matter of time before Grisselle realizes she's been deceived. As far as she knew, I came with Kadie to help complete her mission. But now that she knows Kadie failed, we'll have to move quickly. If you didn't know already, she has the ability to shut down the portals."

Nevin glanced at Gareth. Whatever happy history was between Nevin and Etienne, it seemed clear Nevin wasn't going to just throw caution to the wind without good reason. "And what would you have us do to forestall Grisselle's plans?"

"I need to get to the human world. I told those of my court who I could reach out to that they needed to make their escape from Winter. Rena was sending a few people out each day— some through a hidden tunnel, others faking their deaths and being tossed out with the dead bodies so they could leave under the cover of darkness. I need to make sure they get as far away from Winter as possible."

"We would like to help you and your people," Nevin said. "And I promise, if you tell us everything you know, we'll let you leave here via a Summer portal."

"I'll do whatever you ask."

My gaze shifted between Nevin and Etienne to an ancient looking map, which sat on the table. Strange wooden pegs held it in place.

Nevin took a seat and gestured for the others to do the same. "Let's get down to business."

Dark circles painted the underside of Etienne's eyes as he slumped down next to him. The rest of us followed suit.

"So, tell me about Winter," Nevin said.

It was going to be a long night. I hoped Etienne was able to provide us with the information we needed. And I hoped someday, we might find a way to get the old Kadie back. But the more I heard about the horrors of Winter, I began to doubt that it'd even be possible.

"So you're sure that these are the only weak points of the Winter Castle?" Nevin asked for like the billionth time as Etienne went over the layout of the palace.

"Yes. When Kadie tried to escape, she found that the drains in the Bone Yard led out to a creek outside the castle. The queen had the grates secured, but since you have power, you'd easily be able to unlock it. You could move some soldiers in unnoticed after dark."

"And what about her numbers?"

"I've already told you everything I remember," he said, eyes burning with fatigue. "I know you're just trying to make sure you have everything you need, and I'm not trying to be rude, but time is running out."

I shivered, thinking of the blood and bones and ice. That place would forever be forged into my nightmares. No way did I want anyone else to have to experience it. "Nevin, if what he's saying is true, we're already running out of time." I spoke up from the other side of the table, situated between Gareth and Nevin. "It's already late, and if he's going to leave, he needs to do it soon. Before Ballock or any of the others catch wind of Etienne being here. The sun will be up in a couple of hours."

"The council will ask where we got our information," Nevin said.

"Tell them I brought it back from my scouting party," Gareth said. "I think the element of surprise will be our best weapon. And with some of the council on the outs, I don't trust all of them. Besides, it'll be better if Grisselle believes that Etienne went into the human world and never had any contact with us. She'll never know how much information we have about her armies and the castle layout. For once, she might not see us coming."

"If we let you leave now, would you consider coming back and joining our forces?" Nevin said. "We could use all the royal Fae magic we can get."

"And I can tell you that some of your soldiers from Spring still live," Gareth said. "They hide in the woods and keep Winter from settling in. I can send word to them and let them know you're alive and to meet you in the human world."

I glanced at Gareth. *"Are we sure we can trust him?"*

His thoughts to me betrayed a concern he didn't let show in his expression. *"He did warn us of Kadie's intentions."*

"Well, yeah, but what if that was part of the plan?"

"These are fast becoming desperate times. We need an ally."

Etienne gathered up the map. "Once I get my people settled in, and what's left of my court meets up with me, I'll do what I can. If Winter's going to be defeated, we'll need to stand together. I'll finally be able to do what I should've done a long time ago."

Nevin stood at last. "Then you're free to go. I'll send word to you when we're ready to make our move."

"Thank you." Etienne bowed and took Nevin's arm in his in a handshake of sorts.

"Gwenn, will you see Etienne out through the private gardens?" Nevin said.

"As you wish," she said.

"If you don't mind, I'd like to accompany them," I said. "Just to say goodbye."

"So long as you stick close to Gwenn. Gareth, why don't you stand watch at the gate into the gardens? Make sure no one sees Etienne leaving."

"Of course."

We followed Gwenn through the still darkened hallways. She led us down a private stairwell and over a stone walkway. I sighed as the warm air snaked over my skin. It was nice not to feel the cold bite of winter any longer. The scent of honey spiraled in the air, and I inhaled deeply.

Once we got to the garden, Etienne turned to me. "Before I go, I wanted to tell you that I'm sorry about your friend." His brow furrowed, sadness swimming in his eyes. "I tried to protect her from the queen's wrath and even attempted to help her escape, but I failed her. And for that I ask for your forgiveness. The girl who is imprisoned now isn't the same girl I met in the club."

I nodded, a lump forming in my throat. "Thank you for at least trying. I can't imagine what either of you went through imprisoned there."

"I know you don't fully trust me yet. But I promise to show you that you haven't made a mistake supporting me." Etienne slid a ring from his finger. "This is all I have, but I want to give it to you as a peace offering and to show my gratitude."

He dropped the golden piece of jewelry in my hand. As soon as it hit my palm it glowed then absorbed right into my palm. Warmth coursed beneath my skin. It itched and tingled, sending trails of electricity through my body. I gasped as I watched a new tattoo form. Green ivy looped over the back of my hand and over my wrist, while a golden rose appeared on my palm.

Etienne's eyes widened. "Who are you really?"

"You already know. I-I'm Salome. Queen of Summer."

"I think you're more than that. And should a time come that you need me, I'm at your service."

"Thank you." I glanced back at the palace. "Listen, there's a portal at the top of the path above the waterfall. I'm sure you'll know how to activate it?" I watched Etienne.

"Yes. I'll keep to the shadows. Be safe, my queen. May you be blessed."

CHAPTER THIRTY-SEVEN

Kadie

The clanging of metal doors echoed through the tower, followed by the distinct sounds of footsteps coming toward me. A moment later, I watched as a door appeared in the wall by magic, and Gareth walked in, his sword already drawn.

"I've never liked you," he said. "The only reason I tolerated you was because of Salome. But I promise that any punishment dealt out to you for killing our queen will be handled by me. I will make you suffer," he said from between clenched teeth.

I drew my legs to my chest as if that would shield me from him.

But all he did was move closer, until he knelt beside me. "You better pray you die in your sleep tonight, wench. Because you don't know the meaning of scary—or death—but I promise to introduce you to both."

With that, he walked back out the door, and as soon as he was gone, the door disappeared.

My breathing came in gasps, and I trembled where I sat. They were going to kill me. Grisselle might not get here in time, and I had no idea where Etienne was. Why hadn't he come for me already? Unless they'd already killed him…Fuck. I never should've agreed to this.

I thought back to Etienne's warning. *Some things are worse than death.*

A sob raked through me as I rocked back and forth.

"When night falls, I'll come for you," Grisselle said. *"Don't fret, little sister."*

Part of me wished that she'd leave me. At least here, I could probably convince them to give me what I deserved. But I was bound to Grisselle now. She wouldn't let such a useful tool go to waste. She'd come for me. She would.

Soon the blackened nubs of the candles snuffed out, throwing me into complete darkness. I shivered, listening for any sign of a rescue. But I was met with only the sounds of the tiny feet of rodents.

I whimpered. It was always the darkness trying to consume me. But wasn't I a part of it now? Wasn't my soul as black as the night? Didn't I deserve whatever punishment came my way for all that I'd done?

For long hours, I sat lost with my thoughts, conjuring every nightmarish end that I might meet the next day.

Then I heard Grisselle calling to me. *"My friend is there, Kadie. Cover your head and he will rescue you."*

A cry escaped my lips as I used my arms to shield my head. All of a sudden, I heard a great explosion about me and caught a whiff of smoke and sulfur. Rocks crashed to the floor around me. A scream lodged in my throat as broken stone sprayed against my legs and back. Claws gripped hold of my arms, dragging me up. I glanced around just in time to see a dragon made of smoke clutching me.

From below the tower, I heard the screams and cries of people. Soldiers were shouting orders to bring the creature down, but his great wings kicked up a cloud around us, making it hard to see below. Within moments, he flew through the air, holding me tight, taking me away from my prison—away from my death sentence. Grisselle had come through for me, just like she said she would.

I buried my head against the creature, letting it's rough scales graze against my cheek.

Perhaps this had always been my fate, me being swept away from the club and into Winter. I was meant to be here.

*A*s we sped through the night, I knew the moment we crossed back over the border of Winter. The crispness of the air kissed my skin.

The twisted spires of the castle came into view and the dragon swooped down, landing by the black gates. And there, waiting for me, was my sister, Grisselle. She opened her arms, welcoming me home.

"You've done well, Kadie. You've proven your loyalty and love for me. From now on, you will be my right hand. You will help me bring down Summer. We will prevail."

She cradled me in her arms like I truly was her sister. Like she really did love me. And maybe, in her mind, she did. I was her prisoner, but now I was also her aid. Her heir. Her ally. She'd make sure I was by her side when we attacked Summer and brought it down for good. Winter would win, and I'd get a front row seat for the victory.

I closed my eyes, letting the darkness embrace me. No more would I fear the night, or the shadows, or monsters—because I was the dark. I was the night. *I am a monster.*

CHAPTER THIRTY-EIGHT

Salome

As Gwenn and I headed back toward the castle, the air suddenly became colder. The once starry sky had grown cloudy in a matter of seconds. The stench of sulfur burned my nose. All at once, a loud roar sounded from above, followed by severe gusts of wind.

Stone began to fall from one of the towers.

"Look out!" Gwenn shoved me aside, tugging me beneath one of the small bridges along the bank of the stream. She covered my body with her own, shielding my head.

All around us, I heard screams and rock falling. I buried my face against Gwenn's shoulder, waiting for it to stop.

Soon it did. Patches of fog rolled in, followed by deathly silence.

"What was that?" I whispered.

"A dark entity." Gwenn slowly climbed off of me, her gaze locked with mine. "Are you all right?"

"Yeah, thank you."

We both slid from beneath the bridge to find a pile of rubble and the top of one of the towers completely missing.

Gwenn cursed under her breath.

"What's wrong?"

"That tower was where your friend was imprisoned. Grisselle sprung her, which means she's free and could come back after you."

A shiver crawled over my body. Would Kadie make another attempt on my life? Or did Grisselle have some other use for her? Either way, this just proved that Winter would use any means necessary to destroy us. We needed to fight back—we needed a plan to reclaim Faerie and to right all the wrongs...

When daylight came, Nevin and I sat on a bench in the garden, watching the falls. There were still bits of stone lying about the courtyard, but most of the bigger stuff had been moved. Luckily there hadn't been any serious injuries. A few people had gotten some scrapes and bruises trying to get out of the way of falling rock, but it could've been much worse. I was relieved to know Etienne had made his escape—that he was far from the Winter Queen's wrath.

"Your Highness." Lord Ballock rushed toward us. "The prisoner has escaped."

"I know. Some of us were up late last night and heard the beast attack. Obviously you weren't one of them. A search party has already been formed and is working the borders."

"Your Highness, one of the parties has already checked in, they haven't been able to find any trace of the human— although Lady Antellan swore she felt someone use one of the portals early this morning." He gave me an accusatory glance.

"Are you sure?" Nevin asked.

"Yes. Should we see if we can pick up a trace of the human?"

No," I said. "It isn't necessary. We've got more pressing matters to worry about."

Nevin glanced at me. "She's right, we've got magical borders to rebuild so we don't have any more attacks like we did last night. And we have an army to train."

His mouth turned down in a frown. "But the human made an attempt on the queen's life."

"Lord Gareth and myself are well aware of that. Our queen's safety is of utmost importance; however, the best way to protect her now is to keep her guarded and to reinforce our borders."

"Very well. But I don't think the council will approve of this measure." He stormed away.

"That went well," I said, waving my hand in the air.

Nevin's eyes went wide. "Where did you get this from?" He pointed at my newest Faerie tattoo.

"It happened last night when Etienne was here."

"That's impossible. You've now been marked by three of the four kingdoms." His eyes widened as he investigated my markings.

"Do you know what this means?"

"No, but I'll have our archivist check into it. I haven't seen this since…"

"Since what?"

He glanced at Gareth, who stood watching us. "Nothing, I don't want to jump to conclusions, but let's just say there's more to you than I think any of us ever knew."

"Gareth? What isn't he telling me?"

Gareth met my eye over his shoulder then turned away. *"I can't say for sure. But he's right, this is big."*

"Please don't keep secrets." My teeth grazed my bottom lip.

"I won't. As soon as I find answers, I promise to tell you."

I wouldn't be much of a queen if I didn't live up to what I'd asked him to do. Well, here went nothing. Time to tell them everything I knew, too.

"Okay, there's something you should both know," I said. "I didn't want to say anything, but I feel that the more information we withhold from one another, the less likely we are to defeat Grisselle."

"What do you mean?" Nevin asked.

"Before Gareth came back injured, I had something strange happen to me." I chewed my bottom lip, hoping I didn't sound crazy. "A door appeared in the hallway and I was led into a hidden room. Inside there were these things called Memory Boxes, and there was this voice, talking to me."

Nevin's eyes widened. "You were granted access to the Room of the Past? Before you were crowned queen?"

"Yes. But here's the thing: there were specific things this room or whatever wanted me to know. For one, the Memory Box I saw showed the funeral procession of Genissa—and her body wasn't in the casket."

"It had to have been. We saw it with our own eyes," Gareth said.

"Did you really? Or is it possible that someone was able to manipulate a glamour and make you think you saw it? Because I watched the vision play through several times and each time, the body disappeared right when it reached the bend in the road. And that's not all, there was more information on the Blade of the Four Kingdoms."

"What do you know of the blade?" Nevin stared at me.

"Gareth didn't tell you?"

"I might've forgotten that detail when we got here."

"The sword kind of appeared to me." I paused. "It's hidden

in my room right now."

He ran a hand through his hair, watching me closely. "You're full of all kinds of surprises, aren't you?"

"Maybe, but the thing I wanted to tell you is that this voice, it spoke a lot of riddles…and I think they might be some type of premonition or something. I mean, it predicted Kadie hurting me…"

"It what?" Gareth moved closer.

I took a deep breath. "The voice said: 'Beware of the girl who calls herself friend'."

Nevin cursed. "What else did it say?"

I shook my head. "More than I totally remember. Something about seeking the Matron of Faerie. The voice said the archivist holds the key. The warden holds the map. And the sister…I can't remember that part."

"The sister holds the doorway open," Nevin finished. "That part's from a legend. But the rest… What else did the voice say?"

"It said the other is made of darkness. Do you know what this means?"

Nevin's jaw clenched. "Parts of it perhaps, but this sounds like something we'll need to sit down and put our heads together for. The sooner the better."

"You promise to tell me if you figure something out, right?"

"Yes," Nevin said.

I hoped he would, because the sooner I could figure out my purpose in Faerie, the better. Grandma might have some answers, but I wasn't sure when I'd see her again. Maybe I could convince Nevin to let me go back for a brief visit…But I didn't hold my breath for that to happen. Sunshine warmed my skin as I closed my eyes, letting Summer wrap around me.

"Maybe we stand a chance against Grisselle now. With

Etienne back in the picture, we might be able to take her down, if the three of us use our power," Nevin said from beside me.

"I think we stand more than a chance." I smiled, opening my eyes. "I think we might win."

He chuckled. "Come with me. It's time we strengthen the magic around our borders today."

"Would you like me to ready the horses?" Gareth asked from beside me.

"Yes. And have Gwenn go get a few more guards to accompany us." Nevin reached for my hand and placed it on his arm as we walked to the stables.

So much had changed, and I wasn't sure how to feel about it yet. A few weeks ago, I was just some human girl who happened to have a Fae boyfriend. Now I was a powerful queen, readying myself for war.

Once the horses were saddled, we mounted them. Nevin slid into the saddle behind me, and we galloped from the safety of the palace walls. We traveled along the borders, where Nevin showed me how to set a magical shield. As one we cupped our hands together, prayed to the Goddess of Summer, and let the magic flow through our fingers.

We spent the entire day building up our barriers. When we finished, a green-blue glow swirled in the air around Summer. The breeze seemed warmer, the sky brighter, and the flowers more fragrant.

Nevin guided our horse beneath a willow tree. He helped me from the saddle, then turned to me. "Thank you for helping our kingdom. I know this isn't the life you wanted. But I hope you'll grow to love Summer, like you loved the human world."

"I already adore Summer. Everything we're doing, we're doing for them and for Faerie. I touched his shoulder. "We will defeat Grisselle, together."

He leaned forward to give me a hug. Beneath the willow, we could pretend just for a moment that we didn't have a worry in the world.

When he pulled back, my eyes shifted to Gareth, who stood on the hill.

"I love you," I said through the link.

"I know. But the kingdom needs you."

With a sad smile, I fought the tears that threatened to spill out. *"I understand now why you stayed here all those years, trying to run the kingdom while Nevin was gone. Summer means too much to both of us to not do the right thing."*

Darach's ghost appeared on the hill next to Gareth, unbeknownst to him. Soon, I would need to tell Nevin about him. I meant what I'd said earlier. We couldn't keep secrets from each other anymore. Not if we wanted to defeat Winter.

I watched them both. They were my strength, and I knew they'd be with me through everything. I might be Nevin's queen now, but I was also theirs. No matter what happened, I knew I could trust them with my life.

But I also knew Gareth would be an obstacle for me. I wasn't sure how great I'd be able to pretend that he meant nothing to me when we were in public. This was the part that would suck—keeping our love hidden. Not being able to go on dates or romantic walks or spend time dancing. Nope. Everything we said or did would have to be behind closed doors—another secret.

"Let's go home now," Nevin said.

As we made our way back, Gareth came up next to me, his gaze focused ahead of us so that anyone watching wouldn't notice that his attention was on me.

"Our armies should be ready soon, and with Etienne's information, we might be able to make this quick, with minimal casualties."

"*There's nothing to figure out,*" I teased. "*We're gonna defeat Winter, and then we'll all live happily ever after.*"

He chuckled. "*Has anyone ever told you that you read way too many fairytales?*"

"*I don't need to read them anymore—I'm living one.*"

For now, things were calm, but I knew in the months to come we'd have to face our nightmares. We'd have to face Winter, Grisselle, and Kadie too. But now I was ready for it. Spring, Summer, and Autumn had marked me. But so had Winter. I was stronger for it. I belonged to Faerie now—and it belonged to me.

EPILOGUE

Etienne

Up ahead, I saw the glowing circle of stones—the portal. The fading moonlight cascaded through the canopy of trees as if it energized the portal.

I stepped into the circle. Bright light flashed all around me like thousands of pulsating strobes. I spun, falling down so fast that dizziness washed over me. My eyes squeezed shut as I traveled through heat and cold.

Wind whirred in my ears. There was so much pressure on my body and my head.

At last I slowed until my feet hit something solid.

My eyes whipped open, and I went still. Darkness shrouded me. Snow billowed against my legs. I shivered. Fear entangled me like a net. I was back in Winter.

My eyes adjusted to the blackness, and I saw a gazebo. I'd made it. This must be Salome's grandparents' house. As if sensing our arrival, an old woman hurried toward me, carrying a walking stick that glowed.

"Who's there?" she called. When she got closer, she came up short. Her eyes widened to the size of oranges. "You're alive."

Confused, I stared at her. "Yes… The Winter Queen held me prisoner in her kingdom. But I bring news of your granddaughter. She lives, and she lives well as the Queen of Summer."

Doris smiled. "So it has come to pass. She chose Nevin and Summer. And Kadie betrayed her."

I nodded.

"Come along then—let's get you out of the cold," she said.

I followed Doris' hunched form onto the deck and into the house. Heat warmed my cool skin the moment we stepped inside.

"Who's this?" An older man, who I assumed was Salome's grandpa, met us at the door.

"This is Etienne of Spring. He will be staying with us for a while," she said, turning to stare at me. "And where are my manners? I'm Doris, and this is my husband Frank."

Doris hung her thick gray coat up on a hook, and then she caught my arm and led me to a hidden room. She slipped into the cluttered office, complete with rollaway desk, large ledgers, books, and jars of herbs. She grabbed one of the sconces next to the desk, and the wall slid open.

She retrieved a candle from a shelf and lit it with a match. The light bounced off marble stairs that descended into the dark.

I came up short, staring at Doris. "I recognize you now. You're the Grand Matron of Faerie, the Archivist to the Queen of Faerie. You disappeared hundreds of years ago."

Doris smiled. "Because I was needed here. The queen foresaw it. I used to guard our antiquities and our borders against stray humans coming into Faerie. Now I guard the humans against our kind."

"Then you knew this day would come? That your granddaughter would become Summer Queen?" I asked.

"Yes."

"I'm guessing there's more to Salome than being Summer Queen."

"Much more." Doris ushered me down the curving stairs to a long, marble corridor.

Paintings of battles and gardens and the different seasons hung along the wall, while ancient statues lined the way beneath the house.

I gaped at the mahogany furniture and cases of jewels.

"These are things I saved from the Ruined Court."

I stepped ahead of her into a well-lit room, where rows of swords, bows, and armor hung. "You've got weapons."

"War's coming, Your Highness. We must all be prepared. The queen told me this was to be my task."

My pulse thundered in my ears. It'd all come down to this—a final battle. And whether I wanted to be or not, I was a part of it. Doris turned to me, then brought me into her arms and hugged me tight.

"I can guess what you endured to make it this far...The things you must have sacrificed to survive."

"I could've done more," I whispered.

She brushed hair from my face. "So could we all, Etienne of Spring. But we do the best we can with what we're given. You did what you had to do to help keep your people safe, and now, you will have a chance to avenge those you couldn't."

I held tight to her. For the first time in months, I felt safe. And even though I knew this was far from over, I could breathe again. When I took the field of battle, Grisselle wouldn't know what hit her. She would pay for all that she'd done to Faerie— for all the innocent lives she'd taken over the years from both my world and the human world.

When Doris let me go she said, "Everything will be okay,

now."

And somehow, I believed her. Trying times were ahead, but for this moment, I basked in the warmth of Doris' house, of being free from Grisselle. Tonight I'd relax for the first time in years, and tomorrow, I'd wait for my people to arrive.

Grisselle

My mirror shimmered as I took in the scene before me. Nevin had taken the human girl as his queen. Etienne had betrayed me for Summer. Oh, he'd thought he could hide his betrayal from me, but I'd felt him leave Faerie. He thought he was so clever, trying to sneak off. Just like a man to do something like that.

My fingers tingled with magic. They'd all pay for it, though. Darkness washed over me as I dipped my fingers into the black essence on my vanity.

"If I can't win here then I'll take this fight somewhere I can." I spun to face the Nobles of Winter. My new sister Kadie stood by my side. "By week's end, we march on the human world. Call up our armies, trolls, goblins, ghosts…I want all our people ready to go."

Summer would regret the day they went against me. And the human girl Salome would be the first to go. Or maybe I'd save her for last—let her watch everyone she loved succumb to death. Succumb to me. Succumb to Winter.

Acknowledgments

Where to begin... Edits for this book hit right in the midst of a family emergency this year. There were moments when I wasn't sure if I'd get it finished in time—so I thank my editor Liz for her understanding and allowing *Summer Marked* to be pushed back.

I want to also give a HUGE thank you and lots of hugs to my agents Jenn and Fran. I appreciate your support more than I can say or express. Thank you for the encouraging emails and phone calls during everything.

To my brother Phil, sister-in-law Jenn, sister Rachel, and soon to be brother-in-law Dan, I love you guys and feel blessed every day to have you as my family. Your love and support mean the world to me.

To my FABULOUS husband Tim, I love you more than words can say. To my kids Devin, Alyssa, Kris, Barrett, Erin, and Chase, I am SO proud of each of you. You all excel at everything you do and I love you. Thank you for ALWAYS believing in me, even when I doubt myself.

Ah, and where would I be without my FREAKING AWESOME crit group? Thank you for reading and critting EVERY story I write. You ladies make my words so much more than they started. Your love, friendship, and support over the last several years has been uplifting. You're my second family.

And to my readers... I don't even know what I'd do without you. Thank you SO much for your excitement and emails and messages. You guys are AWESOME.